Till You Come Back to Me

(Book Two in the Stafford Brothers Series)

Chicki Brown

Please Note

This is a work of fiction. Names, characters, places, and incidents either are the product of the author's imagination or are used fictitiously, and any resemblance to actual persons, living or dead, business establishments, events or locales is entirely coincidental.

ISBN: 1500422746
ISBN-13: 9781500422745

Praise for Chicki Brown's Novels

A Woman's Worth

"This is my second book by this author. I really like how she tells stories. She really draws the reader in.

Marcus, the Hero in the story, was an all-around wonderful guy. I like that once he saw Gianne the Heroine, he went right after her. Gianne was in remission from cancer and was excited about life again; experiencing new things but was weary of doing the love thing. From the onset Marcus set out to prove he was sincere in his feelings and eventually love for her. READ THE BOOK!!!" - **T. Baker "aficionado of books"** (Amazon review)

"I am a major Chicki Brown fan, so when I saw she had released a new title I knew I'd be in for a treat. What I didn't know was that I'd get more than I'd paid for. Chicki has been blessed with the ability to grant you access into the worlds she creates and you truly want to stay there, long after the story ends. You've been made privy to the details of the story by others, but my unexpected takeaway from this was the fitness and vegan information...two topics that interest me. But it's like that with her books. She digs deep to give her readers more than just a story, she gives you a world. I recommend this book and I can't wait to read what's next." – **Karen Rodgers-Editor** (Amazon review)

You Make Me Feel Brand New

"Short, sweet, well written and absolutely perfect. You really don't notice how short the story is because all the details are covered. The characters were well developed. There was no sense of the story being rushed. I felt like I had read a complete novel. I would most definitely recommend this story to anyone." - **D.Wiggins** (Amazon review)

Ain't Too Proud to Beg

"I love how Chicki Brown's characters have multiple layers and how vulnerable they are. I also love the detail she puts into the cities her stories take place. As I was reading, I could almost see the beauty and feel the chill of snow-covered Telluride, Colorado and see the beautiful palm trees and how blue the water is on the California Coast. Another thing I loved was the way she wrote this book. Oftentimes a book is written from one character's point of view, leaving me to wonder how the other character was feeling at that time. Chicki writes Ain't Too Proud To Beg from Vaughn and Trenyce's points of view alternately so the reader has the opportunity to understand why they each react the way they do and this just adds to the depth of the characters." – **LadyJ** (Amazon review)

Acknowledgements

Nkem Ivara (http://thewordsmythe.wordpress.com/),

Emeka Godwin
(https://www.facebook.com/pastor.e.godwin) and

Stella Eromonsere-Ajanaku
(http://www.flirtyandfeistyromancenovel.co.uk) for educating me on the tribal differences and other specifics about Nigeria. You have all been a blessing!

Also, thanks to Alfreda Asbury for her help with fine tuning the details, and to Estella Robinson for her tireless beta reading.

Finally, to T.J. Walp, of Manuscript Proofing, for her editing magic. She is always so patient and understanding of my mental blocks.

Prologue

Adanna made her last round through the small ward. She stopped at the foot of one of the cots and stretched, rubbing the ache in her lower back. Her legs throbbed from being on her feet for the last twelve hours.

As one of two nurses who assisted the doctors in the Stella Obasanjo Hospital, her responsibilities ran the gamut from handling intake, to serving as a midwife, to assisting with surgeries. She did any and everything the doctors required, including overseeing medications and other materials, which were in persistent short supply.

In spite of the long shifts, hard work, and limited provisions, she loved her job and couldn't imagine doing anything for a living where she couldn't help people. She and her brother, Emeka, had been born in Lagos, the largest city in Nigeria, but when her parents accumulated the money needed to obtain the necessary documentation for the family to travel to London, they left the country. At the time, she was only ten years old and didn't remember much about those early years, but she would always be grateful to them for their decision to remain in England where they eventually became citizens. Her elementary, secondary, and university education took place in London. During that time, she, Emeka, and her parents returned to Nigeria only three times to visit her relatives who still lived there, but she remembered those visits as joyful reunions filled with music, good food, and laughter. Although she had been raised in Peckham and grown up as part of a thriving Nigerian community, her heart remained tied to her homeland. After her graduation from nursing school, she and Emeka returned to the land of their birth. At first, her father had been dead set against her becoming a returnee. They had left their homeland when she was only ten, and his concern centered mostly on her lack of street smarts in a country where the mantra was "Shine ya eye," which loosely translated meant to "be savvy, be smart and don't let anyone take you for a fool." Nigeria was notorious for armed robberies and kidnappings, particularly of expatriates and returnees whom the perpetrators assumed might bring a larger ransom. He had made it clear that the only way he would allow her to move back to Nigeria was if she and her brother lived together. Emeka had never adapted to life in London. He complained about the weather, hated the food, and despised Britons, so saying he was thrilled to be going back home was an understatement.

They had been renting a flat together for nearly two years, when Adanna announced that she was moving in with a girlfriend. He knew there was nothing he could do to stop her, and he vowed to continue his responsibility for his baby sister. Several times a week he came by the small two-bedroom flat she shared with her roommate, Femi, or even by the hospital to check on her. Adanna often thought his appearances in the evening had more to do with satisfying his need for a good home-cooked meal courtesy of her flatmate than with sibling surveillance. Emeka lived a relatively solitary bachelor existence. He didn't have a regular woman in his life and, as far as she knew, his social life didn't amount to more than his involvement in one of the local vigilante groups that patrolled the streets for criminals and guarded homes and businesses in the absence of regular police protection.

The temperature gradually cooled as the sun set, and she finished checking on the patients.

"Goodnight, Dr. Ijalana," Adanna called out to him as she passed the office door.

"Goodnight, Adanna. Be safe."

She drove her 2005 Peugeot Allure thirty minutes to her flat in Lagos. Her working late couldn't be helped. One nurse and one nurse's assistant had to be on duty at all times to assist the doctor.

Femi arrived home before Adanna, and delicious aromas filled the flat when she dragged in around seven o'clock. The best part was, Femi loved to cook and always had dinner for her. Unfortunately, being the consummate social butterfly, she offered an open invitation to their friends too. She loved to feed people, and their friends loved to eat. Tonight was no different.

"Hello, people," Adanna greeted their friends as she entered the flat.

"Hard day today?" Femi asked as she put a cold Coca-Cola into her hand.

"Always, but I got to deliver a baby, a fat, healthy little girl."

Everyone in the room applauded, and Adanna took a bow. "Sorry to be anti-social, but I'm exhausted. I'm going to eat and go to sleep."

"You need a husband, so you don't have to work so hard," one of their male friends said with a cheeky grin.

Adanna laughed. "Having a husband is just *more* work. Good night, Emmanuel." He was probably right, but since she worked all the time, her social life was virtually non-existent. She hadn't been on anything resembling a date in a year, and her interest in dating had waned. She wanted an educated man who was devoted to her alone and who understood her commitment to her job. Unfortunately, she'd never met anyone who fit those criteria. All of the opposite sex, with whom she associated, were either married medical men or single men with a player mentality she couldn't stand.

So, she remained unattached. Adanna wasn't discontented with her life, because her work was so much more fulfilling than she imagined staying at home and changing diapers could ever be.

Femi put an overflowing plate in her hand, and she gave her a grateful smile. "This is why I love you."

"We'll keep it quiet," one of them said as she retreated down the hall toward her bedroom.

Most evenings, by the time Adanna drove home, fatigue had overtaken her. After she greeted whatever guests occupied their two-bedroom flat, she ate, showered, and prepared to repeat the routine again tomorrow. Every night before she went to sleep, she prayed that the hospital would receive the help it needed. Months ago, Dr. Pategi mentioned hearing rumors about the possibility of getting assistance from *Doctors Without Borders*, but he didn't have an official confirmation. In the meantime, while they hoped and prayed their request might be honored, the small staff worked tirelessly to help patients who came to them with everything from trypanosomiasis to AIDS to severe physical deformities, particularly among young children. Her heart went out to these people – her people. Their suffering was unnecessary.

Because the hospital was located in southern Nigeria, which was predominantly Christian, procuring supplies was easier than in the north where terrorist attacks by extremist Islamic factions often disrupted and sometimes prevented small hospitals and clinics from receiving what they needed. Thankfully, the terrorist attacks by Boko Haram Islamists so far had been confined to the north and central sections of the country.

Adanna turned on the television and placed the plate on top of her desk. When she was in the mood, she'd watch CNN, but more often than not, after dealing with the gravity of her job all day, her mood ran more toward *Glam Squad* or

Nigerian Idol.

Once she devoured the delicious meal and took a shower, Adanna crawled into bed, put in her earbuds and clicked onto the love song playlist on her Smartphone. She chuckled as she snuggled under the top sheet. Her friends vowed to be quiet, but she always needed music to camouflage their voices drifting in from the front room. A romantic at heart, she adored the songs that glorified love, and she had become a fan of the American balladeers like R. Kelly, Kem, Jaheim and John Legend. The last thing she remembered as she listened to Kem croon *Share My Life* was that having a man to share her life would put the icing on an already pretty sweet cake. Just one man.

In the morning, flashes of a dream she'd had last night accompanied her as she drove to the hospital. Her mother, a big believer in dreams, always said they were one of the ways God speaks to us, so when Adanna had a particularly vivid one, she paid attention. The details of last night's nocturnal vision were fuzzy, but it centered on a man whose physical appearance gave the dream had special meaning. No one she knew had such a light complexion and eyes that appeared to glow in the dark.

When she arrived at the hospital, immediately she sensed a change in the atmosphere. Dr. Ijalana and Dr. Pategi were huddled together in front of the laptop and barely noticed her entrance.

"Good morning, Doctors."

"Adanna, come and look at this!" Dr. Pategi said with more excitement in his voice than she'd ever heard. Rarely did the doctors consult with her on patient diagnoses. Her involvement focused on treatment, so she approached them expecting to see photographs of a particular medical procedure. Instead, text filled the screen. She leaned in to get a better look. The document was an e-mail from *Doctors Without Borders*. Their prayers and requests were finally being answered. The organization was sending a team of doctors to work at their small facility.

"This is incredible!" Adanna exclaimed knowing what this meant for their patients, many of who had been waiting for years for surgeries they could not afford. "When will they get here?"

"It says in the last paragraph that the doctors should be here the first week in May. They will evaluate all patients and decide which surgeries will be performed and when. We will assist them in the operating room. Before the team arrives, we need to review the patient waiting list and try to get them in for a final evaluation."

"I can start doing that right now, Doctor."

"I had the feeling you'd be excited about this. You are an excellent nurse, Adanna. We could not function without you." He smiled, and the smooth ebony skin around his eyes crinkled. Dr. Pategi was one of the kindest people she had ever met, and Adanna considered it a privilege to work with him. As a husband and father of four, he sacrificed much of his personal time seeing to the needs of the sick, most of who couldn't afford to pay the normal fees. He worked tirelessly to obtain funds from social and religious organizations to provide the care their patients needed.

"Thank you. Did they include background information on the surgeons who will be coming?"

He scrolled down the page and clicked on a link. The attachment opened. "Yes, there is a photo and a CV for each, if you would like to find out more about our visitors. Take your time. Everything is quiet right now." Dr. Pategi stood, made the seat available to her, and left the room.

Adanna replaced him in front of the screen and casually browsed through the physician information. She stopped suddenly when a photo jumped out at her. The man she'd seen in her dream! The antithesis of African standards of male attractiveness, which generally included a wide nose, thick lips, and dark skin, this man had a fair complexion, a beard, and -- she leaned into the screen to get a closer look at his professional photo -- green eyes. Yet, she couldn't rip her gaze from his image. There weren't many men in her country who looked like him. A twinge of guilt stabbed her over admiring his intriguing face, and it wasn't because of his fair complexion.

The issue of skin color had become an issue in Africa. Recently, a South African musician faced severe criticism over her decision to lighten her naturally dark skin, and subsequently a good number of people in her country had followed suit. The sale of skin lightening products was also a lucrative business in Nigeria, and the debate continued on the ethics of it all. Adanna heard it more often than not from her brother. Even though he had spent his teen years in England, Emeka was fiercely devoted to their tribal culture. He believed that the practice of bleaching one's skin was tantamount to denying your heritage. *This isn't the same thing*, she told herself while she stood mesmerized by the doctor's high cheekbones and intense eyes. *This man would be considered extremely handsome no matter what color skin he had.*

She scolded herself for her mental wandering and scrolled down to read the résumé of Dr. Charles Stafford, which was impressive for such a young man. He had gone to medical school, done his residency at a major US hospital and eventually opened his own plastic surgery practice. Now he was giving up private practice to lend his gifts to the people of her nation.

And, in a couple of months, this fascinating man was arriving at her hospital.

♥

May

After a nineteen-hour flight from Las Vegas, Dr. Charles Stafford landed at Murtala Muhammed International Airport. He entered the busy terminal thrilled to finally be able to stretch his legs and desperate to find a Starbuck's. He smiled at the sight of travelers, and those coming to greet them, dressed in both western and traditional African attire. After a thirty-minute search, he gave up on finding his drug of choice. *An airport without a Starbuck's? Not a good sign.*

After he retrieved his suitcase from baggage claims, he took a cab from the airport to the address he'd been given at the briefing. He handed the paper to the driver, who offered some reassuring information as they drove.

"This address is in a part of the city called Surulere. Almost all the roads there are tarred," the driver said cheerfully. "One of the best things about the area is its security. Robbery incidents rarely occur. The area also has access to the water supply from the Lagos State Water Corporation."

Those were givens at home. He's saying this as though it's something to be celebrated.

"Is robbery really as prevalent as I've heard?" Charles asked, hoping to get more details from the local man.

"Unfortunately, yes. I have been robbed more times than I can count. As a visitor, you need to be extra careful when you go out, especially at night. If you go out to the nightclubs or restaurants, don't flash your money around. Those fellows are on the lookout for tourists with money."

"Well, I'm not really a tourist. I'll be living here half of the year and working at a village hospital." Charles had taken care of the necessities like opening a bank account with the Nigerian EcoBank and having the funds transferred electronically before he'd even left Atlanta. He needed to have access to money without any hassle. You could never tell what might happen when you were far away from home.

"Are you a doctor?"

"Yes."

Charles was relieved when the cab stopped in front of a modern, four-story brick building that contained several flats. He figured out the fare and tip using an app on his phone, and paid the driver with the niara he'd had converted from dollars before he'd left the States. "Thank you for your advice. Maybe we'll see each other again while I'm here."

The driver retrieved his suitcase from the trunk, and then reached into his pocket. "Take my card. Call when you need a taxi and ask for me. I wish you the best, Doctor."

Charles perused the card for a second. "I will. Thank you, Mr. Adeyemi." He popped the handle on the pullman bag and rolled it up the sidewalk as he scanned the neighborhood. Two people standing across the street waved and smiled, and he waved back. He assumed they were used to foreigners occupying this building, if DWB used it regularly to house visiting staff. The front entrance was unlocked, which didn't thrill him. He was used to visitors checking in with the doorman at his building. But he wasn't at his building any more.

The e-mail he'd received said he was being assigned flat number 203, and he assumed it was on the second floor, but it instructed him to see the building manager upon arrival.

The manager, a jovial, portly man named Mr. Lawai welcomed him and eagerly helped Charles lug his suitcase to the flat on the second floor. He imagined the man liked renting to DWB staffers, because his rent was guaranteed. He said the other doctor who would be sharing the flat with Charles had already arrived. The door to the second flat was open, and when they got closer he saw an assortment of luggage right inside the doorway.

"Dr. Davies!" Mr. Lawai called.

"Right here," a voice answered back. "You must be Charles Stafford. I'm Randolph Davies, pediatrics. I guess we're flatmates. Pleased to make your acquaintance."

The two men shook hands.

"Have you checked out the place?"

"Yes, that's what I was doing when you arrived. There are two bedrooms, one bath, living room, and a small kitchen. Looks acceptable. Take a look around."

Charles explored his new living quarters, which took all of five minutes. "It's okay. At least they provide dishes and pots and pans. The others haven't gotten here yet?"

"No, but I assume they will be arriving shortly. We might as well unpack. Which bedroom do you want?"

"I'm not particular. They look identical."

Davies hefted his bags from the floor, closed the front door, and flipped the lock. "In that case, I'll take the one on the left." He smiled and dragged his luggage into the room.

Charles followed suit, rolling his bag to the right.

"Make sure you check the bed," Davies said over his shoulder.

"Why?"

"For bedbugs. They didn't mention it in your briefing?"

"No, they conveniently skipped that part," Charles said, frowning and scratching his neck. "How should I do that?"

"Examine the mattress and box spring carefully before you put the linens on. They told you to bring your own linens, didn't they?"

Charles chuckled. "Yeah, they did mention that part."

A knock on the door interrupted their unpacking and

insect inspection. The man standing in the hallway introduced himself as Emilio Cervantes, a cardiac surgeon from Spain. His roommate, Nils Lindstrom, an orthopedic surgeon from Sweden, had also just arrived, and he said they were sharing flat number 209 down the hall. Cervantes reminded them that their transportation was due to arrive in less than an hour. Charles briefly met the other doctors as each one arrived at the flat, Jack Spivey, the infectious disease specialist from the CDC in Atlanta, and Matthias Verheyen, a dentist from Belgium, rounded out the team.

Because Nils had been on numerous tours with DWB, he'd been designated as team leader. The van arrived and during the thirty-minute trip to the hospital, he suggested they spend the time getting to know each other. He began by telling about himself personally and his medical experience. Each man did the same, and by the time the last had spoken, they had reached their destination.

The driver said he would remain in the area while they worked and gave his cell number to Nils. The team exited the van, and they all took a few minutes to silently scan their surroundings. Abject poverty hit Charles like a slap. He'd read a lot about the country, but seeing it in person was another story. The area was a stark contrast from the bustling, modern city they had just left not more than thirty minutes ago. The team leader's voice faded into the background as Charles' gaze roamed the area. A combination of primitive huts dotted the landscape with a few small buildings that appeared to be made from large logs and mud with thatched rooms. It must have rained recently, because the center of the area was nothing more than a huge mud puddle. The few relatively modern buildings in the village were cinderblock construction. Six people dressed in scrubs stood outside the entrance of the white building.

This must be the hospital.

As they approached the building, which from the outside

looked more like it should've housed an auto repair shop, he gave them a fast overview about the village and the hospital in excellent but heavily accented English. "Drs. Pategi and Ijalana are the only two doctors working here on a regular basis. They have two female nurses and two nursing assistants, both male. We will meet with them to ascertain exactly what they need from us."

As the team approached the building, the expectant smiles of the hospital staff greeted them. Charles' gaze was immediately drawn to the heart-shaped ebony face of the woman dressed in bright pink scrubs. She wore her hair natural, closely cropped and appeared to wear no makeup on her slanted eyes and only a deep wine color lipstick on her lush mouth.

"Welcome to the Stella Obasanjo Hospital," the shorter man said. "We are so honored you've come to work with us. I am Dr. Olushula Ijalana. You can call me Lou. This is Dr. Joseph Pategi, and this is our staff. He introduced the two nurses and their assistants.

He couldn't take his eyes off the beautiful dark-skinned nurse whose name was Adanna. Their gazes met, and a distinct look of recognition momentarily swept across her face. When the introductions were done, the visiting team shook hands with the host staff. Charles shook Adanna's slender hand, and she stared up at him with such intensity in her onyx eyes, he couldn't look away. "Charles Stafford. It's a pleasure to meet you."

"You also, Doctor. We are honored that you decided to join us."

He had to mentally slap himself in order to concentrate on what Dr. Ijalana was saying. And he was good until Nurse Okoro turned around and preceded them around the outside of the building. The easy sway of her generous hips grabbed his attention like a mugger with an old lady's purse. Black American women had inherited their voluptuous rear ends from their sisters in the Motherland, but this was the real deal. Charles smiled to himself. It didn't matter how far removed people were from their native land, some things were ingrained. And any man of African heritage would always admire a spectacular ass.

The hospital staff and their guests settled under a white canopy covering two tables laden with bowls and platters. Nurse Okoro introduced their servers, three women from the village dressed in colorful traditional clothing and head wraps. Dr. Ijalana asked the women to serve the assistants first and instructed them to take turns checking on the patients. Charles bowed his head and silently offered a prayer over the food. Even though it smelled wonderful, most likely it contained ingredients he would never have eaten. The facilitator at the briefing mentioned the necessity of being careful not to insult the locals in any way, and one of those ways was by refusing food they had prepared. When he raised his head and opened his eyes, Nurse Okoro was studying him with a hint of a smile.

The new combined staff got to know each other while they ate. Charles took a few minutes talking with the two local doctors and the other nurse before he settled in the seat next to Nurse Okoro.

He nodded toward his plate. "Can you tell me what all of this is?"

"We asked the three best cooks in the village to prepare your first meal, and requested they fixed only chicken and vegetable dishes." He listened intently while she described the assortment of rice dishes, fruits, and vegetables in detail.

"Thank you. Everything is delicious. You have a British accent. You weren't born here in Nigeria?"

She smiled and her cheeks rose like apples on her high cheekbones. "I was born here, but my family moved to London when I was twelve, and we lived there until I graduated from nursing school."

"Why did your family decide to return?"

"They didn't. My parents still live in London, but my brother and I always wanted to come back."

"That's interesting. I've recently moved away from my family too. Have you ever visited the United States?"

"No, but it's on my bucket list." She laughed and her obsidian eyes danced. "Is this your first visit to our continent, Dr. Stafford?"

"Please, call me Charles. Yes, it is, and I'm looking forward to seeing more of Nigeria."

"We have our problems, but Nigeria also has its own unique beauty both in the villages and in the cities. Are you staying in Lagos?"

As she spoke, Charles admired the slant of her eyes and the tempting pout of her full lips. "Yes, the organization put us up in apartments in Surelere."

"Really? That's not far from where I live. Are you satisfied with your accommodations?"

"So far. We only had time to unpack before the car arrived to bring us here."

Charles tore his gaze from her face when Dr. Pategi said, "Doctor Stafford, you will find our nurses to be invaluable to you," he said with a wide smile. "Because our funding and staffing are limited, Nurse Okoro and Nurse Bankole have often had to handle patient care and perform procedures normally dealt with by physicians. Likewise, our nursing assistants have stepped in to take care of traditional nursing duties. We all pitch in whenever and wherever necessary."

The way Dr. Pategi suddenly interrupted him, Charles wondered if he'd been ogling her. He gathered his senses and concentrated on her words rather than her face.

Chapter One

Five months earlier…

The family room of Charles' parents' Atlanta home buzzed with anticipation. The family had all been together a few weeks ago to celebrate Christmas. This time, he had called them all together for a meeting without giving them an inkling of why, but he knew they would all show up out of mere curiosity.

When he arrived, Cydney, his brother Jesse's wife was the first to greet him as she discreetly nursed their newborn in an easy chair in the corner. "Hey, brother-in-law! You have us all on pins and needles here. We're just waiting for Nick. He went to Cherilyn's church this morning." She propped the little pink bundle on her shoulder and patted her back.

"They're still seeing each other?" Charles asked. "I'm impressed. Okay. That'll give me time to log on to my laptop."

"Are you giving a symposium, Dr. Stafford?" she asked with a giggle.

He gave her the side eye. "No, Cyd. I'm Skyping Marc and Greg, so they can be here with us."

Ramona, who was married to his brother Vic, raised her perfectly-shaped eyebrows. "Wow, this must be serious."

"Charles!" His mother, Lillian, came around the corner from the kitchen before he could answer. "I thought I heard your voice. "Do you mind telling your mother what this is all about?"

He kissed her cheek. "I want to talk to everyone at the same time, Mama. As soon as Nick gets here, I'll get Marc and Greg on the computer. Where is everybody?"

"In the kitchen making sandwiches. If Daddy and your brothers don't eat the second we get out of church, they think they'll die. I sent the kids downstairs to watch a movie."

Charles set his laptop on the cocktail table in front of the sofa, plugged it in and hit the power button. "Since Nick's not here yet, I'm going to make a sandwich." He left the women in the family room.

"What's this all about, Charles?" his father, Victor Sr., asked when he entered the kitchen. "Why was it necessary to call the whole family together?"

"Did you guys leave any meat? I could use a sandwich before we get started," he answered, scanning the counter and momentarily disregarding the older man's interrogation. "Nick'll be here in a few."

His older brothers, Vic and Jesse shared a puzzled glance. Vic slid the bread, mustard, and mayonnaise in Charles' direction. They watched him in silence as he slathered the bread with mayonnaise, and slapped together a combination of ham, turkey, and cheese.

"I have to set up this conference call on my laptop." He poured a glass of apple juice. "If Nick isn't here by the time I'm done, I'll just start without him."

The three doctors stared at him and nodded. "Who the hell is he conferencing?" Charles heard Jesse say as he left the room.

Thankfully, his baby brother walked in the door as he headed toward the computer. "It's about time, man," Charles grasped Nick's hand, and they bumped shoulders.

"I had to take Cherilyn home. What's up, man? Why the appearance summons?"

"You'll know in a few minutes. Do you know how to do a Skype call?"

"Sure. Don't you?"

"Yes, but I've never made a conference call."

"And we're conferencing with?"

"Marc and Greg."

Nick's cerulean gaze rested on his. "This must be *major*. Give me the numbers, and I'll do it. Are they expecting the call?"

"I told them between two-thirty and three o'clock."

Nick, the family cyber-wizard, positioned himself in front of the computer. "They'll be on the line in five minutes."

"Okay. Let me get the rest of the family from the kitchen." Charles crossed the room and peered into the kitchen. "We're almost ready. Come on." His father bolted into the living room as though he couldn't wait another minute to find out what this whole production was about. He took a seat next to his wife.

"Hey, Marc. It's Nick. I'm arranging this call for Charles. Can you see me?"

"Uh huh, is everybody there?"

"Present and accounted for."

"Hey, people!" Marc called from the screen. "Gianne is here with me. Say hi, baby." Marc's fiancée leaned in, waved and was met with a chorus of hellos.

"Hold on, so I can get Greg." Nick did his thing, and the last of his five brothers appeared on the screen from his Manhattan apartment. "We're all in the family room." He moved aside and let Charles take his place in front of the laptop.

"I obviously have an announcement to make, but first I want to say that I've been considering this decision for a couple of years." He met Vic's gaze, and his brother smiled. "And I discussed it with Marc when he was here a few months ago." He paused, cleared his throat and met his father's gaze. "I've put my practice up for sale, and I'm moving to Las Vegas to work with Marc for half of the year." A collective gasp traveled around the room, but Charles was determined to finish. "The other half of the year I'll be working with *Doctors Without Borders* performing reconstructive surgery in a small village hospital in Nigeria. As soon as the legal details are finalized with the real estate agent and the legal guys, I'll be leaving."

His mother grabbed his father's hand. Cyd and Ramona put their heads together and whispered. An uneasy silence lingered until Greg spoke from the computer screen. "That's fantastic, man! It takes a lot of guts to make a move like that."

"I agree," Marc chimed in. "If that's where your heart is, go for it."

"Did you talk him into this, Marcus?" his father challenged, clearly shocked by the news.

"Daddy. Daddy!" Charles raised his voice. "This was *my* decision. When I asked Marc if I could stay with him, he asked me how I planned to make any money during the half of the year I'd be in the States. At that point, I wasn't sure, so he made me an offer."

"Dammit, Charles! You're a Board-certified plastic surgeon," the older man blustered. I already have one son whose life goal is to be a gym rat." He leapt from his seat and headed for the bar in the corner where he poured himself two fingers of Scotch and took a long sip.

Undeterred, Charles continued. "*Doctors Without Borders* is a highly respected organization, and if I'm ever going to do this, it has to be now while I'm single with no kids. If I divest most of my hard assets, I can have a nice cushion. After all, nobody needs a Benz or a wardrobe of designer suits to operate in a remote third-world hospital."

"I think it's wonderful, Charles," Cydney said, bouncing the sleeping baby across her lap.

Ramona just rolled her eyes. Pro-bono work of any kind ran contrary to her DNA.

His mother spoke up. "Victor, I think you're losing sight of the real point here. We raised the boys to give back, didn't we?"

"He doesn't need to sell his practice and move to Las Vegas in order to give back," his father insisted. "You can stay here in Atlanta and volunteer wherever you want, Charles. I know of colleagues who donate their time to DWB, but they only do short tours."

"I thought about that, Daddy, but I don't want to go that route. I'm sick and tired of catering to people's narcissism. I want to help people, I mean, *really* help. If I have to enlarge any more lips, butts, or boobs, I'll lose my mind."

His father slammed his glass on the table. "Boy, what is wrong with you? Those lips, butts, and boobs paid off that $200,000 student loan debt!"

Charles stood his ground. "Right. So my time doing vanity surgery has served its purpose. This isn't up for discussion. It looks as though I have a qualified buyer for my practice, and once the deal is finalized, I'll be moving to Vegas."

"So what will you be doing for Marc?" Cydney asked, obviously trying to intervene on the brewing verbal brawl simmering between father and son.

"I'll be the suit, the one who visits corporations to sell them on the value of corporate fitness programs for their employees. Since the major corporations in Vegas are the casinos, they'll be my targets. It should be *interesting,* since this will be my first stint as a businessman rather than a medicine man."

"You'll do just fine," his mother reassured him. "I'm just concerned about the reports I've heard about the dangers of visiting Nigeria. That's where they have all those kidnappings, isn't it?"

"Yes, Mama, but it's not like I'm a movie star or anything." He chuckled. "Nobody would get anything out of kidnapping me."

"Charles," Marc interrupted. "I need you to call me as soon as you get your flight details."

"Will do, man."

"All right, folks. We're signing off now. Gianne and I have things to do."

"Yeah, I bet you do," Greg said from his window on the screen with a snide laugh that elicited laughs from the family. "Check you later."

Gianne peeked into the camera's view. "It was good to see everybody."

"Before you go, tell us how the wedding plans are coming along?" his mother asked.

"Okay. We haven't decided what kind of ceremony we want yet."

She scowled. "Marcus, please don't call and tell me you decided to take her to one of those awful casino chapels."

"Let's just be thankful he's not taking her into the desert and having a cactus officiate over the ceremony," his father joked, always taking stabs at Marc's New Age tendencies and raw vegan lifestyle.

"Stop it, Victor." She swatted his father's arm.

"We're definitely not doing *that*, but we'll let everyone know the details once we get everything arranged. We're not getting married until next summer."

"It takes at least a year to plan a decent wedding, Marc," Ramona said.

Marc grinned. "Okay, we're going now. Bye."

The family called out their goodbyes and his window disappeared. Charles disconnected the call then closed his laptop.

"Why?" his father grumbled. "I'm convinced Marcus had *something* to do with you making this crazy decision."

"You're wrong, Daddy. I asked him if I could stay with him when I'm in the States. He's living in that big house with so much extra space. Oh, that's right, you've never been to his house," Charles added with such a cutting edge it made his father look away. "I thought it was the perfect solution. A couple of days later, he called me with the job offer. Even when he and Gianne get married, I don't think my living there will be an imposition."

Always the statesman, his big brother Vic raised his glass of apple juice and said, "I think this deserves a toast. To a future filled with discovery and the chance to share your talents with the world. Here's to a great new career! To Charles!"

Everyone holding a beverage, except his father, raised their glass and repeated, "To Charles!"

The elder man shook his head as though in disbelief that yet another of his six sons had chosen to go against the Stafford family tradition. He and his brothers, Clifford and Rodney, were successful private practice physicians. Three of Charles' brothers had all followed in their father's footsteps, and Jesse was part of his practice. Vic Jr. had formerly worked as a surgeon with the practice until he was offered a position as hospital Chief of Staff. A recent graduate of medical school, Nick, the youngest brother, had done his internship but was now wavering on selecting a specialty. The other two, had chosen non-medical professions. Greg currently held a coveted position as a primetime television magazine show host in New York. Marc was creating a name for himself as a Las Vegas celebrity personal trainer and raw foods advocate, which their father considered akin to witchcraft.

Now he had upset the status quo by announcing his decision. At least he'd chosen to remain in medicine, but not in the manner the senior Stafford considered respectable. For years, his father and his twin brother Marc had been estranged because of his decision not to pursue medicine. Only recently had they begun to work on settling their differences. The fact that he would be working part-time with Marc put a burr under the old man's collar.

He planned to fly to Las Vegas in a couple of weeks to start brainstorming with his twin about what his function with Canyon Gate Personal Training would be. The prospect of doing something so completely different excited him. So did the idea of leaving Atlanta. Charles had been born and raised there, and the only time he'd spent away from the Queen City of the South was when he did his undergrad work at UGA. After graduation, he returned to Atlanta and attended Morehouse School of Medicine.

The glitz and glamour of Vegas held a certain attraction for him. He liked the idea that he would be in a city where no one knew him. Here in Atlanta he was always conscious of upholding the Stafford reputation. Seeing your doctor in the club with a girl twerking on his crotch was bad for business to say the least. After spending the past five years working nonstop, Charles had every intention of getting his party on during his six months stateside.

He landed at McCarran International Airport in Las Vegas two weeks later. He had taken a week's vacation to give him time with his twin. Because he thought it was the right thing to do, he'd announced the pending sale of his plastic surgery practice to his staff two months ago. He asked if they could stay on until the transaction was finalized with the promise of a glowing reference and a generous separation bonus. One of his physician's assistants resigned, but the other PA and his receptionist had agreed to remain and keep the office running while he traveled.

He called Marc's cell as soon as the pilot announced that they had reached their destination. Marc said he'd wait outside of the hourly deck where he'd parked. After the flight landed, Charles exited the terminal and stepped into cool forty-five degrees just like he'd left in Atlanta.

"Hey!" he called as he crossed the street to the parking deck. "Thanks for picking me up, man." He pulled his twin into an enthusiastic embrace. "Since I'll only be here for a week, I didn't want to rent a car."

Marc popped the trunk on the Cadillac hybrid, stashed the bags inside, and got behind the wheel. "My old Camry is still in the garage," he said, eyeing the rearview mirror as he pulled into the crawling traffic exiting the airport. "Gianne's not using it anymore since we brought her Camaro back from Atlanta. If it's not beneath your Benz-driving ass, it's yours to use while you're here."

"Thanks, man. The SLS is already gone. I sold it last week."

"Hope you got a good price for it."

"The dealership bought it back. I've had a good relationship with them, and they made me an offer I couldn't refuse." He chuckled then changed the subject. "How's Gianne doing?"

"She's great," Marc answered with a fondness in his voice

that made Charles smile. "Kind of loopy over these upcoming wedding plans, but otherwise she's feeling strong and looking sexier than ever."

"Next June, right?"

"Yup. It seems so far off, but she's convinced that's still not enough time to get everything done. Women..." Marc shook his head, and his long hair flipped around the collar of his polo shirt. "She said she'll see you this evening when she gets in from work."

"I'm glad things are going well for you two. Of course, Mama wasn't thrilled when you told her that you two had moved in together, but she loves Gianne."

"It was the best decision I ever made. I couldn't let her stay with her cousin over in the wild, wild west with those little gangsters gunning people down on the street. It's funny, but she's gradually becoming one of the Real Canyon Gate Housewives. Recently she started playing tennis with one of the neighbors." Both men laughed. "How is Daddy adjusting to your career move?"

"He doesn't really discuss it. Just throws those verbal jabs every chance he gets."

Marc threw back his head with a loud laugh. "I am *so* glad somebody besides me is catching it for once!"

"Thanks a lot. Mama is planning a party she thinks I don't know about."

"There's no way you can get out of that. Mama lives to throw parties."

"So, what have you planned for me this week?"

"You, Lance, and I need to sit down and tell you about our ideas for getting more clients for the business, but we'll have to do it one evening because we're booked solid during the day. We can discuss it over dinner."

"I've been doing some research, and I have a few ideas of my own for some out-of-the-box promotions."

"Great. I can't wait to hear them. Do you want to go back to the studio with me or to the house to get the car?"

"I'll hang with you at the studio."

"Okay. You need to grab some lunch first, 'cause we'll be there until at least six. I brought something from home today. What do you feel like eating?"

"Anything that's not hamster food."

Marc shook his head. "Quianna is in town this month," he added casually.

"I know," Charles answered with a devious smirk. "Why do you think I chose to come out this week?"

Marc's eyes widened. "You two have been communicating since your last visit?"

"I wouldn't exactly call it communicating. She texted me a couple of weeks ago and said she'd be back in Vegas for a short while. I texted her back and told her I'd let her know when my schedule was set. That's the extent of our conversation."

A smile lurked at one corner of Marc's mouth. "Humph! Just protect yourself. Quianna's told me stories that I'd love to report to the CDC."

"Unnecessary," Charles said with a raised palm. "I *am* a doctor."

"Just wanted to enlighten you."

After they stopped to pick up his lunch, Marc drove right to the studio. Charles grabbed his laptop bag from the trunk and followed Marc inside. He threw a 'what's up' nod to Lance, who was in the middle of a medicine ball workout with another client.

Marc's next client had already arrived and was doing stretches at the bar on the far wall. "Sorry I'm late, Kathy. I had to run to the airport to pick up my brother. This is Charles."

She stared at him before her gaze swung back to Marc. "My goodness! You two look so much alike you could be twins."

Both brothers laughed. "We are. Charles beat me here by a whole three minutes, so he's the oldest. You can eat in the office, man. Make yourself comfortable. I'll be in once I finish up with Kathy."

"I'm going to check a few things online while I eat." He left the main room, settled behind his brother's desk, and set up his laptop. With so much going on in his life right now, he received constant e-mails from his lawyers, real estate agent and accountant. He had also asked a female friend to suggest a good place to resell his extensive collection of designer suits and shoes. As he scanned his inbox, he clicked on a message from her which contained the names and addresses of a few high-end consignment stores. His favorite pieces would travel with him when he relocated to Las Vegas permanently. Since he would be the suit representing Canyon Gate Personal Training, it only made sense that he held onto a few of the best ones for client visits. When he returned to Atlanta, he planned to go shopping for a more suitable wardrobe for his new life in Nigeria.

♥

Adanna and Lezigha Bankole, the other nurse, met with the doctors to plan what needed to be done around the hospital before their visiting doctors arrived. The option of doing any remodeling was fiscally impossible, and only minor expenses could come out of their so-called budget. A local handyman who performed maintenance around the facility would take care of the repairs. In the interim, the foremost job was to go over patient files and select those in most urgent need of surgery and other specialized care. Tonight, Adanna took home a stack of files to read over the weekend and present to the doctors on Monday morning.

When she got home, Emeka was sitting in the living room talking to Femi, who was busy fixing dinner. At times she thought he was interested in her beautiful, full-figured friend. But she knew better. Her brother was too engrossed in his vigilante activities to have time for a serious relationship. It was her culinary skill and the fact that he wanted to keep an eye on his sister that brought him to their flat at least once a week.

Emeka took his responsibility as her guardian very seriously. They had been back in Nigeria for almost seven years, but he intended to keep his promise to their father as long as she remained unmarried. It didn't matter to him one bit that she was a grown woman. There was no doubt in her mind that he loved her, but sometimes.... Every time he discovered that she was interested in someone, he practically stalked the poor man until he found out everything he thought he needed to know about him. Emeka's main concern was the tribal heritage of her suitors. Since she'd taken the job at the hospital, there had been no one in her life for him to pester. And that fact made her sad.

"Hello, dear brother," she said as she crossed the sisal rug in the center of the room and pecked him on the cheek. "How are you?"

A sour frown appeared on his face. "I haven't heard from you in days."

"Maybe I haven't had anything to say." Adanna waved a hand in the air. "There's no reason to be concerned. How many times do I have to tell you that?" She turned toward the kitchen, "It smells so good in here. What's for dinner, girl?"

Femi smiled, always pleased when someone complimented her cooking. "I made suya and fried plantains with Puff Puff for dessert."

"Ooh, that sounds great -- and fattening." Adanna laughed. "I have to get out of these clothes. Be back in a minute." She went into her bedroom and changed into a pair of shorts and a sleeveless cotton top, thankful that she didn't have to work for the next two days. She and Lezigha normally alternated shifts and weekends.

"When's the last time you spoke to Mum?" Emeka asked once she reappeared and sat next to him on the sofa.

"A couple of weeks ago, I guess. Why? Is something wrong?"

"No. I talked with her yesterday, and she said she hadn't heard from you lately."

"Oh, so that's why you're here."

"I just wanted to make sure you were okay, Adanna. What are you up to this weekend?"

"Nothing you'd be interested in." She took the plate that Femi handed her and exhaled a tired sigh. "I brought a lot of work home. All I plan to do is rest and read."

"No date?"

"Is it necessary for you to always ask me that?"

"With the exception of Mum's brothers, who live hours away, I am your closest male relative. What kind of brother would I be if I didn't look after you?"

She dropped her fork on her plate without taking a bite and stood. "I am twenty-seven years old. I don't need *looking after*!"

"Well, Dad thinks you do."

"That was six years ago. Give it a rest, will you?"

A knock sounded on the door and Emmanuel and another one of their friends entered the flat.

"Hi, Manny, Agu." She grabbed her plate and glass. "Now you have someone else to talk to, Emeka. I'm going to eat in my room, then I'm going to bed. I'll call Mum tomorrow. Goodnight." She left him shaking his head.

Nothing annoyed her more than being treated like an irresponsible teenager. Her brother was doing what he thought was proper and necessary, but she'd had her fill of explaining her every move to him. At her age, it was downright embarrassing to have her male companions, if she could even call them that, vetted by her older brother. Once he had actually given the "father talk" to one of her dates. These were the times she wished she was back in England, where Emeka wouldn't have any idea of what she was up to in her life. Her father wouldn't be as overbearing as her brother.

Adanna spent all day Saturday with files spread out over her bed going over the cases of current and former patients who required some kind of surgery. As she read the doctors' notes and those written by Lezigha, or herself, she recalled personal details about the patients. She always liked to make a personal connection with those who came to the hospital to be treated, especially the children. It softened the edges of an often frightening visit. The needs of the people were so great, and this upcoming visit from the DWB doctors was an answer to prayer. The visiting team was only committed to the hospital for three months, and surgeons were given shorter assignments than other doctors because of their heavy schedules. Some of these patients needed sequential surgeries and required six weeks recovery time in between. Their needs were constantly on her mind, and she wanted every one of them to receive the necessary medical care.

After she made additional notes on points to mention to the doctors, Adanna returned the folders to her tote bag and went into the kitchen to make lunch.

"Do you have any plans for tonight?" Femi asked, watching her rummage through the refrigerator.

"Not a thing. Why?"

"A few of us are going to *Troy*. Come on and go with us. You never go out with us."

"I'm usually too tired, but I might come. I probably need to get in as much entertainment as possible before all of these changes happen at the hospital."

"When are the doctors supposed to arrive?

"The beginning of May, which is good, since we need time to try to bring whatever we can at the hospital up to par."

"Sounds like once they get here, your schedule is going to be hectic."

"Very. We won't know exactly how things will go until they arrive, but I'm excited. So many of our patients wouldn't get the care they need without this team."

"Okay, so I agree that you need to get your party on right away."

That evening, the two women dressed in their trendiest outfits, picked up Manny and Agu and began the drive to one of the top nightclubs where they were supposed to meet up with several of Femi's friends from work. Adanna wasn't crazy about hip-hop music, the club's specialty. But she did like the fact that all tribes, races, nationalities, and cultures partied together there, and that was what made the place tick. Troy also had some of the best DJs. All she wanted to do was dance and work off some of the frustration that working long hours and being man-free had built up.

Once they arrived and ordered drinks, she watched the

crowd trying her best to mask her displeasure at what she saw. Nigerian nightclubs had changed dramatically over the past decade. The more westernized they became, the more extreme the patrons' behaviors became. She nursed a Guinness and watched a woman performing a lap dance on her male companion that filled Adanna's face with heat. She wasn't a prig by any stretch of the imagination. After all, she worked as a nurse and saw every part of the human body on a daily basis, but this was different. The dancing had no grace or flow. It amounted to something just short of fully clothed bedroom antics of women bent forward with their generous bottoms pressed against their dance partners' crotches. For that reason, Adanna turned down the first two men who approached her for a dance.

"Why didn't you tell me this was the kind of dancing they do here?" she asked Femi, speaking close to her ear so her friend could hear above the loud music.

"Because I knew you wouldn't come. We don't have to dance like they do."

"You're right. I'm not about to give strangers that kind of show."

A few minutes later, two more smiling men came toward them with their hands outstretched. Femi rose first and inclined her head toward the dance floor for Adanna to follow. Reluctantly, she returned the man's smile and stood. She made her way onto the crowded dance floor somewhat self-conscious at first. It had been at least a year since she'd been to a nightclub, and she didn't want to appear out of touch. She also didn't want to look like a stripper. Hell would freeze over before she made her bum clap for anyone. After a minute or two, when she noticed her partner was still smiling, she allowed her body to relax and simply moved to the rhythm. When the song ended, her partner thanked her and returned to his seat at the bar.

Manny and Agu left the women for a while and went to

the pool bar on the VIP floor while she and Femi got some fresh air on the waterfront terrace. When the men eventually returned, Adanna danced with them and several others and enjoyed herself without resorting to any of the stripper moves some of the women did in order to get attention.

Afterward, she and her friends congregated at two tables, ordered food, and caught up on what was happening in their lives. Adanna had needed the conversation more than she'd known. Spending time among friends, laughing and joking didn't occupy enough time in her life, but it couldn't be helped. Even though she enjoyed herself immensely, at this point in her life, her job took priority over such selfish matters.

Manny returned from the dance floor and eased into the empty seat beside her. "Can I get you another beer?" he asked, nonchalantly sliding his arm across the back of her chair.

"Yes, please. Thanks," she said, hoping her acceptance wouldn't encourage his interest in her. Femi swore Manny had a secret crush on her, but Adanna didn't put too much stock in her claim. He always told her she needed to be married and start a family rather than working long hours, but he had never asked her out. She assumed he had come to the realization that he just wasn't her type. Manny worked in a bank in Lagos, which was a decent job, but he never talked about what he wanted in the future. He seemed quite content with his current position, and that was fine for him but not for her. And he knew it.

He signaled the bartender and pointed to the empty beer bottles on their table. "Femi told me things are getting ready to step up at your hospital. What does that mean for you?" Manny took the cold beers from the bartender when he approached and slipped a bill into his hand.

"It means a lot more work, but it also means I will get to observe some amazing surgeries. There is a plastic surgeon on the team who will be doing reconstructive surgery on the children and perhaps a few adults, depending on the severity of their conditions."

"You're very impressed with doctors, aren't you?"

Adanna didn't appreciate the resentful edge in his voice. "I'm impressed by what they can do with the knowledge they have, Manny. Being a doctor means nothing if you aren't using your skills and training to alleviate suffering. These men and women have given their time and regular incomes to come here and do this work at no charge. I'd say that's worthy of a little admiration."

"I suppose," he said with a dismissive wave. "You'll be working even longer hours once they arrive, won't you?"

"Most likely, but I don't mind. I want to be there to help them handle as many patients as possible during their stay, but until they get here, I just want to relax and enjoy myself." She grabbed him by both hands and pulled him up. "Come on, dance with me."

They wriggled in among the moving bodies in the center of the room and stayed on the floor for the next three songs. Winded and thirsty, when Adanna stepped off of the shiny wooden dance floor and headed for the bar, she stopped in her tracks at the sight of her brother staring right at her.

She strode up to him with her arms folded and asked, "What are you doing here, Emeka? Are you spying on me?"

He squinted and mimicked her stance. "No, my dear sister. I am not spying on you. I just happened to stop in for a drink. It *is* a public place."

Already hot and sweaty, Adanna's temperature rose as if she were walking over hot coals. "Don't tell me any bloody lies, Emeka! You don't even like nightclubs. I'm sick of you skulking around to find out what I'm doing." She shoved her hands onto her hips and jutted her chin toward him. "Your time would be better spent trying to find a wife instead of playing guardian to a grown woman."

"I promised Dad I would watch over you, and I will keep that promise until you have a husband to look after you." His patronizing smile only made her angrier.

"Don't you understand that I can look after myself? I'm not helpless. I'm not stupid, and this is not 1950, Emeka."

He took her hand. "I know you're not stupid. I love you, and I'm going to protect you until you find a man who will."

"Please go away." Determined to put a stop to his interference for good, she pulled from his grasp. Adanna stormed across the room in search of Femi as if her hair was on fire. She found her friend standing at the bar talking to one of the men with whom she'd been dancing earlier.

"Excuse me," Adanna interrupted. "May I speak to you for a minute, please?"

"What's wrong?" She must have read her furious expression. "Pardon me," Femi said to the man as she hooked her arm through Adanna's. "I'll be right back."

Both women moved to an unoccupied table nearby. "You'll never believe this! My brother is here spying on me."

"Why do you think that? Maybe he just happened to drop by for a drink."

"First of all, Emeka doesn't do nightclubs, Femi. And when I asked him what he was doing here, he all but admitted it." Adanna waved her arms in the air like a demented symphony conductor. "He must've found out from Manny or Agu that we planned to come here tonight. The nerve of him! This is crossing the line. I'm going home."

"Breathe, girl." Femi grabbed her by the shoulders. "You can't leave now. It's late, and it's not safe to be out there alone. Why don't you order yourself another beer and just ignore him? If it were me, I'd show him I didn't care whether he was here watching me or not. I'd go on dancing and having a good time."

After a few seconds, Adanna dragged in a long breath to calm herself. "You're right. He just gets me so upset." She took a napkin from the table and patted her brow. "I'm going to get another drink. Sorry, I disturbed your conversation."

"No big deal. He was boring as hell." Femi laughed. "I think I'll look around for someone a little more interesting." She walked away, swishing her ample hips to the beat of the music.

Adanna took Femi's advice and stayed on the dance floor for the next hour. Even though she'd kept one eye on the crowd the entire time, she hadn't seen Emeka again. Either he had relocated to a less conspicuous spot or he'd given up and gone home.

Actually, she had a good time once she'd decided to stay with her friends and pushed Emeka's interference to the back of her mind. Regardless, something needed to be done about her brother.

Chapter Two

Charles needed to say goodbye to the two women he'd been dating. Both relationships were far from serious, and he didn't think either woman was expecting anything more to develop. At least he hoped they weren't. Even though he hadn't told them he was selling his practice, just hopping on a plane and disappearing just seemed wrong. He made a note in his phone to pick up a small gift for both ladies while he was in Vegas. Jewelry always made negative news more palatable.

While he ate and sorted through his e-mails, his phone rang. "Charles Stafford."

"Hi, baby," his mother's voice said sweetly. "I just wanted to know if you landed okay."

"Was just getting ready to call you, Mama. Yeah, I got here in one piece. Marc picked me up at the airport, and I'm sitting at his desk in the studio as we speak."

"Good. Oh, by the way, I've scheduled your farewell party for next Saturday. We're renting out the new Shark Bar over at Greenbrier."

"Really?" This had to be someone else's idea. He found it hard to believe his mother was even familiar with the south side nightspot popular with the thirty-something crowd.

"Yes. There's not enough room at the house, and I wanted a place where your friends will feel comfortable. They offer catering and valet services. I think it will be a nice send-off."

He chuckled at how much joy his mother got from

planning celebrations. If she hadn't devoted her life to raising a small army of boys, she would've made a stellar event planner. "You're too much. I would've been fine with dinner at the house."

"Don't be silly. You're making a major move, and it should be celebrated in a major way."

"Thanks, Mama. Well, I have to run. I'm observing Marc and Lance in action today."

"All right, baby. When will you be back?"

"Next Tuesday, but we'll talk again before then. Love you."

"You too. Tell Marcus and Gianne I asked about them."

He hadn't bothered to inquire about the guest list, because it didn't matter. Everyone who was important to him would be there. She'd make certain of it. Whoever else happened to show up would be a plus.

Charles threw the empty lunch bag into the wastebasket, popped two breath mints, and exited the office. His brother and Lance were focused on their clients, so he took a seat in the corner on top of a pile of rubber floor mats. As he watched them explain and demonstrate the workouts, his mind drifted to thoughts of the near future. After four years of college, medical school, internship, residency, and constant seminars on new plastic surgery procedures, learning new things didn't unnerve him. But the prospect of becoming a salesman for his brother's company had him doubting his ability. His patients had always come to him of their own volition. They didn't need to be cajoled into having the procedures. He had often found it relatively easy to convince them to have additional work done when it was justified. Many times women who came to him for a tummy tuck could also benefit from lipo on their hips and thighs. They didn't need to be sold, and he believed it was unethical to pressure any patient into having more surgery. Charles considered himself a master of persuasion when it came to the ladies, but that was personal. This was business. But Marc had mentioned that the majority of his clients were female. Perhaps his skills would be transferable.

"Charles!"

Marc's voice roused him from his thoughts. "I was just thinking of ways I might be able to promote the business."

"And I was getting ready to say that Lance is coming home with us tonight so we can hash out some ideas."

Just as Charles got ready to respond, the front door opened and Quianna's overgrown bodyguard ducked his head and lumbered through with her a few paces behind him. She wasn't dressed to work out. In fact, she looked as though she was on her way to a club in a black mini dress that just barely covered her high, tight booty. She'd accessorized it with big silver earrings and a pair of thigh-high snakeskin boots cuffed at the top. Whatever he'd been getting ready to say to Marc flew right out of his head.

"Hello, Charles." Her slight Caribbean accent made everything she said sound sexy. "I'm on my way to an event, but I thought I would take my chances and see if you were here."

He stood and approached her. "I just got here about an hour ago. It's good to see you, Quianna. You look…lovely."

She gave a throaty giggle and tossed back the new long hair that cascaded over her thin shoulders. "Thank you. I was hoping you could accompany me tonight, since I don't have an escort."

Marc and Lance exchanged a glance and waited for his reply. "I'm sorry, Quianna. I have a meeting tonight. How about tomorrow night? Will you be in town?"

"Tomorrow night…" The singer, known worldwide for her theatrical sexiness, pursed her lips as though she had to give it some thought. "I was invited to another affair tomorrow, but you might enjoy it. I'll pick you up at ten."

Charles saw Marc smirk at her assertiveness. "What kind of affair is it?"

She smiled. "Just a party." When she turned and walked toward the door, her protector rushed to precede her so he could check the parking lot. "Dress casual," she said over her shoulder once she'd stepped outside.

The instant the door closed, Marc and Lance burst out laughing. "It's just a pah-tee. Dress kah-shu-wal," Marc imitated her. "That accent gets stronger when she's flirting."

"Okay, back off."

"I'm just saying, man. If you want to be this week's chew toy, it's none of my business. Just remember what I told you," Marc said, referring to his earlier protection warning.

Charles fixed his gaze on his brother and spoke in a clipped tone. "And remember what I told you."

Marc shook his head. "Okay. We're straight. I won't mention it again."

For the next five hours, he observed Marc and Lance at work. They interacted differently with their clients, gentle and encouraging with some and tougher with others. Both of them even did a little borderline flirting with a couple of the women. He was impressed. When the last client left, Charles helped them wipe down the equipment with spray disinfectant, then they left for Marc's house.

Gianne met them at the back door, greeted Lance and welcomed Charles with a hug. "Just dump your stuff in your room and come out to the patio. Dinner is ready by the pool."

"Thanks, Gianne," he said, thinking it was only fifty-five degrees, a little cool to sit outside. "I know you and Marc are used to being alone, so I hope I won't get in your way."

"Oh, please! This house is plenty big enough for the three of us plus a few others."

Charles put his bags in the bedroom he always used when he visited, and noticed that a few things had changed in the room. A small desk with an office lamp now occupied one corner along with a mini-shelf sound system atop a small empty bookcase. Gianne obviously wanted him to make himself at home.

When he got outside, Marc had a blaze going in the firebowl at the center of the patio, and Gianne had a spread laid out on a table.

"You didn't have to go to all this trouble for me, Gianne," he said, looking over the assortment of chicken wings, sandwiches and salads.

She wiped the back of her hand across her forehead. "Yes, I worked really hard. I called a couple of places and told them to make up some platters. By the way, as a word of warning, this one is Marc's." She pointed to a platter filled with hummus, some kind of pate, and an assortment of vegetables. "Enjoy yourselves. I need to prepare for my class tomorrow."

"How are the wedding plans going?"

"We've finally picked a location. At first we thought about having it at the Canyon Gate Country Club, but we didn't want to pay for a membership just for that. Don't tell the rest of the family yet, but Marc and I decided to have it in Lake Tahoe. Vegas is known for weddings, but not the kind we want. You guys have a good meeting."

Charles smiled when Marc gave her booty a playful swat then grabbed her hand and pulled her close for a kiss. It pleased him to see how happy they were together. Marc had been the lover among his five brothers, and Gianne had what it took to make him turn in his player's card. Thus far in his life, Charles hadn't met a woman with that kind of power. At times he doubted such an elusive creature even existed.

Charles, Marc, and Lance settled around the fire and attacked the small buffet Gianne had provided for them.

"I appreciate you guys giving me your evening. I'm anxious to hear your ideas, Charles, and I want you both to be straight with me about how you think this is going to work out." Marc loaded his plate with generous scoops of hummus, zucchini chips, carrot sticks, flax crackers and living bread. "Okay, let's hear your thoughts."

Charles sat back in his chair and glanced at the darkening sky. "This is nice, man." He finished off a buffalo wing and soothed his torched tongue with a long swallow of Bud Light. "I've spent as much time as I could researching the industry, and what I discovered is that the average client doesn't know what good training really is. It seems like the *image* of proficiency and knowledge in personal training sells your services more than genuine talent and skill." Marc and Lance both snickered. "That doesn't mean you should offer anything less than the best, and knowing you the way I do," he glanced at his twin, "top notch is all you'd give them. I have a few suggestions based on what I've learned. You can take them or leave them, of course. Since the public's *perception* of skill is so important, you should establish yourself as an expert in the field, and you can do that easily by writing."

Marc frowned. "Writing? I'm not a writer."

"But you can be by writing articles for local newspapers and magazines. Of course, at the end you always list your credentials to show that you're more than just words. This is the best way to establish yourself as the go-to guy in the business. You can include those writings in your professional portfolio, post them in a visible spot in the studio, and hand out copies at personal appearances."

"What kind of appearances?"

"Didn't you say you buy most of your groceries at Whole Foods?" Marc nodded. "You could do seminars there on raw vegan cooking. I already looked at several of their individual store websites to see what kind of classes they offer. I think they'd jump at the chance to have a certified raw foods chef giving free classes there."

Marc smiled and helped himself to a veggie burger. "As many times as I've been in the store, that never occurred to me."

"That's why you have me, little brother. You could also schedule Lunch & Learn sessions for local businesses with a dozen or more employees and fix the food to demonstrate your expertise."

"Another idea is for the two of you to do a demonstration at the mall. Since you're already on the outskirts of the mall, transporting some equipment to the center court wouldn't be a major problem. You could ask for participants from the spectators, but they'd have to sign release waivers before they do any exercises, because you can't be too careful with people these days. They'll lift a ten-pound free weight and swear that they tore something so they can sue you."

Lance and Marc exchanged a glance and nodded.

"Two more ideas. I need you both to start putting together a list of mavens in the area, the realtors, doctors and baristas who see a lot of people during their day and might be willing to recommend your services to their clients and customers." Marc smiled in agreement. "Last of all, how active are you guys on social media?"

"Not much businesswise. We have a company Facebook page and a website. Personally, is another thing," Lance said, giving Marc a sidelong glance. "Yeah, this fool is on Twitter and Instagram twenty-four seven."

"That's great!" Charles replied, getting the side eye from his brother. "If you're already fluent in cyberspeak, I have a plan for a strategic campaign on both sites. Would you be willing to handle that, Lance?"

"Sure. You have to let me know how you want to do it."

The men all reached for the food table at the same time and ate silently while they considered what Charles had just presented.

Gianne came through the back door with her hands full of plastic storage containers. "I'm heading upstairs to read for a while, but I want you guys to pack up what's left. Lance, take home whatever you want. Charles, you can take any of this for lunch tomorrow, if you want." She placed a hand on Marc's shoulder, bent down, and kissed him. "Good night, guys."

"You're a lucky man, bro. She's sweet, and she's looking great. When we first met, she was so skinny."

"Thanks," Marc said wearing a smile of male pride. "She's put on twenty pounds of muscle in nine months since she came to Vegas and started weight training with me."

"That's not the only working out she does with you," Lance added with a cocky grin.

"All right, man. My sex life isn't up for discussion tonight."

The men laughed and talked briefly about Marc's wedding plans. As the sky darkened, Charles asked questions about their programs and the financial arrangements they had in place for corporate clients. Lance and Marc described the workout program they'd put together to help him with his desire to bulk up. Once they finished off the food and packed up the leftovers, Lance said goodnight and Marc extinguished the fire.

"I think we're off to a good start," Marc said after they locked up and turned out the patio lights.

"Me too, and I appreciate you and Gianne making room for me."

"This is a big step for you, and I know what kind of resistance you're facing at home." He slapped Charles on the back. "You remember where everything is. See you in the morning." He turned and headed down the hall toward his bedroom.

He shook his head, confused at the unexpected twinge of envy that coursed through him when Marc closed the door to the bedroom he shared with the woman he loved. Charles had never been at a loss for female companionship, but observing the relationship Marc had with Gianne only reminded him that he'd never had anything even close to it with the women who had come in and out of his life. His career had always come first, and he didn't have the time to invest in cultivating anything deep. Singleness had never bothered him, even when he was around Vic and Jesse and their wives who had decent marriages. Whenever he was around Marc and Gianne, though, he wondered whether he was missing out.

Charles shut the door to the guest room, now his bedroom, and rummaged through his still-packed suitcases for a pair of pajama bottoms. Suddenly realizing how tired he was from his full day, he decided to shower in the morning. After he removed his clothes and pulled back the covers on the bed, he slid under the sheet and blanket with his mind on his upcoming date with Quianna. Men all over the world would kill for an evening with the hip-hop princess, and she had extended the invitation to him. But after Marc's warning, his outlook about her wasn't the same. He had no reason to believe that evening would include sex, but the way she'd looked at him as though he were something to be devoured, gave him the feeling that was all

Quianna was after. Whatever the evening brought at least he could say he'd been out with her.

In the morning, Charles made his zombie-like entrance into the kitchen in search of coffee after his alarm went off.

"Good morning," Gianne said from behind the island. "We don't drink coffee, but I remember how you mainline the stuff, so we got you a single cup brewer. I made you a cup, and there are plenty more up here in the cabinet. The instructions and sugar packets are right here," Gianne patted a small pamphlet next to the machine. "Cream's in the fridge."

He grinned. "Thanks. I'm not as evolved as my brother, so I still need artificial stimulation in order to get going in the morning."

"So does he. It's just not caffeine." She sent him a wicked smile. "Sorry that I can't stay and chat, but I have to be in early. I'm doing a special program for the kids this morning. Marc's in the shower. He should be out in a few minutes. Have a great day." She picked up her purse and tote bag and as she went through the door leading to the driveway, she called over her shoulder. "Have fun tonight."

♥

One forty-five. Too late to call Dad in London. He was the only one who could put her brother in check. Adanna decided to delay talking to him. If she called him now, he would know that she'd just returned home. She was already aggravated enough and didn't feel like hearing his mouth. After she removed her makeup and brushed her teeth, she fell into bed, going over in her mind what she might say to her father.

Normally she loved Sunday mornings when she didn't have to report to work at the hospital. Femi usually fixed a scrumptious breakfast, and they would spend a leisurely day listening to music and catching up on reading. Today, Adanna rose early, made herself a cup of coffee, and sat on the edge of the bed contemplating how to tell her father about Emeka. She dialed the number and waited. Her mother answered.

"Ǹdâ, Mum. I know you're getting ready for church, but I wanted to talk to Dad about something. Is he busy right now?"

"Are you all right, baby?"

"Yes, well…no. I need to talk to him about Emeka."

"What about your brother? Is he in some kind of trouble?"

"No. He's getting on my nerves, and Dad is the only one who can put a leash on him."

"I see," her mother said, sounding as if she already knew the reason behind her daughter's call. "He's having his second cup of coffee. I'll get him. Hold on."

Adanna heard her mother's muffled voice in the background as she waited for her father to come to the phone.

"Well," her father's cheerful voice rang out. "To what do I owe the honor of my only daughter calling early on a Sunday morning?"

"Ǹdâ, Dad. How are you?"

"I'm fine. Just getting ready for church. I wish you were doing the same."

Adanna smiled and shook her head. Her father served as a deacon in the Church of England and tried his best to get her to also become a member. She wasn't one for all that tradition. In fact, she had been considering visiting one of the larger non-denominational churches in Lagos. She let his comment pass. "Daddy, I need to talk to you about something. If you don't have time now, I can call back."

"What's wrong? You sound troubled."

"I am. It's Emeka. He's gone off the deep end, and I can't take it anymore." She tried her best to refrain from whining.

"You and your brother always got along so well. What's changed?"

"What's changed is that I'm twenty-seven years old. Emeka is treating me like a minor child, and he's resorted to following me around when I'm out with my friends. Can you please talk to him and tell him to back off?"

"Adanna, he means no harm. I only agreed with you going back home if Emeka accompanied you. A woman alone isn't safe there."

"I don't live alone, and I don't travel alone unless I'm going to work, but he's even shown up at the hospital to check on me. It makes me look like a fool in front of my coworkers."

"Our agreement was that you could return home if you and Emeka lived together, but you chose to dishonor that." His sudden sharp tone surprised her.

"We lived together for *two years*, Dad. By then I'd adapted to being back here and didn't need to stay with him any longer."

"So you say. Emeka told me differently. Your brother and I agree that until you find a husband, it will continue to be his responsibility to look after you."

"Dad," she rolled her eyes at the way she whined, "why can't you two let go of those chauvinist ideas and come into the twenty-first century with the rest of us?"

He sighed into the phone. "Because the date on the calendar has nothing to do with what's proper. Until you meet a good Ibo man, and he takes on the role as your husband and protector, our agreement stands. I'm sorry, Adanna."

"Not as sorry as I am. I'll let you finish getting ready for church. Tell Mum I'll talk to her during the week. Goodbye."

She ended the call with tears stinging her eyes and her mind wondering exactly what Emeka had told her father about how she had adapted to being a returnee to Nigeria. Yes, it was a new millennium, but Nigeria was still very much a patriarchal society. It didn't matter that she earned her own living and paid her own way. Males still had a lot more freedom than females, and she hated that fact. Still, she insisted on making her feelings known. She picked up her phone once again and hit the memory button for Emeka's cell.

"Good morning," she said, forcing an artificially cheerful greeting. "Do you have any plans for this afternoon?"

"Uh…no," he responded in a sleep-roughened voice.

Adanna smiled at the thought that she'd disturbed the sleep he probably wanted desperately after being out so late on last night's espionage mission. "Why don't you come by for dinner? I know Femi is fixing something delicious."

"All…right." The suspicion behind his words was clear. "What's the occasion?"

"No occasion. I just know how much you love her cooking. Come by about three."

"Okay. Thanks."

That afternoon, Adanna, Emeka, Femi, and Agu sat at the small dining table enjoying a sumptuous meal of chicken stew with coconut rice. Once she presumed her brother had eaten enough to put himself in a pleasant mood, she opened the topic she wanted to discuss in the presence of her friends.

"So, how's work going, Emeka?"

He shrugged and offered a small smile. "It's work. Nothing really exciting ever happens in the accounting department of an oil company."

"Well, something exciting is getting ready to happen on my job. We recently found out that a team from Doctors Without Borders is coming to assist us. That means so many of our patients who couldn't afford to have certain procedures and surgeries will be taken care of."

"I think it's great," Femi agreed, knowing her friend's heart was always with the sick and hurting. "You didn't tell me what countries they are coming from."

"According to the background information, they're sending doctors and a nurse from Germany, Spain, Great Britain, Sweden, and the US."

Her brother grunted. "As usual, foreigners are riding in to save the poor, helpless Nigerians as if we can't take care of ourselves."

"Emeka, if we could take care of ourselves so well, their help wouldn't be necessary. There are so many suffering people, especially in the villages. They need the help of anyone who's willing to give it. Honestly, I don't understand you. After living in London for so many years, why are you so against anything or anyone who is not Nigerian? Peckham was thirty-five percent African and probably the closest place to here than anywhere else in the world."

"Because they try so hard to indoctrinate us into their way of living. Look at us, for God's sake. We speak with British accents."

"So what?" Femi interjected. "That doesn't make you any less Nigerian or any less Ibo."

"I just mentioned it, because in your incessant snooping you might see me with some unidentified Caucasians. I wanted you to know who they are, so you don't call out your vigilante friends on them." She caught the lightning quick glance he exchanged with Agu.

Emeka's face spread into a smile. "You watch too much TV news. We don't stalk people. Our job is to respond to crime alerts and handle the criminals." Many citizens had these alerts on mobile phones. If a citizen witnessed a crime, all they had to do was dial a certain code and the group would receive the alert.

"If you say so. I just want you to know that you might see me with some unidentified people, and I don't want you and your boys to make a big thing of it. You have to back off and let me live my own life. This is the last time I'm going to warn you."

His piercing black eyes narrowed. "I'll do whatever I feel is necessary to keep you safe."

Adanna understood Emeka's concern for her. He wasn't being unrealistic about the danger, but he couldn't protect her every single minute of every single day. When he'd left her flat on Sunday evening, he was disturbed once again by her independent spirit. Yes, Nigeria was a far cry from London, where the City Police maintained a constant presence on the streets. Here, particularly in the smaller villages, law enforcement, other than that provided by vigilantes, was poor or generally non-existent. Nevertheless, she had come back to the country to use her skills to help those who needed it the most, and she wasn't going back on that decision. Nor was she consenting to having her brother shadow her everywhere she went. At least she would be back at work in the morning, and when she was busy, Emeka and his excessive devotion, retreated to the back of her mind.

Chapter Three

Charles dressed in a pair of slim-fit jeans and a long-sleeve white cotton dress shirt topped with a black vest, since Quianna had told him to dress casually. He'd visited the barbershop before he left Atlanta, so his hair and beard were still neatly trimmed.

At exactly ten o'clock, a limousine pulled up to the house, and the door chimed moments later.

"I'll get it," he called out to Marc and Gianne, who he knew were lurking somewhere where they could observe undetected.

Quianna's enormous bodyguard filled the doorway when he opened the front door. "Charles Stafford?" he asked.

"That's me."

"Ms. Wright is waiting in the car."

Charles almost laughed. He'd forgotten Quianna's last name, since it was hardly ever mentioned. Remembering Marc's warning, he doubted she could live up to her moniker. He waved to Marc and Gianne and let the driver precede him to the car.

"Hello there," Quianna greeted him with a smile as the driver opened the rear door. "Don't you look handsome?"

Once the door closed, and he was in the quiet confines of the limo, Charles gave her an appreciative onceover. She wore a clingy, low-cut top and skin-tight pants with openings that revealed a glimpse of skin every few inches as though it was made of extra-large Band-Aids. "And you look amazing."

She smiled. "Thank you. I guess I should tell you that we're going to a party that Sinister is giving at a house he's leasing in Summerlin. It's gonna be turnt up, so brace yourself," she said with a wide, unguarded smile.

Charles didn't want to admit that he knew nothing about Sinister other than what he'd seen on the news about the famous rapper. Sinister had a reputation for pushing the envelope in his music and in his personal life. The music and entertainment world was foreign to him, and normally the last thing Charles wanted was to be identified with questionable associates. In Atlanta he had been careful to separate himself from anything that might reflect poorly on his medical reputation. Now that he was seventeen hundred miles away from his former patients, what harm would it do to let his hair down a little?

He'd been invited to the homes of many wealthy Atlantans, but when the limo pulled up in front of a modern stone and glass mansion, he thought Marc's house could be the guest house for this place. The way the sprawling residence was lit up against the dark sky, Charles guessed that the rapper wanted to put it on display even though he wasn't the owner. Cars and limousines surrounded the property, and red jacketed valets opened the car doors to allow Quianna and him to exit. Of course, as they stepped out, so did her bodyguard.

"Charles, you remember Max, my bodyguard," she said by way of an offhanded introduction.

"He nodded in the big man's direction and received a silent nod in return.

The bumping bass of loud music punctuated the night air in the quiet exclusive neighborhood. Max preceded them to the door where a bored-looking woman who appeared to be the hostess invited them in. The pungent aroma of marijuana stung his nostrils as they entered. "He's out back by the pool." She gave an apathetic wave toward an open wall at the rear of the expansive living room filled with people eating, drinking, and smoking. Quianna took his hand and led him through the crowd. The closer they got to the doorway leading out to the pool area, the louder the music got. Charles studied the crowd standing around the glowing blue light of the enormous free-form pool. Most of the women had so little on, he could've been at a pool party–or a strip club.

Quianna spotted their host on the far side of the pool and led Charles toward him. Sinister had an entire magnum of champagne turned up to his mouth and the excess flowed over his chin and down his tattooed chest.

"Hey, Sin," she called to him loudly so he might hear her over the music.

"Quianna!" Sinister lowered the bottle and stretched his arms open to welcome her. "You're looking hot, girl!"

"Thanks. This is my friend, Charles. Charles, this is Sinister."

"Welcome, man." The rapper grabbed his hand, brought it up to his damp torso and leaned in to bump their shoulders together. Charles had to resist his instant desire to wipe his hand on his pants. "Help yourself to whatever amuses you," he said with his famous gravelly laugh.

"What would amuse me right now," Quianna said in Charles' ear, "is some food. Let's see what's on the buffet."

The spread left nothing wanting, and both of them loaded up their plates and searched for somewhere to sit. Every sofa and chaise around the pool was occupied, so he and Quianna headed back inside. This time, they ventured into the back of the house.

"That sounds like the theater," She said in response to the

sound coming from the room. "Maybe we can park in there."

Like a lost child in a strange place, he followed behind her, balancing his plate and champagne flute. But when they entered the semi-darkened theater, Charles had to blink to be certain what he saw was real.

Three guys with no pants were sitting up on the backs of the red leather recliners. At first he couldn't figure out what was going on, but Quianna's curiosity got the best of her and she moved further into the theater to get a better look. In the flickering light of the movie playing on the screen, a woman was eagerly sniffing and licking cocaine off of the men's penises. Each time she finished, they reapplied the pricey powder. They groaned and laughed as she went back and forth down the row. Charles couldn't believe what he was seeing, especially when he realized the woman was a well-known pop singer whose songs he had in rotation on his iPod. He retreated a few paces, intending to silently back out of the room before anyone noticed them, but Quianna settled into one of the cushy recliners with her plate on her lap as though she were about to enjoy a feature film. Not exactly what he wanted to watch while he was eating. He forced himself to pull his gaze away from the licentious scene and focus instead on the wall-sized screen in front of them. This evening had already proven to be more than he expected, and they hadn't been at the party for an hour yet.

Quianna devoured her food seeming to enjoy it as much as the spectacle going on in the seats near them. When one of the men pulled up his pants and zipped them, he glanced at her and smiled. She chuckled and smiled back as if what she had just witnessed was an everyday occurrence. Perhaps it was in her world, but Charles was still having difficulty swallowing the first-class feast on his plate. He cleared his palate with a few fast gulps of champagne, blanked his expression, and whispered in her ear, "The show's over. Let's see what's going on outside." He inclined his head toward the door and stood, this time taking the lead.

Well past midnight, the party was now in full swing and the noise level had increased several decibels. Empty space in the expansive living room was now standing room only and dancing couples jammed the center of the room, so Charles headed outside once again. He welcomed the chill of the fresh air and dragged in a deep breath that helped to clear his head of the claustrophobic feeling he'd had inside the house. Groups congregated beside heat lamps spaced around the pool area. Charles took two more glasses of champagne from one of the roving waiters. He pointed at an empty cabana, slipped an arm around Quianna's slender shoulders, and turned her toward the curtain-shrouded bed.

"Do you mind if we sit out here for a while?"

"Whatever you want." She sat on the edge of the bed, kicked off her heels, and scooted back onto a stack of pillows until her feet left the floor. When she stretched her hand out to him, he saw the invitation in her eyes. "Come, lie with me."

Charles removed his slip-on loafers and joined her. She leaned forward and yanked the ties holding back the curtains.

"I'm cold, Charles. Hold me."

He sunk back into the pillows and drew her into his arms glad that he'd had the foresight to slip a few condoms into his wallet before he left the house. Even with the heat lamps and firebowls, in his mind the temperature still wasn't conducive to outdoor sex. But he wasn't about to complain. They would warm up soon enough. The sensation of Quianna running her bare foot up his leg instantly removed the chill. Charles pulled her closer and his hand traveled up her calf and over her thighs, his long, nimble fingers found their way inside the slits which allowed him to feel her soft, warm skin. As he dipped his head and covered her lips with his own, he imagined undressing her in the cabana right there in the middle of the crowded party. What kind of underwear did she have on? Probably some tiny yet ridiculously expensive bra and panties. But his exploring hands soon discovered neither panties nor bra beneath her outrageous outfit. The discovery sent his libido into the stratosphere. He draped a leg over her hip and tightened his embrace bringing her body flush against his.

Quianna met his exploring tongue, moaned into his mouth and curled her slim, agile body around him like a friendly cat. She ran her tongue around the curve of his ear and unbuttoned his vest and then his shirt. Charles hissed when her fingertips circled his nipples. His hands searched the top of her pants and found a zipper. Just as he pulled down the zipper, took the waistband in both hands and wiggled it over her slim hips, shouting and cursing erupted outside the cabana's closed curtains. The next thing he knew, Max's imposing figure yanked open the curtains and bellowed, "We've got a shooter! I need to get you out of here!" He grabbed Quianna by both hands and literally pulled her from between Charles' legs, which sent his raging erection into oblivion. "Come on, man," Max roared and extended a beefy hand to him.

The sound of gunshots rang out as the three sprinted toward the only opening in the security-fenced-in property to the limo. The driver saw them coming and jumped into the driver's seat like a wheelman in an armed robbery.

Charles and Quianna collapsed in the back seat, breathing hard. She opened the bar and handed him a fistful of napkins. "Are you used to this kind of thing happening?"

After they both wiped the sweat from their faces, she finally answered. "More often than you'd expect. I'm sorry the evening is spoiled."

Someone might be dead, and that's all she had to say? Quianna seemed too blasé about the whole situation. Going out with a music industry star was nice, but not worth risking his life.

This wasn't the kind of evening he'd expected, and it would definitely be the last one he spent with her. At least he'd had the presence of mind to grab his Alexander McQueen loafers before they fled.

"Why don't we go back to my place for a while?" She stroked his cheek.

He checked his watch. "I have my first training session with my brother in about five hours. I think I need to get a little sleep, because I know he's going to kick my butt. The driver can take me back to Marc's."

He knew from the way she pursed her lips that she wasn't pleased with his decision. "Are you sure? You won't be disappointed." She whispered the words against his neck, then placed a soft kiss beneath his ear.

"Yeah. Maybe we can do this again sometime," he said, choosing his words to let her know this was the last time they would be seeing each other socially.

Her body stiffened, and she leaned away from him just enough to let him see how displeased she was. "Uh huh." Quianna picked up the limo phone and told the driver to return to Canyon Gate.

Only the music from the radio filled the inside of the car on the return trip to Marc's house, and when the chauffeur pulled up into the driveway, Charles dropped a quick kiss on Quianna's forehead and opened his own door. "I'll see you at the studio next week."

She just glared at him, so he closed the door and walked toward the house.

The next morning, as Charles downed several cups of coffee, he sat in the kitchen with his laptop and read on TMZ that one of the pro athletes at the party had spent much of the night "hogging" the microphone in the DJ booth. One of the rappers reportedly felt "disrespected" by his actions, which led to an argument resulting in the rapper punching the NBA star in the face. Members of both men's entourages responded, and security had to separate the two groups. But they became involved in a second brawl and shots were fired. Several partygoers were wounded, none fatally.

"Hey. You're looking a little worn this morning." Marc chuckled. "How was your date with the Princess of Hip-Hop last night?"

Charles grunted. "We went to a party in Summerlin. Sinister is renting this outrageous house there. I was just reading what TMZ said happened."

"What do you mean? You said you went."

"We did, but I left jogging barefoot behind her security guard, with my shoes in my hand after they started shooting."

"Shooting?" Wide eyed, Marc plopped down on a stool at the island beside his twin.

Charles spun the computer around. "You can read this while I take a shower. I'll give you the details on the drive to the studio. My head's aching too much for me to get behind the wheel."

Lines formed between Marc's brows. "Do you really want to do this today? There's no need if I have to go easy on you."

"Don't worry about me. I went through worse than this in med school."

"It's up to you, man, but I'd suggest you lay off the coffee and drink water instead."

And so began his training with his health food fanatic twin.

♥

For some unknown reason, Mondays always brought an influx of injuries and complaints, major and minor. Today was more challenging than an average Monday. In the middle of an already demanding afternoon, while she was changing a patient's dressing, an anguished scream pierced the quict.

"Somebody help me!"

Samuel, the nurse's assistant on duty and Adanna came skidding to a stop at the front desk where a very pregnant young girl who appeared to be in active labor was bent forward with her hands on her knees. Rivulets of sweat ran down her face and dripped onto the floor.

The girl, who couldn't be much older than fifteen, couldn't seem to move from the spot.

"It's okay. You're here, and we're going to take very good care of you," Adanna said, trying to calm her down. Look at me. I need you to breathe and don't push until we can examine you. Breathe with me." She did an exaggerated demonstration of the breathing technique.

All of a sudden a puddle of liquid appeared between the girl's feet. There wasn't enough time to take a thorough medical history. Adanna assisted the doctors in all births, and she had often delivered babies in the doctors' absence. This time, both doctors were involved with other serious cases, so she and Samuel would have to handle the delivery.

Adanna didn't recall having seen the girl before, which meant that either she was new to the village or she hadn't received prenatal care there are the hospital. "What is your name?"

"Kinah," the girl answered as Adanna scribbled the name at the top of an intake form.

"Last name?" The girl refused to answer. "Do you have a doctor that's been caring for you, Kinah?"

The girl shook her head vigorously. Suddenly, she bent forward with her hands on her knees and let out a scream.

Getting her personal information was important, but Adanna knew she didn't have time. "This baby is coming soon. We need to get you into the delivery room and up on the table."

"I can't walk! It hurts too much."

"Yes, you can. We'll help you. Just try not to push."

"No. I can't!"

"Samuel, get a wheelchair. I've got her."

"Kinah, look at me. I need you to breathe like this through your mouth." Adanna once again demonstrated the quick pant.

Samuel brought the wheelchair up behind Kinah and pushed it right up to touch the back of her knees, but then she refused to sit.

"Please, I can't sit down!"

"All right. You'll have to walk." Adanna put one arm around the girl's back and held her other hand tightly as she moved the mother-to-be forward with mincing steps toward the small room they used for labor, delivery, and recovery. Getting her up onto the table would have been comical if Adanna hadn't known how close this baby was to being born.

"Help me, Samuel. Get her bum onto the edge of the table. I'll take her legs." After a couple of tries, he finally leaned their patient back against the table. "Take her shoulders and lean her back." He managed to get a firm hold and did as instructed while Adanna physically raised her legs off the floor and onto the table. "Keep her breathing."

Samuel demonstrated the panting breaths as she yanked off the patient's sandals and wrestled her feet into the stirrups, a quick examination revealed that the young mother was not only fully dilated but the baby's head was already crowning. She'd gotten there just in time.

"Good girl," Adanna said, trying to calm her voice as she pulled on a pair of gloves, and removed her panties. "Keep your eyes on Samuel and breathe, okay? This will all be over in a little while." She silently prayed that would be the case and no unforeseen complications would arise.

He kept one hand firmly on the girl's shoulder to prevent her from sitting back up. With the other, he filled a bowl with clean water, dipped in a cloth, dabbed her parched lips, and mopped the perspiration from her face and neck.

After Adanna cleaned her off with a Betadine solution, she announced, "It's time to stop pushing, Kinah. I need to make it easier for the baby to come out and so you don't tear." She injected a local anesthetic and used a scalpel to make a small incision.

"All right. Breathe in through your nose, hold your breath and bear down. "For the next ten minutes, she did as instructed in between groans that sounded like a wounded animal until Adanna said, "Now breathe deep and do it again."

The baby's head emerged, and Adanna asked her to stop pushing again. She gently stroked the sides of the baby's nose downward, the neck, and under the chin upward to get rid of any mucus and amniotic fluid from the nose and mouth. She told the mother to resume pushing, and kept her expression intentionally composed. When the rest of the baby was delivered and breathing, Adanna announced, "It's a girl!" but she didn't lay the newborn on the mother's stomach, as was standard procedure. Instead, she clamped and cut the umbilical cord then met her assistant's gaze with a look she hoped he understood. "I need you here for a minute."

He moved to the end of the table, studied the baby closely and nodded his acknowledgement of her unspoken request. "I'll massage her belly while you clean the baby and take her vitals," he spoke to the mother. "The afterbirth will be delivered soon, just try to relax.

Adanna wrapped the baby in a folded sheet and took her over to another table where she weighed and measured the infant and examined her more thoroughly. Her vital signs, color and reflexes were good, but this little one, who was in such a hurry to make her entrance into the world, had severe facial deformities. From what Adanna could ascertain it appeared to be both a cleft lip and cleft palate, birth defects still all too common in births in Nigerian villages.

"Is she all right?" Kinah called from across the room.

"She's breathing just fine and all her vital signs are normal. I'll bring her to you as soon as I get her cleaned up." Adanna said, frantically trying to think of a way to break the bad news to the young mother. Knowing there wasn't an easy way to soften the blow, she picked up the little bundle. "There is a small problem, but nothing that can't be taken care of." She approached the table where Samuel was still massaging her belly and placed the baby in her arms.

Kinah peeked into the sheet and drew it away from the baby's face then screamed, "A small problem? I knew something was wrong with it the whole time! Get it away from me!" The way she shoved the child back at Adanna, if she hadn't been standing so close, the baby would have landed on the concrete floor.

"You don't mean that, Kinah," Adanna said, cuddling the baby close to her chest. "She's your daughter, and she's perfectly healthy otherwise. This issue can be fixed."

"How? I don't have any money. Her father didn't want a baby to begin with, and now neither do I." Her anguish came out in a moan that nearly brought tears to Adanna's eyes. "Samuel, we need to switch places. You take the baby, so I can deliver the afterbirth and stitch her up."

It took about twenty minutes for Adanna to complete the post-delivery care for the distraught girl. Before she was done, Dr. Ijalana entered the room. She explained what was going on, and he examined the infant.

"Please calm down, Kinah. What Nurse Okoro told you is true. Your baby is fine, and she needs you right now. The nourishment you have to offer is the best for her. Even though your milk won't come in until tomorrow, it would be beneficial for you to nurse her as soon as possible."

"I don't want to touch her. She looks like a monster."

"Why did you say her father didn't want her?"

The girl turned away from them. "He's a white man," she mumbled. "We only had sex a few times, but when I told him I was pregnant, he told me it wasn't his and that he didn't want to see me anymore."

Adanna shook her head at this story, which was all too common and explained the infant's fair complexion. "I'm so sorry."

"Don't be sorry for me. It's my fault for sleeping with him just because he gave me a little money."

Dr. Ijalana sent his nurse a questioning gaze, and she had a good idea of what was on his mind. "After I give you a shot of Pitocin to decrease the bleeding, I'd like to do a couple of tests, just to confirm that everything is as it should be, Kinah. You just lay back and relax. We're going to take good care of you, and you should be able to go home in a day or two." He crossed the room, went to one of the cabinets where non-prescription medications were kept, and came back with an HIV/STD test kit. So many young girls trawled the streets of the villages and cities, making their livings by prostituting themselves. With AIDS so rampant on the continent, odds were that if she was a prostitute, she might be infected. If the mother tested positive, it would be necessary to perform an HIV DNA PCR test before the newborn was forty-eight hours old. The test would be repeated when the infant was one to two months old, and again at age four to six months.

"I need to ask you a few questions, Kinah. Have you been sexually active with any other men besides the baby's father?"

She turned back to face them, and her eyes widened. "No!" Her emphatic reply left Adanna feeling relieved. This baby had enough going against her to also be condemned to living with HIV.

"We're not judging you," Adanna reassured her, "but we need to know for the baby's sake."

"I haven't been with anyone since him." Which probably meant there had been men before him. "I'm telling you the truth."

Dr. Ijalana proceeded to do the test while Adanna tried to explain the baby's condition.

"The baby has a cleft lip and palate. Although no one knows exactly why clefts happen, they have a tendency to run in families. Hormonal imbalances, nutritional deficiencies, and certain drugs when used during pregnancy are possible causes as well."

"I don't use drugs! Are you saying it's my fault she came out like that?"

"Sweetheart, Nurse Okoro wasn't accusing you of using illegal drugs, and she's not saying it's your fault. There are even prescription drugs that are suspected of causing this birth defect. We don't know exactly what causes it, but we do know that it can be repaired."

"It doesn't matter. I'm not taking her home."

Stunned, Adanna said, "You can't desert her. She's just a helpless infant." Dr. Ijalana rested a hand on her arm to stop her from saying anything more.

The girl turned her face to the wall again. "I won't take her. If you make me, I'll get rid of her."

Adanna knew this kind of reaction to an unwanted pregnancy to be true. Abandoned newborns were often found along rural roads, and most often they were dead.

"We're finished now. You have two stitches, and Nurse Okoro will tell you how to care for them before you're discharged. Would you care for something to eat, Kinah?" Dr. Ijalana asked. "You must be hungry or at least thirsty. Samuel can bring you soup, fruit, and some water."

"Thank you."

Once Adanna and the doctor left the room, he said, "Let her think about it overnight, and try to talk to her again tomorrow."

"I doubt it will make any difference, but I will. What a sad situation."

"Yes, and all too common these days. Perhaps you can talk to her about birth control too. At least give her some condoms when she leaves."

"If she doesn't take the baby, what will we do?"

Dr. Ijalana sighed, removed his glasses, and ran a hand over his face. "We can't force her. There's nothing we can do but send the infant to a children's home."

The thought of the innocent child starting her life in an orphanage tore at Adanna's heart. The poor baby didn't even have a name.

"Lezigha will be here soon. Let her know the situation. Between the two of you, maybe you can at least get her to name the child."

By the time Kinah had finished her soup and fruit, she appeared so exhausted that Adanna didn't have the heart to engage her in any more conversation. She removed the tray, covered her with a sheet, and told her to get some sleep. There would be plenty of time to talk to her tomorrow when she was stronger and more rested. The teen mother's aversion to her baby angered her. With the exception of possible feeding difficulties, the deformity wasn't something that would prevent the little girl from living a normal life. Adanna went to the tiny crib to check on the baby. Actually, she was beautiful with big eyes and a headful of light brown hair. As she listened to the little one's heartbeat and took her temperature, she considered how much she wanted her own children. How could Kinah react so harshly to someone she had carried in her own body for nine months? But Adanna knew very well of the hardships that faced most village women. Girl babies still weren't valued as much as males were, and she had delivered a female child with a physical deformity. With no husband and not even a supportive boyfriend in the picture, Kinah knew that the prospects for the future were grim for her and the child. God only knew what her family situation was.

When Adanna returned to work the next morning, Lezigha updated her on their handful of patients. Her concern though was for their lone maternity patient. She decided to attempt to get as much information from their new patient as possible. There had to be a way to help her and the baby.

"Kinah had some discomfort, so I gave her a dose of ibuprofen during the night and tried to talk to her about the baby." The other nurse's mouth twisted. "She didn't want to hear anything I had to say. The baby had a little difficulty with the bottle because of the cleft, but I think she'll adjust."

"So I guess having overnight to think about it didn't do any good." Adanna shook her head. "It's so sad. I'll try to reason with her one more time before she's discharged. How did Mr. Lawal do last night?"

"His fever is down and he's taking liquids."

"Great! Well, I'd better get started. See you tomorrow."

Dressed in her usual scrubs, Adanna started in on her regular morning routine, giving each patient a cheerful greeting before checking their vital signs and recording it on the chart. Samuel had already arrived and was taking care of fixing patient meals. His services were invaluable to the hospital. If they worked at a larger facility, his duties would be restricted to emptying bedpans, taking vitals, feeding and bathing patients, and helping patients to the bathroom. But here at Stella Obasanjo, the staff did whatever was required of them. Samuel did all of this and more without complaint.

The small hospital had only a dozen *rooms*, each of which was separated by curtains that offered a semblance of privacy. Rooms divided by a cinderblock wall were reserved for the more critically ill, and there was one tiny room that served as a quarantine room. Once Adanna had seen to all of the patients, she checked on Kinah. "Good morning, Kinah. How are you feeling today?" She perused the patient's chart.

"Better, I guess."

"Good. I'm going to fix you a Sitz bath. It will soothe your stitches."

"When can I leave?"

Adanna noticed that she only spoke in singular terms. "Your vitals were normal, and your uterus is contracting to its normal size and position, but one of the doctors has to check the stitches to see that they held and you have no sign of infection. After you eat breakfast, we need to get you up and moving to make sure you can walk to the toilet, urinate without the need for a catheter, and eat and drink without being sick."

"What's a sit bath?"

"Just what it sounds like. You sit in a basin of warm water and soak. It will feel good, I promise." Samuel came in with a tray and set it on a stand next to the bed. "Let me help you sit up." Adanna put two pillows behind her back, positioned the tray across her lap, and sat in the chair beside the cot as Kinah delved into her breakfast. "Now that you've had some time to think about things, have you changed your mind about your daughter?"

"Why would I change my mind? I wanted a son, and I ended up having a damaged girl with no father." She gave the melon on her plate an angry stab. "All men want sons. At least if a man is interested in me, he wouldn't be turned off if I had a boy. No man wants a woman with a crippled child, especially a crippled girl."

"She's not crippled, Kinah, and she's a beautiful baby. You didn't even look at her."

"I saw enough. She looks horrible."

Adanna hung her head. When she looked up, she met the young woman eye to eye and pinned her with a long, hard stare. "I'm sorry you feel that way, but this child is your flesh and blood. When we discharge you, she must be discharged with you." She stood and walked toward the curtain then turned around. "Could you at least give her a name?"

Understanding her patient's mentality was difficult. Adanna had become a nurse because she loved people, particularly children. They were the ones who suffered inordinately on the continent. So many died from war, violence, sickness, and disease before they even got a chance to experience life. It hurt her to see any child endure hardship through no fault of their own. Most often it was because of the poverty, ignorance, politics, or the greed of their parents. She always dreamed of one day being able to help hundreds, maybe even thousands of children. She had no earthly idea of how this might happen, but it was her favorite fantasy.

After Adanna gave Kinah her Sitz bath, she took care of the needs of the other patients. With her patients taken of, she finally sat down with Dr. Ijalana and discussed their individual progress. Next they went over the files of the current and former patients whom they would recommend to the visiting DWB team. Unfortunately, many of their patients stays had to be prematurely shortened due to limited medicines and even more limited bed space. The gravely ill or injured were transferred to one of the larger city hospitals, if they could afford to pay. Some were sent back home to die. If it hadn't been for the support the hospital received from outside organizations, they wouldn't have been able to keep the doors open. And soon, more help would be arriving courtesy of Doctors Without Borders.

Chapter Four

Charles groaned in pain as he lifted the strap of his carry-on bag over his shoulder before he boarded the flight back to Atlanta on Tuesday afternoon. Saturday, Sunday, and Monday, he had lifted weights, worked with the heavy punching bag and spent time on various machines in the studio. Marc instructed him on how to bob and weave and distance himself from the bag as though he were fighting a real person. He always wore gloves, so there was no danger of him damaging his hands. Marc promised if he continued some form of training every other day, the pain would soon disappear. He hoped it was true.

During the flight, he thought back to the reactions from his brother and Lance to his retelling of the bizarre night with Quianna. Both of the men agreed with his decision to end any social contact with the singer. Yes, she was beautiful and sexy, but the girl was much younger than him, and she lived on the edge. He liked to have fun as much as the next guy, but their ideas of what was considered acceptable were light years apart.

When the flight attendants came around with the beverage cart, Charles popped two ibuprofen tablets for his aching muscles and reclined his seat. Tomorrow he had an appointment with the practice broker. Hopefully, all would be in order and they could proceed with finalizing the sale of his plastic surgery practice.

The magnitude of things he needed to do before his final move to Las Vegas could easily be overwhelming. Rather than dwell on it, he closed his eyes and mentally willed the medication to take effect. He didn't open them for three hours when the woman sitting in the next seat nudged him to let him know the seatbelt light had come on. They were preparing to land in Atlanta.

An hour later, Charles walked into his condo. He dumped his carry-on bag inside the door, then gave the place a long, thoughtful glance. Less than two years ago, he'd bought the place, and he'd loved every minute of living there. The view from the thirtieth floor, the high-end contemporary décor done by a former girlfriend, and the amenities made his home a showplace. He would miss the doorman, twenty-four-hour concierge, state-of-the-art fitness center, movie theater, clubroom, and pool. He shook his head and stretched out on the oversized taupe-colored leather sectional to take in the view of the Buckhead skyline through the wall of windows. As the sky gradually darkened, he gave himself a mental pep talk. *What's wrong with you? You might be giving up some of this material stuff, but you're about to have an experience that money can't buy. If it doesn't turn out to be what you expected, you can always come back.* That thought snapped him back to reality. This decision was a major life change that couldn't very easily be cancelled just because every piece didn't fit into place perfectly. The momentary sense of regret that breezed over him left as fast as it came. He took his phone from his pocket and dialed.

"Hi, Mama. Just wanted you to know I'm back," he said, being faithful to a tradition. His parents had been sticklers for their sons always letting someone in the family know when they arrived at their destination when they were traveling.

"That's good. You sound tired, so I'll let you go, but I want to talk to you tomorrow about the party."

He groaned inwardly but put a smile in his voice. "I need to go by the office for a while tomorrow, then meet with the practice broker. I'll stop by after that. Will you be home around three?"

"Yes. See you then."

Charles rose from the sofa, retrieved his carry-on bag, and walked into his bedroom. Since he owned the condo, he'd made the decision to rent it out. Dealing with the sale of the practice was enough to handle. The real estate agent he'd hired was also a friend, and he'd found someone who agreed to a one-year lease.

His meeting with the practice broker the next morning confirmed that the deal was done. He'd have to fly back to Atlanta for the closing, but that was a minor inconvenience. Everything was falling into place.

The following Friday, the entire Stafford family along with friends, his former staff, coworkers, and assorted relatives sent him off with a goodbye party that rivaled a wedding reception. The only family missing was Marc and Gianne, but considering he was going to live with them, he didn't see the need for their presence.

Charles and his brothers often marveled at the way their mother could put together a first-class event at the last minute. Miraculously, she always knew whom to include on the guest list and who to leave off. They often teased her about having the skills of a CIA agent. The evening was filled with good food and good music, along with old and new friends who had come to wish him well. He promised them all he would be back to Atlanta whenever his schedule allowed.

Charles had the things he couldn't do without shipped ahead three weeks ago, and he boarded another flight and returned to Las Vegas. This time, Gianne was with Marc when he picked him up at the airport, and they took him to dinner to celebrate his official arrival.

After the hostess seated them and they ordered beverages, he said, "I have to be in New York for a few days, so I'm going to call Greg to see if I can camp out with him for a couple of days."

Gianne sent him a curious glance. "I thought you went to New York to meet with them already?"

"That was to attend a general Information Day. This is to do my official briefing. The briefings and debriefings are only conducted in New York and London."

"That's really exciting, Charles," she said with a smile. "I admire you so much for what you're doing."

Marc nodded in agreement. "Me too, man. It's not easy making such a big lifestyle change, but I have the feeling this might turn out to be the best thing you've ever done. How'd Daddy act at the party?"

"Oh, he mumbled and complained while we were sitting at the table, then got up and made a glowing speech."

"Ha! Sometimes, I actually think he's jealous of us. Think about it. When he was our age, he didn't have the freedom to pick up and move to the other side of the world. He already had a wife and a couple of kids. Plus he had all that *representing the race* pressure. I bet there were times when he wanted to strike out and do something a little unorthodox, yet he stuck with the program and didn't waver. You have to admire that kind of tenacity, I guess."

Charles cleared his throat. "I can't believe I'm hearing that from you. Guess Mama's prayers worked after all."

Marc laughed. "Don't ever let her hear you say that. She thinks she has a direct line to Heaven."

"So how does Doctors Without Borders work?" Gianne asked, digging into her salad. "Is it strictly volunteer, or do they help you with some of the expenses?"

"They pay for all travel, visas, and relevant vaccinations then I'm responsible for routine health maintenance vaccinations. The organization also takes care of roundtrip air tickets from home to mission and hotel in NYC during briefing/debriefing. I'll be paid a monthly salary of approximately $1,500 plus per diem in local currency and full medical insurance."

"I was under the impression that you had to foot the bill for everything. Not bad, at least you have spending cash." Marc frowned. "Where will you be living once you get to Nigeria?"

"I won't know until I arrive. DWB takes care of my accommodations in the field. All they said is that it's shared housing *mostly* with private rooms.

"Ooh, that sounds scary," Gianne said with rounded eyes. "You might end up with a roommate."

"I'm trying to think of it like being back in med school again where a bunch of interns or residents shared an apartment. No doubt it's going to be an adventure. I just hope I'll be able to make a meaningful contribution to the people who need help."

Marc nodded. "I'm proud of you, man, and Daddy is too, even if he won't come out and say it. He's not *that* upset with you, because you're still a doctor. It's just your giving up the practice that bugged him out. He can't imagine you without a well-appointed waiting room decorated with nice artwork and two fine-looking assistants. When he was our age, he was still struggling."

Charles snorted in amusement. "I still can't get over how you and he have mellowed out toward each other."

"They finally understand each other better than they did before," Gianne said with a thoughtful smile.

Marc laughed. "And all it took was thirty-five years."

"Well, I don't know about anyone else," she continued. "But I'm glad you worked out your differences. The tension between you and your daddy was more than I could stand."

They finished dinner with a celebratory toast to Charles' new career, and departed for Marc and Gianne's house, his new part-time home. He said goodnight, retreated to his room then called Greg in New York. His older brother answered sounding groggy.

"Sorry. Did I wake you? It's Charles."

Greg cleared his throat. "Are you kidding? It's only a little after ten here. So, what's up?"

"I have to come back to New York in a couple of weeks for my orientation. Can you put me up?"

"Of course, but I need to check my schedule. What days will you be here?"

"The third through fifth of April. Will you be in town?"

"Hold on. Let me check."

Charles listened while Greg must have been checking his phone. He heard a muffled voice and soft laughter in the background. It distinctly sounded like a woman. "Did I interrupt something, man?"

"Huh? Oh…no, not really. Yeah, it looks like those dates are fine. We can get our party on while you're here. Now that you're no longer in the ATL *representing the family name*, you can let your hair down, and loosen up a little."

He chuckled. "Sounds like a plan. I'll call you back as soon as I book a flight. Thanks."

Since it was still too early and he was too full of nervous energy to turn in for the night, Charles flipped on the television, opened the sliding doors, and went out onto the balcony. He gazed into the distance at the disappearing glow of the sun descending behind the mountains. The glittering lights of the Atlanta skyline had been his view for the past two years. Here there were no high-rise buildings, each with its own unique illuminated crown to distinguish it from the others and no glow of tail lights speeding north on the interstate. Yes, this view had a type of beauty, but it would take some getting used to.

The fact was soon he'd have a lot of new things to get used to. From what he'd learned in the first meeting with DWB, his new life required him to make a major paradigm shift. A lack of the comforts of home, strange foods, language differences, extreme weather, and more would soon be part of his daily existence. He had never even served in the Armed Forces, so the closest he'd ever come to roughing it was when he and Marc went away to camp for a few summers when they were in elementary school. Neither of his parents enjoyed rough and tumble treks through the wilderness. Their vacations were always at five-star resorts with every amenity. Nevertheless, Charles looked forward to living in a foreign country and meeting a different culture of people. Most of all, he couldn't wait to do some significant surgery.

♥

"Doctor, I have to recommend our newest patient for reconstructive surgery. The cleft is severe. No doubt she will have breathing problems without surgery. Lezigha said she had some problem taking the bottle last night. It's difficult for her to latch onto the nipple. We've been monitoring her respiration, and she seems to be struggling a bit. But I guess she's going to struggle her entire life, considering neither her mother nor father wants her."

He agreed. "Yes, that little one has enough strikes against her already. So, the mother hasn't changed her mind. We'll have to see what we can do on her behalf."

Adanna checked on Kinah and the baby for the last time, and once again asked if she had come up with a name. The girl averted her gaze and just uttered a mumbled "No."

Lezigha arrived for her shift, and they discussed the patients as they did every evening. But this time Adanna said, "Keep a close eye on the baby. Her breathing is a little labored. And it looks as though you and I need to come up with a name for her."

On the way home, Adanna hoped Femi had dinner ready. That way, she could jump into the shower, eat, and relax. This evening she wasn't in the mood for sociable chatter with the strays who regularly occupied their living room. She couldn't seem to focus her thoughts on anything but Kinah's baby. When she arrived at the flat, thankfully Femi was there alone.

"You look tired," her flatmate said as Adanna dragged into the kitchen.

"I'm totally knackered. It was a trying day. The girl I told you about—"

"The one who had the baby?" Femi asked as she peered down into the saucepan and stirred the contents with a wooden spoon.

"Yes. She doesn't want the baby and won't even give her a name."

"Oh, that's terrible. There are too many orphans running the streets already. Why would someone do that to a baby on purpose?"

"She doesn't think there's any other choice, because she's not married and the father has denied paternity. He's a white man, and the way she tells it, their relationship wasn't exactly a committed one. For all the background information she gave us, she might very well be a prostitute. It looks as though Lezigha and I will need to give the poor baby a name."

After she changed out of her uniform and took a shower, Adanna and Femi had a rare dinner alone together. They talked about Emeka's appearance at the club and her phone call to her father, a friend's upcoming birthday, and the upcoming rent payment for the flat. Adanna retreated to her room and took out a set of clean scrubs to wear to work in the morning. She attempted to read for a while but couldn't concentrate. Their tiny patient's future weighed heavy on her. What would happen to this sweet little girl if her mother didn't want her? Nigeria was facing an emergency situation in which millions of children were in dire need of care and special protection.

Most likely, they would have to find an orphanage willing to take her. The Jamido Children's Home near Lagos was a possibility. It housed about seventy babies, children and young adults, all orphans who lived together as a family. The thought of that baby growing up as an orphan made Adanna sick to her stomach. As she lay there mulling over what she might do to help the infant, the perfect name came to her – *Chichima*, which meant sweet and precious girl. Pleased and satisfied with the name, she drifted off to sleep, but the ringing of her cell phone disturbed her much needed slumber. A call in the middle of the night was never good news. She grappled around on the top of the table beside her bed until she found it.

"It's Zigha. I'm sorry to wake you, but we have a situation."

Adanna bolted upright. "What's happening?"

"Kinah is gone! I checked on her a couple of hours ago; then when I came around for my two o'clock rounds, her bed was empty. Did she say anything to you to make you think she might run?"

"No, but I had the feeling she might do something like this. Does Dr. Pategi know?" she asked, rubbing the sleep from her eyes.

"Yes, he took a flashlight and searched outside the building, but she was gone."

"What about the baby? Did she leave the baby?"

"Yes, the baby is still here."

She let out a sigh. "That little one is probably better off without her. Try to hold her as often as possible, okay? She needs the human contact. I'll stop at the grocery and pick up some more formula on my way in."

All the way during her thirty-minute drive out of the city, Adanna couldn't think of anything else. She wanted to hurry and get to the hospital early so she could give Chichima a little TLC. The baby needed skin-to-skin contact, to hear soft words whispered in her tiny ears, and to be cuddled near a beating heart. She didn't understand her attachment to the infant, but the desire to protect and nurture this baby was so strong it couldn't be denied.

Dr. Ijalana was sitting at his desk with his forehead in his hand when she arrived in the morning. His usual oversized cup of coffee occupied its normal spot next to his laptop as he studied the screen.

"Good morning, Doctor," she said softly from the doorway, hoping she wouldn't startle him.

He glanced up. "Good morning, Adanna. How are you?"

"Concerned about the baby."

"Yes. Lezigha told me she called you last night."

"What happens in these kinds of situations?"

"Well, if the infant needed continued medical care, we would keep it here and administer the necessary care. But since she is in relatively good physical condition apart from the facial deformity, we have no option but to find her a spot in one of the children's homes."

Adanna's heart sank despite the fact that she knew the decision was inevitable. "Oh, but she's so fragile. Couldn't we allow her to remain here until she is stronger?"

Dr. Ijalana smiled. "She is small, yes, but she's not ill. Since the mother is gone, have you chosen a name for the baby?"

"Yes, I want to name her Chichima. It's so fitting for her."

"Then Chichima it is. I'm going to send word to people I know in the surrounding villages to see if anyone knows Kinah. If that's her real name. Meanwhile, you should contact Ijamido, SOS Children's Village, and House of Mercy.

Between reading and re-reading patients' files, Adanna placed numerous calls to local children's homes in an effort to find a spot for Chichima. Every orphanage she called said they were filled to capacity and added the baby to their waiting list. Physically, ChiChi was gaining weight and no longer appeared to be struggling to breathe, so there was really no justifiable reason for her to remain in the hospital.

Adanna spent every lunch hour with the newborn, cuddling her and singing to her. All scientific evidence stressed how vital it was for newborns to experience human touch. Those who were deprived of ample physical and emotional attention often suffered from developmental delays and were at higher risk for behavioral, emotional, and social problems as they grew up. Even as a nurse, she didn't understand all of the physiological details, but research pointed to the lasting effects of early infancy environments and the changes the brain underwent during that period, and that was enough evidence for her.

One afternoon, while she was in the middle of eating lunch and feeding the baby, Dr. Ijalana entered the room. He leaned against the wall, watched the scene before him for a moment then frowned.

"Adanna, I'm concerned about your attachment to her. You two seem to have bonded with each other. As a medical professional, I know you're aware of personal involvement with patients being more of a hindrance than a help when it comes to effective patient care."

She raised the infant to her chest and held her close as she spoke. "This is an extraordinary situation. And I believe there's a reason why none of the children's homes can take her."

He scratched at his cheek. "And that reason is?"

"I don't know yet, but there is something very special about this child. I understand she can't stay here indefinitely. Until there's an opening for her, I'll provide her nappies and formula so it doesn't have to come out of the hospital budget."

"That's very generous, but the budget doesn't concern me as much as your emotional connection to her. If you become too attached, it will be traumatic for both of you when she has to leave."

Adanna dropped soft kisses on the infant's cheek and rubbed gentle circles on her back. "I'll be all right. As a matter of fact, I've been considering a temporary solution. Would you be willing to let me take her home in the evenings and bring her back in the mornings? That way, Lezigha won't have to deal with the feedings and nappie changes overnight."

Dr. Ijalana rubbed his forehead and hesitated before answering. "All that will do is cement the bond between the two of you even more."

"She needs to bond with *someone*. She's all alone in the world." Adanna met his worried gaze. "Right now there aren't any other options. What else can we do but keep her until she can be placed?"

He shrugged and came closer. "She is feeding better, isn't she?"

"Yes, she's adapted to the bottle, even though she's pulling in some air through the cleft. I've just been burping her well to reduce the bubbles in her tummy."

Dr. Ijalana crossed his arms and smiled. "You'll make a wonderful mother someday, Nurse Okoro."

She sighed. "Well, I need to have a husband first."

"That too will happen when the time is right. Let me talk your suggestion over with Dr. Pategi. I'll give you our decision before you leave this evening."

For the rest of her lunch hour, Adanna talked and sang to Chichima then kissed her tiny, soft cheek and promised that she would do everything in her power to help her. Only, at the moment, she didn't have a clue how on earth she might do that. After she rinsed out her lunch container and put it into the tote bag she carried every day, Adanna checked on the other patients. Two new patients had been admitted in the past twenty-four hours, which meant she would be busy every minute for the rest of her shift. She washed her hands and returned to the ward.

Changing dressings, giving meds, and taking blood samples filled the next few hours, and while her hands busied themselves, she thought about her brother. She hadn't heard from him since the day she invited him to dinner. Had her father changed his mind and given Emeka a warning after all? What other reason would he have just disappeared from her life so suddenly after being a constant presence? She doubted that possibility, but stranger things had happened.

That night, after Adanna gave Lezigha the patient rundown, she checked with Dr. Ijalana.

"Did you talk to Dr. Pategi about my suggestion?" She held her breath and waited for him to answer.

"I did. He said he's willing since space is at a premium around here, but his concern is the same as mine. What will you do when the children's home calls and says they have an opening?"

"I'll deal with it when the time comes. Until then, I need to make space for her in my flat. Thank you so much, Doctor."

He gave his head a pitiful shake and smiled. "You're welcome, Adanna."

Chapter Five

The first week in April, Charles boarded a plane from Las Vegas to JFK in New York. Since Greg hadn't offered to pick him up, he caught a cab, a trip that cost him fifty-three dollars and called his older brother from the taxi.

"Hey, man. I'm here. Should I come to your office or go to the apartment?"

"I already spoke with my doorman, and he's expecting you. He'll have building security let you in. You can chill until I get off work. Help yourself to whatever's in the refrigerator. I should be there around four o'clock."

Charles gave the driver the address then relaxed and took in the scenery, such as it was coming from the airport. Once they arrived in Manhattan, the buzz of the city had his blood pumping. When he'd come to New York for the information day, it had only been an overnight stay, and he hadn't had the time to catch up with Greg. He'd never even seen Greg's apartment. In fact, he hadn't bunked with his big brother since their college days.

When the cab arrived at 1520 York Avenue, Charles paid the driver, who had taken his bag from the trunk and placed it on the brick checkerboard sidewalk.

Within seconds, a uniformed doorman approached him. "May I help you, sir?"

"Yes. Charles Stafford. I'm here to visit my brother Greg."

"Certainly, Mr. Stafford. Welcome to New York. Your brother informed us of your visit. My name is Roland. Let me get your bags."

"Thanks." Charles let him pick up his carry-on bag while he kept his laptop bag on his shoulder and followed the middle-aged black man inside the lobby that was decorated with traditional furnishings. *Not as nice as my building,* was the first thought to come into his head. The second was the sobering fact that the Atlantic was no longer his building, and Atlanta was no longer his home. A guest room in Marc's home would serve as his residence for the foreseeable future, but that didn't really bother him. Charles knew very well that real estate costs in Manhattan were astronomical, especially in a building of this caliber, and he was pleased to see how well Greg was doing for himself.

Roland called for someone from security to meet him in the lobby. Charles tipped him and followed the other man to the elevator. After some momentary small talk, they exited on the seventeenth floor and the man unlocked the door to Greg's apartment. Again, he pulled a five-dollar bill from his pocket and thanked the security man for his assistance.

A smile came to his face when he looked around at the décor. Just like him and Marc, Greg had chosen contemporary décor, but his place had a distinct Asian theme. The calming sound of trickling water filled the small foyer, and drew his gaze to a Zen fountain made of four bowls. Recirculating water cascaded from the largest bowl down to the smallest and gave those entering an instant feeling of calm. Dark wood furniture filled the space, but everything else was light, and to his surprise, one of the walls in the dining area was painted a bright red and had a huge Chinese symbol painted in black on the wall above a gigantic plasma TV. *Nice.*

He dropped his bags and secured the locks, then sauntered from room to room. The first thing he noticed was there was no balcony or terrace. Since space was at a premium, apartments in Manhattan were notoriously small when compared to those in Atlanta. Charles assumed his brother had chosen the older building for its spacious rooms. What he assumed was the master bedroom contained only a large platform bed, chest, tall palm tree, and a flat screen TV on the wall. Sliding shoji screen doors separated both bedrooms from the living area.

He eased down onto the low sofa, took out his phone, and did the requisite check-in. "Hi, Mama. I guess you're out and about. Just wanted you to know I'm at Greg's. I'll be here for three days. Talk to you soon."

Greg wouldn't be home for a couple of hours, so Charles decided to grab some lunch. Greg had left an extra key with a note for him on the refrigerator. He added the key to his chain, locked the door, and took the elevator back to the lobby.

"Roland, can you tell me where I might get a decent sandwich close by?"

"There's a *Subway* right over there," the doorman pointed across the street. "But if you want something a little more civilized, you can try the *Gracie Café* up at 1530. They also deliver, if you don't feel like walking."

"I think I'll walk and explore the neighborhood. Thanks, man."

Unlike Atlanta or Las Vegas in early April, a chill still hung in the air, but at least it was sunny. He walked to the café, ordered lunch to go, and followed the signs to Carl Schurz Park, where the famous eighteenth century mayor's residence, the Gracie Mansion, stood. Charles found a bench where he had a perfect view of the East River, the Roosevelt Island Lighthouse, the Triborough Bridge, Randall's and Ward's Islands. Several people nodded, smiled or spoke while he ate, making him wonder why people insisted New Yorkers were unfriendly. After he disposed of the brown bag and soda can in a nearby trashcan, he strolled the promenade along the river. When he checked his watch, it was already four o'clock, so he started back toward the building. Before he reached York Avenue, Greg called his cell.

"Where are you? I came home as soon as I could, and you aren't even here," his brother said with a chuckle.

"Around the corner. I got some lunch and went to the park. Be there in a minute." Charles picked up his pace. He hadn't seen Greg since he'd gone to Atlanta for the celebration of their brother, Vic's installation as Chief of Staff of the hospital where he, his brother Jesse, and their father were all on staff. Until his move to Las Vegas, Marc and Greg were the only two of the brothers to relocate from Atlanta.

Charles found Greg sitting in the living room watching the news. "Hey, man. It's good to see you," he said as Greg stood and they embraced.

"You too. Have a seat." Greg returned to the sofa and slapped the cushion beside him. "Tell me what's going on with you."

"I have to take a leak. Be right back." Charles went into the guest bathroom off of the living room. When he returned, Greg was on the phone. He removed his jacket and sat.

"Let me call you back," he said, sounding as though he were in a hurry to get rid of the person on the other end. "We'll set something up before the week is out." He put the phone back on the cocktail table looking uncharacteristically uneasy then glanced over at Charles.

"The other night when we were on the phone, I heard a woman's voice. Are you sure my staying here won't be an imposition?"

"Oh, she was just here for the night." Charles brushed it off with a shrug. "So, how'd you like the area?"

"It's nice. Not seeing any houses is a little strange to me though."

"You're a southern boy to your heart."

"Not any more. I've been in Vegas for a couple of weeks now, and I'll be leaving for Lagos soon. Atlanta is the past."

"How's it going working for Marc?"

"I haven't done much yet. He's been concentrating on getting me in shape."

Greg reached out and squeezed his bicep. "Yeah, I see that."

"You're looking pretty fit," Charles said, scanning his brother's lean body. "What do you do to work out?"

Greg laughed. "I'll tell you about it sometime. Right now I'm going to take a fast shower and catch a couple of hours of sleep. I'm taking you to my favorite clubs tonight, so I suggest you do the same."

He did say clubs, as in plural, didn't he? Charles tried to beg off. "I have to be at the orientation at ten in the morning."

"Don't worry about it. We'll be in by three."

"Three? Come on, man, I have to at least *try* to look alert tomorrow."

Greg rose and started down the hall to the bathroom. "You'll survive. I'll see you around seven. We can get dinner first." He continued down the hall laughing.

Four hours later, the two brothers took a cab to *Uva*, one of the city's most popular wine bar restaurants. After they were seated, Greg told him. "I know how much you like Italian. You're going to love this place."

They started out the meal with a traditional bruschetta, then split an antipasto. Greg ordered sea scallops wrapped in smoked prosciutto. Charles stuffed himself on the best fettuccine with shrimp he'd ever tasted. They both finished with tiramisu.

"You don't really expect me to go out dancing now that I've pigged out, do you?" Charles asked, licking the rich coffee-dipped ladyfingers and cream from his lips.

"Don't worry, where I'm taking you, you'll work it off."

"You seem to forget I've been in private practice for the past few years. I was too busy to do much partying."

Greg eyed him with a skeptical squint. "Don't bullshit me. You were too busy trying to uphold the Stafford name and not embarrass Daddy."

"Well, all of us know how that is."

"Why do you think Marc and I moved away? Neither one of us could conform the way Vic, Jesse, and you did."

"We *wanted* to go into medicine."

"Are you certain?" Greg's eyes narrowed to slits. "I mean, we were never given a real choice."

"Honestly, I never wanted to be anything but a doctor, but I understand how you and Marc feel. If medicine isn't in your blood, you have no business going into the field. Where are you taking me anyway?"

"Our first stop is a place called Bembe. The women there are so fine that you'll lose your damn mind. After that we might drop in at Shelter in the South Village." Greg's blue-gray eyes gazed into the distance for a second. "And if you want to bring somebody back to the apartment with you, feel free."

Charles snickered. "I doubt it. I'm not really into that kind of stuff, man."

"I guess what Daddy always says is true. You *are* the serious twin."

"Not all that serious, but I *am* a doctor. I know what you can catch from hooking up with strange women."

"Nothing you can't catch elsewhere," Greg sounded unconcerned. "Since you're such an informed medicine man, you *must* know how to protect yourself."

"Come on, man. I know everything there is to know about that, but I just don't care for the kind of girl you can take home after a couple of dances in a club."

"So, you want a *good girl*." He sang the last two words doing his best Robin Thicke imitation, which brought a smile to Charles' face.

"Not too good, but yeah, I'm not into the skanks, okay?"

"We might have to part ways tonight, then, because," he popped his fingers and crooned, "*I'm up all night to get lucky.*"

Surprised by his brother's candid admission, Charles grinned. "I have my own key, and I can get my own taxi."

"When do you leave for Nigeria?" Greg asked, seemingly satisfied with his answer.

"The first week in May. I need to get my shots, and they have to let me know what my living arrangements will be. I'll be sharing a place with other foreign personnel."

"You won't know who they are until you get there?"

Charles winced. "No. This whole deal reminds me of my college days."

"Yeah, but if you can't stand your roommate, you won't be able to report them to student housing and ask for another."

"Probably not." They laughed at the idea.

"So exactly what will you be doing while you're there?"

"Doctors handle clinical activities, supervision, and training of the local medical personnel, with some administrative duties. I'll be living in Lagos, but working in a village hospital. Mainly I'll be performing surgeries on the most critical cases."

"I wish you luck. That's going to be a real change from the luxury you're used to, man."

"It will, but I'm looking forward to the challenge. What's going on with your job?"

"The show is number one in its time slot and ranked third in New York daytime magazine shows. We're slowly climbing."

"I don't get to see it as often as I'd like, but when I have watched, it was pretty enlightening. You cover a lot of different topics."

"And a lot of beautiful women." Greg grinned. "And speaking of the fair sex, I like to get to the club early so I can see who's coming in."

"You're a mess! I had no idea you were such a player."

"And that's the way I want to keep it. Mama and Daddy don't need to know any details about my personal life, okay?"

"I got you."

The brothers took another cab to the Williamsburg section of Brooklyn to Bembe, one of the hottest clubs in the City. It was only nine-thirty, early for the dance club crowd, but Greg didn't seem to be concerned. He suggested Charles try some sort of fresh fruit drink, and he sat back to peruse the entering crowd. Charles was more interested in the offbeat décor made mostly of found and recycled objects that spoke of the New York area. The DJ played a combination of global music that appealed to their multicultural patrons, something uncommon in Atlanta clubs. There, the clubs were usually predominantly one race with a sprinkling of others.

It didn't take long for the place to get overcrowded. By eleven o'clock, a steamy, bumpin', gyrating crowd danced to live drummers jamming between sets and along with the DJ. The last thing Greg said to him before he ventured into the sea of women standing around the bar was, "The bouncers here mean business, so don't look like you're stalking any of the ladies."

Charles ordered himself another drink. This wasn't exactly what he had in mind when he imagined spending quality time with his brother. Was Greg always on the hunt like this?

Well, I might as well enjoy myself, since it looks like I'm on my own for the rest of the night.

He wasn't a salsa expert, but he could hold his own, so he downed the rest of his drink and approached a curvy Latina who'd met his glance more than once while she chatted with a group of girlfriends. He asked her to dance, and they settled in for a close, slow, sensual sway in the shoulder-to-shoulder crowd. The music was way too loud for conversation, so they just danced to the next two songs. During a brief lull in the music, he asked her if he could buy her and her girlfriends a drink. They left the dance floor and returned to where her friends stood at the bar.

Charles scanned the crowd but didn't see Greg anywhere. He ordered the cocktails, and he and the woman, whom he'd learned was named Soris, engaged in typical singles' banter. How he answered the inevitable, "What do you do?" question depended on where he was. Women always seemed to be impressed when they learned he was a doctor, but that disclosure often brought complications. It automatically gave them the expectation that his funds were unlimited. Or, when they discovered he was a plastic surgeon, some became instantly insecure, as if he were judging their physical beauty. Tonight he wasn't trying to be professional or impress anyone, so he simply answered, "I work in a hospital." Usually that was enough to kill any further questions.

He snatched a fast look at his watch. It wasn't even midnight yet. Soris and her friends seemed nice enough, but with the traveling, the alcohol in his system, and his looming ten AM meeting, he just wasn't in the mood to party. Before he could come up with a way to excuse himself from the group, someone tapped him on the shoulder. He turned to find Greg with his arms around a black woman on his left and a white woman on his right. Both appeared to have had one too many tropical drinks.

"Charles, your brother wants to tell you something," the black woman said.

"I was looking for you, man. I think I'm going to leave now."

"That's why I came to find you. Sha'Ron and Becky said they'd like to join us tonight. I thought we could hit Shelter then go back to my place."

Greg's verbal emphasis and the women's smiles made it clear what he meant. Charles' jaw tightened. Hadn't he just told his brother where he stood on nightclub pickups? Greg obviously wasn't listening or he'd chosen to ignore what he'd said. "Not tonight, man. I have an early meeting. You go ahead and enjoy yourself. Ladies." Charles nodded to the two tipsy women then headed for the exit. He pushed through the sea of writhing bodies and hurried out onto the street, hoping he could hail a cab before Greg and his companions emerged. Thankfully, a taxi stopped for him within five minutes.

Not too long after he entered the apartment and took a shower, he heard voices in the living room. He cracked the bedroom door enough to peek out and see that his brother had indeed brought both women back with him. Greg had chosen to ignore his refusal, and that made him furious. Just like when they were kids, Greg never took anything he said seriously. He still thought of Charles as his baby brother. At first he considered locking the door, but that would look as though he was hiding. Instead, he left the door unlocked, climbed into bed, turned out the light, and waited for Greg to come get him. Instead, the sounds of loud, energetic sex kept him from falling asleep. The next thing he knew, it was morning and the alarm on his cell phone woke him.

The morning came too soon for Charles' liking, but he forced himself out of bed and trudged into the kitchen in search of coffee. Thankfully, Greg owned a one-cup brewer. He was still trying to comprehend what he'd heard last night. As he sat at the kitchen counter and waited for his caffeine infusion to be done, Sha'Ron, one of the women his brother had picked up at the club, emerged from Greg's room looking disheveled and hung over. She mumbled a greeting, stumbled toward the door, and left. After a few minutes, Greg joined him in the kitchen. Charles couldn't believe the first words to come out of his brother's mouth.

"I'm thinking about having Sha'Ron and Becky back over tonight, and I'm happy to share if you've changed your mind. They're both open."

"Thanks for the offer," Charles said with a forced smile. "But I'm really not interested," he said, deciding at that moment to cut his stay short.

"Well, Becky is still here, and I really don't want her to cool off before I get back." He laughed. "What time is your meeting?"

"Ten o'clock, and I'm running late." He studied Greg's haggard appearance. "I hope your makeup person is on her A-game today, because you look like hell, man."

"Maybe, but it was worth it. You should've joined us."

Charles frowned at Greg's serious expression. "Not my thing. Look, I'm going to grab a quick shower and hit the street. Your doorman can get me a cab, right?"

"Yeah. What time do you expect to be back?"

"No idea. I'll hit you on your cell once I know."

"I won't be able to answer between two and three. That's when we go live."

"No problem." Charles drained his cup, carried it to the sink, and proceeded to wash it then return it to the cabinet.

"Boy, Rosalinda would love you."

"Who's that, another one of your booty calls?"

"I've hit it a few times, but no, she's my housekeeper, and she's always telling me how sloppy I am."

He's even doing his housekeeper. The changes he'd noticed in Greg monopolized Charles' thoughts while he showered and dressed. His older brother had always been pretty laid back, but he'd never been reckless. This side of Greg was troubling, but Charles wasn't judging him. After all, he was single and had the right to sleep with whomever he wanted. It just seemed as though his new life as a New York television personality had given him a different mindset, one of which none of the family was aware.

Roland hailed Charles a taxi to the organization's US headquarters on Seventh Avenue. The briefing turned out to be more informative than Charles had expected. He met the only other American on his team, an infectious disease specialist from the CDC in Atlanta, and discovered they wouldn't be meeting the others until they arrived in Nigeria. The other four doctors hailed from other countries and were doing their briefings in London,. The all-day briefing concentrated on teaching the participating medical personnel the necessity of conforming to specific government regulations, and learning to live and work with people of different cultures. Emphasis on risk management and security made it clear that adherence to the field guidelines for personal and team conduct and safety wasn't negotiable.

Charles made it through the briefing even though lack of

sleep threatened to sabotage him. When he returned to Greg's apartment, his brother had just gotten in from the studio.

"I've had to change my flight to get back to Vegas. Marc and I need to hash out some things before I leave for Nigeria." He hated lying to his brother, but he didn't want to go through a replay of last night. If he couldn't change his flight, he'd get a hotel room for the night. "It was great seeing you again, man. Next time, you have to come to Vegas and visit Marc and me."

"Yeah, maybe I will. I guess I should make it out there before Marc jumps that broom and gets all henpecked. It was good spending a little time with you too."

A little time was right.

"What time is your flight?"

"Seven-fifteen," Charles lied. "I think I'll do some shopping before I leave for the airport. They gave us a list of items to buy at the meeting."

Greg gave him a bear hug. "Have a good flight."

And, just like that, their visit was over.

Charles was able to change his flight for a hefty fee, but the expense couldn't be helped. He needed to put some space between Greg and himself. Greg had always been a fun-loving guy, but as far as Charles knew, Greg had never engaged in risky behavior. He flew back to Las Vegas that evening troubled by the changes he'd observed in his brother. He didn't want to mention what he'd seen to Marc just yet.

♥

Adanna peeked in on Chichima one last time, then signed

out. Halfway to her car, she realized she'd forgotten her tote bag. She spun around to head back inside and, from the corner of her eye, she thought she saw a man retreat behind a grove of trees. His action seemed so obvious and yet so strange, she stood still and waited to see if he would reappear. A few moments passed, but she didn't see any movement.

Girl, you're just tired. You need to go home and make the best of your two days off, because you're seeing things.

This was the week she had to work the weekend shift, so she took advantage of having the flat all to herself. Femi wouldn't get home until after five o'clock. Until then, she'd do laundry, wash her hair, and rearrange her room to make space for a portable crib. She finished those tasks a little after one o'clock and decided to visit the Katangua market to search for baby clothes and a crib. The market was considered the best one in the country and the place to go for *okrika* - secondhand clothes - and one could often purchase items as cheap as three for the price of one. She loved the place for its lively atmosphere.

Adanna rushed outside to the car park, and before she put her key into the lock, she saw a man scurry behind the building. This time, convinced of what she'd seen, she jumped into the car, hurried to lock the doors, and pulled out her phone.

"Emeka," she said when her brother answered. "Where are you right now?"

"At work where I'm supposed to be. Why?"

"I think someone is following me."

"And you thought it was me?" The timbre of his voice rose in offense.

"Well…you were the first person to come to mind. It's not like you haven't done it before."

He sighed. "Where are you now?"

"In the car outside my flat."

"Do you see him anywhere around?"

Adanna gave a 360-degree scan of the area. "Not right now, but I know he was watching me, because he tried to hide."

"Can you describe him?"

"Why?"

"You might need to call someone."

"*Someone* like who? You're always telling me the police are useless."

"They are, but I can tell you who to call if you don't feel safe, Adanna."

"No thank you. I don't want to be involved with your friends."

"Are you sure? My friends will take care of people better than the police. They will look out for you, especially since you're my sister."

"I appreciate the sentiment, but he hasn't tried to approach me or anything. If I see him again, or if the situation changes, I'll call *someone*. Okay?"

"Promise me you'll be careful. Don't take any chances."

"I won't. Maybe I was just imagining it."

Adanna ended the call and drove to the market. She retrieved her canvas tote bag from the backseat and joined the bargain hunting throng still a bit unnerved by the incident. Her tension eased as she strolled up and down the makeshift aisles, and smiled at the traders who yelled over each other and sang or danced to get attention to what they were offering. Even with everything going on around her, she couldn't resist looking over her shoulder every few minutes. No matter what she'd told Emeka, she hadn't imagined the lurker, but it wasn't time to focus on that. She had to concentrate on spying out items piled on the ground and on tables.

Just as she'd hoped, Adanna returned to her flat with a bagful of clothes and a fold-up crib for Chichima. She wanted the baby to always be dressed as though she were someone's cherished princess. They'd had some sad cases at the hospital, but this little one's circumstances saddened her like no other. It might've been because the child was helpless. Or perhaps because she had such a desire to become a mother herself. The idea of Kinah turning her back on her own baby was unimaginable. Until one of the children's homes had an opening, she intended to make ChiChi as comfortable and feel as protected as humanly possible.

Femi pulled into her spot outside of their building just as Adanna exited the car. "What have you been doing all day?" she asked through her open car window.

Adanna lifted the overflowing tote bag in the air. "I went to Katangua to do some shopping."

A devoted mall shopper, Femi scrunched up her nose. "What in the world could you get *there*? Are those baby clothes?" she asked, peering down into Adanna's bag.

"Come inside and I'll tell you."

Her best friend sent her a suspicious glance. "Oh, no. I have the feeling there's a story coming."

Once they were inside, Adanna flopped down on the sofa and slipped off her sandals. "You're right. There is a story. Since Chichima is going to be with us at the hospital for a while, I asked the doctors if I could bring her home in the evenings so Lezigha won't have to care for her during the night shift."

Femi eased down beside her. "You're going to bring a baby here?"

"If it's all right with you. Chichima is so good-natured. She hardly cries at all unless she's hungry. I promise she won't be a bother, and it will only be overnight," Adanna rattled on. "In the mornings she'll go with me to the hospital. It is just temporary until a space opens up for her at one of the children's homes."

The overwhelming compassion in Femi's eyes answered before she even spoke. She crossed her arms over her ample breasts. "I guess it would be useless to tell you not to fall in love with this child, huh? You have such a kind heart." She took a deep breath then smiled. "It might be nice having a baby in the house…as long as she's not a screamer."

Adanna spent her second day off washing baby clothes, disinfecting the portacrib, and rearranging her already too small bedroom. When she returned to work the next morning, she had convinced herself that she'd be able to handle the baby and the job without a problem.

Part Two

Chapter Six

Charles found it a bit surreal to now be sitting at a table in Nigeria enjoying an authentic meal with his new colleagues and beginning the other half of his new career. His colleague's conversation faded into the background as he considered how radically his life had changed in six short months. Enough to make any man's head spin, but he smiled at the thought that it was exactly what he'd aimed for. To completely change his life. Someone had purchased his Atlanta medical practice. Strangers now rented his high-rise condo. He'd become a part-time sales rep for Marc's business, and the two women he'd been dating were history. Not that there had been anything wrong with his life. He just wanted something different, and the woman sitting next to him was as different from his former dates as his new sales job was to being a plastic surgeon. Those differences fascinated him. At the moment, his libido was in high gear thanks to Adanna Okoro.

He rejoined the conversation going on around him, but when he glanced at Adanna, her gaze was fastened to his face as though she were hanging on to his every word. It had been a while since he'd received that kind of undivided attention from any woman. Usually they demanded his attention be focused solely on them.

"Nurse Okoro, what do you see as the main medical needs of the people in this village?" he asked, waving away a buzzing fly and trying to bring some dialogue to their mutual staring contest.

"There are many. Of course HIV and AIDS treatment, but

for women, I believe second would be gynecological and obstetrical care. Many of them don't see a doctor at all during their pregnancies, and they have no knowledge of their need for proper nutrition. As a result, many babies like Chichima are born with physical deformities. Immunization for children is also a major priority."

"Is there no immunization program available for infants and children?" Jack asked. As the infectious disease man on the team, he knew very well the necessity of protecting the youngest members of a community from preventable illness.

"I'm afraid not, Dr. Spivey. Those kinds of programs are offered in Lagos and other larger cities, but many of the villagers don't even own vehicles to get them into the city. If the services don't come to them, they do without."

Charles shook his head, the reality of the people's plight becoming even more real to him. This was the reason he signed on with DWB. He wanted to make a difference in the lives of suffering people.

♥

Adanna hoped she hadn't been staring at Dr. Stafford. She found it impossible to take her gaze from his eyes as he spoke and recalled her first response to seeing his picture on the computer. Even more handsome in person, he exuded a quiet, masculine confidence, and seeing him in person only confirmed what she'd thought upon seeing his photo for the first time. He was an incredibly handsome man, slender, well-built, and tall, at least 185cm, she estimated. She wanted to know more about him, but she deferred to her boss and listened as he questioned their guest.

"I probably shouldn't say this, but you're quite young to be such an accomplished plastic surgeon. Your CV is very impressive."

"Thank you, sir." His eyes twinkled. "I've been busy for the past few years, and even though my practice was successful, I wanted to use my skills to help those who really need them rather than merely performing vanity surgeries."

"You said *was*. Are you no longer practicing?"

"I sold my practice to come here for half of the year. The other half I'll be working with my brother's health and fitness business."

Adanna spoke up. "Then you might be interested in knowing how our hospital got its name, Doctor."

Charles nodded and his gaze returned to her face. "Yes, I would."

"It's named for the former First Lady of our country. Mrs. Obasanjo died following complications of plastic surgery in Spain. Her death drew attention to the increase in cosmetic surgery among Nigerian women."

"That's too bad. Elective cosmetic surgeries are increasing all over the world, and often, patients don't research the credentials of their doctor. But even with the most skilled surgeon, unforeseen things happen that can't be avoided. What concerns me is that plastic surgery patients are getting younger and younger."

"How do you feel about that?" she asked, wanting to hear the masculine timbre of his voice.

"As a plastic surgeon, I suppose I should be happy, but I'm not. Maybe I'm old fashioned, but I don't believe young teens should undergo any procedure that alters their appearance unless it's medically necessary."

"What is your reasoning?"

He turned toward her and leaned forward as though no one else was at the table. "Most young teens don't have realistic expectations. If they have low self-esteem or no friends, and they expect cosmetic surgery to fix those problems, then surgery is not the right answer. In those cases I would recommend counseling. I've only performed two surgeries on kids under sixteen, and those were reconstructive procedures."

"Such as?"

"One was a case of maldevelopment of the breast in fourteen-year-old girl. The other was gynecomastia in a twelve-year-old boy."

"I've read about that. Isn't it an overdevelopment of the breast in males?"

"Yes, and it can be traumatizing for an adolescent boy."

"I admire you for setting your own standards. Many doctors only see the money."

A shadow of a smile crossed his lips as though her statement pleased him. It wasn't just his extreme good looks that held her attention. He was fascinating—smart and principled—but she didn't want to appear disinterested in their other guests. Adanna made it a point to talk with each of the other doctors before their lunch ended. She wanted to stay and listen to him talk all day, but Drs. Ijalana and Pategi were ready to start the patient tour. As they stopped at each patient's bed, one of the doctors explained the reason for their admission, the course of treatment and prognosis for recovery. When they got to the last bed, and Dr. Pategi said it was the final patient, she realized he wasn't going to include Chichima. As soon as the team surrounded the bed, she tapped Dr. Stafford's arm and whispered, "There is one more patient, but she's only here because there is no other place for her to go. She should have been discharged weeks ago. I'd like for you to meet her, if you don't mind," Adanna said, hoping he read the pleading in her eyes.

"Of course I'd like to meet her."

She quietly stepped outside of the curtain, and he followed her behind another curtain. Adanna approached the white metal crib, gently lifted, then cuddled the baby against her shoulder before she turned toward him. "This is Chichima. She was born here recently and was abandoned by her mother. Her father isn't even aware of her birth. ChiChi is generally healthy and isn't undergoing any kind of treatment. We are waiting for an opening at one of the children's homes." She handed the pink-clad bundle to him.

He took the baby, and when he looked down at her face, he seemed to lose his breath.

"This is the worst cleft lip and palate I've ever seen," he spoke softly and smiled at the baby. Chichima's pudgy little cheeks puffed as she tried to smile back.

He dropped down in the chair beside the bed and spoke in a soft voice. "Hello, little one. I think your luck is about to change." Adanna watched in amazement as the baby's crooked expression seemed to reach inside him and snatch his emotions right through his chest. "Nurse Okoro, where can I wash my hands?"

"My name is Adanna. There's a sink in the next room to your right." She took the baby, sang a soft lullaby and stroked her cheek while she waited for him to return.

"Did anyone ever tell you that you sound like Toni Braxton?" He peered through the curtain. "You have the same low, smoky voice."

"No," Adanna said, thankful her skin was too dark to show the heat that burned in her cheeks. "I'm not a singer."

Dr. Stafford stepped through the curtain. "I bet Chichima would disagree."

"She needs human contact," she explained as though he had asked a question. "When she goes to the children's home, she won't get that. I want to do what I can for her before she has to leave. At night she goes home with me, to make it easier for Lezigha."

He stared at her for a long moment. "Can you get me a pair of gloves and a flashlight?"

"Certainly." She handed the baby back to him, disappeared through the curtain, and returned in a matter of seconds with a small light and a pair of disposable gloves.

"Hold her arms still so I can examine her."

Adanna sat in the chair with the baby across her lap while he pulled on the blue gloves and knelt in front of her.

"Okay, ChiChi, let's see what's going on here." He touched the baby as though he was being extra careful. "I'm not used to dealing with infants. Before I left the States, I'd been reading up on the most prevalent facial deformities among Nigerian children. I never expected my first patient to present me with an opportunity to perform the exact surgery I wanted to do."

The rest of the team appeared when he was in the middle of shining the light inside the child's mouth. Dr. Davies, the pediatrician was the first to speak. "What do we have here?" He knelt beside Charles and visually examined the baby. "Looks complicated." Dr. Lindstrom, the general surgeon joined them.

"Yes," Charles answered. "It involves the lips, palate, and alveolus." Charles stood. "She's a good-natured baby. Didn't even cry."

Dr. Davies took the light from his hand and checked Chichima's eyes, then examined her belly before he and Dr. Lindstrom rose. "She appears to be in good general condition otherwise. Pretty little thing."

Adanna grinned as though the doctors were complimenting her own child. "Yes, she is. Do you think you can help her?"

"I won't be able to tell how difficult surgery might be until I get x-rays," Charles said. "But I'd rather wait until she's older, maybe around six months. That will allow the palate to change as she grows. Doing the repair later on will help prevent speech problems as she develops. Whenever I do it, I'll need both of you to scrub in with me along with Matt. How long will she be here?"

"We have no idea," Dr. Ijalana answered. "The nearest children's homes are full at the moment."

"There are many other patients who have been waiting for months and even years for different procedures," Dr. Pategi emphasized. "We've selected the most urgent cases, and have their records ready for you to study."

"Excellent," Dr. Lindstrom said. "I'd like to take those back with us. Tonight we need to get our flats organized and find out where we can get dinner in the area."

Charles glanced at Adanna. "Nurse Okoro said she doesn't live far from there. Maybe she can give us some suggestions."

"Of course. I'd be glad to."

"Excellent," Dr. Lindstrom said. "Then you will be our dinner guest tonight at a restaurant of your choice. If you don't have other plans, that is."

She put the baby back into her crib and covered her with a sheet. "No, I don't. Thank you, Doctor Lindstrom. If no one is allergic to seafood, I know the perfect place to take you." When she looked up, Dr. Stafford had a pleased expression

"So, where do you perform surgical procedures?" the team leader asked Dr. Ijalana.

"That is our last stop. We have two rooms in which we operate. Please follow me."

Adanna accompanied the group into the first small room.

She noticed Dr. Stafford's gaze as it traveled from the overhead light hanging above the operating table in the middle of the floor to the canisters of oxygen in one corner. He silently studied the limited equipment - a crash cart, mobile x-ray machine, cardiopulmonary bypass pump, ventilator and an x-ray box built into the wall, the bare minimum necessary to run an OR. His facial expression didn't show it, but she imagined he was thinking he'd had twice the amount and quality of equipment in his own practice.

Now that the tour was done, Dr. Lindstrom accompanied Drs. Pategi and Ijalana to the office to get copies of the files for their prospective patients while the rest left the building and waited outside. "Adanna, since it's almost time for your shift to end, why don't you go with our guests and start your tour guide duties," Dr. Ijalana said with a chuckle when they rejoined the group. "We'll hold things down here until Lezigha arrives."

Even though she was a bit unnerved at the idea of having dinner with six strange men, she smiled. "Thanks. I think I'll take them to OceanBasket on Victoria Island."

"Great choice. Enjoy your dinner, everyone. I guess I'd better get to work. I look forward to working with you tomorrow." He shook hands with each of them and returned to the building.

No way was she about to have dinner with a group of strangers after working all day and eating lunch outside, without going home to shower. "I'd like to go back to my flat to freshen up and change, if you don't mind," Adanna said. "Will your driver be bringing you to the restaurant?"

"Yes, he's been assigned to us by the organization. Would you be so kind as to inform him of our destination this evening? He can also pick you up."

She nodded and walked with the group to the van where

their driver was asleep with the windows open. Dr. Lindstrom gave a loud rap on the door to wake him. "We're done here for the day, but Nurse Okoro needs to tell you where we will be going for dinner tonight."

"They will be dining at OceanBasket on Victoria Island." She turned back to Dr. Lindstrom. "Is seven o'clock good for you, gentlemen?"

He glanced around at his team members who all nodded their agreement. "Seven it is. We appreciate your willingness, Nurse Okoro."

"Please call me Adanna. I will meet you there at seven. Dress is casual." She spoke to everyone, but her gaze involuntarily went to Dr. Stafford.

The six doctors climbed into the van, and she watched it drive away before she went inside to get Chichima. This had proven to be an eventful day. It was great to have a team from all over the globe there to help them, but Dr. Stafford's interest in Chichima made her giggle to herself.

Femi was already at the flat when Adanna walked through the door with the baby in one arm and her tote bag and the other bag she used for ChiChi's belongings. "Mercy, what are you beaming about?"

"Am I? I guess it's just been a very good day."

"What happened to make you grin like that?"

"Well, the doctors arrived, and one of them took a real interest in ChiChi. He wants to do her surgery, but I need to ask a huge favor."

"What?"

"The team has asked me to be their unofficial tour guide, and they invited me to dinner tonight. Could you watch ChiChi for me? I'll owe you."

Femi gave her mouth an exaggerated twist. "Make you a

deal. I will if you promise to introduce me to one of the doctors."

"Femi! I don't know these men. They could be married for all I know."

"Well, that's what you'll find out tonight if I babysit," Femi said with a devious glint in her eyes. "Is it a deal?"

"Oh, why do I always let you get me into these kinds of predicaments?"

Her flatmate folded her arms and waited for an answer.

"Okay, okay! I'll see what I can find out tonight, but I can't promise you anything. These men might not even like Nigerian women."

Her flatmate stretched out her arms to both sides and spun her voluptuous body around. "What's not to like?" She reached for the baby. "Come to Aunty Femi, and please be nice to me tonight while your fake mummy is out running around with the rich doctors."

Adanna rolled her eyes. "How would you know whether they're rich or not?"

"Anybody who's not rich couldn't afford to come to Nigeria for months, girl."

"You're crazy," she said, waving her friend off but considering there was probably a kernel of truth in what she'd said. "I have to jump in the shower and put on something decent. She needs a bottle at six. If you're nice to her, she'll probably sleep until I get back. Thanks. I just hope nobody mistakes me for an ashawo having dinner with six men."

Chapter Seven

*A*ll the way back to Lagos, while the doctors engaged in an animated discussion of what they had seen at the hospital, Charles' thoughts were about the baby with the severe cleft. He was confident he could perform the surgery, but what concerned him more was his strong attraction to her. Marc often joked about the women they dated resembling their mother. The physical opposite of Lillian Stafford, Adanna had skin as dark as a panther's and rather than being model slender, her body boasted enviable curves.

"Charles!" Randy's voice broke through his contemplation. "That baby with the cleft has been on my mind. If we're going to operate on her, we need to do it before she goes to the orphanage."

"I was thinking the same thing," Charles responded, blinking away the mental vision of Adanna's swaying hips. "But Lou and Joseph seem to feel that other patients should take priority over her."

"Yes, I noticed that. We might have to do some convincing, mate."

"I don't think it will be a problem, but how do you feel about having to perform it there?"

The others had stopped their conversation and now listened. "The conditions aren't the best, but we knew that going in. Between the three of us, I have no doubt we can restore her face."

Nils chuckled. "This is my seventh tour, and take my word for it, the operating room at Obasanjo Hospital is a palace compared to some of the places I've been. When I went to Haiti, we operated outside under sheets and tarps strung together with rope and duct tape. We should be able to do any surgery in those rooms."

"I'll have to take your word on that, Nils," Charles said. "I guess I've been spoiled."

Randy shook his head, sending his curly brown hair falling over his forehead. "We all have. When we walked into that ward, the only thing I could think was, crikey, the worst hospitals at home are far above what Lou and Joseph have to work with."

"All I can say is God bless that staff," Emilio Cervantes said. "It's a miracle they manage to get anyone healed. They have my admiration."

Matthias agreed. "This is my second tour. The first time they sent me to the Philippines after typhoon Haiyan for disaster relief. This will be a breeze compared to that situation. I still have nightmares about what I saw there."

"I went to New Orleans after Katrina," Jack finally spoke up. "The concern was about the spread of disease from contaminated flood waters. Anytime you participate in disaster relief, you'll never be the same again. So much death…" He turned his head and stared out the window.

Charles marveled at what Drs. Pategi and Ijalana had been able to accomplish given the lack of just about everything he normally took for granted. He didn't consider himself a prima donna, but he was used to working with the latest in equipment and medication. The operating room, which wasn't much bigger than the master bath of his Atlanta apartment, contained equipment that appeared to be dated, but if they were functional, he guessed they would serve the purpose.

This is going to take some major adjustment. Try not to look shocked. You knew what you were signing on for. Being here will test your mettle. If you're as talented as people say you are, you can perform under any conditions. Think about what surgeons in war zones have to deal with. They operate in tents in the middle of sand storms, monsoons, and enemy fire. Suck it up and grow a pair, man.

None of them spoke again until they reached the outskirts of Lagos when Nils asked the driver, "How long will it take to get to the restaurant from our flat?"

"About twenty minutes. Rush hour traffic should be dying down by then."

"How about we all grab a shower and meet outside at six-thirty? You can hang out at our flat until we're ready, if you like," Nils said to the driver who nodded.

The six doctors boarded the van again after they took ninety minutes to change into more appropriate dinner clothing. They all seemed to be looking forward to a good meal. As soon as the driver started the engine, Matt said, "Let's get this show on the road, so Dr. Stafford can share some personal time with Nurse Okoro."

"What are you talking about?" Charles asked, feigning innocence. It surprised him that his interest in Adanna was so evident.

"Give me a break, mate," Randy said with a chuckle. "Your eyeballs might as well have been attached directly to her arse."

The van filled with masculine laughter, which became louder when Jack said, "Look at him! He's blushing."

Irked by his inability to hide his embarrassment due to his fair complexion, Charles decided it was best not to deny what the other men apparently thought was quite obvious. "What can I say? She's a beautiful woman."

"Yes, she is. See if you can find out if she has any sisters." Matt's wicked expression took Charles by surprise.

"You have to find that out for yourself, man. I'm a surgeon not a matchmaker."

When the team reached the restaurant and didn't see Adanna in the foyer of the popular eatery, Nils asked the host if he had already seated her. He checked the list and said he hadn't then showed them to their table, handed out menus and sent a waiter to take drink orders.

A few minutes passed before Charles looked up and saw her enter the dining room. The red dress she wore complemented the rich shade of her skin. Exotic-looking gold earrings finished off the outfit. The gold open-toed sandals drew his gaze to the shapely legs he was seeing for the first time. At the hospital, she wore pants. Aware that everyone at the table was watching him, he rose first and walked over to meet her.

"You look beautiful," he said, immediately realizing it was probably an inappropriate comment to make to a woman he'd just met earlier in the day, but it was out and he couldn't take it back."

"Thank you. I hope I didn't keep you waiting too long."

It was worth it. "No, we just arrived a few minutes ago."

They approached the table, and the rest of the men stood as Nils pulled out the chair next to Charles' for her. "Thank you for making the reservation, Nurse Okoro."

"It's Adanna, and you're welcome. I thought it would be better than taking our chances at getting a table." The men remained standing until she was seated.

Charles didn't miss how his colleagues all checked out her long legs before she drew them under the table. "This is a nice restaurant," he said. "Do you have any recommendations?"

Her lips, which now matched the ruby color of the dress, pulled into a smile. "Honestly, I've never been here before, but I've heard so many people rave about it, I thought it was a good choice."

The waiter brought their beverages, and he asked what she wanted to drink.

"A Coca-Cola, please."

Nils waited until the waiter returned, and they ordered their meals before he launched into his fact finding mission. "Adanna, I always like to sit down with a local resident when I do these tours with DWB. Tell us about Victoria Island."

"It's one of the most exclusive and expensive areas in Nigeria. It is also one of Nigeria's most active banking and business centers. Most major Nigerian and international corporations are headquartered on the Island. There are first-rate restaurants, shopping malls, hotels, bars, night clubs, movie theatres, schools, and businesses located on the island, so investing in property is very profitable."

"What are the most important things you think we should know?"

Adanna contemplated his question for a moment, sighed, then said, "I was born here, but I grew up in London, so I understand how Nigeria is different from western countries. I must qualify what I'm about to say with this. There are a lot of good Nigerian people, but most of our problems exist because there isn't much of a middle class. There is basically just poor and rich. Many people are desperate, and they will do anything to survive. That includes theft, kidnapping, and cybercrimes. You'll see for yourself how rich Nigerians live here on Victoria Island and in Ikeja." She took a deep breath, and Charles made it a point to take his gaze from the hint of cleavage peeking at him from her sundress.

"Traffic is horrible, and there aren't many traffic laws. We often drive inches apart from one another." She laughed. "Some roads have no lanes, so drivers are all over the road. If you have cash, you should use the Red Taxis. They're modern and drivers have been through driver training courses. Otherwise, hire a driver, since driving yourself will be a beacon to the police to pull you over for no reason and attempt to fleece you."

"The police?" Jack asked with a confused frown.

"Unfortunately, yes. Government corruption is rampant here on every level. Didn't the organization tell you about the vigilante groups here? They have become necessary due to inefficiency and misconduct in the police departments."

"Wow!" Charles said, taking a sip of his beer. "Are these groups dangerous?"

He admired Adanna's thoughtful expression. "I guess it depends on what side you're on. Sometime ago I saw a TV news show where our vigilantes were compared to the Guardian Angels in the US many years ago. They do keep order at times when others won't, but they can also abuse their power. It's just one of the realities of living in Nigeria."

She continued after the server brought their appetizers and salads. "Developing your negotiation skills is a necessity. You'll find that you will have to negotiate for just about everything, especially getting a decent taxi price. It doesn't matter if your destination is five or fifteen minutes away, you will be quoted a ridiculous price of between four and five thousand naira."

The men all grumbled in response and Nils said, "That's the reason our organization provides transportation back and forth to the hospital for us. When we're on our own time, we'll definitely heed your advice."

"To eat and drink in Lagos can be expensive, and at night the *working girls* can be overbearing." She dipped into her crab appetizer, savored it and continued. "Use cash everywhere; otherwise, expect to have your cards robbed. If you use a debit or credit card, request that it be swiped in front of you, but it's best to make use of an ATM and get cash. Just make it a point to cancel the card once you return to the States."

"How about shopping for groceries and necessities?" Charles asked. "We need to stock up on some staples in our apartments."

"From where you're staying, it's a short walk to Shop Rite, the grocery store. They have the best quality at the lowest prices." She paused then giggled. "Oh my, I sound like an advert."

Charles listened while Adanna answered each of his colleague's questions with ease. She didn't seem to be at all intimidated by being the only woman among a group of men who were firing questions at her like bullets from an AK-47. The way she answered them so honestly yet with a touch of humor impressed him. He loved the way she spoke and would've been satisfied to listen to her proper accent all night. She seemed to love her work and truly cared for her patients. So far everything she said or did impressed him. He couldn't ignore the light fragrance wafting from her skin, a fruity, floral scent that made him want to lean in and bury his nose in her neck. *There has to be something wrong with her. Nobody could be that perfect.* Charles came to the conclusion right then that he had to learn more about her.

♥

The atmosphere in the restaurant, the delicious meal and the six men who were totally focused on her words almost made her forget that other diners in the room were staring. She knew good and well what they were thinking—that she was hired to *entertain* a group of foreigners. So many Nigerian girls were forced into prostitution by greedy men who took advantage of their economic desperation. The prettiest and most skillful of them worked the upscale hotels and nightclubs, and Adanna knew the people watching assumed she was one of them. But there was nothing she could do about their presumptions. Besides, she was enjoying herself too much to be concerned.

"Those were some of the best prawns I've ever eaten," Charles said, wiping his enticing mouth with his napkin. "Would you care for dessert?"

The light touch he gave her hand sent a shiver up her spine, and judging by the way his gaze darted to hers, he'd felt it too. "Thank you. I think I will. I'm a card-carrying chocoholic."

He signaled the waiter and asked for a dessert menu. She ordered the Mississippi Mud Pie while he chose the New York Cheesecake. The others did the same, ordered after dinner drinks, and continued their conversation. Adanna couldn't recall when she'd had a more pleasant evening, but it was time for her to leave. She didn't want to leave Femi with the baby for too long.

"I hate to run out on you, but I convinced my flatmate to babysit Chichima tonight so I could join you. It's getting late. I'd better head home. Thank you for a lovely evening." She stood and reached for her purse.

Dr. Cervantes rose and so did the rest of the men. "Thank you for educating us, Adanna," he said.

"Yes, we appreciate your insight," Dr. Lindstrom added. "I guess we will see you in the morning."

"You will. Goodnight, gentlemen." A more powerful shiver shot through her when Charles placed his hand on the small of her back and escorted her to the entrance.

"I'll walk you to your car. Are you in the lot?"

He smiled when she said, "Yes, I'm the blue Peugeot."

They walked outside into the warm evening air. "I could really use your advice on where to buy a car. The van and driver are only to be used to go back and forth to the hospital from our apartment. Since I'll be here for three months at a time, I'll need a way to get around." He stopped beside a car. "Is this you?"

Adanna nodded. "I'd be glad to. Maybe we can talk about it at lunch tomorrow."

He smiled again and closed the space between them. She gazed at her feet to avoid looking directly into his eyes for fear of being hypnotized. "I enjoyed this. Could we do this again soon, just the two of us?" He leaned in and ran a finger across her bottom lip.

She held her breath, stunned by the action and the question. Was he asking her for a date? That's certainly what it sounded like. Her answer came on the breath she finally exhaled. "Yes, that would be nice." She unlocked the car door and got in, hoping she hadn't sounded like a breathless ninny.

"Until tomorrow."

Adanna drove home eager to talk to Femi about the feelings this intriguing man had stirred up inside her. On one hand, his invitation felt a bit hasty. On the other, the prospect of going out on a date with him sent her heart racing. Granted, all she knew about him was what she had read in the information forwarded to the hospital from *Doctors Without Borders*, but it had been a very long time since she'd met a man who exhibited everything she desired. At least he appeared to. She didn't know what to make of the whole thing.

Her musing came to a screeching halt when she pulled into the car park. Why was Emeka's car there? He never came to visit when she wasn't at home. She drove up alongside his Toyota and rolled down her window.

"Ndâ," she greeted him. "What are you doing here so late?"

Emeka slammed his car door and walked toward her wearing a tight expression. "Maybe I should be asking you the same thing. What's gotten into you, Adanna? How do you think Dad would feel if he knew you'd been out alone with six men–white men?"

She blinked at the force of his words. "All of them are not white. And how would you know where I've been?"

"Don't worry about how I know. Have you lost all sense of decency?" His voice grew louder with each word. "Did it even occur to you what people might think seeing you with those men?"

Adanna threw her car door open, and Emeka jumped back to avoid getting hit. "*Those men* are my colleagues. You have to be crazy to follow me around," she snapped.

Her brother continued as though he hadn't heard a word she'd said. "You obviously need someone to keep an eye on you, since you're using such bad judgment."

Adanna planted her feet wide and raised her chin. "You have no right interfering in my life, Emeka."

"I have every right and Dad agrees with me. Until you have a suitable husband, I am going to keep an eye on you and the people you associate with."

The muscles in her arms quivered when she balled her fists. "How dare you talk about the people I associate with. You're the one with the questionable friends. Go out there and keep an eye on the criminals instead of your own sister. *O dighi ihyem mere*," she yelled, insisting in their native language she hadn't done anything wrong.

"Spare me the tantrum, Adanna. One day you will appreciate my concern. Don't trust those men. They're foreigners, and they don't respect our culture."

"You've never even met any of them."

Her brother sneered. "I'll find out what I need to know. Use your head, Adanna. Why do you think they invited you out tonight?"

"Because they wanted to learn more about the country. That's all."

"That's all, huh? Even the man who walked you to your car?"

She recalled the heat that passed between her and Charles as he'd said good night. "He was just being considerate. If no one had escorted me to my car, you'd have something to say about that too."

"Be careful, Adanna. Don't get involved with these men. They can only cause you problems."

"You're the only one causing me problems. Stay out of my life," she bit out through clenched teeth, turned and then walked toward the building. When he followed her, she whirled around and shouted, "You're no longer welcome here. Don't ever come to my flat again."

"Adanna! Adanna!" He threw his arms into the air as she stormed away. The last thing she heard him say before she closed the door was, "I won't allow you to bring shame to our family name."

Femi was sitting in the living room watching *Scandal*, her favorite show, when she walked in. Her life would be in danger if she interrupted her gladiator friend, so Adanna sent her a silent wave and tiptoed into her bedroom to check on Chichima. She smiled at the sight of the baby sleeping on her tummy with her little bum poked up in the air. After she pulled the light blanket up to the baby's shoulders, she went into the kitchen and waited for a commercial break.

As soon as the scene faded to a close, Femi asked, "How'd it go? Did they enjoy their dinner?"

"I think so. They ate like hippos!" Adanna said, keeping

one eye on the TV screen. "When your show goes off, I need to talk to you."

Femi glanced up and studied her face. "Are you all right?"

"Yes, but I have to run something by you."

"Okay. I *have* to see what's going to happen with Olivia."

"I know." Adanna chuckled. "I'll go take off my makeup and change."

Thirty minutes later, she sat bare-faced in her pajamas at the other end of the sofa while Femi catered to her British upbringing and made them both a cup of tea.

"ChiChi didn't give you a hard time, did she?"

"Not at all. I thought she might carry on, since she doesn't know me, but she took her bottle and didn't even cry when I changed her. What a sweet baby."

Adanna smiled, but her thoughts quickly returned to the scene with her brother.

"What's bothering you?" Femi handed her a steaming cup of chamomile brew.

"I guess you didn't hear Emeka and me yelling at each other before I came in."

"No. He was here? He didn't come to the door."

Adanna raised the cup to her lips and took a sip. "He was waiting outside to ambush me." She shook her head. "I don't know what to do about him taking his older brother duties to the extreme. Either he followed me to the restaurant tonight or he had someone else do it, because he knew exactly where I went and whom I was with. Remember when I said I thought someone was following me. Now I know it wasn't all in my imagination."

"Oh, he's gotten out of hand now. What are you going to do?"

"I don't think there's anything I can do. My father approves of his methods. I can only go on and live my life and not worry about Emeka's obsession with being my protector."

"I wish there was a way I could help you."

"You can. I told him he's no longer welcome here, so please don't invite him over or let him in if he shows up at the door."

"I will, if you're certain. After all, he is your brother."

"I'm very certain. I'm going to bed now. Tomorrow's a new day. Oh, by the way, Dr. Stafford asked me out on a date," she said over her shoulder as she left the room.

Femi gasped and shot out of her seat. "What? Come back here! You can't drop something like that and just walk away. Where is he from?"

"He's one of the two Americans on the team, and he's black."

"Oluwa o!" Femi clutched her chest evoking God in her Yoruba tongue. "Those Americans move fast, don't they?"

Adanna grinned. "It's fine with me. He's a very interesting man, and I wouldn't mind getting to know him better."

"I was going to say have pleasant dreams, but I guess I don't have to."

"Oh, shut up."

Adanna retreated to her bedroom and took one last peek at the baby before she climbed into bed. Tomorrow promised to be an eventful day in more ways than she could imagine.

By the time she and Chichima arrived at the hospital the next morning, the visiting doctors, all dressed in scrubs this time, were sitting outside each poring over patient files. She took the baby from her car seat, grabbed her tote bag and Chichima's nappie sack, then scanned the area. Although she expected to see the lurker peering at her from behind a bush, nothing seemed out of the ordinary, so she didn't have to force the smile she put on to greet their guests.

"Good morning, Doctors. Looks like you've already started working."

Charles smiled. "We wanted to get a jump on the day. Do you need a hand?" he asked, eyeing everything she carried.

"No thanks. I'm getting the hang of it. "

Despite her refusal, he rose anyway and reached for the two bags in her left hand. "Lead the way." He followed her inside and placed the bags in the chair next to the crib where the baby stayed during the day. "When you have some free time today, I'd like to talk to you about her surgery."

Her stomach fluttered, hoping it wasn't bad news. "Will you still be able to perform it?"

"Yes, don't worry. There are some other things I need to know about her though."

"All right. We can talk at lunchtime."

The remainder of the morning, while Adanna and Samuel saw to their current patients, the doctors all worked together going over the patient files and establishing an order in which procedures and surgeries would be performed. They wanted to examine each patient, and Drs. Pategi and Ijalana asked Samuel to begin contacting them to set up appointments. One of the major problems was having enough empty beds. The procedures needed to be staggered to ensure adequate space on the ward.

When Adanna broke for lunch, the doctors still had their heads together over the stacks of folders. Disturbing them would be out of order, so she went to get her lunch from the refrigerator and then took Chichima from her crib. Now that the baby was getting older, Adanna liked to give her a little fresh air while she ate her lunch. She put her on a blanket in the shade of one of the trees and noticed Charles' gaze following her as she passed by them with Chichima in her arms. Several minutes afterward, he left the medical pow-wow and joined her.

"We learned our first important lesson today," he said, squatting down beside her onto the blanket.

"And what was it?"

"We need to pack a lunch before we leave our flat. It's not like we can just run around the corner to the nearest fast food joint."

She laughed. "Normally that might be a problem, but we have food left from yesterday's lunch in the refrigerator. Help yourself and tell the others. You'll see the microwave in there too."

He stood to his impressive height then went to speak to the others who had finally recognized it was lunchtime. They trailed him inside and reappeared behind him one by one holding plates.

"You said you wanted to talk about ChiChi. We don't know much about her."

"Didn't you say she's bi-racial?"

"Yes, but what does that have to do with her surgery."

"Nothing. I was just wondering what effect that might have on her chances of adoption once she's at the orphanage."

Adanna gave him a sad smile. "There are millions of orphans in this country. It's unlikely that she will ever be adopted. Most families are struggling and taking in another mouth to feed is inconceivable. The majority of children remain in the children's homes until they have to leave."

"Why would they have to leave?"

"Because there aren't enough homes and not enough room in the existing ones. When children are old enough to be on their own, they are released."

"To go where?"

"Into the street. They live in the alleys of the cities and roam in packs looking for any way to survive. Not long ago, President Jonathan revealed that 7.3 million of the 17.5 million children in Nigeria were orphans. They often suffer horrible child abuse. In order to stay alive, they turn to petty crime or panhandling. Almost a half a million are infected with HIV/AIDS. Thousands of young girls are trafficked to Western Europe each year, most of them enticed into commercial sex work with stories of a wealthy life in Europe. Child trafficking from Africa to Europe has become modern-day slavery."

"That's insane."

"There is no other solution. Our government is not equipped to care for them all."

"Are they unequipped or just uncaring?"

"Both, in my opinion. Charles, there is one thing you will learn about Nigeria. There are many extremely wealthy people here. After all, we are an oil nation, and those who have made their fortune live as though they don't see what's going on around them—to their own people. Their wealth has made them lose all compassion."

Charles shook his head. "Selfish people like that live in the US too, but at least our government offers minimum subsistence programs and most children are put into the foster care system. They live with families that are paid to care for them." He frowned. "Sometimes it works. Sometimes it doesn't."

As he spoke, Adanna sensed a deep empathy within him that touched her heart. "There is foster care here, but the system is flawed. Some parents are so hopeless about the future of their children; they send them to England to live with white foster parents."

"I'd like to wait until she's at least three months old before I operate on ChiChi," he said, returning to their original topic. "But I take it there's a chance she might be gone by then."

That thought made her heart plummet. "Yes, it's possible."

He scrubbed his beard and studied the infant, then picked her up. "Well, Miss ChiChi, it looks like you might be on my table sooner than I expected." His long fingers tickled the baby under her chin, and when she cooed back, Adanna laid a hand over her heart. Everything about him was so appealing to her. If they were going to work together, she needed to keep her feelings hidden, only she didn't know if that was possible.

Chapter Eight

Charles placed the baby back on the blanket and lifted his plate. He needed to restrict his time with Adanna during work hours so he didn't appear unfocused on his assignment. His team members had already noticed his interest and hadn't been hesitant to point it out. Of course, the time he and Adanna were discussing patients was considered business, and he intended to use that time to discover more about her.

"How has it been taking her home every night?"

"Fine. She is such a sweet baby. My flatmate even watched her when we had dinner last night, and she said she wasn't a problem at all."

So, she didn't live alone.

"What does your boyfriend think about your new motherhood status?"

She dropped her gaze to the blanket and answered softly, "At the moment, I don't have a boyfriend."

He wanted to pump his fist in the air and shout, 'Yes!' Instead he simply responded with "Well, that makes it less complicated." When the other doctors finished their lunch and filed back inside, Charles rose and said, "We're supposed to follow up with a few patients today to schedule them for procedures."

The visiting team, along with the two resident doctors spent the rest of the afternoon meeting and evaluating the first few patients who had been ranked highest priority.

Charles found it difficult to mask his emotions as he listened to the patients' stories. In his career thus far he'd dealt with patients who had a certain amount of disposable income or at least had good insurance. Most of the sad stories he'd heard were of the, *I'm so ugly* or *I'm so fat* variety. This was a whole different ballgame. By the time Nils called it quits for the day, Charles had seen a woman with a benign grapefruit-size neck tumor, a man who needed a skin graft for third-degree facial burns, and a teenage boy whose face had nearly been destroyed after he'd been mauled by a dog. And this was only their first day meeting patients. He had to study the procedures, which meant for the next few nights he'd be online brushing up on what he needed to know. If he put in enough hours, perhaps by the weekend he and Adanna could spend an evening together away from the hospital.

Before he left with the team, he found Adanna briefing Lezigha for the night shift. "Excuse me. I didn't mean to interrupt. Just wanted to say goodnight. We're on our way back to Lagos."

The other nurse smiled and said, "I need to check on Mrs. Eze," and quickly disappeared.

Adanna closed the file in her hands. "How did it go?"

Charles blew out a long breath from puffed cheeks. "A little more than I'd expected, but I can handle it with some help from Randy and Matt." He hoped he sounded more confident than he felt at the moment. And the next wave comes in twelve hours."

"Tomorrow's another day. Get some rest." The smiling curve of her full lips ripped his thoughts from the complexities of surgery to wondering whether they tasted as delicious as they looked. He wanted to lower his head until their mouths met but knew it would be a huge mistake. One of the priorities as representatives of Doctors Without Borders was to keep their behavior above board. His attraction to her called for patience, a virtue he'd never found necessary to develop when it came to women. Being a single black doctor in Atlanta where women outnumbered men by ten to one, he'd never had to be patient for too long. The fairer sex and their sensual gifts were readily available. Charles reined in his carnal urges and returned her smile. "You too, Adanna. Be careful going home."

All the way back to Lagos, excited conversation filled the van. All five doctors shared an adventurous spirit, and they looked forward to fulfilling their oath in new and demanding ways.

After they stopped at the store and bought enough food and beverages to last a couple of days, the five men headed to their flat. Mr. Lawai, the building manager who lived on the first floor, met them in the hallway. "Good evening, Doctors. A man was here earlier inquiring about you."

"Did he say where he was from?" Nils asked.

"No, sir, but he seemed particularly interested in Dr. Stafford."

Charles frowned. "Me? What did he want to know?"

Mr. Lawai crossed his arms over his portly belly. "He asked for the *black American doctor*," so it was obvious he didn't know you personally. And he wanted to know what time you usually leave in the morning."

"I don't know anyone here in Lagos. Was he American?"

"No, he was Nigerian. I told him I didn't know your schedule, so he just thanked me and went on his way."

Charles shared a confused glance with the other doctors. "If he comes back, see if you can get some more information. I have no idea who might be looking for me here."

"I don't give out information on my tenants to anyone without an official request. Be careful, Dr. Stafford, he might be out to do some kind of scam on you."

"Thanks, Mr. Lawai. I appreciate that." Charles shook his head. "That was strange," he murmured before the team split up at the top of the stairs when they reached the second floor.

Nils unlocked the door to the flat he shared with Emilio. "Get some rest, my friends. We have another busy day tomorrow."

Jack and Matt gave a tired wave and headed down the hall. When Charles and Randy entered their flat, Charles groaned, remembering what they still had to do to get themselves settled. "Let's put this stuff away and eat. I'm too tired to do anything else tonight."

Randy agreed and dropped his grocery bags on the kitchen counter. "Today was an eye-opener. We're going to have our hands full, mate."

"It already looks like three months won't be long enough." Charles shook his head. "I want to operate on the baby with the cleft before she goes to an orphanage."

Randy opened a can of tuna and reached for a bowl from the cabinet. "Adanna seems to be very attached to her. I was surprised they allowed her to take the baby home with her." He washed the bowl, dried it, then dumped the tuna and mayonnaise in.

"It's such a small facility, and the circumstances are out of the ordinary. Child Protective Services wouldn't allow her to do that in a big hospital, but if you ask me, Adanna loves that baby as though she were her own flesh and blood."

"It's going to be hard on her when that little sprog has to go to the children's home."

"Little what?" Charles' tone came out sharper than he intended.

"Ease up, mate," Randy said with a laugh. "That's Aussie slang for a child."

"Oh. It'll definitely be hard."

"Are you really that interested in doing the baby's surgery, or are you just trying to impress her nurse?" Randy asked with a sly smile as he added salt and pepper then mixed the salad.

He rolled his eyes. "You ask a lot of questions."

"No harm."

"There is no procedure that can give a more profound positive impact on the emotional well-being of a child than the correction of a cleft. So in answer to your question, yes, I really want to operate on that little girl. Impressing Adanna would just be an added benefit," Charles added with a snort of laughter.

"She seems like a sweet woman. When are you taking her out?"

"This weekend, I hope." Charles opened two of the meat pies he'd bought at the market and sniffed them before he maneuvered around his roommate in the small kitchen and placed them in the microwave.

"Wish you luck. Don't forget to ask her if she has a friend."

"You were serious about that?"

His skeptical expression made Randy snicker. "Dinkum."

"What the heck does that mean?"

"It means true, honest, for real."

"Oh hell, I'm going to need an interpreter to live with you, man."

Randy poured himself a glass of Coca-Cola, grabbed his sandwich, then slapped Charles on the back. "You're okay for a Yank, Stafford! Let's see what's on the telly."

When the microwave beeped, Charles joined him on the generic beige leather sofa in the sparsely furnished yet comfortable living room. They spent the next hour surfing the channels. Randy's easy-going nature gave him the feeling that they would be compatible roommates. At least that was one issue he wouldn't need to be concerned about. He needed to be more conscious of allowing his attraction to Adanna to be so obvious, though. His colleagues had already taunted him, and he didn't want his personal life to be the subject of their downtime discussions. Tomorrow he would try to figure out who had been questioning the building manager. He spent the rest of the evening on his laptop researching his prospective surgeries.

The next morning, before the team left for the hospital, Charles asked Mr. Lawai to describe the man who'd paid him a visit. His description of a dark-skinned man of medium height and build about thirty years old could have been one of the thousands of locals Charles had seen in the city since he'd arrived.

Hours flew by while Charles and the other doctors screened patients, performing follow-up exams and took x-rays and sonograms. He tried hard to concentrate on the job at hand rather than the lack of everything he was used to having readily available at work. Not that they couldn't work around it, because they could. And they would. It was just a paradigm shift for him and the others on their first tour.

By noon their stomachs were growling louder than the portable x-ray machine, and he and his team were ready for a break. Today, the team had prepared and packed their lunches. Emilio and Charles headed for the refrigerator first, but when they stepped outside to claim their favorite spot at the wooden table beneath the trees, the sound of raised voices got their attention. Adanna was in the middle of a heated discussion with a man dressed in street clothes.

Charles couldn't hear what they were saying, but the way she flailed her arms, it was evident that she was upset. Jack, Matt, Nils, and Randy joined them, and all of the men watched as the discourse got louder by the second. They all turned toward him as though asking, "Aren't you going to do something?"

He waited for a moment, hesitant to intervene. The irate man could be her boyfriend, and he wouldn't appreciate a third party interrupting their lover's quarrel. Finally, spurred on by the questioning gazes of his colleagues, he rose from the bench and approached the two. "Excuse me, Adanna. Is everything all right?"

"Yes!" the man snapped, sending him a death stare.

"No!" she responded. "My brother obviously doesn't understand that this is my workplace and not the place to discuss family issues."

Ah, he was her brother. "It's time for lunch. We were wondering if you were still joining us," Charles said as pleasantly as possible considering he already had a problem with the man for upsetting her.

"Yes, I am after I feed ChiChi. This is my brother, Emeka. This is Dr. Charles Stafford. He's here—"

Daggers shot from the man's onyx eyes. "I know who he is," he spat out.

"Do you? How?" Charles asked boldly, meeting her brother's angry gaze.

"It doesn't matter. I came here to talk to my sister. This is none of your business."

"Emeka, don't be so rude! We can talk about this when I get home. I need to get back to work now."

Charles didn't move.

"This isn't over, Adanna." Emeka strode away, got into his

car and pulled off with the tires kicking up a cloud of dust in the dry red soil.

"I'm sorry." She glanced at the ground and shook her head.

"No, I owe you an apology. All I saw was a man bothering you, and I thought you might need a distraction."

"That's kind of you. My brother can be overbearing at times. It seems someone saw us together in the car park at OceanBasket the other night. He found out who you were and came here to chastise me."

Charles frowned. "For what? You had dinner with coworkers, and I saw you to your car. Does he have a problem with me?"

"Not with you personally, but he made it a point to remind me that the only Nigerian women you see out with six men, especially white men, are prostitutes. Emeka doesn't want me to associate with any men who aren't of our tribe." She glanced at her watch. "ChiChi must be starving. I need to feed her."

He chuckled. "That baby certainly hasn't let the cleft stop her from eating. She's far from starving."

"Yes, she's getting to be a little roly-poly. Well, I'd better get inside. Thank you for checking on me."

He watched her go into the building, then returned to the table. "That was her brother," he said in answer to their questioning expressions. "It seems he saw me saying goodnight to her at the restaurant, and he didn't like it."

"Why? Did you have your tongue down her throat, mate?"

"No! We were standing at the car talking. From the little she just told me, he has a problem with foreigners."

"Aren't you the lucky one," Randy said with a snide chuckle.

"Do you think he was the man who questioned Mr. Lawai?" Nils asked

"It's the first thing that came to mind. He fits the description."

When Adanna didn't join them for lunch, Charles returned to work and put the incident out of his mind while they saw the rest of the patients scheduled for follow-up visits that day.

Two days had passed since the last of the patients selected for surgery and treatment had been seen, all eight doctors met to set up a schedule for the order of the procedures. Charles made an impassioned plea to Drs. Ijalana and Pategi for immediately performing the cleft repair on Chichima, stressing the severity of the deformity and the looming possibility of her leaving the hospital any day for an orphanage. They agreed and decided that procedures would begin on Monday of the following week to give themselves the weekend to get mentally and physically prepared.

Charles looked forward to the two-day respite, but not for the same reason as the others. Before they boarded the van at the end of the day, he went in search of Adanna.

"I thought this is where you'd be," he said, finding her changing Chichima's diaper. "Do you think you can get a sitter for tonight or Saturday evening? I'd like to take you out."

The smile that met him when she glanced up warmed him to the core. "That would be nice. I'd have to find out, but I can let you know. Tonight is a bit of a short notice. Femi might have plans. She may be willing to watch her for a couple of hours tomorrow or Sunday afternoon."

"Great. What would you like to do? Dinner and a movie, dinner and dancing, lunch and shopping. I'll leave it up to you."

He didn't understand her look of surprise, but brushed it off. "Here's my cell number." He'd written it on a piece of note paper in anticipation of this moment.

Adanna folded it in half, tucked the paper into the front pocket of her tote bag, and then lifted the baby from her crib. "I'll call you this evening." She left through the back door while he exited through the front to board the van.

Only another doctor would've understood the excited chatter as they rode back into Lagos. Charles' confidence was buoyed by his small victory in getting their hosts to agree to allow him to operate on Chichima even though she hadn't previously been on the pre-op list. But the smile he wore all the way back to their flat had more to do with the fact that this weekend would be his first date with Adanna.

♥

Chichima slept while Adanna drove home thinking about Charles' invitation. She wanted to get to know him, so going to see a movie wasn't a good idea. The club atmosphere wasn't conducive to conversation either, and she had no idea what he meant about lunch and shopping. Even though she didn't date a lot, Adanna was well aware that many women took advantage of any opportunity to have someone fund their retail addiction. Only she wasn't one of them. Shopping was nice, but in her opinion, expecting a man you hardly knew to pay for it was just crass.

Femi was standing in front of the stove when Adanna entered the flat. "I need to build you a throne in front of that thing," she said with a giggle as she rested her tote bag and ChiChi's nappie sack onto the sofa.

"Yes, I *am* the queen." Femi grinned and raised a wooden

spoon in the air like a scepter. "I felt extra energetic tonight, so I decided to make everyone's favorites—rice and goat stew, pounded yam and egusi soup, fried fish, and MoiMoi. We'll have leftovers for a week."

"Really? Oh, that sounds great." It tickled Adanna when Femi talked about everyone, as though their friends were their family. "I'm starving. We were so busy today at the hospital that I ended up only eating half of my lunch."

"It should be ready in about an hour."

"Wonderful. I'm going to feed her first." Adanna sat the infant carrier on the floor, went to the refrigerator, and then filled a bottle with formula. "We need to talk before anyone else gets here. Emeka showed up at the hospital today." She filled a bowl with hot water and set the bottle in it to warm.

"Again? What is wrong with him? Doesn't he ever go to work?" Femi tasted one of the dishes simmering on the stove, wrinkled her nose, and promptly added more spices.

Adanna shrugged. "He gets special treatment because he's involved with the vigilantes. He probably tells them he has to respond to an urgent call. We got into an argument when he said that he knew about my dinner with the doctors at OceanBasket."

Femi's eyes rounded. "He followed you?"

"Either he did or someone saw us and told him. Charles and the other doctors were eating lunch outside. When Charles saw us arguing, he came over to see if I was okay. Emeka acted horribly toward him. It was so embarrassing." She lifted the bottle from the water, dried it off, then shook a few drops on her wrist. "He said we'd talk about it tonight. I know what I said about his not being welcome here, but I have to make him see that I'm not going to take his nonsense."

"Good. He's gone overboard, and it has to stop."

Soft babbling sounds from the other room told Adanna the baby was awake. "Right on time. That child knows when it's feeding time." The doorbell rang as she left the kitchen to take the baby from her car seat. When she opened the door, Emeka stood on the other side.

"Come in. I was getting ready to give Chichima a bottle, and I only have a few minutes, so I'll say what I have to say."

Emeka waved to Femi then sat at the end of the sofa. He kept silent as his sister checked Chichima's diaper, positioned the baby on her lap, and then put the bottle in her mouth. Because of the cleft, it often took a few tries before she got a firm tug on the nipple.

"You'd make a great mother, Adanna."

She glanced at him, surprised by his gentle tone. "Someday. Until then, I'm just trying to help a baby who has no one. But you didn't come here to talk about ChiChi."

"No." He straightened and reverted to his usual superior mannerisms. "What you did the other night was not like you. I don't understand why you are trying to bring shame to our family."

"Oh, give it a rest, Emeka!" The baby jumped at the force of her words, and Adanna gave her cheek a reassuring pat. "I only invited you in because I wanted you to know in no uncertain terms that I'm not taking this anymore. If you had any respect for me as a woman, you'd know I would never do anything to shame our family. What you, or whoever you had spying on me, saw was an innocent dinner with my coworkers. At the end of the evening, Charles walked me to my car because it was getting dark. He's a gentleman."

Emeka shook his head pitifully. "And I see you're already on a first-name basis with him." Are you on a first-name basis with all of them?" Emeka cocked his head to the side.

He had a point, but she wouldn't concede to him. "What's

the big deal? We're around the same age, and Americans are very informal."

"You are not wise in the ways of the world, Adanna. Every day I see Europeans and Americans using our women for their pleasure and discarding them when they are through. They have no respect."

"Working with that group has made you suspicious and skeptical. All you see is the worst of what's going on out there, and you transfer that onto everyone else." She opened her hand when her nails bit into her own palm.

"I made a vow to our father to protect you, and I'll do whatever is necessary to keep that vow until you have a husband."

Femi uttered a loud snort from the kitchen, where she was obviously listening to every word they said.

"And how will I ever get a husband with you stalking me like a madman?" Adanna put the baby on her shoulder. Not wanting Chichima to sense her anger, she patted the infant's back with an extra-gentle touch.

"What is wrong with a good man…like Manny?"

"Manny?" she asked in disbelief. "He's like a brother to me. I am not even remotely attracted to him. Besides, the man has no motivation."

He puffed up before her eyes. "Why, because he has a desk job like me? Are men like us not good enough for you because we're not *doctors*?"

The baby released a loud burp, and Adanna resumed feeding her. "It's time for you to go, Emeka." Her voice deepened. "I'm warning you to stay out of my private life. Please leave."

Her brother stood over her with his arms folded. "Don't force my hand, little sister."

Adanna rose with the baby in her arms and met him eye to eye. "Is that a threat?"

"All right! All right!" Femi wiped her hands on a towel, rushed from the kitchen and got between the warring siblings. "You'd better go, Emeka. Now."

He moved to the front door, opened it and said, "Stay away from that American. Don't push me."

She slumped back onto the sofa with tears trickling down her face. "What am I going to do about him? He just won't listen."

"You stood up to him. I'm proud of you, girl. If you stand your ground, he's going to give up sooner or later."

"I don't know." Adanna sniffled. "He is so set in his ways that he doesn't even care if what he does hurts me. What he believes is more important to him than I am. Sometimes I regret ever coming back here. I should've stayed in London."

"Then you'd have your father to deal with. You came here because you wanted to help, and you're doing that. Don't let his craziness stop you from living your life."

"That's what I wanted to talk to you about. Could you watch ChiChi for me tomorrow or Sunday? Charles asked me out. He said we could do lunch or dinner, whatever your schedule allowed."

"Oh, he did, did he?" Femi smiled. "I guess I could keep her for a few hours. If you want to have dinner tomorrow night, you can get her all set for bed before you leave. All I planned to do was relax and watch a couple of movies."

"Thank you."

"I think you like this Dr. Stafford, and I'll do whatever I can to help the relationship along." She moved her hands around in a circular motion and gave her a devious smile.

"We don't have a relationship. It's just dinner, but I do like what I've seen so far. He's brilliant, compassionate, and *very* good looking."

"Dinners lead to relationships, my sister, and with those qualities, you need to see where this is going. At least let him come to pick you up this time, so I can check him out." Femi's bountiful breasts bounced as she gave a hearty laugh.

Adanna burped the baby again, took the bottle to the sink, and then rinsed it. "He doesn't have a car yet. That's one of the things he said he wanted me to help him with. I promised to call him after you and I talked."

She gave Adanna a little shove. "Go call then, and tell him Aunty Femi is on the job."

After she placed the baby in her crib, Adanna took the paper with his phone number from her tote bag. She sat on the edge of her bed. then dialed.

"Charles Stafford."

A shiver ran through her when he answered. "Hello, Charles. It's Adanna."

"Hey, I was hoping to hear from you tonight." The mellow lilt of his voice caressed her. "Did you talk to your friend about sitting with Chichima?" The expectation in his voice was clear.

"I did. She said tomorrow night would work for her."

"Okay. What do you want to do?"

"I'll leave that up to you. No shopping though."

"No? Don't tell me you're the one woman on earth who doesn't love to shop."

"I didn't say that, but I finance my own spending sprees."

"And when was the last time you did that?" Adanna hesitated. "Yeah, that's what I thought. From what I've seen, you're the kind of person who's always so busy taking care of other people you don't have any time or energy left to take care of yourself."

Do I look that neglected? He had a point though. I haven't bought any new clothes in a while, but why do I need them? I wear uniforms to work and rarely go anywhere else.

"That's a sweet offer, Charles, but I'd rather go to dinner and maybe listen to some good music."

"All right. You pick the place, but I'm afraid you'll have to pick me up. We don't have use of the van on the weekends."

"No problem. Give me your address, and I'll be there at seven." She wrote down the information and smiled as she clicked off the call and headed for her closet. The night she'd gone out with the team, she'd dressed casually since the restaurant was informal. This time Adanna wanted his sexy eyes to pop out of his head when he saw her.

Her search ended ten minutes later when she came to the conclusion that not a single outfit in her closet had eye-popping power. Tomorrow morning she and ChiChi would make a visit to The Palms mall. Now Adanna needed to figure out where she wanted Charles to take her. Femi spent more time at Lagos nightspots than she did, so it only made sense to consult her friend for advice. Adanna heard the doorbell ring twice while she got ChiChi settled for the night. She changed into yoga pants and a tank, put the baby in her crib then joined Femi in the kitchen. Manny and Agu had arrived and were seated in their usual spots atop the stools at the kitchen pass-through.

"Can you guys smell what she's cooking all the way across the city?" she asked with a smirk.

"No, Adanna," Manny replied. "Femi called and said she was making a feast. We did contribute, you know."

"You should, as much as you two eat here." She laughed. "Well, since you're here, I have a question for all three of you. Where is the nicest place to listen to some music and get a good meal that's not a dance club?"

"Why do you want to know?" Agu asked with a narrowed gaze.

"I have a date tomorrow night," she said as nonchalantly as possible so she wouldn't sound as though she were making too much out of the news. "He told me to pick the spot, but considering how limited my social life has been, I didn't have any idea."

"It must be one of those new doctors at the hospital," Manny said, giving her an unusually cold stare.

"Yes, it is."

"I suppose money is no object then," he added with a snide smile.

"It doesn't need to be cheap," Adanna added, knowing how budget-conscious most of their friends were. "He said to pick a nice place."

They threw out several names and she wrote them down to look up online. "If you want somewhere romantic, I'd say Explorers in the Federal Palace Hotel on the island," Femi suggested as she served them heaping plates of her culinary creations. She knew more about the nicer spots than the men did. "Plus, they have good music and good food, so you wouldn't need to go somewhere else to eat."

"Isn't that very expensive?"

Femi brushed off her hesitation with a careless wave. "Umm, you did say he's a doctor, didn't you? Are you excited?"

"I am," Adanna answered purposely averting her gaze from Manny's. He had no right to have an attitude just because she'd accepted a date with someone other than him. For the past two years, at least once a month, he had asked her to go out with him. She flatly refused him each time. Both Manny and Agu were nice men, but she thought of them more as brothers than anything else. Sexual attraction was the last thing she felt toward either of them. Not like what she felt when Charles was anywhere in her vicinity. That warm, tingly sensation was what a woman wanted to feel with a man to whom she was attracted.

"Tell me about Dr. Charming," Agu said with a teasing twinkle in his eyes after he'd blessed his food. "Where is he from?" He eagerly dipped into Femi's goat stew.

"He's an American from Atlanta, Georgia."

"I have people in Atlanta," he commented absentmindedly.

"What kind of doctor is he?" Manny asked.

Femi grinned when Adanna bit into a piece of crispy fried fish and hummed her approval. "A plastic surgeon who specializes in facial surgery."

"You're going for the big money, I see." The cutting edge to his words irritated her.

"What is your problem, Manny? I'm not *going for* anything. He seems like a nice man, and when he asked me out, I didn't see any reason to refuse."

Manny grunted and took a huge spoonful of egusi soup.

"If you ask me, it's about time our girl went out and had a good time. You've heard the old saying about all work and no play."

"Is he white?" Manny continued his grilling.

"What if he was, Manny?" Adanna crossed her arms and glared at him. "What would that mean?"

Femi jumped up waving her arms as though she were a referee. "Will you two please stop this? Her love life is none of your business, Manny. And it's just a date! Is everybody ready for a second helping? After that we have chin chin for dessert."

"What it means, Adanna," he plowed on. "Is that Emeka is right. Regular Nigerian men aren't good enough for you."

"Emeka? You've been talking to my brother about my personal life? That explains why we're having this crazy conversation. You've been talking to a crazy person!" She took her plate, snatched some dessert from the platter on the stove, and then left them.

Being alone in her bedroom with Chichima was better than listening to the nonsense Manny had heard from her brother. Of course he would agree with Emeka, because he'd had a crush on her ever since they met. Men! Ridiculous Nigerian men and their patriarchal ideas. Even some young men still held onto beliefs that put them in a position of superiority over women. Perhaps her feminist attitudes developed from her years living in London, but she refused to accept traditions that only served to keep women in *their place*.

She finished her food, got ready for bed even though it was still early and turned on the TV to watch until the baby awoke for her ten o'clock feeding. But even though one of her favorite Friday night shows played out on the screen, all Adanna could think about was how her date with Charles might go.

Decked out in a fitted sapphire dress and matching stilettos some twelve hours later, Adanna gave Femi last minute instructions, kissed the baby and drove to the address Charles had given her. She'd called him before she left the flat, and he said he would be waiting outside. When she pulled up and saw him dressed in an azure blue shirt topped with a tan sports jacket, she smiled. It appeared as though they had intentionally coordinated their outfits. As he approached the car, his long legs making an easy stride, she shivered. Okay, she was going against everything she'd been raised to believe. He wasn't Ibo. He wasn't even Nigerian. Heck, he wasn't even African. At least he was African-American, but he didn't even slightly resemble the men she'd known all her life. Why was she so attracted to him? Stupid question. Of the traits on her mental list of qualities she desired in a man, he possessed them all: educated, successful, highly motivated, kind, and good looking without being egotistical. At least that's the way he seemed. She didn't really know him, so all of that unselfish, gentle healer persona could just be a front.

"Good evening." He leaned inside the open passenger window. "I'll drive. It's not right for you to do the driving on our first date."

"Do you really want to do that? You've never driven here before, have you?"

"No, but I think I'd better get used to it."

Adanna smiled, put the car in park, and slid over.

Charles got in on the driver's side, and his simple fresh, clean scent that reminded her of freshly pressed linens filled the interior of the car. After he adjusted the seat and the mirrors, he turned toward her and let his gaze travel from her face to her feet and back again. "You look… fantastic."

She squeezed her thighs together as the low sensuality in his voice caressed her. "I was about to say the same thing to you."

"Where are we going?"

"I thought we'd try the The Federal Palace Hotel. I've been told they have good music and excellent local and international food. Turn right at the end of the street. Before we get started, though, there are a few things you should know about driving in Nigeria."

"Teach me." His voice lowered, and he met her gaze with a look in his eyes that made her stomach flip. She swallowed her nervousness. He needed to know how to get them to Victoria Island in one piece. "The first thing you should know is every other person driving is crazy. You are the only sane one behind the wheel. Don't say anything to any of them. You want to get to where you're going in one piece. If you have to change lanes, *do not* use the signal." Charles frowned and waited for her to explain. "All it does is alert the cars following you, and they'll speed up."

Adanna directed him through the congested Lagos streets as she continued her on-road tutorial. It didn't take Charles long to get the hang of maneuvering in and out of the disorderly traffic. "You're good. Most foreigners usually end up in crashes their first time out."

"Thanks." His smile mirrored hers and erased her last remnants of tension. She didn't know why she'd been so nervous about tonight. Charles' easy-going personality certainly wasn't responsible. Everything he'd said or done since the team arrived at the hospital demonstrated his pleasing bedside manner, especially the way he handled Chichima.

Miraculously, they arrived at the hotel without incident. The valet opened the passenger door and Charles came around and extended his hand. "Let's have a drink in the bar before we eat."

Adanna shivered inside when he put his arm around her waist and escorted her inside the beautifully appointed lobby. A sign directed them to the Ancestors Spirit & Wine Bar. They took seats on the bright yellow stools at the enormous circular bar. Once they had ordered cocktails, he leaned back and studied her for a long moment with a pensive smile.

"Tell me about Adanna. So many girls as beautiful as you would choose to be models or actresses. Tell me why you chose to be a nurse."

She pondered his question for a few seconds before she released a deep breath. "I hate seeing people suffer. There is so much suffering here, not just in Nigeria but the whole continent. I think I told you that my brother and I were both born here but grew up in Great Britain." Charles nodded. "All those years in London, I couldn't get the images I'd seen as a child out of my head. So much sickness, disease, and deformity." She paused and took a sip of her wine. "My parents didn't have the means to send me to medical school, so I did the next best thing. I went to nursing school."

"You always knew you were coming back here?"

"Always. I never mentioned it to my father, because he's very old fashioned. He would never have agreed to my coming back here alone. Emeka always wanted to return, so he and I came up with a plan to convince our father to allow us to come back together. He agreed with one major stipulation."

"Such as?"

"That Emeka be my guardian."

"How old were you when you returned?"

"I was almost twenty." His eyes widened. Embarrassed, she dropped her gaze from his.

"So, what does that mean? Do your dates have to meet his approval?"

"Traditionally, yes, and even though I told my father I don't appreciate Emeka's interference in my life, he stands firm."

A shadow of recognition crossed his handsome face. "*That's* why he seemed to know who I was."

"Yes, unfortunately my brother takes his promise to our father very seriously."

Charles chuckled. "I take it he keeps a close eye on you."

"Too close. In fact, that's what we were arguing about yesterday." Adanna glanced around self-consciously at the other people seated in the lounge.

His eyes shifted back and forth a few times, as though he were debating with himself, then he said, "Maybe I shouldn't mention this, but our building manager said a man came by asking questions about me. I asked if he was American, and the manager described him as being Nigerian, about thirty, muscular build. That's not very specific, but I don't know anyone here and it seemed very strange to me."

Adanna's jaw tightened. She had no doubt the inquisitive stranger was Emeka or a member of his vigilante squad. "That's very possible. Can we talk about something else?"

She had no idea what to do about the invasion of her privacy.

Chapter Nine

"Okay." Charles sensed Adanna's discomfort over discussing her brother. He tapped his fingers on the glossy mahogany bar to the sound of the music playing somewhere in the background, then said, "Why don't you give me your advice on buying a car. Having you drive us everywhere just won't do." He wanted her to know this was the first of many dates, if he had his way. It was clear by the way she leaned forward slightly that she understood the meaning behind his words.

"As you've already seen, the roads here aren't the best, especially once you leave the city. My best advice is to get a sport utility vehicle, something with off-road capability and the best tires you can afford."

"I've noticed Toyota is pretty popular here."

"Yes, so are Volkswagen, Kia, Honda, and Hyundai."

"My brother swears by Toyotas. He bought his fifteen years ago. It has a billion miles on it, but he still keeps it in the garage as a back-up car. In fact, I drive his old Camry when I'm in Vegas."

She tilted her head. "You don't have a car?"

"I sold it before I came here."

The lines between her brows deepened. "And I thought you lived in Atlanta?"

"I did until right before I came here. When I decided to sell my practice and work with DWB, I knew I'd need some kind of income to live on while I'm in the States. My twin brother lives in Las Vegas and owns a fitness training business. He took me on as his sales rep and PR man. That's why I moved there."

"You're a twin?"

"Yes, I'm the oldest by three minutes."

"Are you identical?"

"Yes, but it's easy to tell us apart. Marc is bigger than me, because he's carrying a lot more muscle. And he wears his hair long."

"Really? Do you have a picture of him?"

Charles laughed. "As a matter of fact, I do, on my phone." He reached into his pocket, took out his phone and scanned through the recent photos. "Here's one we took in his studio."

Adanna took the phone and examined the photo with interest, looking up at him, then down at the screen a few times. "That's amazing. Twins are fascinating."

"What intrigues you so much?"

"The connection between them is something scientists are still trying to comprehend."

"One of these days, remind me to tell you about when Marc and I were kids. I think we should get a table before it gets too crowded." Charles picked up his drink and stood.

Adanna did the same. "Do you want to buy a new or used car?"

"Used."

A sympathetic smile curved her lips. "You really made an extreme change in your life, didn't you?"

He nodded. She didn't know the half of it. Strangely, he wanted to tell her the whole story. After Charles gave his name to the hostess, he continued. "My father is a doctor—an oncologist. My two brothers, Vic and Jesse are surgeons, and my baby brother, Nick, just finished his internship, but we're not so sure he's going to continue. I guess I just followed the path that was laid out for me without giving it much thought. Then, fifteen years down the road, I discovered I wasn't satisfied with my life. I wasn't a renegade like Marc or Greg."

"Greg?"

"All of us stayed close to home except Greg and Marc. Greg is a television host in New York City."

"Your parents must be amazing people to have raised six boys who are all successful."

Charles shrugged. "They did a good job, but it wasn't without conflict and some hurt feelings. Marc got the worst of it, because he didn't want any part of medicine. He started out in college as pre-med, but changed his major in his sophomore year. My father thought he'd gone crazy. From that point, on they locked horns whenever they were in the same room."

"What about Greg? Your father wasn't upset that he went into entertainment instead of medicine?"

"No, and we never understood why until recently. He was disappointed with Marc for two reasons. When Marc decided to go into exercise physiology and natural healing methods, my father looked at it as a betrayal."

Adanna scratched her head. "I don't understand. He's still in the business of helping people take care of their bodies."

"It didn't make much sense to us all these years either, but he and my two uncles are doctors. My father wanted his sons to continue the tradition. In his mind, Greg choosing entertainment was less of a slap in the face than Marc rejecting established medicine and going for what he considers trickery. They hadn't spoken to each other in years until recently."

"What changed his mind?"

Charles smiled. "A woman. Marc met Gianne, the love of his life. She was recovering from a battle with cancer, and she just happened to be one of my father's patients."

"Really?" Adanna leaned forward with her beautiful lips parted and rested her chin in her palm. "This sounds like a TV movie."

"You're not kidding. Gianne started out being one of his clients. Marc had to request her medical records from my father. She temporarily moved from Atlanta to Vegas so he could teach her about eating a raw diet and help her rebuild her body. They fell in love." Adanna smiled.

"To shorten a very long story, he and Marc had it out, and Daddy finally admitted the reason he was so hard on Marc was because he considered him the most gifted of all his sons. All those years everyone believed he just thought Marc was a screw-up."

"Wow! That's some story. So how is Gianne doing?"

"She's in total remission. They're planning a wedding. And Marc and my father are talking again."

Adanna gave a pensive sigh. "Family relationships can be so complicated."

Charles had a good idea what was going through her mind. He put his hand atop hers on the table, and its softness sent a jolt of awareness through him. He really wanted to put it to his lips and place a kiss there. "I apologize for yesterday. If I'd known he was your brother, I wouldn't have interrupted." Charles wasn't going to let on how much he instantly disliked the guy, and he assumed the feeling was mutual.

"I'm glad you did. It was starting to get ugly."

"He certainly didn't want to meet me."

"Please don't take it personally. Emeka has a one-track mind. He's a member of a vigilante group, and he likes to play tough. He has a gift for pushing my buttons and setting me off." She uttered a self-conscious laugh.

"Uh huh. Tell me about it. Even though my family is pretty tight, we can get on one another's nerves the way no strangers ever could."

The hostess approached them and said their table was ready. He closed his hand around Adanna's and they followed the hostess.

After they perused the menu, she continued their conversation. "Are all your brothers married except your twin?"

"Only Vic and Jesse, the two oldest, are married."

"Do they have children?"

"Vic has three and Jess has two."

"I hope you don't mind me asking all these questions. Family is very important in Nigeria, and I'm always interested in hearing about families from other countries."

"Are you ready to order?" Adanna nodded, and he signaled the server. Once they had placed their orders, he continued. "Years ago I dated a Latino girl from a big family like mine. From what I saw, other than language and food, there wasn't any difference between her family and mine. It's just my opinion, but I believe people are more alike than different."

Adanna agreed. "I've always felt that way; although, I don't know many families that aren't African. When I lived in London, I did have a Jewish friend. Her family seemed so much like mine. They valued their sons more than their daughters, loved family celebrations, and discouraged dating or marrying other religions. Until I became friends with her, I thought only Nigerians did those things."

"Even now, Nigerians esteem their boys more than their girls?"

"Yes. Of course laws have changed over the years, but it's understood that sons are appreciated more than daughters because they carry on the family name. You don't have any sisters?"

"No, my father only makes boys. I know my mother always wanted a girl, but now she has Ramona and Cydney, my sisters-in-law. She dotes on them like they're her own, and when Marc gets married, she'll have another one." He chuckled. "Mama and Gianne hit it off right away." Adanna's wistful expression signaled it was time to change the subject. "Will you come with me when I go car shopping?"

She gave him a blank stare. "I don't know anything about cars. When I bought mine, I took one of my friends with me. He was more knowledgeable than I was."

He loved that she was so unassuming. Not naïve, but not self-centered. "I wasn't asking you to come along for your automotive expertise. I'd like you to come along, because I enjoy your company, Adanna."

When she glanced up at him, it felt as though her eyes were penetrating his soul. "I like being with you too, Charles. It's nice to spend time with a man who talks about more than football or his favorite TV show."

"Well, I must admit I *am* a football fan, but I'm talking about American football. I'm not into soccer at all."

"Since this is the first time you've mentioned it, I know you're not one of those crazy fans who paints his face and goes around screaming the team's name in other people's faces. I have two friends, Manny and Agu, who are the type of sports fans I want to choke."

Their meals arrived, and while they ate, he asked her about

her years living in London. They talked about how he was adjusting to life in Nigeria. Charles marveled at how well they related to each other and how easily their conversation flowed. More than anything, he was spellbound by her appearance—a long, regal neck, plump lips and dark skin like rich, semi-sweet chocolate. It shimmered beneath the dimmed recessed lights of the restaurant. She must have applied some kind of lotion that gave her body such an ethereal glow. He wanted to reach across the table and run his fingers from her high cheekbones down her neck and over her arms. Had she rubbed it all over? Did she shimmer like that beneath her clothes too? An image of her glistening naked body stretched out on his bed sent a surge to his groin.

"Charles?"

Her voice snapped him back from his lustful mental wanderings. "I'm sorry. I was just thinking about what you said about sports fans. What is it that you love so much you would paint your face and shout?"

"Truthfully, knowing that I helped someone who needed it."

Charles met her gaze. "But you do that every day. I've watched you at the hospital. You're not a nurse by profession. You're a nurse by nature. It's who you are, not what you do."

"Thank you. That is such a kind thing to say."

"I'm just telling you what I've seen. The way you care for ChiChi is amazing. You have a gentle bedside manner. I know the patients appreciate it."

"What I do seems like a drop in a bucket when there are so many who need help. I want to do more, but I'm only one person."

Could a more perfect woman exist? Her words struck such a

chord in him and the seed of an idea germinated in his mind, but he needed to give it some serious consideration before he mentioned it to her. Instead, he asked what she wanted for dessert and signaled the server. "That's the reason I gave up my practice. It felt selfish to be making all that money from people's vanity when I could be doing something to relieve suffering instead."

He waited anxiously to share his surprise while her while the waiter took their dessert order.

"I have some good news," he said once they ordered. "I pleaded Chichima's case with Lou and Joseph, and they okayed her surgery. We're going to operate on Monday."

"Really?" Adanna flung her arms out to the side and turned her face to the ceiling. "Oh, Charles, that's fantastic! Will I be able to scrub in with you?"

"Of course. I wouldn't have anyone else. You should know that I can only perform the lip repair now. All the research I've done says operating on the palate too early might cause growth problems with her face and could result in speech problems. It's better for her if I wait until she's at least a year old."

She stared down at the Chocolate Espresso Tart the server had placed before her and drew her lips in. "But she probably won't even be here a year from now."

"If she goes to a children's home, how far away would it be?"

She didn't look up at him. "Somewhere in the area, probably not more than fifty miles away."

"You said adoption isn't likely, so no matter where she goes, I could still handle her case."

"Chichima is more than a case, Charles." Adanna took a bite of her dessert. "She's special, and she needs your help."

He studied her drooping shoulders, then hooked a finger under her chin so that she looked him in the eye. "I promise I'll take care of her no matter where she is." Without a second thought, he leaned toward her, and when she didn't back away, he moved in and touched his lips to hers. Just as he had imagined, they were soft and tasted like the dark chocolate she was eating. Her lips puckered beneath his, and she returned the kiss. Charles imagined dipping his tongue between her lips for a better taste, but he didn't want to rush things. He took his time and enjoyed the sweetness of her mouth, then broke the kiss. But when she opened her eyes, the look in them stunned him. There was no doubt in his mind that she was hungry for more, so he happily obliged.

♥

Adanna had almost forgotten they were in the middle of a crowded restaurant. Even the sounds of clinking silverware and conversation faded away as nothing but the feel of his lips and the scent of his fragrance enveloped her. But when he brought his mouth up from hers and the sensations stopped, her body reacted unexpectedly. She threw her arms around his neck and parted her lips. Charles dipped his tongue between them, deepened the kiss, and murmured a low sound deep in his throat. A surge of sexual energy radiated from her mouth to the tips of her toes.

Charles' kiss was so unhurried and delicious she couldn't even recall the last time a man had kissed her. What would Emeka think about this scandalous display of affection in a public place? The thought made her smile to herself.

"Femi is probably waiting for me," she said on a labored breath when they finally came up for air.

"Uh huh," Charles murmured running his hand down her bare arm and staring at her lips as though he wanted to feed on them. God, she hoped he did, but not here.

They made quick work of devouring the rest of their dessert, Charles paid the check, and they left the restaurant.

"I don't want your roommate to get upset, but it's still early," he said, checking the dashboard clock. "ChiChi must be asleep for the night. Why don't you call and ask if she'd mind if we made another stop?"

At the moment she wanted nothing more than to be alone with him a while longer. "Where do you want to go?"

"What do you consider the most beautiful spot in Lagos?"

"At night?" She paused and considered the question. "I guess the Lekki-Ikoyi bridge on the waterfront."

"Will it take long to get there?"

"No more than fifteen minutes at this time of night."

Charles gave her chin a gentle pinch. "Okay, call and see if she'll give us a reprieve."

Adanna made the call, and when she didn't hear any hesitation in Femi's response, she hung up and smiled. "Let's go."

Following a short drive, she told him where to park for the best view, then explained how to put the convertible top down. Charles glanced up at the towering structure illuminated in several different colors against the dark sky. "That is magnificent." He rolled down the windows, lowered the radio, and snapped several pictures with his phone.

When he turned toward her and said, "I wanted to go somewhere that wasn't so public. We're always around other people," Adanna knew why they had come to this spot. She wanted to giggle like a teenager who'd discovered the perfect snogging spot far away from her parents' view.

He slipped an arm around her shoulders. "I want to get to know you better, Adanna, but there's something I need to ask you."

"I have no secrets. Ask."

"I have to go back to the States in about a month. I'd like to know you'll be waiting for me to come back."

It took every ounce of her willpower to disguise her joy with nonchalance. "I will, if that's what you want."

"I guess I need to explain myself." Charles sighed. "Are you seeing anyone else?"

For a moment she questioned whether or not to answer him honestly but quickly reconsidered. She'd be a fool to say anything that might discourage the most interesting man she'd ever met. "No…I'm not." If he had the courage to ask her, she had the right to do the same. "Do you have a woman back home?"

He shook his head. "I was dating someone, but it wasn't serious. We parted ways before I left."

She had enjoyed their time together so much the prospect of his leaving hadn't crossed her mind. Now that he'd brought it up, an ache invaded her chest. "How long will you be gone?"

"Three months. Marc has plans to test my powers of persuasion when I get back. I'd just started my job as his sales rep before I came here. His business is taking off, and he needs all the help he can get." His gaze remained on her face for a long moment. "I'll miss you."

She hadn't expected to hear those words. "I'll miss you too."

His hand rested on her knee. "Adanna, I want to be able to talk to you while I'm gone."

"I have a cell phone, you know."

"I know, but if we Skype or Facetime, I'll be able to see you."

The inevitability of his leaving hadn't come up in their conversation before. She really didn't want to think about it. "I've never used either one. You'll have to teach me how to do it."

"Of course. I'll teach you anything you want." His voice lowered to a soft, seductive tone that sent her temperature soaring. She opened her mouth to say thank you, and he filled it with the gentle massage of his tongue. Adanna relaxed in his arms and let herself enjoy the moment. His right hand cupped the back of head, and the tips of his fingers explored the texture of her short natural hair. When his left hand left her knee, moved beneath the hem of her dress, and stroked her bare thigh, a low purring sound filled the car.

Oh, my God. Was that me? She should have been embarrassed by her behavior, but oddly she didn't care. The sound seemed to encourage him, and his hand traveled higher. Adanna opened her legs just enough to allow him to access the spot that now throbbed as strong as her heartbeat. She laced her fingers into his hair, and the soft, short waves caressed her fingers. Since the first day she had seen his picture, she'd been dying to see what it felt like. Charles teased her tongue into a frenetic dance, then just as the desire became excruciating, he pulled away and rested his forehead against hers, breathing hard against her skin.

"This isn't the way I wanted this to happen," he whispered against her heated skin. "Not in the car." He withdrew his hand from beneath her dress and dragged in a deep breath as though he were trying to slow his galloping heartbeat. "We're in a car steaming up the windows like a couple of kids."

Adanna laughed against his neck. He was right, but what other choice did they have? Both of them had flatmates. And, as much as her body screamed for what it wanted, she knew things didn't need to go any further between them tonight. This was only her second time going out with him, and the first time hadn't been an actual date. So why was she ready to get physical with him? That wasn't like her. Confounded by her own feelings, she ran a finger down his cheek. "You're probably right. Maybe we should head home now."

Charles tightened his embrace and gave her a slow, penetrating kiss. "I want you more than you can imagine, Adanna. Just not like this." The lights from the bridge and surrounding waterfront buildings illuminated the perfect angles of his face.

She rested her head on his shoulder as he turned the key and started the engine. Only the music from the radio accompanied them during the drive back to his flat. Neither of them seemed to feel the need to speak.

When he parked in front of the building, he kissed her again. "Good night, Adanna. Lock your doors and be careful." He exited the car without another word, walked around to the passenger side, and then opened her door.

Adanna watched him go into the building before she got behind the wheel. Her emotions were on a rollercoaster ride. She gazed up into the starry sky, exhaled, and pulled off. All kinds of thoughts filled her head as she wound the Peugeot through the streets.

He's moving fast. Maybe he only wants to have sex.

Perhaps he is really interested, but if you give him what he wants, he'll lose interest.

You've only been with two men in your entire life, girl. You have the right to enjoy yourself.

By the time she arrived at her flat, her head was spinning. Hopefully Femi had fallen asleep, and she wouldn't have to face an interrogation. Adanna gently put her key into the front door and opened it quietly so as not to disturb her friend.

Femi was stretched out on the sofa with the television playing on a low volume when she entered. The second Adanna tried to tiptoe across the room, she sat upright. "I know you're not going to try to get past me without saying how it went tonight?"

Startled, Adanna stopped. "I thought you were sleeping and didn't want to wake you. There's nothing to tell. We had a nice dinner. I'll tell you about it in the morning."

Femi eyed her with a suspicious squint. "Okay, you had dinner, but why did you call and say you'd be a while longer? Where did you go after you left the restaurant?"

"Just down to the waterfront so Charles could see the bridge."

"What's wrong? You seem upset. Did he do something?"

It was useless trying to shut Femi down when she was on a fact-finding mission. Adanna slumped on the other end of the sofa. "He did something all right." She rested her head back and closed her eyes. "Things got a little hot…and if he hadn't put a stop to it, we'd probably be doing the unspeakable in the front seat of my car right now."

"Get out of here!" Femi exclaimed wearing a ridiculous grin. "Well, nobody could blame you if you did. It's been quite a while."

"It has, but that's no reason to forget about how my mother raised me. I'm not an ashawo. Once we got close, it was as though I forgot who I was. All I wanted at that moment was to get closer. I would've crawled inside his skin if it was possible. Charles had more decency that I did."

"Do you really like him, Adanna, or are you just horny?"

"I *really* like him, and even though I *am* horny, it's not just about that. He's smart and seems to be so kind."

"So what is the problem?"

"Well, Emeka for one thing. He's not going to be happy about this."

"Why does he have to know? I'm certainly not going to tell him." Femi crossed her arms and pinned her with a pointed stare. "I guess you're right. He knew about everything else. Do you still think he's following you?"

"Not lately, but he might have someone else watching me. My brother is bound and determined, and he'll find a way to stay informed of my every move."

Femi made a face. "That's ridiculous."

"Anyway," Adanna shrugged. "How was ChiChi? She didn't give you any trouble?"

"She's an angel, not the least bit fussy but she does like being held."

"And I'm guilty of making her that way. She deserves every minute of cuddling she gets. Charles told me tonight that he's going to do her first surgery on Monday," Adanna said with a pleased smile.

"First?"

"Yes, he needs to wait until she's older to do the cleft palate repair. He promised me he will perform it no matter where she goes. That man is wonderful."

"Are you falling in love with him, Adanna? That sappy expression on your face looks like more than just admiration."

"Love is such a powerful word. I'm attracted to him, because he's the sexiest thing walking, but we are only coworkers who just met a short time ago."

"What does time have to do it? Don't you believe in love at first sight?"

"No. You can't truly love someone you don't know. It's impossible, but I believe I could easily fall in love with him, if he's the man I think he is."

"Well, I would really like to meet him. Why don't you invite him over for dinner one night? I'll cook my best dishes."

Adanna gave it a few moments' consideration. "From what I've seen, he has a hearty appetite. I think he'd enjoy that. Just don't invite the whole neighborhood, please."

"How about just Manny and Agu?"

"Okay. Perhaps that will show Manny that he and I don't have a chance together." She chuckled and rose from the sofa. "Thanks again for keeping ChiChi. I'm turning in now." Before she made it to the bedroom, her cell phone rang. The display showed Charles' name and number. "Hello. I made it home safely, if that's why you're calling."

"Good. I forgot to ask you something. Would you and ChiChi go with me tomorrow to look for a car? We could have lunch and make a day of it."

Adanna met Femi's questioning glance. "I'd be happy to go car shopping with you, and why don't you come here for dinner afterward? Femi wants to meet you, and she's one of the best cooks in Lagos State."

"You don't have to ask me twice. Of course you'd have to pick me up again. Do you mind?"

"Not if we're going to find you a car." They both laughed,

"Thank you. What time should I expect you?"

"After I give ChiChi her lunch at noon about twelve-thirty. She usually sleeps for a couple of hours after that, so she won't be fussy. Plus, she loves riding in the car."

"I'll see you then. Sleep well."

"You too."

Adanna clicked off the call and gazed at Femi. "I guess you'll be grocery shopping tomorrow morning. Do you need some money?"

"Whatever you can give me. If I cook enough, we'll have leftovers to eat during the week. I can't wait to meet this man," Femi said as Adanna left the room.

Adanna murmured an appreciative sound when she pulled up in front of the building the next afternoon and saw Charles waiting outside. Today he wore a black t-shirt that hugged his body and showed off his chest and arms. When he opened the door, she saw the letters CGPT printed across the front.

"You know her like a book," he said, turning and glancing into the back seat. "She's out cold." He leaned in and kissed Adanna as though it were something they did every day. "How are you today?"

"I'm great." She smiled up at him. "Last night I had a wonderful date with a fascinating man."

"Is that so? I hope he treated you right."

Adanna was thankful she was already sitting or she might have fainted when he gazed into her eyes. "He certainly did."

One corner of his mouth lifted into a lopsided smile. "So I guess that means you'll be seeing him again."

"As a matter of fact, I am."

"Good for you. I hope it works out."

"So do I."

Her stomach did a little flip, and she turned the key in the ignition to have something to do with her hands. "Where do you want to go first?"

"The biggest Toyota dealer."

"All right." She put the car in gear and drove for a few

blocks before she asked, "How good are you at haggling?"

"Not good at all."

"Let me give you a few tips. Never accept the first price they give you or even the second. Be as resistant as you can without losing the deal. Don't believe everything the seller tells you, and don't be afraid to complain."

"Thanks. Sounds just the same as dealing with car salesmen in the States."

An exuberant young salesman drove them around through acres of used cars in the hot sun. While Charles examined each one, Adanna stayed beneath the roof of the golf cart and kept the baby in the shade. Charles asked her opinion on each vehicle. Ninety minutes and fifteen cars later, he chose a 2009 FJ Cruiser.

Going inside to wait for him to complete the paperwork was a relief, since the baby had awakened and started fussing. "I'm taking ChiChi to the ladies' room to change her diaper."

"Okay. I'll find you when I'm done." Charles and the grinning salesman disappeared down the hall.

With ChiChi now clean and dry, Adanna found a seat in a corner of the showroom. While she fed the baby a bottle of cool apple juice. She considered how easy her interaction with Charles was. It had never been that way with the men she'd dated in the past. Too often they didn't want to share everyday things like going to shop for a car, because doing so was too familiar. Too intimate. Too much like a real relationship. It all seemed natural with Charles. So relaxed.

"Mrs. Stafford. Mrs. Stafford!" The smiling salesman stood in front of her. Her head jerked up when it finally dawned on her that he was speaking to her. "Your husband is almost done. It takes a little longer to check foreign credit references. He wanted me to tell you he'll be out shortly.

Would you care for something to drink?"

Even though she knew she should correct him, she liked being called Mrs. Stafford. "I would. Thank you."

He left and returned with a cold can of soda. Adanna didn't miss how he gazed at ChiChi's face and quickly looked away. Once he was gone, she held the baby close. "Don't you worry, sweetie pie. After Monday, people won't stare at you anymore. Dr. Charles is going to fix your mouth. It'll take some time, but he promised he'll do whatever you need. He's a good man. A really good man."

Chapter Ten

Charles left the office holding the keys to his new vehicle. He'd bought new insurance a couple of days ago, and after the salesman faxed his new info to the local broker, he was good to go. Granted, the Cruiser was several dozen steps down from his SL-class Roadster, but this time he was buying for function and not for style. What it lacked in flash, the big SUV made up for with four-wheel drive off-road capability which was perfect for navigating the village back roads. Like everything else he had done lately, this purchase represented his new life.

He approached Adanna in the showroom and jingled the keys in the air. "As soon as they finish doing the final prep, we'll be ready to go. Are you ladies okay?"

"We're fine."

"I'm going out back to the service bay and try to put a fire under them. If there's any problem, I'll come back and let you know."

He returned to the service department and found the maintenance techs busy sprucing up his purchase. Still beaming, his salesman came up beside him and in an effort to fill the time with small talk said, "You have a nice family, Doctor Stafford."

"I'd say thank you, but they aren't my family," Charles said with a smirk. "The beautiful lady is a coworker and the baby is our patient."

The salesman's eyes widened. "Forgive me for the presumption, Doctor."

"That's quite all right. If I have my way, the lovely Nurse Okoro will be Mrs. Stafford by this time next year." The two men shared a knowing laugh.

"You said you are a plastic surgeon. If you don't mind me asking, can the baby's face be repaired? We see so much of that here in Nigeria." For the first time since Charles had arrived at the dealership, the salesman wore a serious expression.

"Most definitely. In fact, I'm doing her first surgery tomorrow."

"How many surgeries will it take to fix a deformity like that?"

"Hopefully just two, but it all depends on how she grows. It's necessary to wait until she's a little older before the second procedure can be done."

"I wish you much success. That will make a great difference in her life."

Charles had the impression that the man's interest came from some kind of personal experience, but he didn't want to pry. They chatted about how Charles was enjoying his first visit to Nigeria, and once the car was ready, he pledged the dealership's continued support to Charles. They shook hands, and Charles asked him to tell Adanna to meet him outside the front entrance.

He followed her to her flat, and when he parked, he walked a circle around the vehicle, snapped several pictures and e-mailed them to Marc.

When they entered the apartment, a mixture of tempting fragrances caressed his senses. A curvy brown-skinned woman with breasts Charles silently thought were better than any work he'd ever done greeted them with a smile.

"*Ẹ ku abọ!*" She wiped her hands on a kitchen towel and rushed toward them.

"That means welcome in her language," Adanna explained. "This is Femi, my flatmate and very best friend." She turned to the other woman. "I'd like you to meet Dr. Charles Stafford."

He extended his hand. "It's just Charles. It's nice to meet you, Femi. It smells fantastic in here."

She shook his hand and sent Adanna an openly-approving glance that made him snicker. "Thanks. I didn't expect you back so soon. Dinner won't be done for at least an hour. While it finishes cooking, I need to take a shower before Manny and Agu get here. Keep an eye on the stove for me." She pushed a colorful potholder into Adanna's hand.

"Will you please stop introducing me as a doctor?" he said after Femi left the room. "We're not at work."

"I was taught to use someone's official title in introductions. Does it bother you?"

"Yes, when I'm not in a professional situation. It feels like bragging."

She studied him for a moment. "It wasn't coming from you, but if that's what you want."

"Thank you. You said Femi welcomed me in her language. She's not Nigerian?"

Adanna chuckled. "Yes, she's Nigerian, but she's not Ibo like me. She's Yoruba, and her native tongue is different from mine. There are at least three hundred recognized tribes in Nigeria, but Ibo, Yoruba, and Hausa are the main ones."

This was news to him, and he gave her an incredulous stare. "Really? How do people interact with each other, considering the different languages?"

"Almost everyone speaks English. That's what's taught in school since Nigeria was a British colony at one time. We also speak our tribal language among our own people."

Charles nodded. "Interesting. I'm learning something new every day."

She removed ChiChi from her car seat and got ready to put her in a bouncy seat on the floor. "Let me take her. We need to have a little talk."

Adanna passed ChiChi to him. "You two enjoy your conversation while I get us a cold drink."

He took the baby and placed her on his lap facing him. "I just wanted to talk to you without any of my doctor friends around. Monday is your day, and I promise to take very good care of you." She cooed and smiled up at him, her tiny mouth pulling to one side and exposing her gums. "You're going to have a beautiful smile." *And a better chance at being adopted.*

"You should've been a pediatrician," Adanna said softly, handing him a glass of red liquid with slices of orange and lemon.

"I don't think so. I'm a knife man." "You should be honored. Femi made Chapman in your honor."

"What is Chapman?"

"I think you'd call it party punch. It's delicious. Taste."

He took a small sip and savored it. "Mmm. I've never tasted anything like it. What's in it?"

"You have to ask her. I've never made it myself."

Adanna reached for the baby. "Let me change her and warm up a bottle so we can eat in peace."

"Remember, nothing after midnight except water."

"I know the rules, Doctor. Be right back. Relax and enjoy your drink."

While she took care of the baby, Charles took in his

surroundings. He wondered how much of the décor was Adanna and how much was her roommate. The accessories were an interesting mix of African vases, natural fibers, and tropical plants combined with colorful pillows, chrome furniture, and lamps. It looked like something you might see in a magazine. When the thought came to him that her taste wouldn't clash with his, he frowned. Where had that come from?

A loud knock sounded on the front door before two men entered in the middle of an animated conversation. They stopped talking when they saw him. "You must be Dr. Stafford," the taller one said.

"Charles." He stood and shook hands with them.

"Manny," the shorter one said, giving him an expressionless scan.

"Agu," the other followed. "Pleased to meet you."

"Ah, I thought I heard a knock," Femi said as she rejoined them in the living room wearing shorts and a tank that accentuated her curves. "I see you found the Chapman."

"Yes. It's delicious. What's in it?" Charles asked.

"Grenadine syrup, Angostura bitters, Fanta orange soda, Sprite, Ribena black currant, orange and lemon. When it's made right there's some alcohol in it too." She tied an apron around her waist. "Now that everyone is here, we can eat. Manny, I need your help for a minute."

"I thought I was a guest," Manny grumbled and trudged behind her into the kitchen. "You're going to put me to work?"

Adanna grunted as she reappeared and put ChiChi back into her seat. "Don't even try it, Manny," she said, heading for the refrigerator. "You practically live here."

Charles couldn't help but notice how Agu busied himself

with entertaining the baby, as though he wanted to avoid conversation. He also picked up on the way Adanna, Femi, and Manny huddled in the kitchen. Manny returned wearing a sour expression. When Adanna came back with the baby's bottle, he angled his body away from Charles and asked her, "So, what did you do today?"

She put the bottle in the baby's mouth without removing her from the chair and held it at an angle. "We went with Charles to Mandilas to look for a car."

"Did you find something?" Femi asked from the stove where she was filling serving bowls with something that smelled wonderful.

"A Toyota FJ Cruiser," he answered. Not brand new, but it looks good and runs great."

Agu finally spoke, "Good choice. If Adanna hasn't told you, in Nigeria the kind of car you drive determines how much power you have on the road. If you're driving something small, expect other drivers to disrespect you."

This was news to Charles. "Are you for real?"

"Learning how to insult will also come in handy," Agu continued. "You have to give back what they give you, and never take road rage personally. When you battle on the road and overtake, or as you say, pass that person, just forget about it. Don't carry it on later down the road." When overtaking, always turn to look at the person eyeball to eyeball."

Charles shook his head. "That would get you shot in the States."

"You have to use what you've got to get what you want," Femi chimed in. "People aren't going to let you divert, but since you're blessed with such good looks you can just flash them a smile and wink. Most likely the odds will be in your favor."

Manny rolled his eyes.

Charles lowered his gaze. "You have to be kidding. That's crazy."

"No, she's not," Adanna added. "Road rage here is like a game. You have to be the bully. Some drivers even have the factory-installed horn in their cars replaced with one that's more like a tanker horn so they can blast people. For instance, if the car in front of you is going too slowly, turn on your bright lights and honk your horn till he gets out of the way. You have to show them who's in charge."

"The only time you pay for damages to someone's car is if you destroy any of the lamps, but if it is a bump or a scratch, just apologize and go on your way," Agu added. "I've never been to the US, but I've visited London. The driving there is much more civilized."

Manny hadn't said a word to him since he'd arrived, so Charles decided to be the bigger man. "Are they telling me the truth, Manny, or just messing with my head?"

Manny's jaw clenched, and he hesitated before he answered. "It's true. I just doubt if Femi's advice would work. "

"Dinner is ready," Femi interrupted, seeming to sense the tension between the two men. "Everybody come and carry a bowl to put on the table, please."

"Everything smells great," Charles said, trying to lighten the mood as he rose and moved toward the kitchen. "What is all of this?"

Femi described each dish she had prepared. Once they had taken the bowls from her, she joined them in the dining area next to the kitchen and said a short blessing over the table. "Charles, Adanna said you are operating on ChiChi tomorrow. I hope it goes well." She smiled and passed a bowl to him.

"Thanks. So do I. She's very special to Adanna, and I made her a promise that I'd do whatever I could to help."

"What is it with you Americans that makes you think you always have to rush in and save everyone?" Manny crossed his arms and asked with a sour sneer.

Manny's attitude hadn't been just a figment of his imagination. He smiled and imitated Manny's posture. "Oh, I don't know. I guess it's something in our DNA."

The women acted as buffers during the meal, and they finished eating without any punches being thrown; although, Charles really wanted to land a few right between Manny's eyes. But he made his living with his hands, and he'd be damned if he would risk his profession because of this joker's personal problems. Once they had dessert and Charles praised Femi's culinary skill, he said goodnight to the group.

Adanna put ChiChi in her crib and walked him out to his new transportation. "I'm sorry Manny was so rude. I'm afraid he's a bit jealous."

"Jealous of what?"

"He's been asking me out for the past year, and I kept telling him no."

"Is that so? Why didn't you want to date him?"

"He's a nice man, but he's just not the kind of man I could become serious about. I figured why lead him on."

"Why? If you don't mind me asking." Charles stopped beside his car and leaned back against the driver's side door.

"He is too content with the status quo. Twenty years from now he will still be working in the same bank doing the same job. He never tries for a promotion or even considers looking for a better job. Manny lacks motivation, and when we've talked about it, he just doesn't seem to understand what I'm saying. It's not his job that's the problem. It's that he has no desire to strive for something more. It's sad really."

The emotion in her eyes took Charles by surprise. "Do you have feelings for him?"

"Not *those* kind of feelings. I care about all my friends, and I can't comprehend people who don't want to change or advance or accomplish something in their lives. They just go from one year to the next repeating the same pattern, and wonder why things don't change."

"You want more, don't you?"

"I do. That's the reason I came back to Nigeria after I graduated from nursing school. Of course, it would've been easier to get a job in a London hospital, only I wanted to do my part to help my people. Every day I dream about how I can do more."

"I know that feeling very well. Everyone doesn't understand it. Most people thought I was crazy for giving up my practice, but I felt like something was driving me. I had to follow my instincts." He slipped an arm around her waist and drew her close until her body molded tightly to his. "I don't know about you, but I get the feeling our meeting was part of the cosmic plan."

Adanna smiled up at him. "That's funny. I've been thinking the same thing lately."

Charles dipped his head and captured her open, searching lips. Her hands caressed the muscles in his back, and he had to restrain himself from cupping her bottom in both hands and lifting her so her legs were around his waist. If it had been totally dark outside, he might have, but since someone had been watching them, he didn't want to give their spy any fuel for the fire. He cradled her face between his hands and traced the outline of her lips with his tongue then released her from his grasp. "I'd love to stay right here doing what we're doing, but we have surgery in the morning." The dreamy expression on Adanna's face, along with the way his body was begging for her attention, kept his feet cemented firmly in place.

"I know," she said with a sigh against his chest. "Go home and get some rest." She placed a soft peck on his chin and backed away. "Goodnight, Charles."

"Goodnight." He didn't move until she closed the apartment door. A hug and a goodnight kiss at the end of the evening were nice, but it was starting to drive him nuts. He looked up at the sky and groaned. The desire to put his hands all over her body, and for her to do the same was driving him crazy. They couldn't go on like this.

♥

Early the next morning, Charles, Randy, the pediatrician, and Matt, the dental surgeon, were personally setting up the instrument trays in the operating room when Adanna arrived with the baby. The hospital had a limited assortment of the necessary instruments, but each of them had brought their own and any special gear they couldn't live without from home. They had studied Chichima's x-rays for so long they were cross-eyed. The three scrubbed in, and Emilio, the cardiac specialist, stood by in case a problem arose.

Adanna assisted in silence, thankful that she was able to participate. Since she had a personal relationship with the patient, a larger hospital wouldn't have allowed her to be involved in the surgery. Charles said he wanted her to be able to see what the surgery entailed, since they would probably be doing others. And she assumed he also secretly wanted her to observe him in action.

She studied his long, gloved fingers as he set about

repairing Chichima's lip. The baby had been given general anesthesia. Dr. Pategi, who had begun his medical career as an anesthesiologist, monitored that part of the surgery. Charles narrated every step of the procedure as he trimmed the lip tissue and closed the awful gap in his tiny patient's mouth. "The stitches are very small so the scar is as invisible as possible," he explained. "They will absorb into the tissue as the scar heals and won't need to be removed."

Mesmerized by his calm, confident skill, Adanna studied his every move as though she were committing them to memory. She had never witnessed anything so miraculous since she'd become a nurse. At the conclusion of the surgery, the doctors congratulated him on a job well done and discarded their scrubs. Adanna followed them outside where they all stretched and twisted the kinks out in their tired bodies.

"You were amazing," she gushed. "I've observed surgeries before but never anything like that."

"Thank you." She loved the humble way he averted his gaze with a hint of a smile. The man didn't seem to have an arrogant bone in his gorgeous body. "She'll need one more surgery to close the palate once she's past her first birthday." He bent over and touched his toes a few times. "I'm starving. Let's take an early lunch. We have two more surgeries this afternoon."

While the doctors ate, Adanna looked in on the other patients. She talked to the two who had arrived for surgery later in the day, and questioned them to be certain they had followed the pre-op instructions. After reassuring them about the procedures, she instructed Samuel to get them admitted and settled in.

For the remainder of the day, she looked in on ChiChi every fifteen minutes. Charles said she could give her clear liquids by bottle soon after surgery. He said after she tolerated small amounts well, she could add formula. The baby had swelling at the incision site and some bloody drainage coming from her nose and mouth, but Adanna knew this would decrease in a short time. Unless ChiChi's pain level seemed to increase, she administered infant's Tylenol every four hours along with the antibiotic Charles had ordered. The most important thing was to keep the incision clean with mild soap and water and a thin layer of antibiotic ointment.

When Lezigha arrived, Adanna informed her that she would be staying overnight to look after the baby. No need to overburden her, as they would also have two other post-surgical patients on the ward. Charles came to check on them and even managed to sneak a quick kiss before he left for the night. He looked exhausted and contented at the same time. She loved that he received so much satisfaction from using his gifts to heal others. His nature agreed with her so much that for the first time in her life, she wanted to do everything she could to please a man.

After she changed out of her scrubs into a pair of pants and a t-shirt, she warmed up leftovers from Femi's feast and pulled an empty cot alongside the baby's crib. As she ate, her mind replayed how she and Charles had ended the night. Without a doubt, they needed some private time together or they might end up doing things in public that should only happen behind closed doors. She giggled to herself, recalling the sensation of his erection pressed against her belly, and she knew it was why he remained standing beside the car after she'd gone inside her flat. Of course, she didn't intentionally want him to suffer, but what else could she do? Their situation wasn't ideal to say the least, but they could come up with a solution. They had to. Soon.

As far as the baby was concerned, Adanna understood that as a nurse it wasn't normal to become so attached, and she questioned her devotion to the child. She had done everything a doting mother would have, yet she wasn't driven to pursue adoption. What was wrong with her? Why didn't she want to do whatever was necessary to make this poor, unwanted child her own?

She also dreamed about Charles. Dreams in which he had her pinned against a wall, whispered shocking things in her ear and filled her with everything that made him male. The pleasure was so intense she moaned, screamed, and actually woke up with a breathless jolt. Mortified, she glanced around the small curtained room, hoping the audio had only been in her subconscious. Never in her life had she had a dream so erotic. She felt out of control when it came to Charles' influence on her emotions. Even so, that lack of control thrilled her. If he'd pulled down her panties and taken her outside up against the car the other night, she probably wouldn't have tried to stop him. What did that say about her? Was she in love with him, or had the excruciatingly long stretch she'd been without male companionship made her lose her mind and her morals? One thing she was sure of though. She wanted him more than she'd ever wanted anything in her life. Adanna gave her head a furious shake, got up and checked ChiChi, and then lapsed into sleep.

Chapter Eleven

A full day of surgery left Charles with an aching back and throbbing legs. He couldn't wait to get back to the apartment take a long, hot shower and hit the bed, but he remembered he hadn't eaten dinner. A ready-made meal from the grocery store would serve the purpose tonight. In spite of the fatigue in his legs, he parked the Cruiser in his assigned spot behind the apartment and walked to the Shoprite rather than deal with the awful Lagos rush hour traffic.

The complete hot dinners sold in the store weren't anywhere close to gourmet but would silence his growling stomach. On his way through the aisles, he picked a few other items from the shelves then headed for the register. His purchases fit into one bag, and he added a copy of the US edition of *People* magazine before the cashier totaled the order. The aroma of his meal tickled his nose while he walked back toward the apartment going over the day's surgeries in his mind. He couldn't wait to make the food disappear and hit the bed.

The screech of car tires jerked him from his thoughts.

Two men wearing black ski masks jumped out at the curb and rushed toward him. Charles threw the grocery bag to the sidewalk, but before he could steel himself for whatever they had, the heavier of the men landed a powerful punch to his stomach. The blow knocked the wind out of him. Immediately, Marc's instructions came to mind. In an effort to protect his hands, he dropped into a crouch, raised his leg, and sent a lightning fast kick to the man's groin. He went down with a thud. Instantly, the other man grabbed Charles around the neck from behind. He lost his balance, and a split second later, the tall, wiry one yanked something over his head. Charles stood six-foot-two, but this guy had at least four inches on him. It all happened so fast it took him several moments to get his bearings. "What the hell?" he shouted.

"Shut up!" One of them yelled as he twisted a cord of some kind around Charles' wrists.

"What do you want? There's cash in my wallet," he offered once he caught his breath. They obviously didn't just want to rob him, because they would've gone for his watch and the gold chain he always wore around his neck. But the watch was a cheap one he'd bought after they'd been warned in the orientation about wearing expensive jewelry out in public.

"I said shut your mouth!" another voice said in heavily-accented English. "We don't want your wallet."

"What is it you want?"

"You will find out soon enough, *Doctor*." They knew who he was. The man said the word with such contempt Charles thought he might have some kind of personal ax to grind; only he hadn't had enough contact with the locals for any of them to have a problem with him.

DWB had cautioned them about rampant kidnappings, and if that's what this was, they weren't going to kill him. They wanted real money—what they could extort from his family or his employer, not what he normally carried in his wallet. He needed to keep his wits and play along until he could figure out where they'd be taking him.

The drive seemed about twenty minutes long before the car came to a stop. The one seated beside him had such a distinct body odor, Charles wanted to vomit. Beavis and Butthead communicated in their native language, then one grabbed him by the arm and dragged him out of the backseat. Keys rattled, a door opened, and they took him inside some kind of structure. One of them pushed him into a chair and removed the bag from his head.

The unfinished room, which reminded Charles of some kind of bunker, contained a chair and an Igloo cooler sitting beneath a ceiling fan. One corner of the cement floor was covered by a blue mat that looked like the ones Marc used in his studio. A thin rolled up blanket lay in the center of the mat. The opposite corner of the cinderblock box held a toilet. Narrow panes near the ceiling provided the only light.

Charles again tried to get his captors to reveal their plan. "If you're looking for a ransom, I can get what you need from my accounts in the US"

"He has *accounts*," the short, heavier man hissed through his knit mask. "Perhaps we *should* ask for ransom."

"We stick to the plan," the other snapped. "Dr. Stafford, it has come to our attention that you have been soliciting our women for sexual attention." He slowly circled the chair like a cop in an old detective movie.

Charles' jaw dropped. "What? That's insane! I don't *have* to solicit women."

"Did you hear what the pretty boy said?" Butthead asked of his partner.

The phrase ignited a flame inside Charles. He'd always despised being called out because of his good looks. Growing up in Atlanta, where many of his own people still had issues with skin color, he and his brothers were ridiculed through middle and high school. He hated that his honor roll, National Honor Society, and Dean's List status were ignored while his looks took center stage. Nobody ever seemed to be able to get past his face to see that he had a brain. Their ignorance angered him and his twin. He kept his calm and internalized their heartless verbal barbs, but Marc instantly got physical with their tormenters. His twin had meted out countless, *who are you calling a pretty boy?* beat downs during their school years after which they received the ensuing punishment for street fighting from their parents.

"There is no need to deny it. We've seen you in public making sexual advances on a Nigerian woman."

This was about Adanna.

He met their hooded gazes without blinking. "Oh, now I see. You're talking about one *particular* woman."

"You are well aware of what we're talking about, and you will stay in our custody until you agree to end your association with her."

"Go to hell. Adanna is a grown woman. She has the right to date anyone she chooses."

"Dating? Is that what you call it?" the heavy one asked. "It doesn't appear to be a proper courtship. You seem intent on disrespecting her in public."

"I know where this is coming from." Charles' voice hardened. "You can tell her brother that I plan to continue seeing Adanna as long as she wants." He saw a brief flicker of recognition in their eyes and knew he'd hit the bulls-eye.

"We represent the men of this nation. If this young woman has family, I am certain they will appreciate our intervention."

"Is that what this is—an intervention? It feels like *kidnapping* to me."

"Call it what you will, Doctor. It looks as though you need time alone to reconsider. Hopefully, you will change your mind." Beavis drew a pistol from the back of his pants and trained it on Charles while Butthead lumbered over, undid his hand restraints, and stuffed them into his backpack.

He rubbed his wrists and kept his gaze trained on the gun. *I'm in good enough shape now to kick one of their asses, but there are two of them. And one is armed.* "I'm due in surgery early in the morning. People will be looking for me."

"I will ask you one more time. Are you ready to end your involvement with Miss Okoro?"

"No." He could've said what they wanted to hear, but he refused to give in to their ridiculous demand. The best thing for him to do at this point was to play his own game. "What are you getting out of this? I mean, whether you represent some organization or Emeka Okoro, you can't be getting much for doing this job. I can pay you twice what they offered."

"This is not about money, Dr. Stafford."

"It's *always* about money. If you release me now, I'll pay you a thousand American dollars—each."

Charles didn't miss when Butthead's gaze momentarily darted to meet his.

"You are not in a position to negotiate." The lanky one kept the gun pointed at Charles' chest. "You have overnight to think about it. We will return tomorrow to hear your decision."

He addressed Butthead. "Of course, I don't have that kind of money on me, but I can get it in a matter of minutes."

The odoriferous giant took an unopened bottle of water from his backpack and set it on the floor not far from Charles' chair. He tapped his cohort on the shoulder, and they backed toward the door. "There is no way out of here, so I advise you to relax and give your answer serious consideration."

Only after the door slammed and he heard the key turn in the lock did Charles stand and stretch. He was convinced this was all the work of Adanna's brother, but he was thankful Emeka Okoro wasn't crazy enough to get someone to take him out. At least he had some kind of standards. This whole elaborate plot was merely to scare him, thus the small efforts at keeping him comfortable.

He worked the stiffness out of his back, and he studied the room carefully. There truly was no way out. The door locked from the outside and didn't even have hardware on the inside. The only way to reach the windows would be with an extension ladder. Thankfully, it had a working toilet and ceiling fan. Most likely someone had built the concrete box specifically for this nefarious purpose.

He paced twelve steps to the wall in one direction, then twelve steps to the other. *What if they don't return? By midday the room would be a brick oven…* Thinking like that was useless. They'd be back. If not, what was the point in snatching him to begin with?

Angry, tired and hungry, Charles gazed down at the mat and blanket and resigned himself to stop fighting the exhaustion. At least he could rest while he contemplated a way out of this mess. Once he stretched out on the mat and covered himself with the blanket, his body relaxed and his thoughts came more clearly. By now his colleagues must have already figured out that something had happened to him. But if there were no eyewitnesses to his abduction, they wouldn't have any information to give to police, who according to Adanna were useless anyway. His best option was to bargain with his captors and convince them to release him.

♥

Around eight o'clock, Adanna had finally gotten ChiChi to sleep. As soon as she curled up on the cot beside her crib, her phone rang.

"Hello, Adanna. This is Randy Davies. I'm sorry to bother you, but by any chance have you talked to Charles?"

"No, I haven't," she said, immediately aware that something was wrong. "He's not there with you?"

"I don't want to alarm you, but his car is sitting outside, and he hasn't come back to our flat since we left the hospital."

Alarmed, she jumped up from the cot and went outside where she wouldn't wake ChiChi or any other patients. "Oh, my God. He said he was going to stop at the store to pick up a few groceries, but that would have only taken him thirty minutes at best. Have you called his mobile?"

"There's no answer. It goes right to voicemail."

Adanna's pulse escalated. "You said his car is there?"

"Yes. Nobody on the team noticed whether or not it was there when we got in around six-fifteen. Maybe he decided to do some shopping."

"That's possible, but if you don't hear from him soon, please let me know."

"Don't worry, Adanna. There's a reasonable explanation why he's not here."

"Thank you, Randy."

Adanna clicked off the call and immediately dialed Charles' phone. Voicemail. She left a brief message, then re-entered the building to look for Lezigha. "By any chance, did Dr. Stafford say anything to you before he left?"

The other nurse frowned. "Anything like what?"

"About where he might have been going when he left here."

Lezigha shook her head. "What's wrong?"

"I don't know, but his flatmate said he hasn't shown up yet and his car is there."

"I saw him talking with Dr. Ijalana before he left. He

might know something."

Adanna nodded and headed for the office. "Excuse me, Doctor," she said, poking her head in the door. "Did Dr. Stafford mention going anywhere when he left tonight?" She explained the call from Randy.

A deep furrow appeared between his thick brows. "Not tonight. I'd better call Dr. Davies and let him know to call the police if he doesn't show up in an hour or so." The worry she was feeling must have shown on her face. "I know you and Dr. Stafford have become close. Don't worry until they know what's happening, Adanna." Dr. Ijalana had asked Samuel to program all of the visiting doctors' numbers into his phone. He picked it up and hit a button. "Dr. Davies. Lou Ijalana. I just finished talking with Nurse Okoro. Has Dr. Stafford arrived yet? Hmm." He avoided looking up at her. "If you don't hear from him within the hour, I suggest you call the authorities. There is a good possibility he's been kidnapped." He glanced up when Adanna clamped a hand over her mouth. "I can't promise they will be much help, but you need to report it if he doesn't show up soon." He listened for a moment. "Did the organization inform you of the rampant kidnappings here? Anyone who gives the appearance of having money is a target. Yes. I hate to say this, but if he has been abducted, they will contact someone with a ransom demand. Unfortunately, the police will most likely just advise whoever gets the ransom request to settle with the kidnappers. Please call me back if the situation changes."

Lou set his phone on the desk and gave Adanna's hand a fatherly pat. "Don't worry. If he has been taken, all they want is money. You need to sit tight and wait to hear something. Try to get some sleep."

She took one more look at ChiChi and returned to her cot, but watching the inside of her eyelids lasted all of five minutes. All she wanted was to see Charles' face. Her stomach would stay in a knot and her eyes would remain open until she did. Adanna tossed back and forth on the cot as she fought the sobering realization. She was falling in love with the handsome, green-eyed American doctor.

Adanna had asked Lezigha to wake her in the morning in time to take a shower and grab something to eat before her shift started. ChiChi's fussing woke her before Lezigha arrived. She had been up to give the baby a dose of pain medication at ten o'clock and again at two. The first thing she did was check her phone, but there were no messages. She called Dr. Davies.

"Good morning, I know it's early, but I wanted to know if you heard from Charles."

"I'm sorry, Adanna. We called the police around nine o'clock last night. They sent someone out to take a report, and they took a look at his car. The officer didn't sound very positive. All he suggested is that we wait to see if there's a ransom call."

"Did you contact his family?"

"I didn't, but Nils contacted the New York office of the organization. Any emergency notifications have to come from headquarters. I told them to give my phone number to his parents."

"Oh, my God," she said softly, choking back tears. "I'm so afraid for him. He has to be all right."

"Hold on to good thoughts, Adanna. If we get any word, one of us will call you."

"Thank you, Randy. I'll do the same."

She showered, changed into clean scrubs, fed the baby, and then started her shift, stopping every half hour to call Charles' cell phone. After repeatedly getting no response, she bit her lip and dialed her brother. "Emeka, it's me. It's important. I need to talk to you about something. Are you at work?"

"Yes, but I can talk. You sound upset. What's going on?"

"I need your help. I know you have contacts, and I need some information."

"What kind of information?"

"Doctor Stafford, the one you met the other day at the hospital, is missing."

"When did this happen?"

"Yesterday evening after he left work. He parked his car outside his flat and disappeared. Oh, Emeka, I'm so afraid he might've been kidnapped."

"So what do you expect me to do, Adanna?"

"Couldn't you ask around among your friends to see if anyone's heard about a kidnapping? They seem to have their ears to the ground."

"That's not exactly something people go around bragging about. Kidnappings are only successful if they're kept secret and the negotiations are kept between the abductors and whoever is being asked to pay the ransom."

"I know you dislike him, but he's my friend and I am so worried about him. Will you help me, please?" Adanna knew she was whining, but she couldn't help herself.

"I doubt if I can find out anything, but I'll ask around. I don't see why you're so concerned about him to begin with."

"He's a human being, Emeka, a kind and gentle person who doesn't deserve anything bad to happen to him."

"It might take some time, so be patient."

She uttered a small sound of relief. "Thank you."

For the rest of the day, Adanna forced herself to concentrate on performing her regular duties. She assisted on two surgeries, and checked on their existing patients. In between responsibilities, she looked in on ChiChi and called Charles, hoping each time that he would answer and have an explanation for his whereabouts the last twelve hours, but she knew it wasn't going to happen. Visions of what might have happened to him plagued her. She knew all too well that armed robbery was the number two scourge in the country, and often those incidents ended violently. It seemed wrong to pray that someone be kidnapped, but it was the lesser of two evils.

Would Emeka even bother to help her? His initial reaction to Charles had been downright nasty. He didn't have a rational reason for disliking Charles, and she was determined to make him acknowledge that fact. If she could just get the two of them together, Emeka would see what a good, decent man Charles was. That's all she needed to do.

Chapter Twelve

*T*he next thing Charles knew, the sound of the heavy door opening pulled him out of a deep sleep.

"Get up, Dr. Stafford!"

He blinked and momentarily tried to get a grasp on his surroundings. After a quick glance, it all came back to him, and he bolted upright. The tall man stood over him holding the same gun and still smelling like the downdraft from a garbage truck. The odor emanating from his lanky captor was beyond what he'd experienced with some of the street people when he volunteered his services at the homeless shelters in Atlanta. Those folks grabbed a shower whenever and wherever they could. This brother obviously just didn't believe in bathing.

"You Americans eat this." He placed a box of KFC and another bottle of water on the seat of the chair. "Eat. I will return in a while, then we'll talk." He inched backward to the door keeping the gun pointed at Charles' chest. The door closed with a whoosh.

Charles stomach growled. He hadn't eaten anything since lunchtime yesterday. He didn't normally eat fried chicken, but it smelled so good. *I'd better eat. There is no telling how long I might be stuck here.* When he got to his knees, pain radiated through his middle from the punch that had brought him down last night. He limped over to the toilet, relieved himself, and used some of the bottled water to rinse his hands before he tore into the meal. By the time he finished the three-piece dinner, the door clicked and opened. Beavis returned with his gun drawn.

"All right, Dr. Stafford. You've had enough time to think. What is your decision?"

"You're right, I have. This whole *we are protecting the virtue of Nigerian women* thing is bullshit. I want to speak to Emeka Okoro. He should be man enough to talk to me face-to-face."

Charles leaned back when the putrid one waved the barrel of his gun around. "We told you before, we don't know this Emeka Okoro. Your time is running out, Doctor. If you want to leave this room, you must agree."

"Bring Okoro here, and let me deal directly with him." The man came closer, and Charles leaned back again, not for fear of being shot, but because the rank odor invaded his personal space.

"You are making a big mistake. I believe you need more time with your thoughts." He turned and left as quickly as he had come.

Alone once again, Charles was suddenly aware of how the temperature in the room had risen. It must have been past noon by now and the sun sat high in the sky. Thankfully, at least the ceiling fan moved the warm air around. He sipped on his water and returned to the mat on the floor. What if they were telling him the truth? What if Adanna's brother didn't have anything to do with his abduction? If he didn't, the demand he'd just made was useless. He had to consider the possibility, and if that was the case, what could he offer them besides money to let him go? Charles made up his mind that when they returned, his approach would be different. No matter who was behind this, he wasn't about to give up the one woman who appealed to his intellectual, emotional, and physical desires. He hadn't been looking for a serious relationship, but it seemed he'd found one just the same. Adanna was the kind of woman he would be proud to take home to meet his parents. She was strong and determined yet feminine, kind, and gentle. He'd seen her stand up to her brother and deal with obstinate patients. She had been confident and self-assured at a dinner with six male doctors. And seemed just as confident cradling a fretful baby to her breast and singing a comforting lullaby. Everything she did, she did it well.

The next time the door opened, Butthead appeared in the doorway. "Dr. Stafford, I have come for your answer."

"Good," Charles said, doing his best to meet the man's hooded gaze. "Your partner is a very stubborn man, or perhaps he's just financially comfortable and doesn't need money. Since he's refused to hear me out, I thought you might be more reasonable." The man shifted his considerable weight from one foot to the other.

Charles had his attention, so he continued, "I understand you're carrying out instructions, whether for an organization or an individual. Maybe you're doing this because of some kind of conviction, or maybe you're just helping someone. I don't know, but I'm prepared to pay you alone the two thousand American dollars if you help me get out of here. Remember, I've never seen your face. I can't identify you. Your buddy seems intent on doing this for some kind of glory, but I think you understand as well as I do that glory won't put food on the table."

Silence. The man folded his arms atop his protruding belly.

"I am not guilty of disrespecting any Nigerian women. The only woman I am involved with is Adanna Okoro, and our interest in each other is mutual. She is a beautiful, intelligent woman whom I would *never* disrespect, and if all goes as I hope, I plan to ask her to marry me. Of course, I'll need to be taken to my bank in order to withdraw the funds. Any EcoBank branch will do. Is it worth two thousand dollars for you to get me out of here?"

The man sniffed, moved from one foot to the other, and studied Charles for a long moment before he spoke. "Three thousand."

Charles smiled to himself, but kept his expression blank. "Three thousand and you agree to let me walk away from the bank?" Charles kept talking and watching his jailer's eyes move around the room but never focus on anything in particular. That was enough to let him know the man was giving his offer serious consideration. "If we're going to do this, it has to be done in a way that won't attract attention. Where is your partner?"

"That is none of your concern."

"I think it is, because if we're going to do this, it has to happen before he comes back. That is, if you don't want to share the money." Charles waited for a response.

"We must leave now," Butthead said after a long pause. "I must restrain you and cover your head again until we reach our destination."

Charles wasn't thrilled at that prospect, but if it got him out of this concrete box, he'd have to go along with the program. "I understand."

"Turn around, Doctor, and remember I am armed."

"I don't need a reminder." Charles obeyed and let his hands once again be secured behind his back with the bungee cords and his vision obscured by the hood. He heard the door opening and waited for directions.

"Come. Lie down across the backseat and don't get up until I tell you." He nudged Charles toward the vehicle, opened the door, and then pushed his head down as though he were a cop getting a suspect into a patrol car. "All right, Doctor, it is best if we go to a branch out of the area. It is somewhat of a drive, so just relax."

It seemed odd to Charles when he actually did relax. With the realization that these guys didn't want to kill him and the fact that he was finally out of the bunker, he didn't even regret the three thousand dollars he was about to relinquish. They rode for what had to be thirty minutes at little more than a crawl. From what he surmised, it was late afternoon. The streets were in their usual horrendous state with the beginning of rush hour.

His driver maneuvered the streets in silence until he said, "Listen to me," he began in an ominous tone. "I will park the car and untie you. If you make any sudden moves, I will shoot you. The bank is around the corner, so I will walk behind you. If you try to run, I will shoot you. When we get there, if you write a message on the withdrawal paper or say anything out of order to the teller, I will shoot you. Once you get the cash, put it into an envelope, hand it to me, and walk toward the exit. When we get outside, I will return your phone. You go to the left and walk until you get to the fountain under the big oroko tree before you use your phone. Understood?"

"Understood." Charles didn't have an inkling what an oroko tree was, but he could identify a fountain.

Butthead parked the car, and Charles heard him fumbling around in the front seat, then get out and open the back door. "You can sit up. Turn around." He made quick work of freeing Charles' hands and removed the hood from his head. "Step out of the car and start walking. When you get to the corner, turn right. Slowly. Do not turn around to face me. Do not speak to me. I have the gun in my pocket, and I will keep it on your back until we are done."

"Gotcha." Charles followed his instructions. He turned the corner and saw the Ecobank branch about a hundred feet ahead, yet he had no clue as to where he was. He strolled toward the bank, hoping his disheveled appearance didn't draw attention. At the bank entrance, he opened the door and held it for a woman who was exiting before he proceeded inside sensing his captor a few feet behind him. When he began to fill out the withdrawal slip, it occurred to him that he didn't know the number of the new account offhand, so he mumbled aloud, "What's the damn account number. Gotta look in my wallet." No comment from his shadow, but Charles had no doubt if he slipped up, he would end up with a bullet in his back. He drew his wallet from his back pocket with a slow hand and laid it on the high-top table. It took him a moment to find the card with the pertinent information the bank had sent him. "Ah, here it is," he said as though talking to himself.

Once he completed the slip, he approached a male teller. From the corner of his eye, he saw that his companion had replaced his ski mask with a straw hat and a pair of sunglasses. Charles went to the teller and slid the paper toward him. He greeted Charles with a pleasant smile. "Good afternoon, sir."

Charles returned his smile "Good afternoon."

The teller glanced at the slip and typed into his computer. "Do you want your cash in any particular denominations?"

"It doesn't matter."

Moments later, the teller counted out the bills with the swift efficiency of a dealer in the poker tournaments he sometimes watched on ESPN. "Three thousand. Is there anything else I can do for you today?"

"May I have an envelope, please?" Charles asked.

"Certainly." The teller handed him a crisp white bank envelope. "Have a good evening, Dr. Stafford."

He seemed a bit startled when the man called him by his title, then remembered he'd created the account in the name of Charles E. Stafford, MD, ASPS. "Thanks. You too." Charles breathed a sigh of relief and walked toward the exit.

"Stop outside and hand me the envelope once we clear the doorway," a voice said behind him.

A few feet onto the sidewalk of the busy street, Charles handed the envelope to the anxious man who in turn returned his cell phone.

"It was a pleasure doing business with you, Doctor."

"Wish I could say the same."

"Remember to turn left at the corner and go up to the fountain before you make a call."

Charles walked a few steps and sensed the man was no longer behind him. Sure enough, when he looked over his shoulder, Butthead was gone. Either he'd slipped inside one of the buildings or into an alley. After he'd walked the three blocks, as he'd been told, he took out his phone and dialed Nils.

"Charles?" his team leader asked in a breathless voice when he answered the call. "Where are you?"

"Honestly, I don't know, but I am now one of the statistics they warned us about in orientation. Some guys abducted me and took me out of the area. It took three thousand dollars to get one of them to release me."

"Lord, man! Are you hurt?"

"Just my pride—and my bank account." He heard voices of his colleagues shouting questions in the background. "I'll tell you all about it once I get back to the apartment. Hold on, let me ask someone where I am." He stopped in front of an elderly man sitting on a bench outside of a variety store. "Excuse me, sir. Can you tell me what town this is?"

The man squinted and studied him for a moment. "This is Festac Town."

"How far am I from Lagos?"

The man frowned again. "You are in Lagos, my boy."

Charles nodded and thanked the old man. "Nils, he said I'm still in Lagos, a section called Festac Town. I'm going to find a taxi and get back to the apartment," he said to Nils. "Please tell Adanna I'll call her when I get back there." He continued walking, and each block he crossed seemed to change as he got farther away from the bank. The area had gradually changed from a commercial district to a seedy strip with clusters of women loitering outside. It didn't take a rocket scientist to figure out that this part of the city was nothing but a commercial sex district. He glanced up at the street sign. First Avenue. A couple of the women dressed in outfits that didn't leave much to the imagination were bold enough to solicit him, promising to give him *treats*. One of them even lifted up her microscopic dress to show him her wares. His first thought was that his brother Greg would be in heaven here. Charles walked for a while longer, and the pungent aroma of weed coming from a parked car drew his attention. He looked into the vehicle as he passed a couple having sex in broad daylight. That prompted him to do an abrupt about-face and get away from the area before something else happened to him. From what he could tell, he'd have a better chance of finding a taxi closer to the bank. Even though he never saw the fountain, his kidnapper was probably long gone by now. Charles picked up his pace and soon found himself back in the commercial business district where he hailed a cab and instructed the driver to take him back to the apartment.

Thankful to be back in familiar territory and to see his new truck still parked in its space, Charles bolted the door to his apartment and called Adanna. "I'm back at the apartment." He took the phone from his ear at the squeal of elation she gave that was so contrary to her usual calm manner.

"Thank goodness! I was so worried about you, Charles. Are you sure you're all right?"

The sweetness in her tone made him even more anxious to see her. "I'm fine, but I need to talk to you about what happened. Can you come by here before you go home?"

"Of course I will. Did Dr. Lindstrom tell you he filed a police report?"

"No, we only talked for a minute. Let everyone know I'm okay. I need to find something to eat and take a shower right now, before I start smelling like one of those assholes who grabbed me." He chuckled, the first time he'd found anything to laugh about in the past twenty-four hours. "See you tonight."

♥

Adanna placed her phone back in the pocket of her scrubs and wiped the tears from her eyes before she alerted Dr. Lindstrom and the rest of the team that Charles was back at the apartment. In a little over an hour her shift was ending, and she could see him. The whole incident sounded so bizarre. Why would someone kidnap him and not request a ransom from his family or the organization for which he worked? How had he gotten away? Now that she knew he was safe, she couldn't wait to hear him tell the story.

When Lezigha arrived, Adanna brought her up to date on the latest with Charles then asked her if she could leave ChiChi at the hospital overnight. Her coworker agreed and promised to monitor the baby closely for any increase in her pain level. By the time she arrived at the flat, Femi was already there. Adanna also gave her the lowdown on Charles. She had a million questions, none of which Adanna could answer.

After she showered and changed clothes, she drove to his flat. She knocked on the door, and he opened it wearing only a pair of cargo shorts and a towel around his neck. He grabbed her into his arms as though they hadn't seen each other in weeks. The other doctors hadn't arrived yet, so they were temporarily alone.

"I was so afraid," she said, pressing her cheek against his freshly-showered chest. "Did they hurt you? How did you get away?"

He put a finger to her lips. "Shh. I'll tell you everything. Just let me kiss you first." Still standing in the doorway, he lowered his head, drew her bottom lip into his mouth, and sucked it gently. "Let's go outside on the balcony, so we can talk before the rest of them get here." He stopped in the kitchen, took two bottles of cold water from the refrigerator, and opened the doors to the terrace.

Adanna studied his face as he folded his lanky body into the chair across from her. She might have been wrong to expect him to be happy, but he appeared to be disturbed. "What's wrong? You're not as happy as I thought you'd be about getting released."

"I wasn't released. I bought my way out." She frowned. "I paid my own ransom." He leaned back heavily in his seat. "Let me go back to the beginning." He started with the moment he left the store and described everything that happened up to the point when his abductors told him their motive. "They claimed to represent *the men of Nigeria*, and I was their target because I'd been seen disrespecting their women in public."

"What did they mean by that?" She had to be honest with herself. She didn't know him beyond what she'd seen at the hospital. For all she knew, he could be a notorious player.

"They didn't mean *all* Nigerian women. They meant you."

She gaped at him. "Me? What makes you think that?"

"Because you're the only woman I'm seeing, Adanna—Nigerian or otherwise." He hesitated, pursed his lips. "And I believe your brother was behind it."

"Charles! That's an awful thing to say and a serious accusation to make." Emeka's behavior and the strange things that had happened in the past few weeks sped to the forefront of her mind. "He has been acting strange lately. Stranger than usual."

"Think about it, Adanna. Someone's been asking questions about me, and you've had the feeling you were being followed. He hated me from the moment he saw me, and he has a problem with us seeing each other. Those guys didn't rob me or ask for any money. Their only demand was that I stop seeing you. Unless you have an ex who doesn't want you dating another man, who else would have that much of a vested interest in your social life? You might not want to admit it, but this has his name written all over it."

She shook her head and tried to deny what was beginning to sound like a reality. "I hate to think that, but you're probably right. Emeka has gone overboard in his responsibility for me and his tribal allegiance. Both have become an obsession with him. I could disregard his extreme views and even brush off his coddling, but having you kidnapped is unforgiveable." Tears welled in her eyes at the possibility. "The whole thing makes sense, though. If the men who grabbed you were real kidnappers, their first move would have been to demand a ransom. If he really loved me, he would never do such a thing."

He put an arm around her and she rested her head on his shoulder. "I just don't know how we could prove he was involved to begin with."

"I know how, because I know my brother. On the phone I couldn't see his face, but if I confront him in person, it will be easy to tell if he's lying to me. The sad thing is, even if he admitted to arranging your abduction, no one will hold him accountable. In this country kidnapping is like a plague, and people have almost become numb to it. Lawlessness is out of control. The authorities consider kidnapping a private issue to be handled between the parties involved. They feel if no one was harmed, it's only money."

Charles shook his head. "An attitude like that only encourages people to commit crimes."

"Was there anything they said or did during the time they held you that might be a connection to Emeka?"

"Nothing. Each time they left me alone, I went over every single word. They didn't say much to me other than repeating their demand to stay away from you."

"Charles, are you here?" Randy's voice yelled from the front door.

"Out on the balcony," Charles called back.

Randy appeared in the balcony door with the rest of the team behind him. "Good to see you breathing and in one piece, mate. Come inside and spill the details."

Adanna followed him inside where all five doctors were waiting with expectant expressions. Charles took the next few minutes to recount the whole story.

"I had to report the incident to the New York Office," Nils informed him. "They might have contacted your family. You'd better call them as soon as possible to ease their fears."

"I hope they didn't. My mother must be losing her mind."

"So, you're out of three grand and don't even know who set the whole thing up?" Jack asked, looking particularly angry.

Adanna met their questioning gazes. "We have a pretty good idea. I am the reason Charles was put in harm's way," she said, unwilling to look into their eyes. She described their suspicions about Emeka and her brother's guardianship and vigilante membership. After she explained how Nigerian vigilante groups differed from what the term usually represented in other countries, Emilio, the least talkative of the group, asked, "You're saying he feels his tribal and family commitments take priority over the law?"

"Sadly, yes, and my father agrees with him, so my wishes are irrelevant."

"The consequences of a male-dominated society," Matt added in his thick Belgian accent. "Legally you have no recourse, Adanna?"

She exhaled a heavy sigh. "I might if I went to court, but doing that would destroy whatever remains of our family relationship."

Charles squeezed her hand. "What would it take to make Emeka accept us being together?" He was stepping into territory she'd rather not address, especially in the presence of others.

"In our case, nothing."

"What do you mean, in our case? What would people in other cases do?"

"I'd rather not get into that, it doesn't apply to us," she said, hoping to end his questioning.

Charles raised her chin. "Tell me, Adanna. If there's something I can do to change his mind, I want to know what it is. Please."

She glanced around at the five pairs of eyes staring at her and shrugged. "Fine. We would need to be engaged, and you would have to pay a dowry to my family."

All eyes zoomed in on Charles, who didn't appear the least bit bothered by her disclosure. "And how is that handled?"

Adanna clasped her hands in her lap and avoided the intense look in his eyes. "Most urban Nigerian families no longer ask for a bride price. It's an old tradition."

"How much is required?"

He couldn't actually be considering it? Could he? He asked the question so casually, as though we were talking about paying the power bill. Excited yet embarrassed, she glanced up from her hands at Randy's silly grin and it sent a rush of heat into her face.

Nils stood and inclined his head toward the apartment door as a signal to the rest of them. "Perhaps this is something they need to discuss in private. And perhaps you should consider taking tomorrow off, Charles."

"I'm fine. You've already had to cancel two surgeries because I wasn't there. I also need to do a follow-up on Chichima."

"Don't concern yourself with the baby, Matt said. "She's doing fine. I examined her this morning."

"It's up to you, Nils said as he opened the door and stepped into the hall. "Nobody will blame you if you take a day to get yourself together."

"Thanks, but it's not necessary. I'll call my family and see you in the morning." Nils nodded, and Jack, Matt, and Emilio filed out behind him.

"I'm going to fix something to eat, and then I'll be out of your way," Randy said apologetically as he moved into the kitchen and searched the refrigerator.

Charles refrained from continuing their conversation and called his mother while Randy slapped together a sandwich, took it and a bottle of beer into his bedroom, and shut the door.

Once he'd convinced his mother that he was alive and breathing and effectively shut down his father's *I told you so's*, Charles took Adanna back out onto the balcony, "Tell me how this dowry payment works."

The idea that he cared about her enough to even consider such a solution thrilled her, but making such a move was premature to say the least. They had been out together less than a handful of times. Yes, she had fantasized about

Charles being her husband; only, having him marry her because he was being pressured was not the way she'd envisioned the engagement she had dreamed of since she was a young teen.

"I would never allow you to do that, Charles."

"Why not? It might be a few months before I would've asked you anyway, but the end result would be the same." He grinned.

She stared at him in disbelief. "Really?" He took her by the shoulders and caressed her arms with his big, soft hands, a sensation that brought goose bumps to the surface of her skin.

"Really. I came to Nigeria to experience what I felt was lacking in my life. Now I understand it wasn't just my professional life that needed a drastic change. My personal life was suffering too. I just didn't see it until I got away from it all. Until I met you. You'd make a wonderful wife, Adanna."

Stunned, Adanna didn't respond and just blinked at the words coming from a man who hadn't even said he loved her. He sounded as if the idea was merely the next logical step in his life change plan.

"I think you're remarkable. Every day, as I watch you work and take care of ChiChi, I think about how different you are from the women I've dated in the past."

That didn't sit right with her. "Yes, I'm sure they were beautiful and cultured," she said with a snide edge in her tone.

"So are you, Adanna but in a different way," he said softly as though he were deep in thought.

"How am I so different from them other than not being American?" That seemed to hit a nerve, judging by the way his mouth fell open, so he clarified himself. "I mean that in the best way possible. You're confident in who you are, and you don't put on airs to impress people. I like that. It's so attractive."

She smiled. "What were the women you dated like?"

"I'm embarrassed to say that I always seemed to end up with the same type. I'm sure there are women like that in Nigeria, the ones who run after actors or athletes. In Atlanta, there are women whose only goal in life is to marry a doctor. It's almost like a cult. There's even a reality show about it. They strive to look perfect, by wearing designer clothes and spending a fortune on fake hair and fake breasts." He laughed. "It never occurs to them that they could be doctors or nurses themselves. Some of them will take classes but only to bone up on their social graces so they don't make any faux pas at social events. Most of them are too lazy to do any actual work. Oh, they volunteer for charitable causes to impress the man they're trying to snag. All they're looking for is a dude with M.D. after his name to pay for those designer clothes and shoes. Those women aren't really cultured. They're pretending."

His candor surprised her. "That's why you offered to take me shopping. If you don't like that kind of woman, why did you date them?"

Charles snickered. "I guess because I wasn't looking for a serious relationship to begin with. They looked good, smelled good, and would do just about anything I asked. I know that sounds tacky, but I'm being honest."

"I'm not judging you, because I know what you mean. When you're not expecting anything serious, I think we all tend to relax our standards. A few of the men I've dated left something to be desired, but it didn't matter."

"Exactly, but I don't want to talk about them. Let's talk about us. I have to leave to go back to Vegas in two weeks. It would be nice to know that I'll be returning to a woman I know for certain is mine. I promise when I come back, I'll ask you properly."

Adanna had dreamed about being able to announce to the world that she was engaged, but no man had ever come along and taken her heart. Of course, Manny would have made the offer in the blink of an eye, only she'd always known he wasn't the one. Unfortunately, it had taken her two years to make him understand that fact.

"This is so sudden. I wasn't certain we felt the same way about each other, but you don't understand. There is so much more to this. It's tradition, so it must be handled in a certain way."

"Why don't you explain it to me?"

"Traditionally, marriage among Igbos isn't simply a relationship between the future husband and wife but also involves the parents, the extended family, and their villages. Once the man asks the woman to marry him, if her answer is yes, he and his father will pay a visit to her house. His father introduces himself and his son and explains the purpose of his visit." Charles leaned forward and slid his chair closer.

"The bride's father welcomes them, and asks his daughter to come in. He asks her if she knows the man, and her acknowledgment indicates her agreement with the proposal. The bride price negotiation begins with the groom, his father and the village elders returning to her home on another evening. They bring gifts with them, which are presented to the bride's father."

His brow furrowed. "What kind of gifts?"

"Usually wine and agricultural products. After they share a meal, the bride's price is discussed between the fathers. In most cases, there is only a symbolic price to be paid for the bride, but in addition other items like livestock and agricultural products. Usually it takes more than one evening before the final bride's price is settled, offering guests from both sides a lavish feast."

"That sounds barbaric, as though they're haggling over a car or something," His nose wrinkled.

Adanna shrugged. "Another evening is spent in the payment of the bride's price at the bride's home when the groom's family hands over the money and other agreed items. The money and goods are counted, while relatives and friends partake of food and drinks. Once everything is settled, the traditional wedding day is planned." She sat back in her chair and pinned him with her gaze. "See what I mean? This is what's normally done in the villages, but as I said, most city people no longer follow these customs to the letter. What they do to satisfy tradition, though, is have a traditional wedding in the village of the bride's family along with a Christian or what's often called a white wedding."

Even though she wanted to do the happy dance at hearing him claim her as his, the prospect of his leaving was ripping her heart out. She lowered her head and pinched the bridge of her nose. "I don't want you to leave."

"I don't want to leave either, but I have no other choice. That's the way my contract with DWB is set up, and Marc is waiting for me to get back to work. I want to be able to talk to you while I'm there, though. Since you're here, let me show you how to Skype. When you get back to your apartment, you can download the program to your laptop." He checked his watch and picked up his phone. "It's morning in Vegas. Let me see if I can get Marc."

Adanna watched him dial. Would this separation help or hurt their relationship, one that was suddenly moving at light speed? She had always heard the phrase—*absence makes the heart grow fonder*. Now she wondered if there was any truth to it. As unofficial as it was, Charles had just said he wanted to marry her, and she didn't want anything to change his mind. Not distance. Not cultural tradition. Not crazy brothers. Nothing.

Part Three

Chapter Thirteen

"*H*ey, it's me. Are you at the studio already?" Charles said to his twin when he answered the phone.

"What the hell is going over there?" Marc asked, sounding just like their father. "I got this frantic call from Mama last night saying DWB called to report that you were missing and they suspected kidnapping. Where are you, man?"

"Calm down. I just talked to Mama and Daddy. They know I'm okay. Yeah, I was kidnapped, but it's a long, complicated story. I'll be home next week, and I'll give you the details when I get there. Right now I'm trying to teach my friend how to Skype. Can I Skype you in a few minutes?"

Marc uttered a theatrical groan. "You're kidding, right? Did I just hear you say, 'Yeah, I got kidnapped, but I really want to do a computer class right now?'"

Charles laughed. "It's…*important.*"

"Ahh, your friend is a *woman,*" Marc said after he'd hesitated for a few seconds. "I hear it in your voice." Their symbiosis as twins had always given them a unique insight into each other's psyches. Fooling the other twin was a near impossibility.

"You're right," Charles rose and crossed the room so Adanna wouldn't hear.

"What's she like?"

"Smart, beautiful, loving. That's all you need to know. Can you help me out or not?"

"Hold on, will you? Let me turn on my laptop. While it's logging on, you can tell me more about her. What does she do for a living?"

"She's a nurse at the hospital."

"Nigerian?"

"Yeah."

"What's her name?"

"Adanna. Adanna Okoro."

"Pretty name. Is it serious?"

"You could say that."

"Amazing what can happen in just three months, isn't it?"

Charles knew Marc was referring to his own whirlwind courtship with Gianne, whom he'd met at a family celebration and invited her to come to Las Vegas to train with him two days later. The rest was history. He barked out a hearty laugh. "You aren't lying, man."

"Okay, let me sign in to Skype, and we'll be good to go. Is she coming back with you next week?"

"No. That's why I'm showing her how to Skype. Are we set?"

"We're set."

"Give me about ten minutes to teach her the basics. We'll call you back."

"I'll get Lance to take my next client. Talk to you in a few. I can't wait to meet her."

"Promise me you'll behave yourself."

Marc snickered. "Of course."

"My laptop is in the bedroom," Charles said after he ended the call and returned to the balcony. He grabbed a chair from the kitchen and took Adanna's hand. "We can do it in here." The heat that crept up the back of his neck wasn't just from the sultry evening but from the double meaning of his words. "I mean—"

"Don't worry," Adanna smiled up at him," I know what you mean." She grasped his hand and followed him into the bedroom. "This is a nice flat."

"It's okay. At least Randy and I each have our privacy and enough space so we don't feel cramped." He pulled out the chair beneath the small desk. "You can sit here."

Several minutes later, after he sat beside her and explained what she needed to do on her own laptop, he entered Marc's number and waited for him to appear on the screen.

"I guess you have a picture," Marc said in response to the way Adanna covered her mouth with her fingers, apparently amazed at their resemblance. "Yeah, there really are two of us, but I'm the good looking one."

"This is Adanna. Meet my baby brother, Marc and his fiancée, Gianne."

"Hi," Gianne replied with a smile.

"It's nice to meet you both. Charles wanted to be certain I got the hang of this Skype thing before he leaves next week."

"I'm so glad you're okay, Charles. When your mother called, it scared us half to death."

"Thanks. What are you doing at the studio, girl?"

"No school today. I can't miss any workouts with this wedding coming up."

"I finally get him back for another ninety days," Marc said, studying Adanna's face. "Hope you haven't let him get fat and lazy."

"Certainly not. He works too much."

"He gets that workaholic gene from our father," Marc said with a snide laugh.

"He's been a real blessing to our patients, one in particular, a baby who was born with a facial deformity and abandoned by her mother. He operated on her a few days ago."

Charles and Adanna exchanged a glance when Gianne's eyes widened and she asked, "Someone abandoned a baby? Who would do such an awful thing?"

"A very young, unmarried mother who was abandoned by the baby's father. She felt having a deformed baby who is half white would be a double burden. It's a very sad situation."

"What's going to happen to the baby? Who is taking care of her?"

"I am, until one of the children's homes has a spot for her."

At this point, the brothers were no longer part of the conversation.

Gianne gasped. "Children's home? Do you mean an *orphanage*?" She gave the screen an incredulous stare.

"There are tens of thousands of orphans here," Adanna explained. "Their parents either died from AIDS, were casualties of war, or other unfortunate incident. Some reporters have called them the throwaway children of Nigeria."

"My God. I've never heard anything so awful, especially when there are couples that can't conceive for one reason or another." Sadness filled her big, tawny eyes.

Charles' gaze met his twin's for an instant before he looked away. Gianne's thoughts were palpable.

"Do you have your flight info handy?" Marc asked, obviously trying to change the subject. "I need to know what time to pick you up."

"Hold on for a minute." Charles rummaged through the papers on the desk until he found the paper with his travel information. "I'll be landing at McCarran on Saturday afternoon around one-fifteen, but I'll call you once I'm on the ground. Okay, man, I'd better let you get to your clients."

Gianne held up a finger. "Charles, before you go, I want to ask a favor. Could you take a picture of the baby and send it to me?"

He pressed his lips together and exchanged another concerned glance with Marc before he answered. "No problem, if that's what you want, G. I'd planned to do it anyway, since I always like to keep before and after shots for my patient files. She still needs one more surgery, but it has to wait until she's older."

"Thank you. It was great meeting you, Adanna. I hope we can meet in person one day soon."

"Me too. Take good care of Charles for me, and if you don't need him for the whole three months, please send him back." They laughed and said their goodbyes.

The moment Charles signed off, Adanna asked, "Why would Gianne want a picture of ChiChi?"

"She can't have kids. When Marc met her, she was one of my father's patients. He's an oncologist, and he was treating her for endometrial cancer. My brother, Vic, performed a hysterectomy on her."

"And Marc still wanted to marry her," she said thoughtfully. "That says a lot about what kind of man he is."

Charles nodded, his mind already anticipating his future sister-in-law's questions when he arrived. "Do you know anything about Nigeria's rules for foreign adoptions? I guess I'd better be ready for her questions."

"All I know is it has always been discouraged, but I don't know the reasons."

"We might as well check into it while we're online before we go out and get dinner."

What they found on the Internet only offered unfavorable information to take back to Gianne. After an hour had passed, he shut down the computer. "Let's eat. I have to make up for two days."

"The only thing they fed you was fried chicken?"

"With fries and a biscuit," he added with a spiteful laugh.

She rubbed gentle circles on his back. "In that case, you definitely need a good meal. Let's go to OceanBasket."

Charles ordered enough food for two men, and Adanna made sure it included a salad and vegetables. Once they returned to his apartment and settled in at the kitchen counter, he said, "I need to ask you a favor. While I'm gone will you drive my truck? I don't want to leave it here with the guys, because they're gone all day. If it sits in the same spot every day, I might as well put a *please steal me* sign on it. And it's not good for a car to sit too long without being driven."

A shadow of uncertainty crossed her face. "Do you really want to do that? I've never driven a vehicle that large before."

"You have this week to practice. You'll be fine."

She did her first practice drive to the hospital the next morning. Charles spent the first hour explaining to Lou and Joseph what happened during his abduction, then went to examine Chichima before he began his scheduled surgeries. The swelling in the baby's face had already begun to decrease. Her stitches would be dissolving within a day or two, and Adanna said she was eating as though he'd never even put a scalpel to her mouth.

"Miss ChiChi, there is someone I know who wants to see you," he said softly once he'd completed the exam and propped the pudgy infant up between two rolled up blankets in the corner of the crib. "Her name is Gianne, and she's a very sweet lady." The baby knew him now, and she tried her best to smile as he spoke, stitches and all. "I don't know if anything's going to come of this, but it's worth a try."

He took out his phone and snapped several pictures, then put her on her back and covered her with the colorful sheet. When he turned to leave, Adanna was standing in the curtained opening wearing a smile that weakened his knees.

"You are so good with her, Charles. She couldn't have had a better doctor."

"Thank you. The incisions are healing well, and there's no sign of infection. I'm pleased."

"I hope Gianne doesn't get too invested in the idea of adopting her. From what we read last night, the possibility is small."

"When I go back to Vegas, I'll sit down and have a serious talk with her. Even though she looks delicate, Gianne is a strong woman. If this is what she wants, she'll find a way to make it happen. Take a look at these pictures. Which ones should I e-mail to her?"

Adanna studied each shot as he advanced them on his phone. The third and the fifth are the best ones. Explain to Gianne that she has a little post-op edema."

"I will." He concentrated on his phone for several minutes. "There. She should have them in a couple of minutes."

"Why are you doing this?" he asked, still baffled by Adanna's disinterest in adopting ChiChi in spite of her devotion to the baby.

"Doing what?"

"Not trying to adopt her yourself. You obviously love her."

"I love all of the children in her predicament. She just happened to fall right into my lap."

"That still doesn't answer my question."

She pursed her lips in a way that made him want to lean in and kiss them. But they were at work.

"You might not understand this. ChiChi needed my help, but she's not supposed to be mine. I know that. One day I will have my own babies with my own husband. There is no doubt in my mind that she came into my life for another purpose. Now I know what the purpose is."

Charles studied her pensive expression. "You're an amazing woman." He touched a hand to her cheek.

"This amazing woman needs to get ready for surgery, and so do you. Come on, we have a full schedule today."

"Yes, ma'am." His heart pounded at the startling realization that she was right. Adanna Okoro would have the babies she wanted. And he would be their father.

♥

Late that evening, after Adanna had assisted Charles, Nils, and Randy with two surgeries—the removal of a benign facial tumor and a skin graft on a burn victim—she drove the Cruiser back in Lagos to her flat. "It was a good day. I learn so much working with you." She opened the car door to exit the truck.

Before she could get away, he cupped his hand behind her neck. Her skin sizzled when he snuggled his nose into the concave between her neck and shoulder and breathed in deep. "You did a great job in surgery today," he whispered against her skin. "We work well together."

"Yes, we do," she spoke into his hair as she buried her fingertips in it, "and I love working with you." She wondered how well they could really work together. Helpless and unable to control her hungry mouth and her impatient hands, Adanna's heart thumped the reality.

Achọrọ m gị

I need you.

The thought of him being gone for three months seemed inconceivable, and the only picture playing before her closed eyes was one of her nude body pressed against the hard, lean contours of his. She wanted to see him without a stitch of clothing more than she wanted to breathe, but she couldn't voice that desire.

"Adanna, please don't go home tonight." He held onto her hand. "Come to my place and stay with me."

Her eyes stretched wide. "But Randy is there."

"His room is on the other side of the apartment." Charles' lips caressed her neck as he spoke against her skin. "He'll never even know you're there."

She tilted her head to the side, and smiled. "We don't want to do that, Charles."

He grinned back. "We don't?"

"No." Adanna placed a soft kiss on his mouth and opened the car door. "See you in the morning."

"Okay." He groaned, gave his head a woeful shake and waited until she entered the building before he exited the truck and got behind the wheel.

They'd both have to go to their own flats and relieve the

tension the best way they could. But before she could even do that, she needed to call her father. Femi hadn't gotten home yet, so Adanna went into her bedroom, closed the door, and placed the call to her father's mobile number. Her mother didn't need to know what had happened. It would only upset her.

"Ǹdâ, Dad, it's me. Are you busy?"

"I'm never too busy to talk to my daughter. How are you?"

"Not good, I'm afraid. Something happened to my friend…um…the man I'm seeing, and I am very upset."

"You are seeing someone?" Her father's voice rose in surprise.

"Yes. I'm sure Emeka already told you about him." She continued on without giving him a chance to speak. "He's an American doctor working at my hospital, and he was kidnapped a couple of days ago."

"That's unfortunate, but why would that have anything to do with your brother?"

She ran through the details of the events.

"Well, this doctor sounds like a resourceful young man, but nothing you just told me implicates Emeka."

"Come on, Dad. The kidnappers admitted they had taken him because of me, and they didn't even ask for a ransom. Emeka was trying to scare Charles into no longer seeing me, but it didn't work. In fact, all their plot did was make us even more determined."

"Even if Emeka had a part in the scheme, why do you think he would listen to me?"

"Because he knows you condone everything he does concerning me. Please let him know that's not true."

"Adanna, I will *not* accuse your brother of participating in a crime, and neither should you," he snapped. "Emeka wouldn't do anything illegal. He is family, and you should not accuse him unjustly."

"Dad!" she protested. "He didn't do it himself, but I'm convinced some of his friends did. I don't doubt it for a minute. Charles wasn't abducted at random. Why won't you help me?"

"I am all the way in London. What do you want me to do?"

"Tell Emeka to stay out of my private life. I am going to date whoever I see fit, and he can't stop me."

"You sound foolish and rebellious, Adanna."

"No! I sound like a grown woman with a mind of her own. How can you hang on to those old ways when you don't even live here anymore? This is the twenty-first century, Dad. Women are not men's property."

"I understand that very well. This American you are so taken with, is he black?"

She rolled her eyes. "Yes, Dad."

"You say he is a doctor?"

As if he didn't already know. "Yes. He's a successful plastic surgeon."

"How long will he be in Nigeria?"

"Indefinitely. He's doing three-month terms here."

"After which he goes back home to his wife and children, I assume."

She gasped and squeezed her eyes shut. "That's a horrible thing to say! I've video-chatted with some of his family. He wouldn't do that if he was married."

Her father insisted on planting suspicions in her mind. "If

he is so successful, why did he come all the way to Nigeria to work in a small village hospital?"

"Because he's tired of making a lot of money but not getting any satisfaction from his work. He wanted to do surgery that impacts people's lives," Adanna snapped, furious with his prejudicial notions.

"Hmm. Have you introduced him to your brother?" He sounded as though he might be softening.

"I tried, but Emeka's attitude is awful. He came to the hospital and refused to even speak to Charles."

"Is your relationship with this doctor serious, Adanna?"

"It's going in that direction. Charles is leaving this weekend to go back to the US, and I'm thinking about going with him. I can't live in a place where decent people are just snatched off the street and nobody cares. The police won't even do anything about it." Of course, she had no intention of going with Charles. She'd made the statement only to shock him, but as she spoke the idea began to appeal to her.

He rushed to reply, "Don't be hasty, Adanna. You wanted to return home for many years."

"I did, but I was young and didn't understand how difficult it can be living here."

"You *cannot* move to another country with a man you're not married to."

"I can do whatever I want. You refuse to help me with Emeka, so I don't see that I have any other choice."

"What has happened to you, Adanna?"

"I grew up. Good night, Dad. Tell Mum I send my love." Adanna ended the call, and stared at the phone on her night table for a long moment. Never in her life had she spoken to her father that way, but she wanted him to understand how serious she was. The fact that he wouldn't even consider her feelings just because she was female made her heart ache. *Why do my brother's opinions matter more than mine?* She already knew the answer to that question. Because it was tradition, and that tradition stunk like spoiled ofada stew.

On Friday morning, Adanna sat in the airport with Charles waiting for his flight to be announced. Neither of them was in a chatty mood. His departure and their separation seemed to weigh as heavily on him as it did her. She eventually broke the uneasy silence. "I called my father the other night to tell him my suspicions about Emeka."

His eyes narrowed. "You did? What did he say?"

"That he didn't believe Emeka had anything to do with the kidnapping. I suppose that's what I expected him to say, but I was holding out hope his attitude had miraculously changed."

"No luck, huh?" A smile lurked at one corner of his mouth.

"None. He did ask questions about you though."

"What kind of questions?"

"About your job and your marital status."

"My marital status?"

Embarrassed, she lowered her gaze. "He suggested that you're going home to your wife and children."

"What?" He said the word so loudly, a couple of the other travelers sitting near them turned around. "Why would he assume that I'm married?"

"It's a common problem here," she answered, watching the travelers rushing to and from their gates rather than looking him in the eye. "Foreign men come here on holiday or for business and get involved with local women. They go back home often leaving babies behind. That's what happened to ChiChi's mother."

He frowned. "And he's putting me in the same category without even meeting me."

"It's unfair, I know, but he and Emeka believe the only man who will treat me properly is an Ibo man."

He smoothed the neatly-trimmed hair covering his jaw. "Look at me, Adanna." She gazed up into a pair of smiling green eyes. "I'll just have to prove him wrong. While I'm gone, I want you to think about how I can do that." A voice came over the PA system announcing boarding for his flight. Charles stood, drew her up to meet him. "I'm going to miss you so much. Three months didn't sound like a long time when I signed up, but now it seems like forever. I'll call you when I land. Once I get unpacked and settled in Marc's house, we can Skype," he said, studying her face as though he were trying to memorize every detail before he licked his way into her mouth, and cupped his hands under her bottom.

When he lifted her until her feet left the floor, Adanna locked her hands behind his neck and arched against him. "Until you come back to me, I'll see your face every time I close my eyes."

"We *really* need to spend some quality private time together." Desperation took over as they disregarded the passersby, nibbled and sucked until they were breathless, neither of them wanting to break the kiss. Finally, Charles lowered her to the ground and whispered in her ear. "Find us the perfect place, so you can surprise me when I get back." He hoisted his carry-on back over his shoulder and walked toward the gate.

She wasn't sure whether she had lost sight of him because he'd disappeared into the mass of passengers boarding the flight or because of the tears blurring her vision. In her mind, three months seemed like forever. The sadness she felt at the moment was only tempered by the seed he'd just planted in her mind. She would spend the time he was away, finding the ideal spot for them to make love for the first time.

While she made her way out to the parking deck where she'd parked the Cruiser, Adanna considered her daydreams. In them, she had always imagined making love with Charles somewhere outdoors, but to suggest that to him seemed shameless. She located the truck and drove out of the airport, seeing her fantasies more than the road ahead.

Since it was Saturday and ChiChi was still at the hospital, Adanna decided to make a detour to the Protea Hotel in Ikeja. About a year ago, she had attended an outdoor wedding reception there, and she'd imagined a romantic night at the luxurious hotel. The vision had always included a nameless, faceless lover. Now she clearly saw Charles' hard, fair-skinned body stretched out next to hers on one of the cushy poolside chaises. She had no idea how much a night at the idyllic local palace might cost.

She drove to the hotel, parked the truck and entered through the arched portico. Rather than go to the front desk, she walked across the polished wooden floors of the lobby and went directly to the pool area. Just as she remembered it, the long elliptical pool sat beneath a three-story water feature that was illuminated after sunset. Dark wood chaises with overstuffed cushions surrounding the pool begged to host romantic interludes. Yes, this was the perfect place.

It took all of her restraint to keep a straight face when she inquired at the front desk and was told that the cost of a room for one night ran between five and nine hundred American dollars. She might have to rethink this fantasy.

Some twenty-eight hours later, Charles called. "Hi." She closed her eyes at the sound of his voice.

"Hi. You landed safely?"

"Uh huh. I'm waiting for Marc to pick me up. Did you think about what I said?"

"I did. In fact, on the way home, I stopped by a place I've wanted to go for a long time, but we can talk about that later when we have more time." She didn't know how to tell him about the cost without feeling like a gold-digger. Perhaps she could come up with another idea before they discussed it.

"I can't wait to hear about it. Once I get to the house, I'll Skype you."

"Okay. Remember, it's after eleven PM here, and this is my weekend to work."

"We have to learn to navigate this nine-hour time difference. Keep your laptop logged on for the next hour. Love you, baby."

She clicked off the call, smiling to herself. He loved her…

Chapter Fourteen

The plane touched down in Vegas after the interminably long flight. Charles breathed a sigh of relief and took out his phone to let Marc know he was on terra firma as soon as the pilot gave the okay. Next, he dialed Adanna. They only talked for a brief moment, but he'd picked up on a strange note in her voice. After they said goodbye, he rested his head back on the seat and waited for the plane to taxi to the terminal. Had his suggestion that their relationship become more intimate shaken her up? She'd never been squeamish about them being physically close and had nearly melted into him as they said goodbye. Adanna had given him the impression she wanted this as much as he did. But he could've misread her actions. He knew one thing though. The way he craved her scent, her touch, her body, he couldn't go on much longer with just a goodnight kiss at the door.

Charles scrubbed his face and snapped himself back to reality when the pilot announced they were ready to deplane. Now that he was back in Vegas, he'd have to switch gears and go from healer to salesman. From scrubs to a business suit. From possible lover to temporary houseguest. He puffed out his cheeks and released a whoosh of air as he took his carry-on bag from the overhead storage bin. *You were the one who wanted to change your life.*

Marc was waiting for him at the baggage carousel and greeted him with a brotherly hug. "How was your flight, man?"

"Long," Charles groaned, bent backward, and stretched.

"They fed us, but I'm hungry. Do we have time to stop by Capo's? I've been eating too much Nigerian food, and I'd kill for one of their meatball parmigiana sandwiches right now."

"Those meatball sandwiches will kill you first." Marc's hair flipped over the collar of his polo shirt as he shook his head and laughed. "Look up their number and call it in, so they'll have it ready by the time we get there. Do you want to go back to the studio with me or to the house?"

"The house. I told Adanna I'd Skype her, and it's almost midnight there. After that I'm going to get some sleep so maybe I can avoid jet lag."

"Gianne's out running errands. I'll call her and let her know you're there but not to wake you when she gets in."

Charles Googled the restaurant on his phone and called the order in. As soon as he finished, Marc said, "Now, tell me about the kidnapping. How did you get away?"

"It wasn't as difficult as you might think. First of all, it wasn't a normal kidnapping."

"What does that mean?"

He went on to give his twin the whole sordid story. By the time they reached the restaurant, Marc was slack-jawed. "You're saying Adanna's brother set the whole thing up to stop you from being with her?"

"That's the way it looks, but we have no way of proving he arranged it. I'm still imagining Beavis trying to beat Butthead's ass when he discovered he took the money and ran." Charles snorted a laugh.

"I don't know how you can laugh about it, man. You're down three grand and can't even have the dude charged. She must be something special."

He met his brother's gaze. "She is."

Charles devoured his meal while he chatted with Adanna online. "I know it's late there, but I have to ask you something. You sounded strange when you mentioned your idea for our special night. Are you having second thoughts?"

She stared at the screen for a moment, then dropped her gaze. "No second thoughts on my part. I just think the place I chose might be a little extreme."

He grinned at the screen. "Nothing is too extreme as far as I'm concerned. Why don't you tell me about it?"

"The location is beautiful, but the price is outrageous." She described the hotel and the pool and ended by saying, "One night costs between five and nine hundred US dollars."

"That's what's bothering you? This would be a *very* special occasion. Find out if they have a weekend package. We can decide if we want to book it for the weekend I get back."

Adanna's astonished expression brought a smile to his face. "That's a lot of money, Charles. You already lost enough money because of me."

"I don't think of it that way. I consider them investments in our future. Let me know what you find out. Both of us need to get some sleep now. I'll call you tonight before I go to bed. You should be awake by that time. Love you."

"Love you too. Sleep well."

Three hours later, after Charles awoke feeling discombobulated until he remembered where he was.

Vegas. Right.

He had sympathy for people who traveled a lot. How did they ever get themselves centered? It would probably take him several tours to get accustomed to being on this three-month merry-go-round. His first thought was that he wouldn't see Adanna this morning. He glanced at the clock on the night table and then down at his clothes. It wasn't morning. It was five o'clock in the evening.

After he took a fast shower, he wandered into the hall looking for signs of life in the sprawling desert ranch. Soft music drew him down the hall to Gianne and Marc's office. She was sitting at her desk, seemingly absorbed in whatever she was reading. He cleared his throat, and her platinum blond head spun around to face him. Every time he saw her, he thought not many black women could pull off that color without appearing clownish, but it was perfect with her soft honey complexion.

"Charles! You're awake." She bounced up from her chair, met him in the doorway and swung her arms around his neck. "Glad you're back. How was your flight?"

"Extremely long." He gave her a tight squeeze. "Sorry I wasn't up when you came in, but the time difference has me all screwed up."

"Don't worry about that." She pointed to the leather side chair in the corner. "Sit down. I wanted to tell you how much I liked meeting Adanna the other day. She seems like a sweetheart. I also wanted to thank you for the pictures of the baby."

"You're welcome, and you're right about Adanna. She was a little concerned about me sending the pictures, since ChiChi had just had surgery and was still swollen."

"Are you serious? She is absolutely adorable, swelling and all. I have so many questions to ask you about her."

"We really don't know much about her other than her mother appeared at the hospital one day in late-stage labor. She'd never been there for prenatal care, and when Adanna and the resident doctors tried to get more information from her, she only gave the basics."

"How old was her mother."

"She said she was seventeen, but Adanna said she looked more like fifteen."

Gianne squeezed her eyes shut. "Oh, Lord."

"Has she been tested for HIV/AIDS?"

"That's one of the first tests given. They were both clean."

"Good," she said, giving a thoughtful glance at the pool outside.

"I printed out some information from the US State Department about international adoptions, if you want to take a look at it. Gotta warn you, it's not very positive."

"How so?" Her big doe eyes returned to his face.

"Let me get the papers from my carry-on." He went back to the guest room and fished the printout from his bag, hoping the information wasn't devastating to his future sister-in-law. "Some of the language is a bit ambiguous," he said when he returned and handed her the papers. "Basically is says that American adoptions are discouraged."

"But Adanna told me that there are thousands of orphans there. Why would the country keep people from adopting Nigerian children?"

He shrugged and surmised, "Maybe they feel like our culture isn't desirable."

"Worse than having all those children grow up without parents in orphanages?"

"Possibly."

"That's insane. What did you mean by some of the rules are ambiguous?"

He found the spot he'd highlighted in yellow. "It reads, *All Nigerian states that have adoption laws, with the sole exception of Lagos State, require prospective adoptive parent(s) to be a Nigerian citizen. As a result, adoptions by non-Nigerians may not be acceptable for purposes of US immigration.*" I could be wrong, but I take that to mean that an American can apply for Nigerian citizenship in order to qualify. It also says, *the law is sometimes inconsistently applied.*" To me, that's saying there have been exceptions, and it does say *with the exception of Lagos State*, which is where the hospital is located. If you're seriously thinking about looking into this, you need to have an attorney explain the rules. What does Marc think?"

She bit her bottom lip. "We haven't really talked about it."

"Why not?"

"He knows I'm interested in finding out more about it, but that's all."

"G, if you want to jump into this, you should sit down with my brother and tell him just how serious you are."

"I will. Do you feel like going out for dinner?"

He rubbed his stomach. "I stopped by Capo's on the way here and got a sandwich and salad, but I could eat again. Marc's going to make me burn it off anyway."

"You can count on that," Gianne said with a giggle.

His gaze ran from her head to her feet. "By the way, you're looking real good, girl."

"Thanks. I had my six-month checkup, and I'm still cancer free. For the past couple of months I've been faithful with my workouts. It's October already, and the wedding is in June. I need that gown to fit perfectly."

"Don't lose too much, because I know for a fact that my brother is very satisfied with your curves."

Gianne grinned. "He should be home in a little while. I just talked to him a few minutes ago, and he said he was finishing up with his last client for the day. I assume you two already talked in the car, but you have to tell me about the kidnapping."

Charles made himself comfortable in the chair behind Marc's desk. "I'll probably be telling this story until I'm eighty. I can hear it now, 'Grandpa, tell us about the time you got kidnapped in Africa." They both chuckled, and he launched into the tale once again. Gianne listened intently as he rehashed the whole preposterous event.

"So you think her brother was behind it?" She asked when he finished.

"It's the only explanation that makes any sense. It doesn't make much difference anyway, because the police there tend to look the other way when it comes to kidnapping. Since I paid them, they consider the issue moot."

"That's ridiculous."

Marc appeared in the office door. "What's ridiculous?"

"Hi, honey. That he can't legally do anything about the kidnapping," Gianne answered.

"Yeah," Marc leaned down and dropped a kiss on her lips. "It sounds like the wild, wild west down there."

"I told Charles I think we should go out for dinner, unless you feel like fixing something."

"That's fine. Let me jump in the shower and change into some real clothes." Marc still wore his work uniform, a form-fitting Canyon Gate Personal Training t-shirt, and a pair of running shorts.

"So, tell me about Adanna," Gianne said, while they waited for Marc.

Charles felt an involuntary smile spread across his face. "What do you want to know?"

"Oh, my God, look at that smile."

"She's the epitome of what a real nurse is. I think she just might be the most compassionate person I've ever met since I became a doctor. The hospital is lacking in most of the equipment and supplies we take for granted here, but it doesn't seem to bother her. Adanna and the rest of the staff make do with what they have. It's rare that she complains about the circumstances, and her average day is ten hours long. Other than a surgical nurse, her knowledge of surgical procedures goes way beyond the average nurse's. She's assisted in most of my surgeries, and she's efficient and quick."

"How did she come to care for Chichima?"

"When ChiChi's mother ran off, the normal procedure would've been to have her transferred to one of the children's homes. At the time there were no vacancies at the homes closest to Lagos, so she had to remain at the hospital. Adanna volunteered to look after her and even got permission from her bosses to take her home at night so the night nurse wouldn't be overburdened."

"She sounds very special."

"That's an understatement, girl. Besides that, she's so damn fine she could give Lupita a run for her money," Charles said, referring to the Kenyan actress who was taking Hollywood by storm.

"Lupita was the first person I thought of when I saw Adanna on the screen; only, Adanna is blessed with more curves. You and your brother do love that, don't you?"

Charles grinned. "Most brothers do."

Following a leisurely dinner at Marc and Gianne's favorite vegan restaurant, they returned home. Gianne retired to the bedroom, while the men went outside to the patio where Marc lit the fire pit to ward off the slight chill in the fifty-degree air.

"From what you've said, you seem to be enjoying your first term in Nigeria. Is that just because of Adanna, or do you like doing the work?"

"Both. The surgeries have been challenging, especially since I've specialized in cosmetic vanity surgery for the past few years. I removed a benign tumor from a man's neck that was the size of a baseball. And the other day I performed a skin graft on a patient with severe burns to the face. I've never experienced the kind of gratitude that I've seen from these patients. It's amazing."

"Do you like living there—I mean the atmosphere and the social scene?"

"It's different, and I haven't done much besides go to restaurants and do some sightseeing. Adanna's promised to take me to the beach one of these days. It's hard for her to get away alone, since she has the baby."

Marc's expression sobered. "I need to ask you something. If Adanna is so taken with the baby, why doesn't she adopt her?"

"I asked her that very question the other day. She said she believes ChiChi came into her life for a reason, but she hadn't known what that reason was until she talked to Gianne. Adanna wants to have her own babies."

His twin leaned back in his seat, folded his arms and studied Charles' face in the light of the flickering flames. "And you're ready to help her with that." Charles' silent smile answered him. "Wow. I don't believe it. Mama said we've always done everything at the same time. When are you going to propose?"

"When the time is right. We're not at that point yet, but we have talked about it."

"You haven't slept with her yet?"

"No, and I don't want to pressure her."

Marc gave him a knowing look. "If you're willing to wait on getting physical, you really *do* love her. I'm happy for you, man. Last year this time nobody could've convinced me that we'd be ready to settle down."

"I just hope we can do as well as Mama and Daddy have." Charles stroked the hair on his chin. "It'll be forty-three years for them this summer."

Marc snickered. "Mama had to be a strong woman to deal with him all those years."

"Yeah, but Daddy is different with her than he is with us. When she speaks, he listens. And she doesn't bark often, but when she barks, he backs right down."

"That's because he already knows she's right."

"True…true. I guess that's the secret. Picking a woman you respect who you can trust to always tell you the truth no matter what."

Charles shook his head. "I'm not so sure about Vic and Mona or Jess and Cydney though. Mona runs the show, and Vic seems okay with that. Cyd is so tame she just goes along with whatever Jesse says."

"Mona had Vic whipped from day one." Marc got up and added a log to the fire. "The minute he saw her, he was done. She could've put a leash around his neck, and he would've smiled while she was doing it."

"She *is* beautiful, man."

"Yeah, and she knows it. I think Cyd is just happy to be married to a man who can provide for her. Considering her background, you can't blame her. She came from nothing and had a rough life, so being pregnant every other year and staying home taking care of the kids probably seems like heaven to her."

"I can't imagine Adanna being a housewife. She's too committed to her work."

"Gianne loves what she does, but she'd trade it all in for a family. She desperately wants a baby. Now that she found out about ChiChi, I need to investigate all there is to know about Nigerian adoptions. This is the first time she's shown any interest in adoption. Until now, every time I brought it up, she said the wedding plans were enough to deal with, but deep down inside I know it hurts that she can't have her own babies. She wanted the whole experience–feeling the first kick, the big belly, and even the delivery and nursing part."

Charles studied the lines on his twin's forehead. "Maybe you need to pursue the issue on your own and talk to someone at the Nigerian consulate in Atlanta just to find out what your options are."

Marc massaged his temples. "I've thought about it, but if she found out I'd gone without her, my life would be in danger."

Charles chuckled. "Aww, come on. Gianne is one of the sweetest women I know. You make it sound like she has a split personality."

"There's more truth to that old saying about not making a black woman angry than you can imagine." He pursed his lips and glanced up at the darkening sky once again. "I guess it wouldn't do any harm to find out what the whole process entails. There's really no way she could know about it unless I told her. On another note, I've been working on those articles, if you want to take a look at them."

"That's great," Charles said, surprised that Marc had forged ahead with the project without his prompting. "How many did you write?"

"Six so far. That was a great idea, man. I've never been much of a writer, but once I sat down and got started, ideas began to flow. Gianne edited them for me, since she's the English expert in this house, so they should be in pretty good shape."

"I think I'm just going to take it easy tomorrow, so maybe I'll spend the day reading them and get back to my workouts on Monday morning." Charles checked his watch. "Right now I need to Skype Adanna. It's eight a.m. on Sunday there."

♥

Adanna waited anxiously for Charles' calls. She had also set up call forwarding to automatically forward his calls to her mobile just in case she wasn't able to get to her laptop. This morning she got up and turned on the computer before she went into the bathroom. After she washed her face and combed her hair, she applied some lipstick in an effort to appear as though she hadn't just rolled out of bed.

At promptly eight o'clock, a call alert window appeared on the screen. She clicked on the Answer With Video button and smiled directly into the camera. "Good morning. Well, I guess it's still Saturday night there. Did you get any sleep?"

"A couple of hours. I'm getting ready to crash for the night. Maybe by tomorrow I'll be back to normal. "What are you up to today?"

"Nothing much. Since ChiChi isn't here, I think I'll just clean up my bedroom and relax a bit." She didn't want to tell him her actual plan for the day.

"How was she yesterday? No fever?"

"No fever, and she's doing well. Randy is keeping a close eye on her. The good news is I think I've found a woman in the village to watch her during the day. She had a clean, safe house, and I could just drop her off down the road on my way to work."

"Do you know anything about this woman?"

"I've asked around, and she seems to be well-liked. Her husband died recently, and she is in dire need of a way to make some money."

"If you think she's a good choice, find out what she's going to charge, so we can let Marc and Gianne know."

"Okay. I'll go by to see her tomorrow on my lunch hour.

"How's Mr. Mohammed doing?" he inquired about the burn victim on whom he'd performed a skin graft.

"He was experiencing some discomfort, so Nils increased his pain meds."

"Good." Charles rubbed the back of his neck. "I'm more tired than I thought, so I'm going to sign off now. Have a good day, baby."

She forced a smile. "I will. Talk to you tomorrow." Adanna logged off, and closed her laptop. Today she also planned to drop in on Emeka unannounced and find out for sure whether or not he was lying to her about his participation in the kidnapping.

After a long shower, she moisturized her skin with her favorite body butter, threw on a pair of slacks and a top, and went into the kitchen to make a cup of tea. The sound of running water in the other bathroom let her know that Femi was up and getting ready for church. Often she had considered attending the big, non-denominational church with her, but echoes of her father's voice always stopped her. He was a deacon in the extremely traditional Church of England. Even as a child Adanna had never enjoyed the staid, outdated services of a church where the Queen was considered the Supreme Governor and the church and State were linked. Most of the people attending were older. She couldn't remember seeing many fifteen to thirty year olds in their parish. The one time she had visited Femi's church at the enormous gold and burgundy sanctuary on Ayodele Okeowo Street, the joyful singing, clapping and dancing seemed a little extreme and the size of the congregation was overwhelming. But all in all she'd enjoyed it. She had all intentions of going back until she'd mentioned the visit to her father who called it a cult and warned her to never set foot in the building again.

"I'm going to see Emeka. Are you cooking today? Do you need money for groceries?" she asked when Femi exited her bathroom.

"No, we're good. I'll see you this afternoon. Hope it goes well. Don't hurt him."

For a moment, Adanna considered driving her car, but changed her mind. If her brother was ever going to come to terms with her relationship with Charles, he needed to know just how serious it was. Several minutes later, she parked the Cruiser outside Emeka's flat. After she dragged in a long fortifying breath, she headed up the steps to the front door.

His eyes widened at the sight of his sister standing on the doorstep so early on a weekend morning. "What are you doing here? It's not even ten o'clock yet."

She pushed past him, and strode into the living room. "I need to ask you a question," she said as she plopped down into his prize leather recliner. "And I want you to sit down, look into my face, and answer it."

Emeka turned his back to her. "What are you talking about?"

"Sit down, Emeka. Unless you're ashamed to face me."

"Why should I be ashamed of anything, Adanna?" He eased down into the chair facing her.

"That's what I'm here to find out. Look. At. Me."

He cocked his head and rolled his eyes as though he thought she had a screw loose.

"Look me in the face and tell me you didn't have anything to do with Charles being kidnapped."

He dropped his gaze and stammered, "H-how can you ask

me that? I am your brother!"

"Why can't you look at me?"

"What's wrong with you? You already asked me about this, and I answered you."

"On the phone, where I couldn't see your eyes. Tell me again, Emeka." This time she reached out and held both of his hands in hers and waited for an answer.

His gaze darted to hers for a fleeting moment, then dropped to the sisal rug. "He is not the man for you, Adanna. Why isn't a man from among your own people good enough for you?"

Heartbroken, she released his hands as though touching them had burned her. "It has nothing to do with Ibo men not being good enough. I just haven't met anyone who's spoken to my heart the way Charles has. He's a generous, successful, smart man, and he loves me. You see he negotiated his release with your friend. You could learn a lot from him."

"He did nothing other than throw his money around the way Americans always do. Wake up, Adanna!"

She hung her head. Now she knew for sure that he set up the kidnapping. "Why won't you let me be happy? Your prejudice against all foreigners is going to do nothing but hurt you, Emeka."

"And so is your association with them."

She stood and looked down at him. "This makes me so sad. I had always hoped you would be friends with the man I married."

His head jerked up, and he wore a stricken expression. "You're going to marry him?"

"When he asks me. Yes, I am. I have to leave now."

He grabbed her hand. "You're making a mistake, Adanna."

"No, I'm not, and I told Dad that I intend to do as I please. You two will no longer control my life." Adanna yanked her hand from his grasp and walked out with him on her heels. As she put the key in the driver's side door, he yelled, "Did he buy that for you? Are you living as a kept woman now, Adanna?"

She glared at him, got behind the wheel, and then drove away, blinking back tears. Why couldn't her family be happy for her? As yet she hadn't heard her mother's opinion, but more than likely she would side with her father. Her mother was an old-school Ibo wife, and she usually bowed to his decisions and opinions. She considered disagreeing with him to be disrespectful.

Nigeria had come a long way in some respects, but in other ways old traditions and expectations still lingered. It was definitely a land of contrasts and extremes – modern versus antiquated, over-the-top wealth versus mind-boggling poverty, westernized culture versus indigenous traditions. Would she experience this kind of treatment from others if she and Charles did marry? Adanna shook her head. She would cross that bridge when she reached it. If she reached it. After all, Charles had only mentioned marriage in general terms. He hadn't proposed.

Femi wasn't home from church when Adanna arrived at her flat, so she launched into a deep cleaning of her bedroom. She liked to keep the room as clean as possible for ChiChi's sake, but today she had to do something to work off her frustration. She hated confronting Emeka, but he'd left her no other choice. After she fished her iPod from her purse, she selected the latest album from D'banj. His blockbuster hit, *Top of the World* got her dancing and singing at the top of her lungs while she cleared her dresser, the baby's dressing table and the few items sitting on the window sills. Once she finished dusting, she stripped the linens from their beds and tossed them into the washer. By the time she put clean sheets on the beds and vacuumed the floor, Femi stood in the bedroom door shouting to get her attention over the music.

"Do you want to talk about it?"

Adanna turned down the volume. "I didn't hear you come in." She frowned. "Do I want to talk about what?"

"Whatever it is that has you cleaning like a tornado." Femi folded her arms, leaned against the doorframe and waited for an answer.

"I can't fool you." She put down the spray cleaner and sat on the end of her bed. Femi joined her. "I went to visit Emeka this morning to see if he could look me in the face and swear he didn't have anything to do with Charles' kidnapping."

"He couldn't," Femi surmised.

Adanna shook her head. "For years, I've imagined one day bringing that special man home to meet my family. In my mind they always welcomed him with open arms. Guess that was only wishful thinking."

"I'm sorry, girl. Think about it this way. If Emeka and your father refuse to acknowledge Charles, you won't have to endure all of the tradition."

"This will probably sound crazy, but I wanted to do all of it – he and his father bringing gifts to my father and negotiating for me."

"You could still have both wedding ceremonies, though, if that's what you want."

"Not without the blessing of my family. All of this anxiety is probably premature to begin with. Charles hasn't proposed. I don't have a ring. He could decide tomorrow that he's never coming back to Nigeria."

Femi grabbed her shoulders. "Now you're talking crazy. He wouldn't have bothered to introduce you to his brother if he wasn't planning to stick around. If he was just using you to occupy his time while he's here in Nigeria, why would he arrange video chats with you while he's gone? Don't let your frustration with your family spill over onto him."

"You're right." Adanna managed a weak smile. "I guess I'm just discouraged."

"Yes, you are, but you are in a relationship with the kind of man you've always wanted. Enjoy it, and just see where it leads."

"I'll try harder to look at the bright side."

Adanna's positive declaration ended up being short-lived. The very next morning, while performing her rounds, her phone rang.

"Miss Okoro?"

"Speaking."

"My name is Miss Balogun, the Intake Coordinator at the SOS Children's Village."

"Hello, Ms. Balogun."

"I have your name as the contact from Stella Obasanjo Hospital for an abandoned infant named Chichima."

"Uh…Y…yes," Adanna stuttered and took the phone outside, fearing what she was about to hear.

"I have good news. We have an opening for the baby. Would you be able to bring her this week?"

Panicked, Adanna responded, "Well…um…she just had surgery, and…she isn't in any condition to be moved right now," she said, giving the woman a half-truth.

"Surgery? Does she have physical problems?"

"Nothing serious. Adanna replied, stunned by the call.

"She was born with a cleft lip and palate. The first surgery was performed recently."

"I see. Do you have any idea when she will be able to travel, Ms. Okoro?"

"That's up to her doctor, and he isn't in the country at the moment. When do you need an answer?"

"As soon as possible. This spot only became available as the result of an unfortunate incident. If Chichima doesn't fill it, I have no idea when another might become available."

"An unfortunate incident?"

"Yes. One of our infants passed away."

"Oh, that's terrible. I'm so sorry to hear that. Please, Ms. Balogun, I need time to contact her doctor. Can you wait for at least twenty-four hours?"

"That shouldn't be a problem. I'll wait to hear from you."

Adanna stuffed the phone in her pocket and held her head in her hands. *You knew this was going to happen. You should've been prepared.* Immediately, she looked at her watch and calculated the time in Las Vegas. It was the middle of the night, but this was an emergency. She dialed Charles' mobile number.

"Adanna?" he answered in a sleep-roughened voice. "What's wrong?"

"I'm so sorry for waking you, but it's important. The SOS Children's Home just called. They have a spot for ChiChi, and she has to be registered this week."

He cleared his throat. "Baby, isn't this what you wanted?"

"At the beginning, yes, but now I think it would be a mistake sending her there. If Marc and Gianne really are interested in adopting her, I need to reconsider."

"So what would you do?"

"Keep her with me and take her to the babysitter while I'm at work during the week."

"But you're not her legal guardian. If they wanted to adopt her, wouldn't they have to deal with the state?"

She was silent for a moment. "Not if I adopt her first."

"Adanna," he said, suddenly sounding wide awake. "You're willing to do that?"

"Think about it, Charles. If I adopt her, she won't have to go into the orphanage, and I might be able to make private arrangements with your brother and Gianne."

"I think you're giving Gianne's interest too much weight. They haven't made a decision, and we don't know what the laws are regarding private adoptions."

"We need to talk to them as soon as possible. Can we do a video chat tonight your time?"

"Wow, I guess so. I don't want to wake them now. When they get up for work, I'll run it by them, okay?"

"Okay. Thank you, Charles."

"You never cease to amaze me, woman. I love you."

"I love you too. Call me back after you talk with them."

Adanna reentered the building and went straight to Chichima's crib. The baby stayed awake most of the time now that she was getting older. She looked up at Adanna and smiled.

"My precious girl, things are happening for you. I hope I can work this out." She lifted the baby and kissed her forehead, still being careful of her face. After she gave her a bottle, Adanna continued her rounds, all the while going over in her mind how this whole situation might possibly turn out. Charles called back and said he, Marc, and Gianne would call at ten o'clock Las Vegas time.

At lunchtime, she drove up the road into the village and talked with the prospective babysitter again. The woman had been recommended by a couple of other women in the village. She was middle aged and lived alone. That evening, after she checked on the baby for the last time, she left work eager to get home and Skype with them. She ate dinner with Femi and watched a little TV before she logged onto her laptop and got a few hours of sleep. Her alarm clock was set to go off a few minutes before seven a.m. her time. By the time the call alert popped up on her screen, she had made herself presentable and was sitting at her desk in the bedroom.

"Good morning," Charles said. "Marc and Gianne are here. I explained what's happening with ChiChi."

"Hi, Marc. Hi, Gianne," she said when they appeared on the screen. I guess you're getting ready for bed, but I really needed to speak to you directly. I am not trying to pressure you, believe me. I don't feel comfortable about sending ChiChi to the children's home now. This is a difficult situation, and I just need to know if you've given it serious consideration."

Gianne leaned in. "If you adopt her yourself, won't it be hard for you to give her up?"

"From the beginning, I never felt that ChiChi was supposed to be mine, Gianne, but I strongly believed I was meant to be in her life for a reason. Until we met, I wasn't sure what that reason was. You two aren't even married yet though."

"We talked about this earlier," Marc interjected. "There's a lot of research that needs to be done as far as the adoption goes, but if you're willing to keep her until we can contact the Nigerian embassy here and get the details worked out, we're willing to pay your legal fees and ChiChi's care. Charles said when she's released from the hospital you'll need to hire someone to look after her while you're at work."

Adanna stared at the couple, stunned by their offer. "You're saying you want to pursue this?"

"We sure do!" Gianne said with a wide smile. "I believe everything happens for a reason. Your meeting Charles and his working at your hospital wasn't an accident, but we need time to do the research and get these wedding plans done."

"When is the big day?"

"The first Saturday in June. It's almost November, and after the first of the year, time is going to fly."

"My main concern," Marc added, "is how attached ChiChi will be to you. It might be too disruptive for her to wait that long."

Adanna studied the lines of concern between his brows. "I thought about that too, but going to a children's home where she'll no longer get one-on-one attention would be even worse."

"She's right," Gianne agreed. "If you're willing to do this, Marc and I will do everything we can on our end."

"Today I met with a woman in the village who is willing to care for her during the day. She is a recent widow and mother of five grown children, and she needs the money. Her house is in good shape, and she appears to be very clean. Since ChiChi isn't even walking yet, I don't think there will be any problem."

Charles' concerned gaze went from his brother to Gianne and back to the screen. "Sounds like we're all agreed. I'll help Adanna while you two find out exactly what has to happen to make the adoption a reality. We need to keep this just between the four of us for the time being." He smiled at her. "I miss you already. You'd better get to the hospital. It's getting late there."

"We'll talk soon." Adanna shut down her laptop, dropped it into the bag she carried to work, and gave a contented sigh, certain they had all made the right decision. Now she had to call the children's home.

Chapter Fifteen

Charles did his best to hide his feelings when Adanna told him about her confrontation with Emeka during one of their Skype calls. After all, even though he was a bigot and a borderline criminal, he was still her flesh and blood. He knew how the lines were drawn when it came down to matters of flesh and blood, and he wasn't surprised that Emeka hadn't given her an outright denial. He believed he was justified in what he'd done, and nothing was going to change that.

Neither was he surprised when Adanna told him she had officially removed ChiChi from the waiting lists of all three children's homes. The situation with her had blossomed into something bigger than either of them imagined. Charles had to agree that she had come into their lives for a higher purpose than a common Third World surgery.

Charles and Marc sat together one night in the home office planning for his first visit with the manager of the local Whole Foods store. His twin was usually relaxed, thanks to a stimulant-free diet, constant exercise, and a happy sex life, but tonight Marc appeared to be on edge. He kept staring out the window at the mountains in the distance and combing his neatly-trimmed beard with his fingers.

"What's up, man? You're a little edgy tonight."

"I'm worried about Gianne. Today she found out that her cousin, Tanya, the one she stayed with when she first moved here, is pregnant. I could tell the news really upset her even though she denied it. She refuses to talk about it, and she's been really quiet. I know she's happy for Tonya, but I could tell she was hurt at the same time."

"Now that Adanna's called off the children's home placement for ChiChi, if all goes well, she can get her adoption plans in the works. There's a good chance Gianne will be a mother by the time you two tie the knot."

Marc straightened in his desk chair. "That would be the best wedding present anyone could give us."

"Are you really sure you want to start out your marriage with a kid? That kind of kills the honeymoon phase."

Marc grinned. "We've been on our honeymoon since she moved in. Okay, let's talk about tomorrow. Are you ready?"

"Yeah, I am. If I rehearse my speech any more, I'll be quoting it in my sleep."

Marc leaned back so his chair touched the wall, folded his arms and grinned. "I guess you have it sewed up. Go get 'em, man."

When it was time for his appointment with the workforce management director of one of the largest casinos in the city, he couldn't tamp down his nervousness. He wouldn't have admitted it to anyone, but even after all of the medical seminars he'd given, his stomach was in knots. Now he was a salesman, and he wasn't sure he could be a convincing one. Doing the hard sell was foreign to him. As a physician, he didn't have to sell his services. Patients came to him, often too many for him to handle and he had to refer them to his colleagues.

The director listened intently during his presentation offering them an opportunity to use Canyon Gate Personal Training as part of their employee wellness program. All I need to do is sell them on the fact that as a medical professional I highly recommend incorporating physical fitness in their employee benefits package. Doing so won't just help the company by reducing the number of sick days used and improving the appearance and stamina of those employees who perform on stage, but it also makes the company eligible for government incentives. When it was all over, he was able to answer all of the director's questions. He shook hands with the man and left, hoping his performance had been polished enough to seal the deal and thankful he didn't have to do this for a living.

In the weeks that followed, he did his daily workout with Marc and Lance, edited the articles Marc had written to submit to local magazines, and continued to fine-tune his corporate presentation. He even did a few dry runs for Marc and Lance, so they could throw questions at him the way a prospective client might. When he met with the manager of the local Whole Foods Market, he secured dates over the coming three months for Marc to give raw food prep demonstrations at the stores.

That evening, after he recounted the visit for Marc, Charles brought up another subject that had been on his mind for some time. "Are you and Gianne going home for Christmas?" he asked, meaning their home in Atlanta.

"Probably. You'll be here, won't you?"

"Yeah. In fact, I'm scheduled to go back to Lagos the first week in January, but I was thinking about flying Adanna and ChiChi in for the week. That way everybody could meet her, and you and Gianne could meet the baby."

Marc's face lit up. "That would be fantastic. Would you fly them here or into Atlanta?"

"Atlanta, if Mama says they can stay at the house."

"She wouldn't refuse. Sounds like a great idea."

"I haven't mentioned this to Adanna yet, so let me make sure she can get away for the week before we make any plans."

Once ChiChi had been discharged from the hospital, Adanna called. "I have a surprise for you, Doctor."

"Is that so? Let me have it."

She held ChiChi up to the screen so they could see each other. When the baby recognized him, she burst into an effervescent giggle that put a lump in his throat.

"Hello, Princess? How are you?"

"Say hello to Doctor Charles."

ChiChi waved her little arms about and smiled at his image. He could see how well she had healed, and that knowledge did more for his ego than winning an NEPS grant. "She looks wonderful, and so do you," he said, admiring Adanna's thin-strapped top that showed off her nipples and more than he'd ever seen of her velvety dark skin.

"And I have a surprise for *you*. Do you think you'll be able to take off Christmas week?"

"Perhaps not the entire week. I don't know. Why?"

"Because my family always gets together at my parents' house in Atlanta. I'd love for you and ChiChi to join us. It's about time everyone met you, and Marc and Gianne met ChiChi."

"Really?" she whispered as though she didn't believe what she was hearing. "That's an expensive flight."

"I can use my frequent flyer miles. What do you say?"

She hesitated. "I would need to talk to the doctors before I give you an answer, but yes, I'd love to! "Wait…I can't take the baby out of the country without the proper paperwork."

"You could if her doctors insisted the surgery needed to be performed at a specific stage, and she needs to see a specialist in the US."

"Dr. Pategi and Dr. Ijalana probably know more about that than I do."

"Okay. I'll call them and take care of that right away"

He knew her well enough now to know when she was truly happy. The apples of her cheeks rose and drew her tempting lips into a smile that exposed even, white teeth. "See how many days they'll let you take, and be sure to tell them you're coming to meet my family." He knew how strongly Nigerians felt about family and hoped it might influence their decision. "I also need to find out what we need to take ChiChi out of the country."

Charles made a call to the Nigerian embassy in Atlanta. He stated ChiChi's physical condition as the reason the trip. The man he spoke to made it clear that official medical evidence had to be presented, along with the baby's birth certificate, a signed letter of authorization from her caregiver with a signature that matched the one on the caregiver's passport.

Lou and Joseph gladly agreed to write a letter that included a detailed explanation of ChiChi's medical condition stating she was visiting the US for a consultation with him. They were convinced it would be sufficient.

During their next video chat, Adanna's beaming face appeared on the screen. "I got an answer today about Christmas."

"Judging by the way you're smiling, it must be good news."

"Yes. I haven't had a real vacation in all the time I've been working at the hospital. Dr. Ijalana and Dr. Pategi want me to take the whole week!"

"Fantastic. Now all we need to do is wait for the approval from the State on ChiChi's travel. I'll see if I can get you a flight out of Lagos on the twenty-third your time, because you have to be here for Christmas Eve. We have a fun tradition that I want you to be part of."

"I suppose you're not going to give me any hints?"

"Nope, but you'll enjoy it. I promise. You need to know a couple of things before you start packing. Atlanta weather is milder than a lot of the country, but it'll still seem cold to you. The temperature might be balmy or it might be freezing, so you'd better pack a little bit of everything."

"I'll pack like I'm going to London, but I need to shop for ChiChi. She doesn't have any cold weather clothes."

"Yeah, about that. Marc and Gianne said they'll take care of her clothes and send them to you in a few days."

"Oh, Charles. They seem to be getting so invested in this idea of adopting her. I hope we're not making a mistake in letting them meet her. What if the adoption isn't approved?"

"Why wouldn't it be? You helped deliver her. You've cared for her since day one, and you're a resident Nigerian. Think positive, baby. It's all going to work out."

"I hope you're right. Gianne will be devastated if it doesn't."

As soon as they finished talking, he called his mother. "Hey, Mama. It's Charles." The brothers always identified themselves over the phone, because they'd been told they all sounded alike. "I'm calling to talk to you about Christmas."

"It's not even Thanksgiving yet. Are you having turkey with us?"

"Sorry, I can't. I guess I'll be eating soy turkey stuffed with wheatgrass or something else disgusting with Marc and Gianne." They both laughed loud and long. "But I will be home for Christmas, and I was calling to ask if it's okay if I bring a friend. Well, two friends, actually."

"You never have to ask that, Charles. Who are they?"

He exhaled slowly. "I haven't told you about her, because

I wanted to see where our relationship was going before I introduced her to the family."

"It's going well, I assume." He smiled at the expectant note in her voice.

"Very well. She's a nurse at the hospital and she has a six-month-old baby girl."

She cleared her throat. "Is there something you forgot to tell us?"

"Come on, Mama. I haven't been there for six months yet. The baby's not hers, but she's taken it upon herself to look after her. She was abandoned at the hospital where we work. Will she be able to use one of the guest rooms for the week?"

"How sad. Of course they can stay. It's been so long since we had a baby in the house," she said in a breathless, excited tone. "I need to get her a crib and a high chair and—"

"Mama! Mama, listen! Don't go to any expense. Maybe Cyd has stuff we can borrow for the week."

"That's a great idea. I'll call her later."

"Please don't tell everyone that I'm bringing *Ms. Right* home. That'll be too much pressure on her. Okay?"

"I won't, Charles. What's her name?"

"Her name is Adanna and the baby's name is Chichima. We call her ChiChi."

"Well, I can't wait to meet them."

"Will you prepare Daddy for me, so I won't have to answer a hundred questions when I get there?"

"I'll take care of it. He'll be on his best behavior. When will you all be coming in?"

"I'll be there on the twenty-second. I'm trying to get her a flight into Atlanta on the twenty-third." He paused for a moment. "Thanks, Mama. I knew I could count on you. When I get definite flights, I'll call and let you know. Love you."

Lillian Stafford was the glue that held the family together. She had always seen to it that holidays were filled with food, music, gifts, and special surprises. After she had ended her teaching career and devoted her life to raising a small army of boys, she'd turned her attention to making their home a place where her sons' friends could hang out. Once they were in their middle school years and his father was forging ahead in his medical career, she began entertaining his colleagues and their wives. To hear his father tell it, by the time she reached her forties, her reputation for throwing parties and organizing volunteer events was legendary. These days she rarely entertained his father's colleagues, but got her joy from organizing charity events, giving birthday parties for the grandkids, and making the major holidays eventful.

Adanna's family relationships were so strained; a fun-filled holiday might be just what she needed. Granted, it would likely be different from a Nigerian Christmas, which he knew nothing about. Charles rested his head back on the chair and smiled. It looked as though his plan was coming together. Now he could concentrate on his upcoming sales calls and look for the perfect Christmas gift for Adanna.

When he lived in Atlanta, there was never a question about where he would spend Thanksgiving. Usually he slept late, and got up in just enough time to shower and dress before he drove across town to his parents' house. The aromas of turkey, glazed ham, roast beef and other carnivore delights greeted him at the door, and he'd spend the entire day eating and drinking with the family. Neither Marc nor Gianne possessed his mother's cooking skill, and even if they had, they would only use it to bring an artichoke or a head of cauliflower to room temperature. Perhaps this year he'd sleep extra late, run out to get a pizza and watch the games.

Weeks later, Charles woke to familiar smells coming from the kitchen. At first he thought he was still in a semi-dream state, until he realized he needed to take a leak. On the way out of the bathroom, he followed the sound of Gianne singing in the kitchen.

"Good afternoon, sleepyhead."

"Hey, what are you up to?" he asked, eyeing the familiar Thanksgiving meal ingredients spread over the counter but knowing she and his brother only ate raw.

"Fixing Thanksgiving dinner for Marc and me. Don't worry. I have a surprise for you." She gave him a wink. "Look in the fridge. The brown bag is yours."

He did as she asked and found a small shopping bag with M&M Soul Food, W. Charleston Boulevard, written on it filled to the top with white-topped aluminum containers. The contents of each were written in black marker–turkey and cornbread dressing, candied yams, macaroni and cheese, collard greens, rolls, banana pudding, peach cobbler, and a gallon of Muddy Waters.

"Are you kidding? You bought all of this for me?"

"Marc and I didn't want you to suffer." She laughed. "We know our diet is a little much for most people, and he said you're used to having your mother's cooking for Thanksgiving. I don't know how this will compare, but M&M won the award for best soul food in Vegas for the past ten years."

He walked over to her and lifted her from the floor into an enthusiastic hug. "Girl, you're the best. Thank you, but what is Muddy Waters.?"

"It's their name for sweet tea mixed with lemonade."

"Oh, I see. This is a lot of food for just one person, though."

"That's why I also got you these." Gianne opened one of the lower cabinets and handed him an unopened set of food storage containers. "You might want to divide everything up and put it into the freezer. That way, you can have a soul food feast a couple more times."

"You're too much. I really appreciate it. Where is Marc?"

"I sent him to find an open store, because I forgot a couple of things. He should be back soon."

Charles took a seat on a stool at the island. "While I have you here, I was wondering if you could do me a huge favor. I want to do some shopping before Adanna gets here, and I'll need a woman's opinion. Do you think you could spare a couple of hours with me at the mall?"

"You do know tomorrow is Black Friday, right? It's the best bargain shopping day of the year. I'd love to go out and see what I can score as early Christmas presents."

"Thanks, Gianne, but you know I'm not really looking for a bargain. What time do we need to leave?"

"Early." She stretched out the word for emphasis. "And I have to warn you. I'm a guerilla shopper, so prepare yourself."

♥

The only place Adanna had ever been outside of Nigeria was London, and even there she'd spent all of her time in Peckham, which was a largely African community. No doubt visiting Charles' family in the US would be a different experience. She practically vibrated with anticipation. All she knew about the United States was what she'd seen on television shows or CNN, and she knew neither gave a balanced view of real life anywhere.

The morning Charles called, she told Femi about his invitation. "Guess what? Charles is flying ChiChi and me to Atlanta to spend Christmas with him and his family. The hospital gave me off the whole week."

"That's wonderful. This will be your first time in the US."

"Yes, and I'm so excited." She drummed her fingernails on the countertop, smiling, but fighting an empty feeling in the pit of her stomach. "I'm nervous about meeting the family. Not the whole family, just his father. He sounds so…so hard to please."

"But you're not going to please him. You're making the trip to please Charles."

"Has Marc's girlfriend met his father?" Femi asked with a twinkle in her eye.

"I think so. Yes, I remember Charles saying that Marc met her at a family party. Why?"

"Why don't you call and ask her what to expect."

"That's a great idea. You always know the right thing to do." She hugged her friend around the neck. "I'll tell you what she says."

Adanna had her preconceived notions of what the family might be like from Charles' stories. Judging by what he'd told her about Marc and Gianne, he had a good perception of their personalities. He described Marc as bold, quick-witted and harmlessly flirtatious. Based on his description of Gianne, Adanna had expected attractive, independent, and kind-hearted, which is exactly how she seemed once the two women were able to talk to each other. Her anxiety revolved around his father. Charles had never told her anything horrible about the man, but what he had said made him sound formidable. What if he didn't like her? She knew from personal experience that a father's opinion carried great weight. But the senior Dr. Stafford and her father were two different people. She had to make herself remember that fact.

A week later, after she'd brought ChiChi home from the hospital, a box arrived at the hospital addressed to her. It contained a handwritten note that read, *We're so excited about you coming to visit for Christmas. Since Chichima has never been in the cold, Marc and I wanted her to be warm and cozy while you're here. If anything doesn't fit her, just bring it with you, and we'll exchange it. Can't wait to meet you in person. Love, Gianne. 702-555-4327*

That was exactly what Adanna needed to convince her to make the call. First she went through the box and showed the baby the items. "Look at what you got, Princess. You are going to look so pretty for our trip." ChiChi's blue-gray eyes followed intently as Adanna held up the little dresses, track suits, onesies, pajamas, shoes, and matching accessories. At the bottom of the box she found a small soft doll with cocoa-colored skin. "What do you think?" The baby kicked her feet and uttered musical syllables in approval. "I need to call Gianne and thank her." She placed the doll between ChiChi's chubby hands and watched her turn it back and forth to examine it closely.

Adanna checked the time, then dialed the number.

"Hello," a female voice answered.

"Gianne? This is Adanna. I'm sorry to call so early, but I wanted to tell you that I received the parcel for ChiChi."

"Hi, Adanna. It's okay, we're awake just not up yet. I'm so glad it got there safely. Honey, it's Adanna," Gianne said. "She got the box."

"The clothes are just adorable. ChiChi is playing with the doll right now. There's just one thing. We're still waiting for approval on her travel from the State."

"We're not worried about that," Gianne replied, cheerfully. "Everything will fall into place. If anything is too big or too small, we can replace it when you get here. We weren't too sure about the shoes."

Adanna smiled at her positive outlook, took a pair of the shoes and held them up to the baby's feet. "They look like they will fit just fine. Thank you so much."

"It's our pleasure. Marc lives in sport shoes, so he picked out those pink sparkled Nikes." Gianne said with a giggle.

"They're awesome. I had another reason for calling you, but I really wanted to talk to you when Marc wasn't there."

"Is something wrong?"

"Not really. I thought I might get your take on the Stafford family. I'm pretty nervous about meeting them."

"Oh, that's all? Girl, I can be honest in front of Marc. In fact, let me put you on speaker, so you can get his input too."

Adanna heard his voice in the background, but she couldn't make out his words.

"Okay, ask away, girl."

"Well, is there anything I need to know before I get there? I know their father is a bit *difficult*."

Marc barked a loud laugh. "He's only difficult with his sons. Gianne thinks he's a prince."

"That's true, Adanna. When I met Dr. Stafford, he was my doctor, and he was the most sensitive, caring man I'd ever met. A special bedside manner is essential when you have to deliver devastating health news. For two years he treated me with more care than your average doctor. At the time his kindness meant more to me than I can even explain. Vic did my surgery, and I'd seen Jesse around the office long before I ever met Marc, but I didn't know them personally. When I got my remission diagnosis, Dr. Stafford invited me to a family dinner celebrating Vic's promotion at the hospital. He didn't have to do that, but he knew I hadn't been out socially since I'd gotten sick. That was the night I met Marc."

"So he introduced you two?" Adanna asked, curious to hear more about how their relationship began.

"Hell no," Marc said. "I saw her sitting at a table by herself, so I introduced myself. We ate dinner together, and I took her back to my parents' house for dessert at the end of the night. My father didn't like the idea of us being together. He thought I was going to hurt her."

"Admit it. You *did* have a scandalous dating track record."

"True, but that's not the point. He had no reason to believe I was going to treat you badly."

"Is there anything that he really dislikes when it comes to women?" Adanna asked.

"Loudness or drunkenness," Marc said, "but you don't seem like you have those problems."

"Not usually." Adanna smiled at the memory of her recent showdown with Emeka outside of the hospital.

"I have another question. It's Nigerian tradition to bring gifts when visiting someone's home for the first time. Any suggestions?"

"My father loves good scotch. Mama likes gold jewelry and pretty things for the house."

"What kind of décor does she have, Gianne?"

"Traditional and timeless, uncluttered, serene colors, classic lines."

"I'm glad you asked her that question," Marc grumbled in good humor. "Anything else you want to know?"

"I don't think so. Thank you both for calming my nerves."

"Adanna, if Charles likes you, Mama and Daddy will too. Don't stress over it."

"See you soon."

The two weeks before Christmas went by quickly. The State had approved ChiChi's travel, so Adanna eagerly prepared for her first visit to the States. At first she'd considered telling her parents where she would be during the holiday, but when she recalled her last conversation with her father, she threw the idea out like one of ChiChi's used nappies. Femi would know how to reach her in case of an emergency, and a crisis was the only event in which she might contact them. Emeka didn't need to know anything at all.

Charles was scheduled to arrive in Atlanta the day before her flight came in, and he'd promised to meet her and ChiChi at the airport. Even though she was apprehensive, Adanna couldn't wait to get to the US.

Chapter Sixteen

Charles' baby brother, Nick, picked him up at the Atlanta airport on the twenty-second. They hadn't seen each other since his going away party when he moved to Las Vegas. Nick lived in a small apartment in the Camp Creek area a few miles away from their parents' house.

"How're you doing, man?" Nick asked as they walked across the street to the parking garage. "I heard you have a lady coming to visit for the holidays."

"Damn! I asked Mama not to broadcast it." Charles shook his head.

"Mama didn't tell me. Daddy did."

His eyebrows rose. "What did he say?"

"He said you were pulling one of Marc's stunts, only your woman has a baby."

Charles sighed. "He has a lot of nerve. Daddy was the one who invited Gianne to the dinner in the first place. He just didn't expect one of us to hook up with her. And, yes, Adanna has a baby, but she's not her mother. The baby was a patient of ours. She's an orphan."

"An orphan?"

"Yeah. Her mother abandoned her at the hospital right after she was born. Adanna's been taking care of her ever since."

"Humph. Daddy didn't mention all of that."

"Of course not. He wants to make it seem like something

crazy is going on, even if it isn't. How's Cherilyn? Are you two still together?"

"Yup. She's good. Just got a promotion on her job and she's getting ready to buy a house." He stopped next to a new BMW convertible. "This is me. I treated myself after graduation."

Charles nodded and smiled, admiring the shiny silver sports car. "Sweet."

A click sounded and Nick said, "You can put your bags in the trunk."

"This is the longest you've even been with a woman. I hate to sound like Mama, but are you two planning to make it permanent?"

"Not yet. I need to figure out what I'm going to do with my career before I make any other major decisions in my life."

"Still can't decide on a specialty, huh? Maybe you should just go into family practice."

"Actually, I'm considering men's medicine."

"Seriously? You want to be the *Dick Doctor*?"

"I can't believe I'm hearing that from you," Nick glanced at him with a smirk, "considering you were the *Boob King* for years, man."

"For real though, from what I've read, men's health is a prosperous field. So many men have issues these days. Do you mind if I ask what has you leaning in that direction?"

"During my internship, we had a patient admitted who was my age at the time, early twenties. He was engaged and about to get married when a near-fatal car accident almost ended his plans. Even though his airbag went off, the steering column bent from the force of the crash and pushed down between his legs. Did severe damage. Naturally, he called off the wedding, because he didn't want to burden his fiancée with a husband who couldn't perform sexually."

"Wow. What was the outcome?"

"His fiancée didn't want to hear that, and she hung in there with him. His family called in a specialist from Connecticut who did major surgery. He had to have a penis pump inserted, but at least he could function again."

"Did they stay together?"

"They were while he was still in the hospital, and he was there for a couple of months."

"Have you mentioned your decision to Daddy yet?"

"No, but I can already hear him calling me the *boner pill pusher*. It's only because men's health didn't exist as a specialty when he was in med school.

The brothers' laughter filled the car. "That man is a piece of work. He'll change his mind when he discovers how much you can make."

"When's your lady coming in?"

"Tomorrow evening around four."

"Are all of you staying at the house?"

"Yeah, but I'll be in our old room. Adanna and ChiChi are taking one of the guest rooms."

"Just wondering. I didn't think Mama and Daddy weren't suddenly changing the *no co-habitation rules*."

"Hell will freeze over before that happens."

Nick pulled into the driveway. "I talked to Mama this morning. She said she'd hold dinner until we got here, so I know they're waiting."

"Anybody else coming?"

"Not tonight."

"Good. I need to relax for a while before the mayhem starts."

"Mama! We're here," Charles called out as they entered the foyer of the spacious traditional brick home. He dropped his luggage at the bottom of the stairs.

His mother came toward him from the back of the house with her arms spread wide. "Charles! It feels like I haven't seen you in years." In spite of the fact that he was almost a foot taller than her, she wrapped her arms around him and hugged him like he was a pre-teen.

He kissed her forehead and walked her into the family room with an arm around her waist.

"Hey, Dad." Nick sat on the sofa next to their father who was stretched out in the leather massage recliner the brothers had chipped in to buy him a few Christmases ago.

"I see you picked up the world traveler."

"Yup, and I'm a hungry world traveler," Charles answered. "How're you doing, Daddy?"

"Glad to have a few days away from the office."

"I've been keeping dinner warm. We're ready to eat." His mother went into the kitchen that opened onto the family room and continued listening to their conversation

Charles removed his jacket and laid it over the back of the sofa. "So you really do use that thing?"

"I certainly do. This is my TV chair." He smiled at his sons. "How're you doing?"

"I'm good. Got a lot to tell you."

"Are you ready to come back to civilization yet?"

"Lagos *is* civilization, Dad. It's a beautiful city. The whole country is in different ways, from what I understand, but I've been so busy I haven't had a chance to do much sightseeing."

"A lot of surgery?" the elder man asked with a spark of interest in the jade eyes his sons had inherited from him.

"So many we can't perform them all. While we're on the subject, I wanted to talk to you and Mama about ChiChi."

"Who in the world is ChiChi, and what kind of name is that?"

"ChiChi is the baby Adanna is bringing. It's her nickname. Her full name is Chichima. It means sweet, precious girl."

"This is the baby your mother said you operated on?"

"Yes, sir. She was born with both a cleft lip and palate. I've already repaired the lip, but I can't do the palate for another six months or so. Her mouth is still a little crooked, but she looks like a different child from when I first saw her."

"Poor baby," his mother said with a sympathetic frown. "I admire Adanna for taking care of her. Everyone wouldn't accept that responsibility."

"Adanna is an exceptional woman, Mama. You'll see."

His father eyed him with a curious squint. "Does she plan to adopt her?"

"As a matter of fact, she's about to start the proceedings after the first of the year."

"And you're prepared to take on a ready-made family?"

"Damn, Daddy. He just got off the plane," Nick said, trying to run interference. "Give him a few minutes to breathe."

So shocked by the interaction between his youngest brother and his father, Charles couldn't even respond. If he or his older brothers had spoken to their father that way when they were younger, they would've received a backhand and a serious tongue-lashing. Was the old man going soft? Finally, he answered, "It's okay. Yes." Charles had to keep Marc and Gianne's plan to himself. It was up to them to reveal it to the rest of the family, if they wanted to. "I admit I have become very attached to her. She's a good-natured baby. The only time I've ever heard her scream was when she was having some discomfort after surgery."

"Come to the table, guys, before this food gets cold."

"I love your spaghetti and meatballs. Thanks, Mama." Charles smiled at her after his father blessed the food. The conversation returned to the subject at hand.

"You really like working in Nigeria?" Nick asked, passing Charles the large ceramic bowl of pasta.

"It took some getting used to, but by the end of the first tour, I was pretty comfortable." He spooned a heaping serving of spaghetti onto his plate and topped the mound with three meatballs. "Most people speak English, so that eliminates a communication barrier. The food is different, but it's good, and there are plenty of non-Nigerian restaurants in Lagos. Driving is a challenge." He laughed. "But I've gotten the hang of it. I even bought a truck, a Toyota SUV, to get around. Speaking of driving," he turned to Nick, "would you be able to drop me at Enterprise in the morning so I can pick up a rental. They gave me a better price than the airport car rentals, and—"

"Since when did you start bargain shopping?" the elder man interrupted as his wife gave him the side eye.

"Since I started living on fourteen hundred a month."

His father cut to the chase. "Charles, we've been sitting here long enough. Why don't you stop avoiding the issue and explain how you ended up getting kidnapped. Your phone call was less than vague."

After he devoured a mouthful of salad, Charles took a sip of the red wine his mother always served with the Italian meal and swallowed. "I'm sorry. I'd had a crazy couple of days. When Nils told me the organization had contacted you, I wasn't up to talking but just wanted you and Mama to know I was safe." He went on to give them a blow-by-blow account of the abduction and his eventual release, but tailored the story to leave out any mention of Emeka. He didn't want anything to come up that might ruin Adanna's visit.

"Three thousand isn't much of a ransom," his father said with a skeptical squint.

Charles contradicted him. "Some people there are so poor, three grand is a fortune. I had the feeling one of the guys would jump at the offer."

"They didn't hurt you, did they?" Concern darkened his mother's eyes.

"Not after that first punch. They seemed to be under instructions not to harm me."

"Instructions from who?"

Charles almost winced at the slip. "I don't know," he lied, keeping a straight face. "But it's over and done with now."

"What are the police doing about it?" Nick asked between bites of garlic bread. "Did you press charges?"

"Against who? I don't know who they were, and kidnapping isn't considered a major crime there. If a ransom is arranged between the kidnappers and the victim's family or employer, they stay out of it."

"What kind of nonsense is that?"

"Nigerian nonsense, Dad. It's a peculiar country with a lot of government problems."

"And you'd rather be *there* than here in Atlanta?"

Charles looked at him directly. "Right now, yes. I love the work and being with Adanna is important to me. She's a very skilled nurse, even though she's never been formally trained as an OR nurse. All of her surgical experience came from on-the-job training. She's smart, quick, and compassionate, and I've had her assisting me since I started my surgeries."

His mother listened with a questioning look in her eyes. "You sound quite proud of her, Charles. That's so important in a relationship, but there must be more than her professional skill that attracted you to her when you first met."

"Okay, Mama," he said with a sheepish smile. "Yes, she's beautiful, graceful, and the fact that she has an incredible body doesn't hurt either."

She uttered a knowing laugh. "I can't wait to meet her and the baby."

"I'm picking her up late tomorrow afternoon. It's her first visit to this country, and I want it to be a great one."

"You say that as though you think we're going to scare her off."

Charles laughed at his father's wicked grin. "Not intentionally, but meeting our tribe can be overwhelming if you don't come from a big family, and Adanna doesn't."

"She doesn't have any brothers or sisters?"

"Just one brother, Mama. They aren't very close, and her parents live in London."

"Oh, that's too bad." His mother's sad expression spoke of her love for her own mini-army. "Don't you worry, if it's left up to me, Adanna is going to have the best holiday she's ever had. By the way, Cydney said she has everything you need, and she reminded me that you'll need a car seat too."

He grimaced. "I forgot about a car seat. Can you tell her

I'll come by to get everything early tomorrow?"

Adanna called when she and the baby arrived at the airport in Lagos. Femi had driven them, and Charles was relieved when she said Femi would wait there until they boarded. From what he'd seen, flying with kids could be a test of mental and emotional strength. Parents of small children often wore the pained expressions of frustration, embarrassment, and anger as they tried to quiet fretful or undisciplined children on flights. He hoped ChiChi remained her normal easygoing self. Close to thirteen hours on a flight was torture for adults. Adding a child to the mix pushed the stress quotient off the charts.

In the morning, after Nick dropped him at the car rental company, Charles drove to Jesse's house. Cydney opened the door looking like her old self. The weight she had gained with their last baby was gone, and after looking exhausted for the past two years, she finally appeared rested.

"Charles! Welcome back!" She greeted him with an enthusiastic hug. "Jess is in the family room with the girls. Come in and have a cup of coffee with us."

He followed her down the hall of the two-story traditional that had the same layout as his parents' house. The sight of his brother sitting in the middle of the floor wearing a tiara and *having tea* with his three-year old daughter took him by surprise. Jesse and Vic shared a serious nature, and to see him doing something so frivolous revealed a side of his brother Charles had never seen. Jesse's youngest sat beside him in a play saucer with so many gadgets she looked like a jet pilot in her own little cockpit.

"Hey, man. You're just in time for tea," Jesse said, appearing momentarily abashed. "Welcome to the other life of Dr. Jesse Stafford."

Charles reached down and clasped his older brother's hand in a lingering greeting. "Looks like a great life to me." He bent and placed a kiss on his niece's forehead. "Hi, Miss Celise."

The little girl's confused stare told him she still couldn't tell her uncles apart. "I'm Uncle Charles. You forgot about me already?" She blinked, said 'Hi', and went back to pouring the invisible tea.

"I heard you have some visitors coming to join us." Jesse raised a tiny floral cup to his mouth and pretended to drink. "Does that mean you're about to join the tea party brigade soon too?"

Charles shrugged. "I don't know about soon, but I wouldn't mind wearing a tiara."

The brothers caught up with what had been going on in their lives, and Charles didn't know how to respond when Jesse asked, "Is Marc coming? I didn't want to ask Mama, because I wasn't in the mood for a lecture."

The lifelong tension between Jesse and Marc was a sore point with the rest of the family. Of the six brothers, they were the only two who didn't get along. The conflict between them had existed since they were young and Marc had undergone heart surgery, which required him to be hospitalized for months. Jesse, who was only five at the time, saw their mother's decision to stay at the hospital with his younger brother as abandonment. In his mind, she seemed to have disappeared from his life. As he got older he mentally understood the circumstances, but he never overcame the hurt.

"He and Gianne will be here sometime tomorrow. They'll be staying at the house too. Why?"

"I need to have a talk with him."

"Aww, come on, man," Charles groaned. "Can't we have

one holiday when nobody's feelings get trampled?"

"That's why we have to talk. He can tell you about it if he wants. Until then it's between him and me."

Charles raised his hands in the air. "If you say so. Just please force me to apologize to Adanna for my family. Has anybody heard from Greg?"

"If he called anyone, it would be Mama."

Charles pulled out his phone and pressed a few buttons. "I'll find out." He waited a few moments. "What's up? It's Charles. I'm at Jesse's house, and we were wondering if you're coming down?"

"I'll be there, but I'm only staying for Christmas Day."

"Oh, you're doing a hit-and-run this time."

"Well, I have to work today, then I have a hit-and-run here that needs to be attended to."

"I understand, man," Charles said, even though he really didn't. Ever since his very brief stay with Greg, Charles questioned his older brother's judgment when it came to the opposite sex, but it was none of his business. "So when will we see you?"

"I'm taking a late flight out tomorrow evening. I should be there around nine. Nobody has to come get me. I reserved a car at Hartsfield."

"All right. See you tomorrow." Charles put his phone in his pocket and stood. "He'll be here about nine tomorrow night. I'd better get this baby stuff and head back. Adanna's coming in around four."

Jesse removed the tiara, rose to meet him, and slapped him on the back. "We'll be there for the Christmas Eve party."

They embraced and Charles called out for Cydney. "I'm getting ready to go, girl. Where's the baby stuff?"

"In the garage right inside the door on the left," she said from the catwalk overlooking the living room. "Don't worry about bringing it back before you leave. We'll pick it up from Mom after the holiday. And don't forget to stop and pick up whatever wine and dessert you want for the party."

"I really appreciate this, Cyd. Mama was about to go out and buy everything."

Cydney giggled. "That's how your mother is. I already wiped everything down with disinfectant, so it's all set. Let me open the door for you from the inside."

Charles went outside and waited while one of the garage doors rose. He went in and found the items where Cyd said they would be. *ChiChi's not even six months old and needs all this gear? No wonder Jess and Vic keep moving to bigger houses.* After he loaded the bed, high chair, car seat, and plastic bathtub into the car, he drove back to his parents' house and put it all into the largest guest room keeping a close eye on the time.

♥

The flight from Lagos departed on schedule. Adanna was thankful Charles had booked her in first class. At least she had a little more room to maneuver with ChiChi in her seat. Mercifully, the airline let the families with young children board the plane first, which allowed her to lumber down the aisle with the bulky car seat and overstuffed carry-on bag. She'd filled it with a few frozen bottles of milk, two changes of clothes, and as many nappies and dry snacks as it would hold.

When she and Femi arrived at the airport, a skycap was right there to help, and she tipped him one American dollar per item as recommended by a travel website. Having never flown with a small child before, Adanna had read everything she could find online so she might avoid disturbing other passengers. After some of the fiascos she'd observed on flights to and from London, it seemed some parents were totally indifferent toward the discomfort they inflicted on other passengers. She was prepared to apologize profusely to anyone sitting near her for any inconvenience she and ChiChi caused. Charles tried to get them seats as far forward on the plane as possible. Farther toward the back the plane was noisier, and it would be a nightmare trying to get off carrying everything. The baby was booked in a window seat, the best spot for a safety seat.

As they boarded, Adanna held the baby close to her chest after reading about the danger of someone dropping a carry-on on them while trying to move it in or out of an overhead bin or smacking the baby with a wayward bag when boarding or getting off the plane. Once they were settled into their seats, she kept ChiChi sucking on either a bottle or a pacifier to relieve ear pressure. The worst part of the long flight was the frequent trips to change her nappies in the small lavatory. Adanna wanted to kiss one of the flight attendants who took an instant liking to ChiChi and strolled up and down the aisle with her and even took her into the coach area for a short visit. She and the baby slept on and off through the flight and landed in Atlanta without any major mishaps, and Adanna walked through the jetway smiling when two passengers remarked that ChiChi was the best baby they had ever seen on a flight. One of them was even kind enough to carry the baby's safety seat for her into the concourse.

"We're here, Princess," she said to the baby who had just awakened again. "Dr. Charles promised to meet us, and I hope he's here." She gave a nervous glance around as they approached baggage claim. "This place is enormous."

"Adanna!" She heard his voice before she saw him waving above the crowd waiting at the carousel in the baggage claim area. "There he is," she whispered to ChiChi as they approached. "And he looks wonderful."

Charles pushed through the crowd and wrapped his arms around her and the baby for a long moment before his lips met hers in a sweet, lingering kiss she'd been dreaming about since he left for Las Vegas.

"I'm so glad you're here. How was the flight?" he asked when he released them and gave the man standing close beside them a questioning glance.

"This nice man carried her car seat for me."

He shook the man's hand. "Thank you."

"No problem. Glad to help. Enjoy your stay in Atlanta," the man replied, then turned to search out his luggage on the carousel that had just jerked into movement.

Charles smiled at ChiChi. "Did you do okay on your first plane ride?"

"She was so good. One of the flight attendants walked her up and down the plane, and two people even complimented me on her behavior. Ooh, that's my bag—the big red one."

He stepped up to the carousel and had to wait for the bag to come around a second time before he grabbed it and lifted it onto the floor. "What in the world do you have in here?" he asked with a grimace.

"Everything I thought I might need for both of us for the week. We are women, you know." She winked.

"I'm parked in the hourly deck across the street. It's not too cold out, but it'll probably feel cold to you." He smiled at the whiskers and cat ears on the hood of ChiChi's fuzzy pink jacket. "Did this come from Gianne and Marc?" he asked, tying the strings under her double chin.

"Yes. Isn't it adorable?"

Charles nodded and smiled, but the smile didn't reach his eyes. "I'm going to ask you this one last time. Do you think you might be making a mistake by not keeping her?"

"I'm not sure about anything. All I know is what I feel inside."

"Okay. I can't ask you to go against your gut feeling. The next big question is, are you ready to meet my tribe?"

"I can't wait. I'm just worried about the Chief."

He let out a loud laugh. "The Chief will probably build you a throne and seat you beside him and the Queen. If there's one thing my father appreciates, it's a beautiful woman with brains." He stopped beside a generic rental car. "Here we are. I'll put in her seat."

On the way to the interstate, Adanna found it hard to concentrate while Charles described his home town. No matter how much she tried to focus, she dwelled on meeting his parents. "I can't get over the fact that it's almost rush hour, and no one is leaning on their horns or trying to run anyone off the road," she said, trying her best to seem unconcerned about the upcoming meeting.

"Don't get it twisted. Drivers here can get ugly too, but those are isolated incidents."

While he talked, she only half listened. He didn't understand how important an introduction to parents was in her culture. She wanted to measure up to their expectations; only she had no idea what those expectations were. She also didn't have the faintest idea what Jesse's and Vic's wives were like or what they looked like, but she had a strong feeling they didn't look like her. In Nigeria she was considered attractive, and Charles always said how beautiful he thought she was. But that was his opinion, not his mother's or father's. But her appearance might be of no concern to them at all, though. Her other concern was how they might feel about ChiChi. All they knew was that she had a baby, and most likely they assumed if she and Charles were considering marriage, that baby would become his responsibility. Telling them the truth would betray their promise to Marc and Gianne to keep their plan secret until her adoption plans were settled.

"Adanna!" Charles' voice pulled her from her musing.

"I'm sorry. What did you say?"

"I was saying that you won't get to see the Atlanta skyline because we're going over to the west side. What's on your mind?"

Adanna turned around to peek at ChiChi. The baby was so quiet that Adanna assumed she had gone back to sleep, but she was wide awake and seemed to be entertained by the tall pine trees whizzing by, all she could see from her car seat. "I was just thinking that I wish we were able to tell your parents the truth about ChiChi."

He took his eyes from the road for a second. "What difference does it make?"

I hate for them to think I'm saddling you with a ready-made family."

He reached across the console and rested a hand on her knee. "That's none of their concern. Dating women with children is practically a given for a man my age these days."

"It is their concern, Charles. Every parent wishes the best for their child."

"And you believe having ChiChi in my life wouldn't be the best?"

"I'm not saying that, but your mother and father might."

"I don't know what else I can say to convince you that won't be the case. Guess you just have to wait a few more minutes and see how it goes." He squeezed her knee, returned both hands to the steering wheel, and changed the subject. "Tonight we should just take it easy, but tomorrow I'd like to do a little shopping. We usually exchange gifts Christmas morning."

"I brought something with me for your mother, but I couldn't bring your father's gift on the plane. I thought I might pick it up here."

"We can go to the mall that's close to the house first. If we can't get everything there, we can go up to the north side."

Since she wasn't a big shopper, the prospect of spending hours at the mall didn't excite her. To her it was more important to spend time with his family. "Does your mother cook a big Christmas dinner?"

Charles chuckled. "Are you kidding? She's probably been cooking for the past few days."

"Do you think she would let me help her?"

"I know she would. My mother is all about preparation. Sometimes I think she loves getting ready for an event more than the actual event." The baby made a little noise that sounded like a laugh. "That's right, Princess, and she's going to spoil you rotten."

When he took the next exit off the highway, Adanna's heart fluttered. "Are we almost there?"

"About ten minutes away. Relax, will you?"

"I'll relax when this week is over."

Charles returned to his tour guide narration as they drove down a busy street. "This is Cascade Road. I spent a lot of time here growing up. Back then there weren't nearly as many stores and businesses, but it was one of the few all black commercial districts in Atlanta."

"That sounds so strange to me when you say all-black. At home *everything* is all black." She laughed.

"Atlanta was an important part of the civil rights movement of the fifties and sixties and was the first American city to be considered a black Mecca. My parents grew up at the tail end of the movement, and their parents made sure they were aware and involved. In turn, they raised us the same way. Giving back to the community wasn't an option. It's what was expected of us."

"Did you resent it?"

"No way. We liked participating in community events. It was a change of pace from our schoolwork. None of us were really involved in sports except Marc. He ran track in high school. School and church activities were the only things we were involved in."

"I've been meaning to ask you about that. We never talked about church. Do you attend one?"

He frowned. "Not regularly. We were raised Baptist, but that's a little too traditional for my taste now."

Her mouth opened in surprise. "Really? I stopped going to church when I moved back home. We were raised Episcopal, and my father is a deacon in the Church of England. You don't know what traditional is until you've endured one of those services."

"I guess I should've mentioned this to you before now, but Mama always expects us to go to church with them if we're home on a Sunday. Would you mind joining us?"

"Mind? I'd love it. I'm sure Baptists are more lively than Episcopals."

"Not much. Not at their church anyway. Growing up, my brothers and I called it *Bourgie Baptist* because it was so uppity." He made a turn onto a street with large brick homes then turned into the parkway of a two-story house that had so many windows, she wondered how many rooms it contained.

"Let's leave everything in the car. I'll come back out and get it later."

They entered the house through a back door and stepped

into the kitchen. She was awestruck by its size and old European style. *Femi would be in heaven in a kitchen like this.*

The man sitting in one of the eight ladder-back chairs at an enormous island rose and walked toward them with a smile.

"This must be Adanna. My goodness, you're even prettier than Charles said." He took her hand and gave it a gentle squeeze. "Victor Stafford, I'm Charles' father."

"I am so honored to meet you, Dr. Stafford."

"First things first, sweetheart," the woman wiped her hands on her apron which read, *It's not burnt. It's just crispy.* "I know you're a nurse, but no one gets called doctor around here. There are too many of them, and all it does is feed their already overgrown egos." She smiled and opened her arms offering Adanna a hug. "I'm Charles' mother, Lillian, and I'm so happy you're spending Christmas with us."

Adanna stepped into her embrace. "Thank you so much for having me. I feel as though I already know you from all the wonderful things Charles has said."

Mrs. Stafford bent down over the infant carrier in her son's hand. "And this is ChiChi. You're absolutely precious."

"Come into the family room," Mr. Stafford said, inclining his head toward the big, open room where a fire blazed in an expansive fireplace with a natural stone surround.

Charles gave her an *I told you so* wink as they followed behind him.

"You have a lovely home. My flatmate would die if she saw your kitchen."

"Thank you. Is she a cook?" His mother took the infant seat from Charles' grasp, set it in one of the easy chairs, and proceeded to remove ChiChi's jacket.

"Not professionally," Charles answered. "But she could be if she wanted to."

The way Mrs. Stafford undressed the baby, undid the safety straps, and lifted ChiChi to her shoulder spoke of experience. "Hello, sweetheart. I am so glad you came to visit us." When ChiChi returned her smile, Adanna thought the woman might melt. "Oh, boy. I don't know if I'll be able to let this little angel go back home."

"I'm going to get their bags and take them up to the guest room," Charles said. "Let me take your coat."

Adanna shrugged out of the lightweight wool coat, the only one she owned that was suitable for cool weather. "Can you look in the small suitcase and get one of her bottles?" A few minutes ago the thought of him leaving her alone with his parents would have struck fear in her heart, but their warm welcome had dialed down her apprehension several levels.

"It's just the two of you in the big house?"

"Yes," Mr. Stafford answered. "And it's about time. We had a houseful of kids for thirty years, and we still have a houseful every holiday."

"That's a blessing. In my family, it's just my brother and me."

"Well, darling, when they start rolling in here, hold on to your hat." Mrs. Stafford returned to the stove. "It gets crowded and crazy."

"I look forward to it. Charles has told me so many stories about what it was like growing up in a big family. The only one I've met is Marc, and that was only by video chat."

"I'm still so amazed at the technology which allows us to do that now."

"Do what?" Charles asked when he came back into the family room and handed her the bottle.

"Video chat," his mother said. "When are Marc and

Gianne coming?"

"Tomorrow afternoon. You're itching to discuss wedding plans, aren't you, Mama?"

"I can't help myself. Vic and Ramona's wedding was exquisite. Jesse and Cydney's was sweet and romantic, and we haven't had one since."

Uneasy with all this wedding talk, Adanna busied herself with digging ChiChi's bib from her bag. She hoped and prayed his mother wouldn't ask her about her and Charles, because she didn't have an answer that sounded sensible. Charles had only asked about Nigerian wedding customs in response to Emeka's reservations about their relationship. He hadn't said another word about it since, and she'd made up her mind not to dwell on the matter.

"May I warm up her bottle?" Adanna asked, hoping it would end the wedding talk. "Thankfully, she drinks regular milk now, but I like to use a clean nipple and take the chill off first."

"I'm already at the sink. Let me do it for you," Mrs. Stafford offered.

She took a clean bottle liner from her carryon and handed the bottle over the counter. The older woman took a nipple brush from a drawer next to the sink. "You have a brush?"

"When you've had five new babies in this family in the past seven years," she filled the bottle with soapy water and gave it a vigorous scrubbing, "it just makes sense to keep the items I needed here for whenever the grandchildren stayed over. It makes life easier." She smiled, rinsed the nipple with steaming water, and handed it back to Adanna. "I see you use those disposable bottles."

"Yes." Adanna wondered if her statement was a criticism. "I really like them."

"When I first saw them, I thought what an ingenious idea.

When my boys were little, it seemed as though I spent my life washing and sterilizing bottles."

Okay, it wasn't a criticism. Relax, Adanna.

Once ChiChi finished her bottle, Mrs. Stafford called everyone to dinner. "We're going to eat in the kitchen. It's just the five of us."

Adanna didn't understand what she meant until she saw the dining room on the other side of the kitchen. The table had at least twelve chairs, but with six sons, their wives and five grandchildren, a huge table was a necessity.

"We're going simple tonight, since I'll be cooking all day tomorrow. Did Charles tell you about our Christmas Eve tradition?" she asked as they settled at the island, which by itself was the size of a normal dining room table.

"All he said was that you have a fun tradition that he wanted me to be part of."

"Oh, well, I'll let it be a surprise then.

Chapter Seventeen

*D*uring dinner Charles' parents asked Adanna how they celebrated Christmas in Nigeria, and he appreciated how attentively they listened.

"I was born in Nigeria and lived there until we moved to London when I was twelve. What I remember the most about Christmas as a child was how a tailor came to take our measurements for Christmas clothes." Charles didn't miss the light that came into her eyes as she remembered. "My mother bought us new shoes and toys as early as August and put them away where we couldn't find them. My cousins and I formed a group and created a special dance and my auntie rehearsed it with us every week. Celebrations took place in the streets, with music and dancing and everyone dressed in their new clothes to eat and celebrate. All of the Christian homes were decorated with palms, Christmas trees, and twinkling lights."

"Not that much different than here," his father remarked.

His mother added, "It sounds lovely. We try to keep some traditions going, especially for the grandkids. Children need those memories. That's why we still open gifts early Christmas morning. The whole family comes here, and we have breakfast together after the presents are opened."

Their response to Adanna was exactly what Charles had imagined. His father clearly appreciated her intelligence and beauty. His mother smiled as she watched her handle the baby, and when he and Adanna spoke to each other. Lillian Stafford was big on relationships. She valued communication, and he knew she was evaluating how he and his new lady responded to each other. He volunteered to change ChiChi so Adanna could finish her dessert.

"Come on, stinky girl. Let's get you out of here so they can enjoy their cake." He carried her in one arm and Adanna's bag in the other into the living room. After he spread a small blanket onto the rug, he dug out the baby wipes and a fresh diaper. His parents didn't need to know this was his first time changing a diaper.

"Promise you won't laugh at me," he told ChiChi in a singsong voice that always brought a smile to her cocoa brown face which to his amazement was the same color as Gianne's. "I've seen this done often enough. It shouldn't be hard." And it wouldn't have been if the baby had been lying perfectly still. After he pulled the tabs open, he had to hold her feet together so he could reach for the wipes and clean her disgusting little bottom. He made the mistake of holding her feet with his right hand, then realized the wipes were also on his right. When he crossed his left arm over the right and reached for the container, ChiChi thought it was the right time to yank one of her feet from his hold. Her heel went directly into the mess in the open diaper. "Oh, come on, Princess! Why'd you do that?"

A laugh behind him drew Charles' gaze up to his father who was standing in the doorway. "Need some help, son?"

"No. I got it."

"You sure?" his father said with another loud chuckle.

Charles snickered. "No."

"I've done this six times, you know."

"When did you ever change diapers?"

"When you were too young to remember."

Charles stared at him for a moment, flabbergasted when his father knelt beside him and pulled a fresh baby wipe from the container and cleaned the baby's foot. "Thanks."

"I'll hold her feet while you do the rest." He studied ChiChi's face as Charles went to work on wiping her bottom and wrapping up the dirty diaper. "You said she was born with a cleft lip and palate?"

He nodded. "I've only corrected the lip so far. The second surgery has to wait until she's about a year old." He opened the clean diaper and spread it beneath her.

"Do you have any pre-op photos?"

"Yes, sir. They're on my phone."

"I'd really like to see them. Looks like you did an excellent job."

Charles pressed his lips together to stifle the smile that could only come from a father's approval. He opened the tabs and folded the diaper around the baby's protruding belly, then reached into his pocket for his phone. After he scanned through the photos, he handed it to his father. "There are a few. Press the right arrow to advance."

The elder man scrutinized the photo and moved to the next. "Amazing. You've become a superb surgeon, son."

"Thanks, Daddy," Charles said, taken aback by his father's generous praise. He and his brothers had always known that their father was proud of them, but his verbal praise wasn't always forthcoming. It seemed the older the man got, the more he mellowed. "I'll probably be doing many of those procedures. Clefts are very common in Third World countries because of the lack of pre-natal care."

"Are you enjoying your work there?"

"Very much, and the fact that I met Adanna makes it even more enjoyable."

He grinned. "I like what I've seen so far. You two seem very similar."

"How so?" Charles never thought of Adanna and himself as being alike in any way other than their professions.

"She seems calm like you. Yesterday you said she assists in surgery, but she wasn't trained as a surgical nurse. That proves she's smart. You two make a good couple."

Charles looked into the eyes of the man who had been his role model and mentor. "I love her."

"I see that, and I think you're making a wise choice. How is she with money?"

"Thrifty. Too thrifty in my opinion. I offered to take her shopping after our first lunch date, and she refused."

His father's eyes rounded. "Really? Why?"

"I gave her a choice between dinner and a movie, dinner and dancing, or lunch and shopping. She gave me a speech about financing her own shopping sprees."

"That's rare."

"Tell me about it. Can you imagine Mona doing that?" Both men snickered at the thought of his brother, Vic's wife turning down an opportunity to spend money. "I could tell she was the kind of woman who put other people's needs before her own. I just wanted to treat her, but she wasn't having it."

"Now *that's* the kind of woman who makes a man want to give her the world."

"And it's just what I plan to do."

His father slapped him on the back. "You and Marc have made good choices. At one time I wasn't so sure about Mona, but I now believe she's the wife Vic needed beside him as he advanced his career. And I wasn't convinced about Cyd and Jesse making it because of her family background. She proved me wrong. Jesse needs that extra attention, and she gives it to him. Plus, she's a good mother. Let's get back to the ladies before they think we disappeared."

Adanna was busy helping his mother clean up the kitchen when Charles returned. While his mother loaded the dishwasher, she wiped down the stove and counter.

"There you are," she said when they entered the room. "I was just about to come see what ChiChi did to you."

"She didn't make it easy, that's for sure. But Daddy and I got her straight."

She whirled around and gaped at him.

"That's right. He reminded me that he's done this six times, and he's an expert."

"That old man has you fooled. Six times total maybe," She elbowed Adanna. "He hasn't changed a diaper in thirty years, and that was only when he had no other choice."

"Uh oh. She's calling you out, man." Charles checked his watch. "I know Adanna is wiped out from that twelve-hour flight. We're going upstairs to watch a little TV and turn in early, if you don't mind. I put Adanna and ChiChi in the blue room. I'll share my old room with Marc." He wanted them to know that he intended to respect their house rules.

"Get some rest. Adanna, if you need anything that's not in the room, please let me know." His mother kissed the baby's forehead. "See you in the morning. I'll be up early cooking."

"If you don't mind, I was hoping I could help," Adanna offered with a touch of shyness in her voice he'd never heard from her before.

"I'd love it, but Charles said you two were going shopping, and the stores will be a nightmare tomorrow. It's probably best if you get out early. There will be plenty left to do when you get back."

He picked up ChiChi's seat and Adanna's bag, then reached for her hand. "Night, Mama. Night, Daddy."

When they reached the second floor landing, he inclined his head to the left. "This way."

"I borrowed a few things from Cyd, Jesse's wife. She even sent one of those baby tubs and said she disinfected everything for you."

"That's sweet of her."

"Believe me, their kids had so much paraphernalia, it was ridiculous. Mona already gave away the baby stuff she and Vic had. After she had their third, she said she was done. Cyd and Jesse kept theirs, since they haven't decided how many they want to have."

Charles stopped outside a bedroom, reached inside and flipped on the light switch. She glanced around. "This is a very nice room. "You got a crib for her? I was going to let her sleep with me."

"I gave you the biggest guest room since the crib takes up space. Greg certainly doesn't need this much room. Neither do Marc and Gianne."

"Thank you. If we're going out early in the morning, maybe I should bathe her tonight."

"Go ahead. The tub is inside the big tub in the bathroom. Do you need any help?"

"No. This will be quick." Adanna laid the baby on the bed and started to undress her.

"I'll see what's on TV while you do that." Charles sank onto the loveseat and picked up the remote control. So far he was pleased with how everything had gone and hoped the peace would remain once the entire family arrived.

After Adanna finished with ChiChi's bath, Charles studied the way she gently lotioned, powdered, and dressed her in new pajamas from Gianne and Marc. Undoubtedly, she would make a fabulous mother, and he still questioned her decision about the adoption, but he had to believe she knew what was best.

She sat beside him with the baby on her lap. "What's on?"

"A lot of Christmas movies and specials. How about The Grinch?"

"What is that?"

"Oh, I guess it wasn't as popular overseas as it is here." He switched the channel.

"This is a cartoon."

He laughed. "Yes, but it's a cartoon with a message. I watched this so many times when we were young I could quote the dialogue by heart." When he slipped an arm around her shoulders, she rested her head on his chest and gently bounced the baby on her knee. Within a few minutes, ChiChi was asleep and Adanna seemed to be absorbed in the animated classic. The sound of footsteps drew Charles' gaze to the open doorway, which had been an ironclad house rule since the day Vic reached puberty. If any of the brothers had a member of the opposite sex in his room, the door had to remain open at all times. And they were warned to expect frequent walk-bys. Charles thought he was hallucinating when his father nodded, reached for the doorknob, and silently closed the door.

Once all was well in Whoville, Adanna put ChiChi into the crib, and he changed the station to a movie. Before the second commercial break, she was out cold. The combination of several glasses of wine, the familiar warmth of his surroundings and her soft breathing gradually lulled him to sleep. When he woke, Adanna's arm was wound around his waist and her cheek against his chest. The light coconut scent of her hair wafted into his nose. Instead of waking her, he rested his head back on the loveseat and enjoyed the moment.

Finally he gave her shoulder a nudge. "Adanna, I'm going down the hall," he whispered so he wouldn't disturb the baby. "Get into bed and get comfortable."

"No," she murmured, half asleep, and tightened her arm around him.

The thought that she wanted him to stay only intensified his desire to remain right where he was. It seemed as though a conspiracy against them making love for the first time existed. Now they were finally alone, but in his parents' house. Not the ideal place for what he hoped would be an uninhibited initiation into the physical side of their relationship. He released a frustrated breath and pried her hand from behind his back. "Baby, wake up," he said more forcefully this time. He eased up from the loveseat. "I'll set my alarm so we can get an early start tomorrow."

She glanced up at him with a dreamy, sexy expression. That look gave him an instant vision of picking her up, carrying her over to the bed, and stripping off her clothes until she lay before him with no barriers between them. Only that was just his wishful thinking. There were barriers between them, and they had nothing to do with clothing.

♥

Adanna rubbed her eyes as Charles hurried from the room. She assumed he didn't want his parents to think anything was going on with them behind closed doors. How had the door gotten closed anyway? They'd been cuddled up on the loveseat for the past few hours. She shook her head and padded across the thick carpet to the bathroom peeking into ChiChi's crib as she went by. The baby was sleeping soundly and hadn't even kicked off the covers.

The wash of bright light in the bathroom when she hit the

switch revealed an assortment of items next to the sink. Mrs. Stafford had seen to it that the basket contained every conceivable personal care item she might need. Adanna washed her face and crawled into bed thinking about what her first full day in the US might bring.

At six the next morning, Charles gave a soft knock on the door. She opened it and gave his body an admiring scan. All he had on were a pair of lounge pants. Her fingers curled seeing the dusting of hair covering his chest. If only she could pull him into the room, lock the door, and have her way with him for the next few hours…

"Good morning. Is she still sleeping?" he whispered, glancing toward the portacrib.

She squeezed her hands into fists and made herself look past him into the hallway instead of at his firm pecs and strong shoulders. "Yes. I was just getting ready to take a shower before she gets up."

"Okay. I'm going downstairs to make coffee. Do you need anything?"

She chuckled. "No. Your mother thought of everything. This is better than staying at a five-star hotel."

"That's Mama. She always has all different kinds of tea. You can pick what you want when you come down."

ChiChi slept through her shower and Adanna was even able to get halfway dressed before she heard her babbling. "Good morning. You must feel comfortable here to sleep so well in a strange house."

Thirty minutes later, the three of them were having breakfast in a restaurant in an area he called Camp Creek. She mixed cereal, applesauce, and milk and fed ChiChi then, at Charles' suggestion, she experienced her first taste of cheese grits, smoky link sausage, eggs, and biscuits.

After two hours, Charles hadn't found anything he wanted

for his mother and father, so he drove another forty minutes to Phipps Plaza, a mall that reminded Adanna of The Palms Mall in Lagos. A few more hours at the upmarket mall, jammed with last minute holiday gift seekers and Adanna had had her fill of shopping. Eager to return to the house to help Mrs. Stafford with the cooking, every time he stopped in front of a display window, she urged him on and reminded him that Marc and Gianne would be arriving soon.

"Fine. I just need to make two calls first." He pulled out his phone and walked a few steps away as though he didn't want her to hear what he was saying. A couple of minutes later, he glanced back at her, dialed another number, and had a brief conversation with someone. "Okay, we can leave now. I needed to make two more stops, but Nick is going to take care of one for me."

Charles ran into the Publix grocery store on Cascade Road on the way back to the house and came out with two bottles of wine and two containers of ice cream. "Mama and Daddy take care of dinner on Christmas Eve and the rest of us supply the wine and dessert," he explained as he got back into the car.

An unidentified car with a rental sticker on the rear bumper was parked in the driveway when they got back to the house. "Looks like they're here already." Charles cut the engine and turned toward her. "I don't know how you want to handle this, but we need to be careful not to give Mama and Daddy any idea of what Marc and Gianne are up to. We should follow their lead."

Adanna nodded. "I'm ready if you are." She waited while he came around to open the door. Before Charles helped her out of the car, he stopped and stared at her as though he was contemplating a question.

"Don't ask me again, Charles. I know I'm doing the right thing. Please don't look so worried. Let's just go inside. I want to meet them in person."

He opened the back door, pulled up ChiChi's hood, and took the napping baby from the car seat. "You should be the one to present her to them. I'll come back out and get the bags." Adanna took her and preceded Charles up the sidewalk. Voices were coming from the end of the hallway in the family room when they entered the house. Marc and Gianne were sitting together on the sofa facing the door. When Gianne looked up and saw them coming into the room, the expectancy in her eyes put a lump in Adanna's throat.

"We're back." Charles placed the ice cream into the freezer and the wine on the sideboard in the dining room. "And look who's here." He and Marc grasped hands all the while keeping their gazes on her and Gianne.

"Adanna, we finally meet in person." Gianne stood and greeted her with a hug. "Is the baby asleep?" She craned her neck and peered around Adanna's shoulder to try to see ChiChi's face.

"As soon as the car engine starts, she falls asleep. It's time for her to wake up anyway." Adanna lifted the baby from her shoulder. "Wake up, Princess. Somebody wants to meet you." She turned the drowsy infant around, and the moment she opened her eyes, Gianne inhaled a sharp breath.

"Oh my! She's beautiful, and look at her eyes. Marc, she has blue eyes!"

Marc took his time getting up as if he intentionally wanted to appear unconcerned. "Wow, they look like Nick's. How're you doing, little lady?" He gave the baby's double chins a gentle tickle.

"Can you take her while I get out of this coat?" She held ChiChi out to Gianne. "I'm not used to wearing a top coat, so I'm burning up now that we're inside."

Gianne stretched out her arms. "I'd love to. Come to Auntie G."

Adanna removed her coat and took it to the closet by the front door. Charles and Marc watched in silence as Gianne removed the baby's jacket, set her on her lap, and began talking to her as though she were an adult.

"I hope you didn't give Adanna a hard time on the airplane. I know it was a really, really long flight. Did they treat you right?"

Adanna returned to the family room. "They certainly did. She won over a flight attendant, who gave her the royal treatment."

Mrs. Stafford sent Marc a concerned glance. "They had no other choice. Look at that face."

"You're right, Mom." Gianne bounced ChiChi on her knee. "She's perfect. You can hardly tell she's had surgery, Charles."

"Her smile isn't completely symmetrical, but it was the best I could do with the amount of tissue that was available. I'm pleased with the results."

The way Mrs. Stafford's gaze followed Gianne didn't go unnoticed. Adanna whispered to Charles, "Your mother knows something is going on. You might want to warn Marc."

He leaned over and said something in his twin's ear. Marc glanced at his mother then moved to sit beside Gianne and spoke to her so no one else could hear. They talked for a couple of minutes before Marc said to the room, "Since everybody's not here yet, this might be a good time to tell you what's going on."

His mother looked up with a hint of a smile that gave away her thoughts. "Yes, why don't you tell us?"

"What are you talking about?" Dr. Stafford asked, oblivious to the situation going on in the room.

"Marc and Gianne have something to tell us, honey."

Marc bit his lip as though he wasn't sure of how to start. "Gianne and I are going to adopt ChiChi."

"I knew something was up," Mrs. Stafford chirped, beaming.

"You always do, Mama. We can't hide anything from you. The situation is complicated, though, because Nigeria prohibits foreign adoptions."

Dr. Stafford frowned. "Why on earth would they do that?"

"We don't really understand it from what we've read online," Gianne answered. "Maybe Adanna can explain it." She glanced at Adanna for help.

"Nigeria isn't the only African nation that discourages foreign adoptions. The U.N. says many of these adoptions aren't legitimate and there have been cases of children sold by their adoptive parents, and children abducted and later sold, put into child prostitution and pornography. Some have even been placed for adoption because they were wrongly considered orphans."

"Most western countries," Marc added, "even though we can offer a higher standard of living, are often considered evil because of the issues she just mentioned. And we can't deny that this stuff is big business in the US, but it makes it almost impossible for people who want to do a legal adoption."

Dr. Stafford scrubbed his forehead. "How do you plan to get around the rules?"

"I'm going to adopt her in Nigeria. Once that's taken care of, we could do a private adoption."

Lines of concern marred Charles' mother's forehead. "But you seem to be so attached to her. Are you sure you're not making a mistake?"

"Right from the beginning after her mother abandoned her at the hospital, I felt so strongly that ChiChi had come into my life for a reason. Even though I didn't understand at the time, I knew she wasn't supposed to be mine. When I met Gianne and Marc, it became clear exactly what the reason was. I have no doubt."

Charles put an arm around her. "I told you she's special, didn't I, Mama?"

"Yes, you did, and I see what you mean."

An embarrassing heat filled Adanna's face. "I know you can't see it, but I'm blushing."

"By the time she works everything out in Nigeria," Marc added, "we'll be married. You can tell the rest of the family later, if you want."

The bell rang, and a few seconds later a tall modelesque woman entered the family room holding two children by the hand. "Hi, folks!" Adanna had never seen such a stunning woman other than on the movie screen. Her long, dark hair had a windblown look that gave her a glamorous, sexy appearance.

"Hey, girl," Charles and Marc greeted her. "Where's Vic?"

"He and Trey went to the store. I didn't have time to pick up the dessert and wine yesterday." She let go of the children's hands. "No running through Grandma and Granddad's house, you understand me?" The little boy and girl nodded their heads. "Speak to everyone."

"Hi, Uncle Charles. Hey, Uncle Mark."

"This is Miss Gianne, remember?" The kids nodded again and mumbled a soft greeting to Gianne.

"And you must be Charles' friend."

"Yes, my name is Adanna."

"I'm Vic's wife, Ramona."

She and Adanna exchanged pleasantries and subtly studied each other as women do. "Hi, Adanna. Welcome to Atlanta. Is this your first time here?"

"Yes. In fact, it's my first time in the US" Adanna admired her skinny jeans that fit like a second skin. She marveled that this woman who had given birth to three children still had an amazing body.

"Well," she said with a photographer-ready smile. "You're going to see how the Stafford family does Christmas. We have a good time, girl."

"I'm looking forward to it," Adanna said, thinking Gianne and Ramona looked nothing alike. She couldn't wait to meet Jesse's wife. The front door opened again. This time another tall, handsome yet austere-looking man came down the hall with a boy about five or six years old. Adanna loved the way he greeted his brothers with a hug.

"Hey, the world traveler has returned! You know you'll have to tell the kidnapping story over again, don't you?"

Charles groaned and introduced them to her as his oldest brother, Vic and his son, Victor the third, or Trey.

Vic took her hand. "We're happy to have you, Adanna." He turned his back to her and said to Charles loud enough for her to hear, "She's fine, man."

"I know," Charles responded with a satisfied male smile.

The front door opened once more, and a harried-looking woman with a milk chocolate complexion and shoulder-length hair entered carrying a baby on her hip and a toddler by the hand. "Jesse's outside parking the car. He's on call this weekend, so he might not be able to stay all night."

"Hi, Cydney," Mrs. Stafford said. "Come here, Celise. Let Grandma take off your coat," she said to the toddler, a little girl who looked like a miniature Halle Berry. "Gianne, you remember Cydney. And this is Charles' friend, Adanna."

The woman hoisted the infant higher on her hip and came closer. "It's nice to meet you, Adanna. This is Aria." Her gaze went to ChiChi who was happily bouncing on Gianne's lap. "Is that your baby?"

"No. I've been caring for her, though."

"Look, Aria," Cydney said, turning her daughter to face the other infant. "You have someone to play with. Honey, look at this precious little girl," she said to the man who had just walked in. He resembled Charles, only his face was rounder and he wore his hair cut so close his scalp showed.

Adanna grinned. "That's exactly what her name, Chichima, means."

Jesse introduced himself, then greeted his twin brothers with a robust handclasp and bump of their shoulders.

The doorbell rang every few minutes. It seemed to be just a courtesy though, since everyone who entered appeared to have a key. The next to arrive was the youngest brother, Nick. Charles made sure Adanna and Nick met each other. Gianne moved to sit beside her. "You're wearing the same amazed expression I did when I first saw them all together," she whispered in Adanna's ear.

Adanna chuckled. "You read my mind. I've never seen such a handsome group of men in one place in my life."

"And there's still one more. Greg won't be here until later."

"I don't know if my heart can take it."

"Yes, Mr. and Mrs. Stafford did some great work." The two women burst out laughing and drew curious looks from the rest of the family.

"We were just talking about what a gorgeous family this is," Gianne explained. The men shook their heads, and the other women nodded in agreement.

The doorbell rang, but this time no one stepped inside. Mrs. Stafford left the kitchen and headed for the front door with a credit card in her hand. "That's probably Fellini's with the pizzas. I need cash for the tip, gentlemen."

Her sons pulled out their wallets and each handed her a couple of bills. "They love to see us coming," Charles told her. "It's a two-hundred-fifty dollar order each time. This is our Christmas Eve tradition. Get ready for the best pizza in Atlanta."

The deliveryman maneuvered his way inside, balancing at least a dozen pizza boxes and a couple of large bags. He followed Mrs. Stafford into the dining room, settled the bill, and then left.

"Okay, everyone. Dinner is served. There's a container of hand wipes at the end of the table. Use them, please."

Adanna's eyes rounded at the spread. Pizza, salads, wines, non-alcoholic beverages, and assorted desserts covered the table. After Dr. Stafford gave a quick blessing, the family obediently complied with her request. They filed around the table and loaded up their plates. Lively chatter, humorous storytelling, and the sound of happy children filled the crowded family room.

"What?" Adanna asked Charles the third time she caught him watching her.

He leaned in so she could hear over the din. "Are you having a good time, or is this all a little too much for you?"

"No. I love it. It's wonderful to have such a big family where everyone gets along."

He snorted. "Well, I wouldn't go that far. At least Marc and Jesse haven't gone for each other's throats yet."

She sent him a questioning look. "Are you serious?"

"Oh, yeah," he said, reaching for another slice of pizza.

"They're the two hot-tempered ones. We've had to break them up a couple of times in the past. Mama doesn't take kindly to anyone knocking her furniture over."

Adanna's jaw dropped. It was hard for her to imagine this room full of educated, successful men actually scuffling on the floor.

"Families are just families. We all have our issues. They're just different from other people's issues."

She smiled, sensing that he was trying to make her feel better about her own problems with Emeka. Even though she appreciated his identifying with her, it wasn't nearly the same. Emeka had not only broken the law, he'd demonstrated just how much he disregarded her feelings. She would've rather gotten into a physical fight with him.

Cydney beckoned to her from the corner of the room where she was nursing Aria. Adanna took ChiChi from Gianne, joined her, and gave ChiChi a bottle. Something felt so right about being there.

Cydney sent her a sidelong glance. "So, what do you think of this bunch?"

"I was just thinking about that. This is very different for me, since it's only my brother and me. Our parents live in London, so I don't get to enjoy big family get-togethers. "I haven't talked to Ramona yet, but they all seem very nice."

"Mona and I get along fine." What was behind Cydney's lopsided smile? "She's just way more sophisticated than I am. We don't have a lot in common."

"What do you mean?"

"She's a *real* doctor's wife. Into all the charity stuff and keeping a high profile in the medical community, you know."

"Truthfully, I don't," Adanna confessed. "Back home I don't travel in the same circles as the doctors. My friends work in other fields."

"I didn't come from that kind of background either. At first I wondered if Jesse would grow tired of me just wanting to be a homemaker, but he likes our life the way it is. Naturally, I go with him to medical functions, but I try to stay on the DL. By the way, did Mama tell you about our annual shopping spree?"

"Not yet. Is this another tradition?"

"Mama! Come tell Adanna about our day-after-Christmas outing."

Mrs. Stafford crossed the room and gazed at the clock. "I wonder where Gregory is."

"He'll be here, Mama," Charles reassured her. "He worked today and had to catch a late flight."

Mrs. Stafford sat beside Adanna, took ChiChi from her arms, and propped the baby on her shoulder. While she gently patted the baby's back, she explained. "Since we all cook and work hard in the kitchen to make Christmas dinner special, the day after is our day off. We take advantage of the after-Christmas sales, and the men handle babysitting duty. Our day on the town starts with breakfast."

She hadn't been prepared for this. Adanna imagined these women frequenting the best stores and sparing no expense. "Oh, I'm not a big shopper. Maybe I'll stay here and help them watch the children."

"You'll do no such thing," Ramona insisted. "This is our time to bond without the guys around. You don't have to do any shopping, if you don't want to. But when you get out there and see the sales, you won't be able to help yourself. Besides, the men finance the day."

Adanna gazed across the room at Charles. "It's just that I don't feel comfortable taking money from Charles. He's not my husband."

Ramona looked at her as though she were tolerating a fool. "Oh, sweetie. Don't start out your relationship by taking a vow of poverty. Let the man take care of you. If he didn't love you, he wouldn't do it."

Mrs. Stafford tempered Ramona's narcissistic comment. "These boys grew up lacking nothing, but Victor and I tried our best to make sure they understood how blessed they were. We taught them to enjoy giving to others. I have to agree with Mona. Don't block your blessing, Adanna."

Gianne weighed in on the matter. "I understand where you're coming from, girl. I had the same issue with Marc when we first started seeing each other. We had only known each other for three days when he offered to fly me to Las Vegas and train me for free. I wasn't used to that kind of treatment from any man I'd ever been involved with. Stafford men love to give, and they get real joy out of providing nice things for us."

Ramona nodded in agreement, then turned toward the other end of the room where the men were seated. "Boys, are you still sending us shopping the day after Christmas?"

They all nodded without comment.

"How much do we get this year?"

"We're going plastic this year, baby." Vic poured himself another glass of wine and answered in an unconcerned tone.

"What does he mean?" Adanna whispered to Gianne.

"They're giving us their credit cards. No limit."

"That can't be true."

"It *better* be true," Ramona said, "because I've been a *very* good girl all year."

"But aren't we exchanging Christmas gifts tomorrow?"

"We are. This is something special. Don't concern yourself, Adanna." Cydney patted her arm. "The guys get off on this. They *really* do. Sometimes it's almost like a competition between them to see who can treat their wife the best. I ain't mad at them."

All Adanna could think about was that the gift she'd bought for Charles wouldn't be nearly enough. She admired the fact that this family was a very generous one, but they also had more than she'd ever had. The vast chasm of difference in their standards worried her. Thinking she would come here and assimilate into their lifestyle was just a silly pipe dream.

Chapter Eighteen

While the women chattered about their shopping day, Charles retreated into his thoughts. Being back in Atlanta felt good, and spending time with the family always reminded him of what was important in life. But tonight he had a nagging feeling that something was simmering just beneath the surface. He didn't know what it was, and he hoped it stayed there at least until they finished opening their gifts tomorrow.

Adanna appeared to be at ease among his family, and for that he was thankful. At the moment she was in a huddle with Gianne, Cydney, and his mother. Ramona had been on and off her phone since she'd arrived discussing a Valentine's Day ball fundraiser for the hospital she was organizing.

Marc and Jesse refilled their wine glasses and left the room together and went downstairs to the basement.

"Wonder what that's all about?" Nick asked, exchanging curious glances with Charles and Vic.

"Let's just hope they keep it civil," Vic grumbled.

A little after ten, the two brothers emerged from the basement wearing unreadable expressions. There were no evident signs of stress and no blood, and since they didn't comment, neither did anyone else. A little while later, Greg walked in looking like the veritable Manhattan bachelor dressed in all black with a gray cashmere scarf thrown casually around his neck that matched his duckbill cap.

"It's about time," his father called across the room. "Good

to see you, son."

"You too, Dad. How're y'all doin'? I can say that now that I'm back in the South." He laughed and removed the Ray-Ban aviator shades he didn't need on a dark, wintry night.

"Hey, Greg," Ramona greeted him with one of her Miss Georgia beauty queen smiles. "Mama said you're only staying until tomorrow night. Is that true?"

"Afraid it is, Mona. I have some business to take care of in the City."

One by one he greeted his brothers with a masculine hug. "How's everybody doing?" He addressed the question to the room. "You're looking good, Gianne. Marc must be taking very good care of you." He sent her a devious wink.

"Thanks, Greg. I'm feeling great."

His gaze settled on Adanna. He walked over to her, reached for her hand and said, "I don't know *you.*"

"All right, lover boy," Charles interrupted, recalling the side of his older brother he'd seen during his recent stay in New York. "Turn down the charm. There aren't any cameras running right now. Adanna, this is Greg, the *personality* of the family." His exaggerated eye roll elicited a laugh from everyone in the room.

"It's my pleasure, Adanna." He kissed her hand, then knelt in front of her. "And this future heartbreaker is…?"

"Chichima. We call her ChiChi."

Greg eyed Charles. "You've been busier than you let on, bro."

"In fact," Marc interrupted, "she's going to be ours, if all goes as planned." That revelation ignited a chorus of questions from the rest of the family. "We told Mama and Daddy last night, but everyone might as well know what's going on. She was abandoned at the hospital where Charles and Adanna work. Since Nigeria discourages foreign adoptions, Adanna is going to file for adoption. After that, hopefully she will be able to arrange a private adoption with us."

Cydney's hand flew to her chest. "Oh, my God! That would be wonderful."

"And with her skin tone and those eyes, she looks like she could actually be yours," Ramona added.

"Well, I hope it works out for you." Greg threw up his hands. "Personally I want that baby vibe to stay as far away from me as possible."

"So there's no one special in your life right now, Gregory?" their mother asked.

"Nope. Nobody special, and that's just the way I like it."

In the morning, he and Adanna rose early so she could help his mother prepare breakfast. While they fixed coffee, tea for the adults, and set out juice boxes for the children, the family arrived one by one and added their gifts to the pile around the tree in front of the bank of curved windows in the family room.

"Ridiculous, isn't it?" the older woman said when she noticed Adanna staring at the towers of brightly-wrapped gifts. "This is what it's like when you have six children."

"I think it's great." Adanna giggled. "The only place I've ever seen this many gifts was a toy giveaway at one of the malls back home."

"Victor and I never went to any extremes when the boys were growing up, but I must admit we have become over-indulgent grandparents."

"That's the truth," Jesse said.

"Don't tell any stories, Jesse! You and your brothers

always got what you wanted for Christmas."

"Huh, I'm still waiting for that Mustang GT."

She slapped his arm. "I'm talking about when you were little and asked for *reasonable* things. And your father has bought more cars for you boys than I care to remember."

"I'm not trying to sound ungrateful," he snickered. "But they were just never what we wanted at the time."

"They had four-wheels and an engine," Dr. Stafford groused from the family room where he'd just finished lighting the fireplace. "That's all you speed demons needed."

"Do you remember that red Firebird the Atlanta Police picked Vic up in for cruising during Freaknik?" Marc asked.

Adanna was lost. "What in the world is a freaknik?

"It started out as a fraternity and sorority picnic here in Atlanta during the eighties," Marc explained. "But by the nineties it had turned into a citywide event with over a quarter-million attendees. Lots of concerts and wild parties, and the street cruising brought the city to a complete standstill two years in a row. Charles and I weren't allowed to go, because we were too young."

Jesse laughed. "All I remember is how pissed Daddy was when Vic called from the police station."

Charles noticed how Adanna studied their interaction. She seemed to be enjoying the banter between his brothers, but a question lingered in her eyes. "What's on your mind?"

"I can't imagine them having a knockdown, drag-out fight. And I can't get over how she handles a houseful of people. Everything is in its place, yet her hair is done, and she even has on light makeup."

"She *is* amazing, but that's her gift. Organizing events and parties is her specialty, and her talent helped my father get where he is today."

Mrs. Stafford peered across the counter. "Does everyone have coffee? As soon as Gregory gets down here, we'll be ready to open the gifts.

When Greg appeared a few minutes later, she put a mug of coffee into his hand and told him to find a seat in the packed family room. The older children sat on the floor closest to the tree. Cydney and Gianne held the babies.

Dr. Stafford took his place at the front of the room and announced. "As usual, the children go first, and it's only fitting that we start with the newest first." Adanna's lips parted in surprise when he passed identically-wrapped boxes to Gianne and Cydney." These are for Aria and ChiChi from Lillian and me." He presented their gifts to the rest of the grandchildren before he began reading the tags on the rest of the mountain of boxes and bags at light speed. When he finished almost twenty minutes later, each adult and child had a stack of unopened boxes beside them. "Okay, that's all. Have at it!"

"I didn't expect all of this for ChiChi and me," Adanna whispered to him. "I only got gifts for your parents."

"Not to worry. Nobody expected you to get them anything."

The box from his parents contained a plush crawling Minnie Mouse doll. Jesse and Charles set them in motion and both babies waved their arms and kicked their legs as they watched the dolls wiggle across the carpet.

"I know neither of them is crawling yet," Mrs. Stafford said, "but it's supposed to help teach motor skills. And it was just *so* cute, I couldn't resist."

The sounds of squealing kids, tearing paper, and the subsequent sounds of appreciation filled the room.

He nudged Adanna so she didn't miss his father's smile when he opened the box containing the twelve-year-old

Johnnie Walker Black Label Deluxe Blend Scotch Whiskey she'd bought him. But when he crossed the room and kissed her cheek, she looked completely flustered. "You didn't have to do that, darling, but it *is* my favorite. Thank you."

A few moments later, everyone in the room turned at his mother's gasp as she opened her gift from Adanna. "Oh, my! This is exquisite." All of the women leaned in to get a closer look and murmured their approval.

Picking out something for a woman you'd never met wasn't easy, but she had definitely nailed it. "That looks just like Mama. How'd you do it?"

"I consulted Femi. In my opinion, I couldn't go wrong with her flair for fashion."

"Where did you get it?" she asked, holding up the seven-strand white crystal bead necklace with a circular brooch securing the strands together.

"It comes from Zahmad Wireworks and Jewelry, a well-known Nigerian jewelry company.[1] Charles described you as regal and elegant, and when I saw it, I knew it was the right gift."

"This is lovely, Adanna. Thank you so much."

Next, the couples presented their gifts to each other. "I couldn't very well bring this on the plane." Adanna handed Charles an envelope.

He frowned and then broke into a wide grin when he saw the gift certificate for a Keurig coffee brewer and ninety-six K-Cups of his favorite Starbuck's Caffe Verona dark blend. "I guess I have been griping and complaining, huh?"

"Yes, you have been whining a lot, but I understand. We don't have Starbuck's in Nigeria. It's the same as trying to find my favorite English tea here in the US."

After he hugged her and thanked her with a long, juicy

kiss, he glanced around the room almost as though he was waiting for everyone else to finish opening their last gifts. He nodded to Nick, who left the room and reappeared seconds later with a bag that he placed in Charles' hand. A hush came over the room when he placed the bag on the floor next to the chair, scooted out of his seat and got down on one knee.

"Charles, what are you doing?" she whispered.

"Remember when I asked you to find the nicest place in Lagos for us to spend an evening?"

Adanna nodded, her eyes watery and wide. "I was going to wait and ask you when I got back to Lagos, but I can't wait any longer." He reached into the bag, took out a velvet box, and opened it. "I love you, Adanna Okoro. Will you be my wife?"

She took her gaze from his eyes long enough to catch a glimpse of the eager faces surrounding them. "Yes! Yes, I'll marry you!" Adanna circled his neck with her arms and sealed her response with a kiss that was accompanied by whistles, cheers, and old-school dog pound barks.

He removed the ring from the box and slid it onto her finger with a dozen phones capturing pictures of the moment in real time. One by one, the family closed in to hug and congratulate them. Once the excitement died down and they got a moment alone, he grinned at how she wiggled her fingers back and forth making the two-carat diamond sparkle.

"It's the most beautiful ring in the world," she said never taking her gaze off the center brilliant cut round center stone, surrounded by two intricately designed white diamonds set in platinum.

"If you'd rather have yellow gold, we can exchange it. I just thought the platinum would look beautiful against your skin."

Adanna shook her head vigorously.

"Then I want you to hear me out on this. We need to plan a trip to London, so I can meet your parents."

Shock replaced her joyful expression. "Do you really want to do that? I mean, after my father sided with Emeka and all?"

"It's the right thing to do, baby, whether they agree with us being together or not. I just need to state my intentions man-to-man."

The admiration in her eyes made his toes curl. "We should do what you think is right, but I can't see Dr. Ijalana and Dr. Pategi allowing me to take any more time off."

"Maybe you won't need to take any more time off. Not if we go this week. Rather than stay here in Atlanta, if the travel agent can change our flights we could go to London for the rest of the week." He glanced at his mother. "Mama's not going to be happy, but it's probably our best option. I'll explain to her. At least we spent Christmas with them, and you'll get to hang out with the ladies tomorrow. Why don't you call them now? I need to know what our options are."

♥

Adanna swallowed hard at his suggestion. God knew she didn't want to have a showdown with her father, but if Charles had the courage to confront him, she had to support him. "I don't want them to know we're coming, but I was getting ready to call and wish them Merry Christmas. I guess I can at least find out if they have any travel plans for the next few days." She took her phone from her purse. "Let's go into another room."

"Merry Christmas, Mum," she said once they were inside

the library with the door closed.

"Merry Christmas, Adanna. Thank you so much for the gift," she said of the cash Adanna had mailed them. "We'll put it to good use. Your father is sleeping right now. I was hoping to hear from you."

Why couldn't you call me yourself?

"Did you do anything special yesterday?"

"Yes, I had dinner with friends and their family." There was no need to go into detail now, Adanna decided. "It was…terrific."

"Was Emeka with you?"

"No, Mum. These were my friends. What are you and Dad doing for the rest of the week?"

"Nothing in particular. Since you and Emeka left, there hasn't been much to celebrate."

Adanna ignored her comment. "Well, tell Dad I called and said Merry Christmas."

"Wait, I'll wake him. I'm sure he wants to talk to you."

Sure he does. "No, that's all right. Don't wake him. If I don't talk to you before next week, have a happy New Year."

"You too. I hope we'll be able to see each other soon."

"We will, Mum." She pushed the end button and sent Charles a guilty glance.

"I know you hated doing that, but it'll work out better this way."

In the morning, while Adanna and Gianne were in the middle of giving Charles and Marc last-minute instructions on keeping ChiChi fed, dry, and happy in their absence, Dr. Stafford announced, "All right, ladies, back off. She's staying with three doctors. She'll be fine. Your car is here. Let's not keep the man waiting."

"Car? I thought someone was driving?" Adanna asked, realizing she was the only one who didn't know the program.

Marc smiled. "Someone *is* driving, and he's yours for the day, so make sure you don't abuse him."

Adanna went to the window to peek out, then shook her head at the sight of the stretch limo in the driveway.

Mrs. Stafford shrugged on her coat. "It's extravagant, I know, but it only happens once a year, so I decided years ago to just relax and enjoy it. Let's get out of here before they change their minds."

The men handed over their credit cards and kissed them goodbye, looking quite pleased with themselves.

"This is my first time too," Gianne whispered as they exited the house. "We can be amazed together."

"Merry Christmas, ladies," the driver said as he opened the rear door and took Mrs. Stafford's hand to help her into the car. "My name is Terry, and I'll be your driver for the day." He then offered his hand to Adanna and Gianne. "My schedule says we have two others to pick up, so just get comfortable. There are mimosas in the pitcher on the bar."

Adanna glanced at Gianne. "Is he serious?"

"There's only one way to find out," Gianne lifted the top of a silver pitcher and laughed. "He's serious. Do you want one, Mom?"

"Of course. It'll get me prepared to listen to Mona's explanation of why she's late."

Adanna checked her watch. "She's not late."

"That's why he's been instructed to pick up Cydney first," the elder woman chuckled and sipped her beverage.

Gianne filled two more glasses and, while they rode for a few minutes, Adanna gazed at the ring Charles had placed on her finger last night. Every hour since she'd left Lagos seemed like a dream, and now the idea of returning rubbed her like sandpaper. By Nigerian standards her life there was good, but it didn't compare to the way these women lived. Until now she hadn't even considered how she and Charles would make life together work. At the moment, going back to living in her flat and working a job where she was on her feet all day was about as appealing as changing bedpans.

"Look at her," Mrs. Stafford remarked to Gianne, drawing Adanna from her thoughts. "She's in another world."

"Truthfully," Adanna said, choosing to be open about her feelings. "I was thinking about going back home. I have to, of course, because of the adoption and my job, but I'm not so sure I want to."

"Does Charles know this?"

"Last night we didn't have time to talk about anything much." She'd let Charles tell his mother about their plan to leave early for London.

Gianne regarded her with a serious expression. "Don't you think you'd better get it out into the open now?"

Before Adanna had a chance to answer, the driver stopped the car in front of another traditional brick house that looked similar to the one they had just left.

"Be right back, ladies."

"This is Cydney and Jesse's house?"

"Yes," Mrs. Stafford slid over to make room for her daughter-in-law. "They've been here about three years now."

"Hey, everybody. You don't know how I've been looking forward to this." Cydney slid into the backseat waving over her shoulder at Jesse standing at the front door holding Aria. "So, Adanna, how does it feel to be the newest inductee into the Stafford family?" she said once their driver headed for their next stop.

"A bit surreal. My life in Nigeria is quite ordinary. It's mostly work and very little play. I'm getting quite spoiled."

"This isn't everyday life for us either, girl," Cydney said, brushing her long hair over one shoulder and taking a sip of the mimosa Gianne placed in her hand. "But we do have special occasions every so often, right, Mama?"

Mrs. Stafford agreed. "Every woman needs to treat herself or allow herself to be spoiled sometimes. I remember back when the boys were still in elementary and middle school. There were days I was so tired, all I wanted to do was cry, and many times I did. It's not easy being married to a doctor, especially a young doctor. Their time is not their own, and you're left with the kids, the house, taking care of paying the bills, giving back to the community, and trying to look decent when you do go out to a social function when most of the time you feel like a washed out dishrag."

"I guess I have to be thankful that Marc chose to take a different route. We spend a lot of time together. I know that'll change as his business expands, but I'm loving it right now." Gianne smiled, and Adanna silently admired how her short platinum blonde hair complemented her honey brown skin.

The car soon came to a stop again. Adanna rolled down the window enough to get a glimpse of the huge brick and cut stone house sitting atop a hill on a deep lot. It appeared to have a three car courtyard, and definitely looked like her idea of the kind of home she pictured Ramona living in.

"I'm sorry for being late. I just couldn't get Maite up and moving this morning." Adanna laughed to herself at the speed at which Mona took the glass from Gianne's hand.

"Yes, it must be terrible to have a slow live-in

housekeeper," Cydney said before Adanna had a chance to ask who Maite was, and she'd said it with such a snide chuckle, she had to wonder if Cydney really meant it in jest.

"You have no idea," Mona prattled on oblivious of her sister-in-law's jab. "All I told her to do was to get the kids up and dressed before I had to leave, but she was in the kitchen because Vic wanted *his coffee*."

"He's paying her salary, isn't he?"

"That doesn't have anything to do with it, Mama. I run the house."

Mrs. Stafford rolled her eyes. "Drink your mimosa and calm down. We're getting ready to have a wonderful day."

Following an animated breakfast at a local restaurant and several hours of shopping at Lenox Mall and Phipps Plaza, the women had to force Adanna to use the credit card. She'd only bought small items—an Atlanta souvenir for Femi and something for Lezigha and the two nursing assistants. When she stopped to admire a dress in one of the department stores, they literally dragged her into the dressing room to make her try it on then to the cashier to pay for it.

Next, the driver took them to one of Mrs. Stafford's favorite Buckhead restaurants. The staff knew her by name and welcomed her party with attentive service when she introduced them as her present and future daughters-in-law.

During the meal, Ramona caught her staring at her ring. "Did he get what you wanted?"

"I didn't even know he planned to propose any time soon. It was a complete surprise. Yes, I love it, but it doesn't even compare to yours." She glanced at Ramona's five-carat rock.

"This isn't the original. I upgraded last year for our anniversary and told Vic it was his gift to me."

A weak smile was all Adanna could manage in response.

She could never do something so hurtful to Charles, but maybe Vic didn't care. Charles could always buy her another ring for their twenty-fifth anniversary, but this one was unique and precious.

The conversation around the table enveloped her like a warm blanket. This kind of camaraderie with women in the same family was something she'd never had. The longer they were together, the more she seemed to crave it.

"My sons have chosen very well, and I am so proud to have each one of you in my family," Mrs. Stafford said, making eye contact with them one-by-one. You're so different, and yet each of you brings something special to our family. I think this coming year is going to be the best one yet for the Staffords."

Adanna took a deep breath. "I guess this is a good time to tell everyone that Charles and I probably won't be staying the whole week. Yesterday, after he gave me the ring, he said he wants to go to London to visit my parents. He's checking into changing our flights now."

Gianne appeared dumbstruck. "You're leaving early?"

Adanna hadn't even considered how their abrupt departure would affect Gianne. She'd only had two days with ChiChi. "Charles thinks it would be best to surprise them, but it won't be a pleasure visit. My father and brother are against Charles and me being together because he's not African."

"But he's African-American," Mrs. Stafford innocently insisted.

"Actually, they only want me to marry within the Ibo tribe."

The women's expressions ranged from astonishment to confusion to disbelief. "Why?" Gianne was the first to ask.

"Because it's tradition. Keeping marriage within the tribe

serves to keep the tribe pure and strong. Believe me, it's nothing personal against Charles. They would feel the same way if I wanted to marry a native Kenyan."

"What happens if you go against the tradition?" Ramona asked.

"I won't have my father's blessing on the marriage, and my family won't attend the wedding."

Cydney gave her arm a sympathetic pat. "That's awful."

"I guess I should be straight with you," Adanna said, deciding to come clean with the women. "Charles didn't tell you the whole story about the kidnapping, because he didn't want to embarrass me." She hung her head for a moment, pulled in a strengthening breath. "We believe my brother was behind the kidnapping." Shock registered on Mrs. Stafford's face, but Adanna continued and unveiled the whole sordid story. Once she finished, she heaved a sigh. "It's more my brother than my father. He's just listening to what Emeka has told him."

Ramona finally spoke with her hand touching her neck. "Oh, I've never heard such a romantic real life story. How many men would pay thousands of dollars rather than deny their involvement with a woman? Charles loves you so much he risked bodily harm."

"We believe they were given instructions not to hurt him, but that's not the point," Adanna insisted. "They had no right to do such a despicable thing to him. What makes it even worse is living in a country where this kind of crime is commonplace. It's barbaric."

Mrs. Stafford appeared confused or perhaps a bit stunned. "Are you saying your father knew and approved of what happened?"

"I don't think he knew, but when I told him why I thought Emeka was involved, he automatically refused to believe it."

"How do you feel about going to visit him?"

All she could do was clasp her hands under her chin and squeezed her eyes shut to push back the tears she felt gathering at the back of her eyes. "I don't want to go, but Charles has already made up his mind. We won't have any of our wedding traditions anyway, so it doesn't matter."

"What kind of traditions?" Her future mother-in-law asked.

"Oh, nothing important. Just things that are done as a matter of course."

"Traditions are important, Adanna. Tell us about them."

She gave the ladies an abbreviated version of Ibo engagement and marriage, which included the parents, extended family, and villages. "When a man asks a woman to marry him, if she agrees, the next step is for him and his father to go visit to her house. The future groom's father introduces himself and his son and explains why they have come. The bride's father invites them in, asks his daughter to join them and asks her to confirm that she knows the man. Her saying yes shows that she has already accepted his proposal. Both fathers, along with the village elders, begin their negotiation of the bride price, but outside of remote villages this part is usually symbolic now."

"Do you mean like a dowry the way it used to be in the old days?" Gianne asked.

"Yes, but other than in the villages it's just a figurative gift these days, if it's done at all."

Ramona's horrified expression almost made Adanna laugh. "They have to *buy* you?"

Mrs. Stafford pinned her with a hard stare. "Mona, dowries were the norm in most of the world until the last century, and they are still an important part of the marriage agreement in some cultures today. Let her finish."

Mona rolled her eyes and busied herself with reapplying her lipstick.

"The future groom and his father come back to her home a second time with gifts for the bride's father."

Charles' mother leaned in, appearing fascinated with the details. "What sort of gifts do they bring?"

"Since these traditions began in small villages, it's usually wine and food products. After they share a meal, the bride's price is discussed between the fathers. Once the final bride's price is settled, there is a big feast."

"That sounds glorious." The older woman's eyes twinkled. "I have a question. Do you think it would have any effect if Victor and I went with you to London? It might make everything seem a bit more formal."

Her offer left Adanna momentarily dazed. "You'd do that for us? I'm sure it would make an impression on my parents," Adanna said, recalling her father's suspicions about Charles' marital status. "That would be wonderful."

But will Dr. Stafford feel the same way?" Adanna couldn't imagine Charles' father getting involved in his sons' romantic lives.

"Don't worry about Victor. I can handle him. We just won't mention anything about your brother's suspected involvement in the kidnapping. Just leave it up to me."

"We'll have a little pow-wow when we get back to the house." Mrs. Stafford got their waiter's attention and requested the check.

"Before we go, I just want all of you to know how much this day meant to me. It's just my brother and me. I don't have any sisters, and I live so far away from my parents. Since Emeka and I moved back to Nigeria, this is the first time I've felt as though I belong to a family. These past few days have been great. Thank you so much."

"Personally, I think you'll give this family an upgrade," Ramona added. "With that sophisticated accent, we might have to make you the official family spokesperson."

Mrs. Stafford now seemed to be in a hurry to end their leisurely girls' outing. After she paid the check and called the driver to pick them up at the restaurant. All five women filed back into the limo more introspective than they had been at the day's start. They watched and listened in awe when she called home. "Victor, we're on our way back. Yes, we had a fabulous day. I need to talk to you about something when we get there. Tell Charles not to go anywhere. Everything's fine. We'll talk about it when I get there."

Adanna said an emotional goodbye and exchanged hugs with Cydney and Mona at the next two stops and promised to keep in touch. When they arrived at the house, Mrs. Stafford took Adanna by the hand and headed right for Dr. Stafford's office and asked Greg to send them in. Gianne reassured Adanna that she would look after ChiChi.

"What's going on, Lil?" Dr. Stafford asked as he and Charles entered the office.

"Adanna and Charles need our help, and I think we should give it to them."

Chapter Nineteen

***"D**o you know what this is about?" His father's hand on his shoulder stopped Charles as he glanced at Adanna sitting across from his father's desk bouncing one knee and biting her bottom lip.

"No. I was just about to ask you."

"This will only take a few minutes," his mother said in a cheerful yet determined tone. "During our lunch this afternoon Adanna told us the whole story about the kidnapping and how her father and brother feel about your relationship." His father's eyes narrowed, but he let her continue. "From the way she explained engagement and marriage traditions among her people, I think it might go a long way if your father and I accompany you to meet her parents. Of course, we can't do the whole village feast and all, but we could present them with special gifts and take them somewhere nice for a celebration dinner."

Amazed by his mother's grace and compassion, Charles smiled. "Mama, that's a wonderful offer, but I already booked a flight for tomorrow."

She glanced at both men. "Since your father had the foresight to take the entire week off for Christmas, maybe you can get us a later flight. What do you think, Victor?"

"I'm still back at *the whole story about the kidnapping*. Will one of you please explain what that means? Why the hell wouldn't her father and her brother accept Charles? He's a doctor, for God's sake!"

Adanna hurried to explain. "Dr. Stafford, it has nothing to

do with Charles personally. Like many people in my country, they believe I should only marry a man from within our tribe. I don't believe I'm bound by those old traditions, and that has put a wedge between my brother, my father, and me."

"What. About. The. Kidnapping?" his father demanded, glaring at his son.

Charles threw up his hands and admitted to his and Adanna's suspicions, being careful to stress more than once that they had no actual proof of Emeka's involvement.

His father stared at his mother as though she'd lost her last thread of good sense. "And you want me to pay for plane tickets and buy gifts for a man who doesn't consider my son good enough for his daughter?"

"That's not what he thinks, Victor. It's a traditional issue, not a personal one, but if we approach her parents with some semblance of formality, it would go a long way in changing their attitudes." She smiled. "We haven't been to London in a decade. And you know what they say about catching more flies with honey than with vinegar."

He ran a hand over his short gray hair, then drummed his fingers on the desktop. "Adanna, how does your mother feel about you and Charles?"

"Actually, I haven't spoken to her about it. My mother is very old school. She believes it's her place to agree with my father no matter how she feels personally."

"Humph," he said, gazing at his wife with a chuckle. "That's an interesting concept. What time does your flight leave?" He looked as though he'd already made a decision.

"Tomorrow evening around five," Charles answered.

His father shook his head. "You know your mother is crazy, right? See if you can book us a flight to get there as close to your arrival as possible. We'll need a hotel for two nights."

"I've booked us at the Intercontinental, because it's only about fifteen minutes from where her parents live. Is that okay?"

"Talk to your mother about that," he said with a wave of phony disgust.

"We're not going to visit them until you and Mama get there. It's best if we present a united front."

"You don't know my father," Adanna said weakly. "He can be very stubborn."

Charles snorted. "So can mine."

His mother stood, walked behind the desk, and planted a kiss on his father's forehead. "Thank you, honey." She took Adanna by the hand. "Let's go to the kitchen, make some tea, and talk about the gifts."

"Damn women," the older man said with a good-natured grumble. "I don't know what makes it so hard to say no to them."

"I never had trouble saying no to women until Adanna. That's how I know she's the one. I want to say yes to everything she asks me. Let's hope this visit makes a difference. It would make her so happy if she had her father's blessing. Guess I'd better get on the phone with the travel agent. I'll let you know what I find out." He walked toward the door, turned around and said, "I know you didn't plan on traveling this week. Thanks for doing this for us."

Not one for outward displays of emotion, the older man simply nodded.

Charles breathed a sigh of relief after he'd made flight and hotel arrangements for his parents then went in search of his brothers. If this was going to be his last night in Atlanta, he wanted to spend it with them. He found Marc and Greg lounging in the family room watching a movie and waited for a commercial to tell them what was happening.

"How about we go out for dinner and drinks tonight? I'll call Jesse and you two can see if Vic and Nick are free tonight."

"I'll call Jesse," Marc suggested much to Charles' surprise.

"What happened with you two on Christmas Day?"

"For some reason, Jess said he wanted to bury the hatchet," Marc explained. "He didn't go into any detail. He just said we're getting too old to carry grudges. I never had a grudge against him to begin with, but I wasn't going to argue with him. We shook on it, and that was the end."

Greg scowled. "Seriously? I wonder what's going on with him."

"Maybe he finally decided to grow up," Charles said with a chuckle. "Okay, let's see if we can get something together for tonight. Where do you guys want to go?"

"Magic City," Greg answered without hesitation. "I haven't been there in years."

Charles winced. "Not Magic City. I hear Cheetah has better food."

"What's wrong with you, man? Nobody goes there for the food."

"I don't care. We can take a vote when we get into the car."

By the time all of the brothers arrived at the house that evening, Greg had used his powers of persuasion to rally them to his choice, and a half-hour later the six of them filed out of Jesse's SUV into Magic City's parking lot.

They had only settled in at a table and started their first round of drinks when one of the dancers came up to

Charles. "Doctor Stafford? I'd heard you left Atlanta and moved to Las Vegas. You probably don't remember me, Onnika Stewart."

"Hello, Onnika. Yes, I remember you," he lied. After you performed hundreds of breast enlargements, one pair looked just like the others. "I did move to Vegas. I'm in town for the holiday. How are you?"

"I'm doing okay. And these are still doing the trick." His brothers' eyes popped when she lifted her double Ds covered only by star-shaped pasties in both hands and jiggled them.

"Glad I could be of service." He waited until she walked away. "See, this is why I didn't want to come to Magic City. I've done procedures on at least a dozen of their dancers."

"Maybe I *should* consider going into plastics," Nick said with a sly grin.

Greg pulled out his wallet. "In that case, they need to give us a volume discount. Let's get this party started. I'm going to find the ATM."

What Charles really wanted at the moment was something to eat. He got the attention of one of the servers and he and Marc ordered an assortment of food. By the time Greg returned, Nick had summoned two strippers for private lap dances. One of them was thin, flat-chested, and covered from neck to ankle with tattoos. She had nothing to jiggle, and just looking at her made Charles itch. Her skin reminded him of some kind of snake, but for some reason, his baby brother was intrigued. The other woman was prettier and had a fuller figure and a much more voluptuous derrière. If he donated to anyone's college fund tonight, it would be hers.

Greg yelled above the music. "What's the matter, Charles? This used to be one of your favorite pastimes."

"Hey, you picked this place. I just wanted to hang with my brothers tonight."

"And since I know what an *ass man* you are," Greg announced. "I asked Gorgeous here if she'd dance for you." All of the brothers shouted their agreement. "Assume the position, man."

Charles relaxed, dropped his arms down over the sides of the chair, and grinned as the dancer sauntered toward him. The funny thing was, as his eyes took in her mouthwatering curves, his mind imagined Adanna doing the tempting performance for him. It had been months since he'd had sex with anyone, and that was the problem. He didn't just want *anyone*. He wanted Adanna. By the time her dance ended, he was visibly worked up, much to the hilarity of his brothers who were showering singles all over the now completely nude performer. He reached into his pocket, took out a twenty, and pressed it into her hand.

After she was no longer in their midst, Greg said, "If you want her to keep you company, I can find out if she's willing."

"No thanks. I wasn't aware we were having a bachelor party tonight. I just got engaged twenty-four hours ago."

"To be honest with you," Marc chimed in. "You're looking pretty tense, like you're in desperate need of some stress relief. And bunking together at Mama and Daddy's house isn't helping the situation."

"I have other things on my mind. Adanna and I are leaving tomorrow for London. It'll be our first night alone together, and I'm going to make it happen."

Greg's jaw dropped, and he glanced around at his brothers as though asking for confirmation of what he'd just heard. "Are you saying after all these months you never gave her the bone?"

Charles reluctantly shook his head. "Our living arrangements haven't exactly been conducive to doing the slap and tickle."

"No wonder you look so drawn," Vic said with a loud laugh. "Are you sure you don't want Greg to work out something for you?"

Charles gave the ceiling an extended glance. "No. I'm good."

"Well, I've made my own arrangements. You're welcome to join us and make it a foursome." Greg rose and headed toward the VIP rooms as though he'd just given something as bland as the weather report.

Vic's laugh bellowed above Jason Derullo and Two Chains blasting from the sound system. "He's always been such a clown."

"He's not kidding. When I stayed with him, I noticed a few things, but I wasn't going to mention it to anyone."

Jesse and Vic exchanged a curious glance. "A few things like what?" Jesse asked, dragging his chair closer.

"While I was in New York for my orientation, I'd hoped to spend some time just catching up with him, but he had other plans. It seems like he hits the clubs every night."

"What's so bad about that?"

"There's nothing wrong with that per se, Nick, but he brings home strange women. The second night I was there he had two of them. "He didn't even remember one of their names, but he offered me one of them like she was an extra bag of fries or something. He's out of control, if you ask me."

Vic looked dumbfounded. "Greg just picked them up in the club? He didn't know them at all? Damn. Raised in a houseful of doctors, you'd think he'd know better than taking stupid health risks." He stroked his forehead. "Did you say anything to him about it?"

"I didn't want to get into it with him, so I just left early," Charles said. "I spend more money changing flights than I do flying."

"Let's give him twenty minutes, and then one of us needs to go get him."

Charles reared back in his seat. "Are you volunteering, Vic?"

"Yeah, I'll go get him."

"Don't any of you tell him what I said," Charles warned. "He's leaving in a couple of hours, so let's keep it on the DL for this visit."

The brothers murmured their reticent agreement. Jesse ordered more drinks, and they all looked relieved when Greg returned flushed and grinning before they finished the round. Later that evening, they said goodbye to him as he left and headed back to the airport, none of them breathing a word to him about their discussion.

Charles valued the rare time spent with his brothers. Before he'd moved from Atlanta, he, Nick, Jesse, and Vic got together at least once a month. Now they might see each other two or three times a year. The bond they shared was unique, and as they got older, their connection had become stronger. Now Greg seemed to be in a crisis, and they needed to come up with a way to address it.

Vic and Jesse had gone home directly from the club. Charles went in search of Adanna and found her upstairs with Gianne. "Am I interrupting anything?"

"Hi." She smiled, and his chest filled with that familiar warmth he'd gotten every time he saw her. "No, we were just talking about the adoption procedures."

Even from the doorway, he saw the sadness in Gianne's eyes. "I hate that you have to leave so soon. Marc and I were just getting to know ChiChi."

He rested a hand on her shoulder. "I know. I'm really sorry about this, but with our schedules, going to London this week was our best option."

"We understand. I hope everything works out with Adanna's parents."

"Family stuff can work your nerves," Marc said from the doorway. "I know better than most people." He snickered, came into the room, and sat beside Gianne on the bed. "You just let your people know the Stafford tribe is something to be reckoned with, and if they refuse to let you join our family, we might have to come over there and kick a few asses." He sobered. "Listen, Adanna. We can't tell you how much we love you for trying to do this for us, and we're ready to do whatever is necessary to make ChiChi ours."

"I love you and Gianne too. This week has been unbelievable. It's so wonderful to feel like part of a family. As soon as we get back to Nigeria, I plan to file the paperwork, and I'll let you know every detail."

"I made reservations at the Intercontinental Hotel Westminster. Mama and Daddy will be staying there too." From the corner of his eye, Charles saw Adanna whirl around.

"Why did you pick that hotel? Couldn't you find someplace more reasonable?"

"It's new, and if it's comparable to the one in Atlanta, that's just what I want."

Before he and Marc left the ones they really wanted to spend the night with, they kissed them goodnight and retired to their old room. Just like they'd done back in the days when they had shared the room, the twins stripped down to their underwear, stretched out on the extra-long twin beds, and turned on the television and watched silently until Marc asked, "Are you thinking about meeting her parents?"

"Yeah. Not as much as I'm thinking about us spending the night together. It probably would have been a better idea to spend extra money and book a suite so we could put ChiChi's crib in the outer room, but it's too late to worry about that now."

"Don't let that baby see anything that might scar her for life, or Gianne and I will have to deal with it for the next eighteen years."

Charles howled. "Since we left Lagos, I've been spending money like a madman. I need to put on the brakes. It's not like it used to be when I could count on doing a dozen breast augmentations and lipos the next week to pay for all the flight changes, gifts, and hotel rooms. Dipping into my savings makes me nervous."

"Other than your cars, you've never gone overboard with spending. You didn't cash in your investments, did you?"

"Hell no, man. Those are part of my retirement fund, and as Daddy never failed to remind us, not to be touched."

"Just making sure you hadn't lost your mind."

"Afraid you're too late, man. It's amazing how the right woman can make a man open his heart and his wallet without giving it a second thought."

♥

Adanna put ChiChi down for the night, then emptied the dresser drawers and closet. While she folded their clothes and placed each item in their suitcases, she went over the events of the past few days. It suddenly occurred to her that she hadn't even thought about work since they landed in Atlanta. Was that a good or a bad sign? The only reason she'd returned to Nigeria had been to use her nursing skills on behalf of her people, but now the idea of living elsewhere was starting to appeal to her.

While the men were out together, Mrs. Stafford had asked a few personal questions about her parents so she and Dr. Stafford could present them with the proper gifts. Adanna gave her a crash course in Nigerian customs for introductions and even printed out something from the Internet. Although she had grown up with these customs, trying to explain them to an outsider in some respects seemed almost silly.

What filled her thoughts even more than the encounter between their parents was the encounter awaiting her and the man she loved. It hadn't been easy trying to show him how much she wanted him without coming across as desperate and sex-starved, which she was. If they got their opportunity, she wanted her desire for him to be unquestionable. Before they had left Nigeria, she had bought a few sets of sexy underwear and one teddy in hopes that the opportunity to wear them might present itself during their trip. As she folded them and placed the lacy, yet unworn items back into her suitcase, she closed her eyes and imagined Charles admiring the lingerie on her body then slowly removing it. All of her life Adanna had been taught that such intimacies should not happen until after the wedding, but she knew she couldn't wait any longer. Rather…she wouldn't.

No one in the house rose early the next morning, and by the time they had all showered and dressed, it was close to noon. Following a late brunch, she and Charles left ChiChi with Marc and Gianne while they made one last run to the store for milk, nappies and a few incidentals. When they returned, she and Charles thanked his parents, and the men watched the women share a tearful goodbye.

For most of the flight to London, she, Charles and ChiChi slept. They landed at Heathrow the next morning and took a cab to the hotel. To their bodies, it was actually after midnight Eastern Standard time, but it didn't matter how jet lagged they were. Their first night in London was also their one and only night alone. Dr. and Mrs. Stafford were arriving the following morning.

A bellman accompanied them to the room with their luggage. He briefly described the amenities available in the modern executive room. Adanna's gaze took in the room decorated in soothing tones of taupe, cream, and wood finishes and zoomed in on the huge king-size bed with its ceiling-high padded headboard.

Charles tipped the bellman then walked over to the window high above the city and stared out at the London skyline.

"What are you thinking?" Adanna asked, coming up behind him and wrapping her arms around his waist.

"It's not a very pretty place."

"Not unless you appreciate old architecture and chilly weather. But who cares about the scenery?" She hugged him tighter, determined to let him know what was on her mind.

He turned to face her. "You're right. Why don't you get ChiChi straight so we can go downstairs and find something to eat. We can shower and unpack later." While she did that, he took ChiChi's still frozen bottles from the cooler bag inside his suitcase, and placed them in the small refrigerator. After he checked to see what kind of coffee the hotel had provided, he rolled the crib from beside the bed to a small alcove between the bedroom and the bathroom.

The lounge offered a light lunch, and once Adanna allowed ChiChi to munch on a few chips, she finished her bottle and her head began to loll to one side. "It's time for her nap."

Charles left cash on the table to cover the bill and they took the lift back to their room. He opened the door, immediately walked over to the window to pull the drapes so the light wouldn't wake the baby. ChiChi was already out cold. Adanna busied herself with putting her into the crib, removing her little shoes and covering her with a blanket, yet she sensed Charles' movement behind her. He'd turned on the sound system, but kept the music at a low volume. Maybe it was just her nerves or her imagination, but he appeared to be moving in slow motion. ChiChi's afternoon nap normally lasted about two hours, and precious minutes were slipping away. Charles removed his coat, and laid it over the back of a chair. He took off his shoes and sat at the end of the small sofa as though he were intentionally avoiding the bed. Finally, after what seemed like an interminably long silence between them, he took her hand. "Let's take a shower."

She grasped the hem of her top to pull it over her head. "No. Let me." He slipped his soft, hot hands under the fabric onto her bare skin, and the glorious sensation made her arch into him. Adanna raised her arms so he could pull her top over her head, and she did the same to him. He'd told her more than once that red was her best color, so she had purposely worn the new red bra and panties in anticipation of whatever the evening might hold. The way his gaze caressed her body confirmed that she'd made the right choice.

"You have the most beautiful skin I've ever seen," he whispered against her neck, leaving a trail of hot kisses down to her cleavage. The tips of his fingers outlined the scalloped edge of her bra, and when they reached the clasp worked nimbly to release the abundance it held. Charles filled his hands and murmured something she didn't understand. Her knees weakened when he lowered his head, took one nipple into his mouth, and teased it with his tongue until it grew hard. To keep her from losing her balance, he drew her closer with one arm, then treated the other breast to the same gentle attention. Taking two steps forward, he moved her closer to the bed, knelt before her, and unbuttoned her slacks. Mesmerized by his gentle yet masterful attention, Adanna leaned back on her elbows so he could slide her slacks and panties over her hips. Now all she wore were trouser socks, which he rolled down her calves and replaced with soft kisses. For a moment, she didn't move, didn't breathe.

"I've been thinking about this," he said between ragged breaths, "since that first day I saw you at the hospital."

"So have I," Adanna ran her hands down his back and around to his belt buckle. "But I never imagined we'd be here." Her fingers fumbled with it for a moment before he worked the buckle loose and unzipped his pants. Her hands shook as she made the first move and slid a hand inside the open zipper. What she found sent a surge of passion through her so strong all she could do was wrap her hand around him and squeeze. She tried not to think about the fact that her hand just barely closed around the throbbing organ in her fist.

"Oh, God," he groaned. "Let's get into the shower or we might not make it back to the bed."

He stepped out of his pants and the boxer briefs that hugged his body as though they'd been painted on and left them in a pile on the floor. He turned on the warm water, lowered his head to her breasts. Her nipples peaked at the softness of his lips and the gentle caress of his tongue as he paid homage. When he raised his head and brought his lips to her mouth, she held his whiskered face between her hands and looked up into those eyes. Eyes that had the power to hypnotize her. Adanna dove into their olive depths and let herself go. That was the moment she knew something had changed. This kiss tasted of his need and how much he'd been holding back all these months.

Their gazes met, time kicked into fast forward, and they were in the shower soaping each other's bodies in a feverish rush. The instant the lather rinsed away, Charles wrapped her in a towel from the rack and lifted her in his arms and carried her back to the bed.

Charles kissed his way up the inside of one leg and down the other. Lost in the sensation, she threaded her hands into his hair, whimpered, and then let her thighs fall open. His tongue stroked her center until she lifted her hips from the mattress, her moans becoming louder.

He shimmied up her body and covered her mouth with his. "Shh…you're going to wake ChiChi."

When she reached for him again, he pressed his body against her so she could only caress his arms, back, and butt. She knew he was ready, but was taking his time to ensure that she was also. His long, talented fingers reached deep inside her this time and her hips met his strokes beat for beat. Finally, her head fell back and her mouth dropped open.

Charles withdrew just long enough to cover himself with a condom then spread her knees wider. Adanna uttered a passionate hiss when he replaced his slick fingers with his weighty erection. She threw her arms around his neck and moved against him in a frantic rhythm.

"You feel so good," he whispered between ragged breaths. "I want to stay in this bed with you for the rest of my life."

The only word she managed to utter was his name, and as she repeated it, it seemed to send him into the stratosphere. Charles hooked one of her legs around his hip, and pulled her into him, the depth of his penetration bringing a scream of pleasure from the depths of her soul. He covered her mouth with his hand, and had to bury his face in her neck as the intensity of her orgasm brought him right along with her. With a long growl, he rode the waves of pleasure with her and tried not to wake the baby sleeping six feet away.

Adanna cuddled her cheek against his chest as their breathing slowed. He held her as though he was afraid she'd try to get up and leave him in the bed alone, but that was the farthest thing from her mind. No man had ever made love to her like this. In fact, it was clear to her that what she'd known before wasn't making love at all. Her rather limited experience with men had been disappointing to say the least. If anyone asked her, she would've said Nigerian men had rightfully earned the stereotype of being selfish and concerned more with their own pleasure. And many still bragged about their aversion to oral sex, but that was just another side effect of living in a male-dominated society. Even the men who didn't want to admit it still believed somewhere in the recesses of their minds that women were put on this earth to satisfy their needs.

She couldn't resist lifting her hand just enough to gaze at the diamond on her fourth finger. Finally, she had what she'd been waiting for.

Chapter Twenty

Charles smiled at the way Adanna pulled the sheet up to cover her breasts, as if the six-month old knew what they'd been doing. She sat up and spoke to the baby in a soothing voice reassuring her that she and Charles' were right there. His gaze followed her while she slipped from beneath the covers and searched for her clothes.

"Where are my panties?" she asked, looking under the bed on her knees.

"You don't need panties." He gave her a salacious grin. "All you have to do is change hers, and she'll be happy."

"Stop it, Charles." Adanna picked up the still damp towel from the floor and wrapped it around herself.

He snickered, settled back into the pillows with his hands behind his head, closed his eyes, and replayed their first encounter. Every minute of their sexual experience had exceeded what he'd imagined. And he had a vivid imagination. The way Adanna had responded to him had done wonders for his ego, but he was still concerned he might have allowed his hunger for her to overrule his restraint. He hadn't exactly taken things slowly. Just seeing her beautiful body had torn away every shred of his self-control. A few hours from now ChiChi would be ready to go back to sleep and their pseudo-parenting would be over for the night. He couldn't wait to make up for whatever he'd failed to do earlier.

Tomorrow they would be walking into one of the most stressful situations he'd had to face since taking his Board exams, so he had all intentions of making their evening both soothing and satisfying. And there was no telling when Adanna would be able to take another vacation. He certainly didn't look forward to returning to their shared apartments.

Adanna carried ChiChi to the bed and plopped her down on top of the covers. "All changed and dry. Keep an eye on her while I find the rest of my clothes and fix her bottle."

He sat up against the headboard and fluffed a couple of pillows behind his back. "I hope she doesn't realize I'm naked under here," he said, peering beneath the covers and sending her a teasing wink.

"Good morning, Princess. Did you have a good time with Marc and Gianne?" The baby cooed and smiled at him as though she knew exactly what he was saying. "I'm sorry we had to take you away so soon." He stroked her curly head.

"Ah, here are my panties. How did they get all the way over on this side of the room?"

"I guess I was in a hurry."

"Yes, you were." Adanna dragged the crib back into the bedroom, turned on the television and scanned the channels until she found a twenty-four-hour children's network. She put ChiChi back into the crib with her bottle, angled her body so she could see the screen, and crawled back under the sheets with him.

"I hope I wasn't in too much of a hurry." He sent her a questioning gaze.

She cupped his face between her hands. "Did you hear me complain–even a little bit?"

"No, ma'am. You were quite noisy, but it didn't sound like complaining to me. In fact, later on tonight we can do whatever you might've wanted but didn't get."

She gawked at him. "It was better than I imagined, and

that's saying something!"

Charles smiled. "Oh, so you imagined it was going to be great?"

"I certainly did." She snuggled close to him, fit one leg between his, and he hardened instantly at the contact.

"Don't start something you can't finish, girl. When she's done with her bottle, let's find a couple of movies to watch. After that, maybe we can order room service for dinner."

"That sounds lovely." Adanna rubbed her cheek against his chest.

Tonight couldn't come fast enough for him.

He and Adanna spent the early evening teaching ChiChi how to play with a couple of the many toys she'd received for Christmas while they watched a movie. The baby was getting older and more adept with her motor skills. She also stayed awake longer between naps. Adanna took a few pictures of the baby happily playing with the ones Marc and Gianne had given her and sent them to Gianne's phone. The family had been so generous, it was necessary for them to confiscate an extra suitcase from his mother just to hold the gifts.

Charles ordered dinner from the Blue Boar Smokehouse in the hotel, got his first taste of British barbeque, which didn't quite meet up to the standard of his southern taste buds. After they ate, Adanna took ChiChi into the bathroom and gave her a bath in the big tub. When he moved the crib back into the alcove for the night, he heard her talking to the baby. "In the morning we're going to visit my parents. This doesn't have much to do with you, but I just wanted to warn you anyway. No matter what you see or hear, just smile and ignore it." She lotioned and powdered her in the middle of the bed, dressed her in her pajamas, and put her back into the crib for the night.

"You're nervous, aren't you?" he asked while he watched her fiddle around with ChiChi's clothes for their visit the next morning. She changed her mind about the outfit three times.

"Yes, I am."

"My parents will be here early. After they eat breakfast and freshen up, we can go and get it over with. Until then, let's just forget about what we have to do tomorrow."

A knock interrupted him, and when he got up to answer the door, he noticed ChiChi's head peeking up in response to the noise. "Go to sleep, Princess. It's grown-up time now."

"Who could that be?"

"Room service. I ordered a little treat for us tonight."

"We just ate. What are you trying to do to me?"

Charles opened the door, took the cart from the hotel employee, and handed him a tip. "Trying to get you to relax. It's just wine and something sweet." He rolled the cart over by the windows, used the corkscrew to open the bottle, and filled one of the crystal flutes. "Try this."

Adanna took the glass from his hand and took a sip. "It's delicious."

"Good. Sit down on the bed and sip it slowly." Charles poured himself a glass and peeked in the alcove to make sure ChiChi was asleep before he followed her to the bed. This time he had to tamp down his earlier frenzy and concentrate on Adanna. He didn't want it to be trivial to her. He wanted her to feel it with every bit of her emotions. Every move he made and every word he spoke needed to be meaningful to her tonight.

She sat on the edge of the bed, staring into her wine glass. Charles eased down on the bed beside her, placed his open palm on her back and moved it in a slow circle. "Don't worry about tomorrow, baby. I know you want it to go well, but regardless of how it goes, no one can stop me from marrying you." He enveloped her in his arms, and the softness of her breasts against his chest sent a wave of desire through him. All he wanted to do was devour her, but tonight was her night. He took the wine glass from her hand, raised her chin, and touched her mouth with a kiss as soft as a whisper, then leaned her back onto the bed never taking his mouth from hers. The tension in her body eased as he kissed his way over her chin, down her neck, stopping only to remove her blouse. Tonight she wore a white satiny bra that contrasted perfectly against her skin. Not wanting to rush, he took his time kissing her breasts through the slippery fabric and grasping her erect nipples between his teeth. The breathy sounds she made only spurred him on, and her sharp intake of breath when he let his hand brush over the sensitive spot between her thighs only made it harder for him to maintain the unhurried pace.

Charles had no idea when they would get this chance again once they returned to Nigeria. If only they had more time together. He slipped his hands under her bottom, squeezing both cheeks of her magnificent booty and flipped her over so she was on top of him. His hands urged her against him until their hips were grinding in a slow precise tempo. Adanna responded with a moan, her heart pounding against his chest. Their kisses, now exploring and ravenous, drove him to accomplish his only goal at that moment—to get her out of those slacks so there were no boundaries between them. Willing himself to slow his pace, he rolled onto his side taking her with him. First he unhooked the satin confining her breasts, then concentrated on the buttons of her pants and had to get up on his knees in order to wriggle them over her legs.

"Tell me what you want," he whispered against her open mouth when he laid back down beside her and ran his hands over her velvety skin.

"I just want to feel you inside me. Fill me the way you did this afternoon." She grabbed his shoulders and pulled him as though she was trying to meld his whole body with hers.

"My pleasure," he said, turning her over once more until she was on her knees. He put one of the fluffy pillows under her head and knelt behind her. In order to bring her hips back against him, he put one arm around her waist and used that hand to caress the swollen spot between her legs. There was no other softness like this on earth. He murmured his adoration for her body and stroked her until she was slick. Adanna's body trembled and her knees went weak, and he stopped just long enough to put on a condom, which he'd deposited in the night table earlier.

Charles had learned concentration and focus as a surgeon, but in this situation, as her slippery folds received him all of that went right out of the window. It was impossible for him to maintain restraint any longer. He sunk himself to the hilt with a visceral growl and pumped his hips in time to Adanna's mewling sighs. As he reached around and took her breasts in both hands, he went deeper feeling every dip and groove within her. The room filled with her low-throated scream when he hit her spot. She seemed to go into another realm shouting words he didn't understand. They could've been in her native tongue or merely words of passion. It didn't matter, because the sound of them took him right to heaven. He muffled his shouts of release against her back then collapsed onto his side and held her tight while he waited for both of them to stop trembling.

They lay in the flickering light of the television enjoying the afterglow until Adanna said, "Promise to keep doing that, and I'll never leave you."

He laughed. "Is that all?"

"Yes, unless you have more surprises like that for me."

"I have all kinds of surprises for you, girl."

"I can't wait."

She didn't have to wait long. They slept for a short time, and he woke her once during the night for more fun and games.

By the time the phone rang with the wake-up call Charles had requested, ChiChi had already awakened them with her happy morning chatter. His parents would be arriving shortly. Not long after he and Adanna finished showering, his cell rang. His parents had checked in. They wanted to eat breakfast and talk about the plan for the day. Adanna dressed the baby in another of her new outfits from Marc and Gianne, and they met his mother and father in the Lobby Lounge. It was already mid-morning. They ordered coffee and pastries, and Charles started the discussion.

"Adanna says it's best if I do the talking when we first get there, then turn it over to Dad," he explained. "She thinks it's best if the women don't say much."

"I found some lovely gifts for them. When should we present them?" his mother asked.

"Once the introductions are done, but before we enter the house. I want to call before we leave." Adanna took out her cell, dialed, and waited. "Mum, it's me. I just wanted to know if Dad was there."

"Yes, he's here. Do you want to speak to him?"

"Not right now. I'm here in London, and we'll be there in about twenty minutes. See you soon." She hung up before her mother could respond.

Charles had never seen his parents so out of their element. If there was one thing Victor and Lillian Stafford were known for in Atlanta, it was handling social events appropriately. This visit would prove to be a learning experience for everyone concerned.

All five of them piled into a taxi the hotel concierge has secured. Adanna instructed the cabbie to the destination on Hollydale Road in Peckham. The short ride brought them to an area of the city that was experiencing gentrification. Cafes, delis, wine bars, galleries, African food stores, and market sellers lined the streets of what had become a vibrant, multicultural neighborhood. Dr. and Mrs. Stafford seemed to enjoy viewing the eclectic Georgian, Victorian, Edwardian, post-war, and contemporary architecture as they rode through the quiet streets of the three sections of Peckham.

When the driver stopped in front of a quaint cottage, Mrs. Stafford breathed an admiring sigh. "Is this your parents' house?"

Adanna nodded with a tremulous smile and sucked in a long breath. "I'll go in front." She stepped out of the taxi. Charles handed her the baby, paid the driver, and walked beside her carrying the infant seat. His parents exited the car with their arms full of beautifully-wrapped gifts.

Adanna used the heavy doorknocker to announce their arrival. Within a matter of seconds, a slender, dark-skinned woman opened the door. This had to be her mother. They had the same hourglass figure.

"Hi, Mum," Adanna said. "I'm sorry for the short…"

Her mother stared at ChiChi, threw her arms in the air and screamed, "Ewo! Ewo! Ọ nọ n'nsogbu!"

"Mum, jikonata onwe gi!" She said, basically telling her wailing mother to get a grip. "I am not in trouble."

A portly man veered around the corner into the foyer at a run. "What is it?"

Her mother pointed to the baby and repeated, "Ọ nọ

n'nsogbu!"

"Le m anya n'iru," her father said with fire in his eyes. "Gwa onye ọbụna ezi okwu!"

"For God's sake! I *am* looking in your face, and I *am* telling the truth!" Adanna shouted over the commotion. "Will you two please speak English?"

Charles squeezed her shoulder and stepped in front of her. "Deacon and Mrs. Okoro," he said, remembering Adanna telling him that Nigerians preferred being addressed by their professional or honorific title until they felt comfortable being on a first name basis. "Please calm down. This is *not* Adanna's baby. She was a patient, and she was abandoned at our hospital. Your daughter took it upon herself to care for her. I'm Dr. Charles Stafford, Adanna's fiancé, and these are my parents." He extended his hand to the man who studied him for a moment then reluctantly clasped it in return. "First of all," Charles continued, "I want to apologize for the surprise visit and wish you a Merry Christmas. I take it you are both well."

"Merry Christmas to you as well." He directed his gaze past Charles to Dr. and Mrs. Stafford.

Dr. Stafford stepped forward. "Deacon Okoro, I am Dr. Victor Stafford, and this is my wife, Lillian. It's an honor to meet you." He reached out and Adanna's father grasped his hand. After a vigorous shake, his father offered the wrapped gifts with both hands. Mr. Okoro accepted them with a smile.

"Dad, can we come in?" Adanna asked, looking embarrassed that they were still standing outside on the walkway.

"Forgive me. Please come in. This is my wife, Jelani."

"Let me take your coats," she offered once they were inside.

"Pleased to meet you." Mrs. Stafford smiled and handed her the bouquet of flowers she'd bought at the hotel gift shop on the way and a gift-wrapped box.

They followed her father into a cozy living room where a fire burned inside a small stone fireplace. "Please, sit." But no one sat until he did.

"Deacon Okoro, my father came here from the United States to talk with you."

Dr. Stafford leaned forward and clasped his hands together and kept his gaze indirect. "My son asked me to come here to properly ask for your daughter in marriage. I understand you have reservations, and I'd like to talk about them."

"It might be best for us to discuss this in private," he said, looking from Charles to his father. Mrs. Stafford, Adanna and her mother all seemed to hold their breath.

"I'll make some tea. Adanna, will you and Mrs. Stafford join me in the dining room?"

Her father nodded and the women reluctantly left the room.

♥

"Now," Adanna's mother said when they entered the dining room, "may I please hug my daughter?"

She put the baby on her hip and hooked the other arm around her mother's shoulders. "I've missed you, Mum."

"I've missed you too, Adanna. You two sit while I put on water for our tea and open my gift."

"You might want to open that first," Mrs. Stafford said.

"All right, if you insist." She sat at the end of the table and worked on removing the gift wrap.

Adanna took a seat next to her mother with ChiChi on her lap and glanced around the dining room where she had shared a decade of dinners with her family. The walls were now a soothing blue instead of the bland beige they had been when she still lived there.

The rustling of the paper held the baby's attention, and she observed like a guest at a bridal shower. When the shiny paper fell to the floor, her mother lifted the top of the box and opened the tissue inside. She lifted an angular polished stainless steel tea kettle from the box. The mahogany handle and whistle were shaped like a dolphin. "Ooh," she breathed. "It's an Alessi designer kettle. How beautiful. Thank you, Mrs. Stafford."

"I'm so glad you like it. And I'd like if you call me Lillian."

"Lillian. I'm going to rinse this out to heat the water, and when I get back I'd like to know more about Chichima."

Charles' mother must have searched all over for just the right gift. And judging by the gleam in her mother's eyes, she'd found it.

While the men were still sequestered in the front room, the women shared tea and biscuits, and Adanna told her mother the story of how ChiChi came to them. She also told her about Gianne and Marc and the adoption plans. Her mother extended her arms, and the baby went right to her.

Much to Adanna's surprise, she said, "You're doing a wonderful thing, Adanna. God will bless you for your kindness."

"Thank you, Mum. She had no one. Her mother threw her away. I couldn't let that happen to her." Almost absentmindedly, she gazed toward the front room. "What do you think is going on in there?"

"I assume Charles' father is telling your father why his son would make you a proper husband. Your father will probably ask lots of questions."

"It's wonderful that your other son wants to adopt the baby; then you will have a grandchild."

Mrs. Stafford smiled. "Charles and Marcus are only two of my sons. I have six, and between them there are five grandchildren."

"Oh, how wonderful! Neither of my children are married, so we have no grandchildren yet."

"Well, Mum. Charles says he wants at least three, so pray that everything goes well in there."

"Adanna's name means *father's daughter*," her mother said to Mrs. Stafford in a thoughtful tone. "And he has always been very protective of her. He wants what he believes is best for Adanna, and he meant no disrespect to your son."

"I understand," Lillian answered looking her mother in the eye. "Since I only have sons, I've never been on the other side of the issue. Parents seem to be more concerned about their girls, and I guess rightfully so. This is a harsh world we live in, and so often the results of a mistake weigh harder on the woman."

"So true," she agreed, handing ChiChi back to Adanna and refilling their tea cups. "Can she eat this?" she asked, holding one of the semi-sweet tea biscuits.

"Yes, but she makes a terrible mess." Adanna blinked at what her mother said next.

"Adanna is a strong woman. She's smart and has always had her own mind, and she fought to return to Nigeria against her father's wishes. The only way he would agree to her return was if her brother went with her, but I knew she would have been just fine on her own."

This was the first time Adanna had heard how her mother

truly felt about the issue. At the time, she hadn't said a word to back Adanna's decision. Shocked, she looked at the woman who had raised her and felt sorry for her. To be married to a man and not be able to speak your mind was the most stifling thing Adanna could imagine. "Thank you, Mum. It means a lot to hear you say that."

Heavy footsteps approached the dining room, and her father stood in the doorway. "Adanna, you need to join us."

She glanced at the older women, and Mrs. Stafford took the baby from her arms. "Go ahead, sweetie. We'll wait for you here."

Adanna followed him in the front room where it appeared that he'd put more wood on the fire. The gift Dr. Stafford had brought was open on the table and a glass sat in front of each man.

"Would you like some wine?" Charles asked as she sat next to him.

He appeared calm, but she couldn't read anything into his expression. "Thank you,"

He poured and put the glass into her quivering hand. She grasped the stem with both hands hoping her nervousness wasn't too apparent.

"Adanna," her father began, "you know how I have felt about you one day marrying. I had always hoped your union would be with a man from among our own tribe." He paused. "What was just as important to me was that whoever the man was, he would treat you with respect, be able to provide for you financially, and also to be able to give you children."

She nodded.

"Dr. Stafford pointed out that carrying on the family name rests with sons not daughters, but carrying on traditions falls firmly into the hands of women. I agree. If I am going to be concerned about anyone's offspring, it should be Emeka's." Her mouth fell open, and she immediately closed it with a blink. "Charles has assured me that he is well able to provide for you, and that he doesn't expect you to continue working unless you want to. He has also said he will not ask you to sign a pre-nuptial agreement." The possibility had never even occurred to her. "We have agreed that the bride price is an outdated custom and should be disregarded. We would all like to hear your thoughts."

Her gaze jumped from her father's face to Dr. Stafford's, then settled on Charles' before she could muster up the words to speak. "I—uh—that's good. No, that's great. I'm happy you were able to reach common ground."

Charles took her hand and entwined their fingers and smiled. "I told your father that since the family already has a wedding coming up in June, it would make sense for us to wait until at least the end of the year. How does that sound to you?"

The grin that rose up from her toes eventually bloomed on her face. "It sounds perfect." She went to her father, and hugged his neck. "There's one more thing, Dad. I need you to have a talk with Emeka."

"Rapu okwu a."

"I can't just forget about it. If he agrees to honor your decision, Charles and I promise never to mention our suspicions again."

"I'll call him tonight."

"Thank you, Dad. I want to tell Mum and Mrs. Stafford." She released him and ran back to the dining room. The two older women squealed when she barreled through the door and said, "We're getting married!"

Charles came up behind her, encircled his arms around her, and kissed her neck. "My father wants to take everyone to dinner at the hotel. Can you call a cab for us? Your father said they'll drive their car."

In the taxi on the way back to the hotel, Adanna rode with her head resting on Charles' shoulder. She couldn't stop smiling. "I can't thank you enough for intervening for us," she said to Dr. and Mrs. Stafford. "There's no doubt in my mind that things wouldn't have gone this way without you. What in the world did you say to him?"

Dr. Stafford smirked. "Basically, I explained how Charles was raised in a Christian home in a family of men in which education and hard work took top priority. But I believe what turned the tables was when I said I told him about my son's professional status and how wealthy he is going to be in the future."

"Well, isn't that something?" Mrs. Stafford said, sending Adanna a wink.

During a leisurely dinner at the hotel, Adanna saw a side of her parents she hadn't seen since she was a little girl. They laughed and shared embarrassing childhood stories about her with Charles' parents, and Mr. and Mrs. Stafford did the same. ChiChi got passed back and forth between the women. Adanna and Charles saw her mother and father out to the car park after they had dessert and coffee. Charles kept silent while they hugged and said their goodbyes. He kissed her mother, shook her father's hand, and promised to keep them apprised of the wedding plans. After he turned away, Mrs. Okoro said: "Ọ mara mma nwoke." Adanna just smiled and said, "Yes."

Once they got into the lift, Charles asked, "What did your mother just say to you?"

"She said you are very handsome."

His shoulders shook as he gave a silent chuckle. "We have to go back to our room to pack, and then we're leaving for the airport," he said to his parents as they rode the lift to their rooms. "As soon as we're done, we'll stop by your room on our way to check out."

"I thought we were never going to be alone! Tell me everything that happened. I'm still in shock," Adanna blurted out the second the doors closed and the lift took them to their room on a higher floor.

Charles shook his head. "My father has done some things in the past that had my brothers and me convinced he needed psychiatric intervention, but today I saw a different side of the man. The wild thing is I could tell he was getting a kick out of the whole thing. The older he gets, the more he surprises me."

It only took them thirty minutes to pack and for Adanna to change the baby before they took the lift back down to his parents' room. His mother opened the door in answer to his knock.

"Our flight is leaving for Lagos in three hours, so we're not staying, but…" Charles said.

Adanna continued, "We just wanted to say thank you for stepping in for us today. You turned the whole situation around."

"You were amazing, Dad."

"And I thought my mother was going to pass out when she opened that designer kettle. Mrs. Stafford, it was the perfect gift for a tea connoisseur."

"Victor and I were just talking about one thing that's going to have to change if you intend to become part of our family."

"Of course. Anything." Adanna scratched at the base of her throat.

"You have to start calling us Mama and Daddy like the rest of our daughters-in-law."

Adanna's hand moved from her throat to cover her lips, and she shut her eyes for a long moment. "I'd love to."

Chapter Twenty-One

*T*heir return to Nigeria turned out to be more disturbing to Charles than he was prepared for. His relationship with Adanna had changed. They were no longer dating. Now that they were engaged and had been physically intimate, going back to sleeping in an empty bed and having another man as his roommate set his teeth on edge.

They went directly to her apartment from the airport, and he made sure she and ChiChi got settled. When it came time for him the leave, knowing they were going to be separated once again erased all of the contentment he'd had for the past week. By the time the taxi deposited him at his apartment, the combination of his thoughts and jet lag had turned him into a post-holiday Grinch. He grumbled a few words to Randy before he closed himself in his bedroom and went back to sleep.

In the morning, the two roommates met in the kitchen. Randy poured himself a cup of coffee and stirred in a couple of spoonful's of sugar. "Morning, mate. How was the trip?"

"Great. I didn't mean to brush you off last night, but I just wasn't feeling being back here."

"Gotcha. Maybe it's time to change your tour schedule or bail altogether."

Charles met his gaze. "I've been thinking about that a lot lately, especially since Adanna and I got engaged for Christmas."

Randy's eyes widened, and he slammed his palm into Charles' hand and gave it a firm shake. "Congrats, mate! I had the feeling it was getting serious. She's a fantastic lady."

"Thanks. Don't say anything to anyone at the hospital yet. We took that step, but haven't talked about what comes next. I need to ask Adanna how she wants to handle it."

"Sounds like it's time to have a yarn with the gorgeous Nurse Okoro then. Unless you plan on having a long-distance marriage too."

Charles laughed, and massaged the headache that had formed behind his eyes. "Oh, hell no." He groaned. "This jet lag is about to kill me." He glanced at the clock on the stove. "I'd better get into the shower. She'll be here to pick me up in a little while. How'd everything go while we were away?"

"Busy, as usual. Nils is having a staff meeting this morning, so that should bring you up to speed."

"Okay. See you there."

An hour later, Adanna blew the horn. Seeing his Cruiser in good condition put the first smile of the day on his tired face. She slid over to let him get behind the wheel.

"Good morning," he said after he kissed the lips he'd dreamed about last night. "We need to get a couple of things straight before we get to the hospital."

"Good morning. I was thinking the same thing. What's on your mind?"

"Hello, Princess," he said over his shoulder to the baby before he put the truck in gear and pulled away from the apartment. "Should we make an announcement? If we do, that's going to bring up some questions."

"Right. We have to tell them, because I'm not taking my ring off for any reason." She held up her hand in front of her face and gazed lovingly at the sparkler.

"Okay." He grinned. "You know Lou's and Joseph's first questions will be whether or not you plan to stay."

"And they have a right to know. I guess we should just be honest and tell them we don't have an answer yet. That's all we can do right now, isn't it?" Her dark eyes searched his as though she were waiting for him to make a decision.

"I guess so. Let's start there and talk about the rest tonight."

The announcement of their engagement at the end of the staff meeting was received with good wishes and a barrage of questions as they had expected. After the meeting, he sat down with Lou and Joseph privately and told them about Adanna's plans to adopt ChiChi, which would most likely take months to be approved and finalized. Beyond that, he admitted they had no definite plans yet.

He and Adanna spent the day getting back into the swing of the normal workday. That night, after ChiChi was asleep, they made the announcement to Femi, Manny, and Agu, who had dropped by to welcome her home. Femi's and Agu's congratulations seemed heartfelt, but Manny's was chilly, which didn't seem to surprise Adanna at all.

Even though they were both exhausted, they sat on her bed talking until late that night. "We need to think about what we're going to do now. My original plans when I came to Nigeria were just to work on a rotating schedule until I decided to do something different. I know what kind of surgery I want to specialize in, but I need to hear your thoughts."

She sighed. "I came back to Nigeria to use my nursing skills to help my people, and even though I realize I'm just one person, I hate to turn my back on them. But the time I spent in the US visiting your family has given me a different outlook on my own life. I didn't understand how much I need the closeness of family. This visit has shown me what's been missing in my life. Other than living in London, I've never experienced life in another country. And I've never been part of a close family. You don't know how badly I want that, Charles. I'm so confused right now."

"I don't think you're confused. I think you're feeling guilty about wanting a different life for yourself." He paused and combed his beard with his fingertips. "I've had an idea in the back of my mind for a while," he spoke softly so he wouldn't wake ChiChi. "I mentioned it to my brothers, but I didn't want to say anything to you, because it was just an idea."

"Tell me."

"How would you feel about starting a foundation to help the hospital? When I threw it out to Vic and Jesse, they said they'd be willing to participate, but at that point it was just a thought. Putting an organization like that together is a huge undertaking and running a charitable foundation takes constant fundraising."

The proposal seemed to light a fire in her. She rose and paced the length of her small bedroom. "Are you talking about something designed specifically for Obasanjo Hospital?" He nodded. "They are lacking so many necessities. Dr. Ijalana and Dr. Pategi do their best to keep their heads above water, but it's never enough. How would this work?"

"We would have to set up a 501c3 non-profit corporation in the States, but I don't know the details. My mother knows more about that kind of stuff than I do."

She stopped pacing and looked him in the eye. "That's a fabulous idea, but who would run it?"

He smiled. "You and a board of directors, of course. You wouldn't be doing the hands-on work anymore, but if you were able to secure sufficient funding, Lou and Joseph could hire more staff and get the supplies and materials they so desperately need. I would still donate my time for volunteer surgery maybe once or twice a year, and you could sign up to work with me."

"If we move back to the US, where would we live?"

"Where do you want to live?"

"I have no idea. Atlanta is the only place I've ever been."

"You can come to Vegas and see how you like it there. Personally, I like the suburbs of Atlanta much better."

She plopped down onto the mattress beside him. "Why?"

"They're two very different areas. The weather, the demographics, everything is different, but I'm an Atlanta boy, so I'm probably prejudiced."

"Atlanta is lovely. The homes and all of the trees are just beautiful."

"Vegas is lively, but it's mostly nightlife. It's a tourist city in the middle of the desert. Definitely not as family-oriented as Atlanta, but you can get to California in no time."

"Are you going to keep working with Marc?"

"I guess that depends on where we decide to live. One thing I'm sure of is I don't want to go into private practice again."

"There is so much to consider. Tomorrow I'm picking up ChiChi's adoption application papers to get the process started. I have to become a US citizen in order for the private adoption to be legal, so I guess it doesn't matter what city we live in."

"Quite a few people will be affected by our decisions. It's only fair to let Marc know what I'm going to do when I go back to Vegas at the end of March."

"That should be our goal then."

Charles returned to his apartment, showered, and sat on the balcony drinking a beer. Even though he was physically tired, his mind was racing so fast, sleep was out of the question. So much had happened since he arrived in Nigeria, and his life seemed to be moving at light speed again. He'd been shocked by the way Adanna had so eagerly accepted his hints about leaving Nigeria. Now that he'd cleared that major hurdle, there were a dozen more looming ahead.

He glanced at his watch. It was five PM in Atlanta. He dialed his parents' number. "Hi, Mama. You got back okay?"

"Yes, we did a little sightseeing before we left London. How are Adanna and ChiChi?"

"They're fine. I called to ask if you'd check into something for me. We're thinking about setting up a 501c3 to help the hospital here. You know all about that stuff. Could you pull some information together on how to do it and e-mail it to Adanna?"

"Sure, honey, but I imagine she would have to be a US citizen first in order to set up anything here."

"Right. Well, anything you think might help her get started would be great."

"Anything for you. Send her my love and give ChiChi a kiss for me."

"Thanks, Mama. I have surgery tomorrow, and I'm wiped so I'm going to bed."

"Take care of yourself, Charles."

"I will. Love you, Mama." He hung up feeling a little more positive about getting the proverbial ball rolling.

A week later, he and Adanna hand-delivered the adoption application along with duplicate copies of her birth certificate, certificate of fitness, proof of employment, ID card, paycheck stubs, bank statements, passport photo, and tax clearance for the past three years to The Special Adviser at the Office of Youth and Social Development in Ikeja. She had everything they requested in order. Now the wait began.

The very next day, after Charles had only been home for about an hour, Adanna called. "Emeka wants to come by here to talk. I guess he's spoken with my father. You should be here."

He had performed three surgeries and was looking forward to crashing in front of the TV, but she was right. He should be there, so he dragged himself up, put on some clothes and got back into the car.

When Emeka arrived, Charles was sitting in the living room waiting for him. Appearing a bit startled by the apparent set-up, her brother asked, "What is this about, Adanna?"

"I don't know. You called me, remember?" She took two beers from the refrigerator and handed one to Charles before she gave the other one to her brother.

Emeka sat with his elbows on his knees and stared at the floor for a few moments before he said, "I talked to Mpa a few days ago." She and Charles shared a glance. "He told me you came to London for Christmas." He twiddled his thumbs. "And he gave you his blessing on your upcoming marriage. Because I believe in tradition, I would never go against our father's wishes. I—I came to—apologize for speaking against your relationship."

"Thank you, Emeka. That means a lot to me, but Charles is the one you should apologize to." She folded her arms, pinned him with her gaze and waited.

Her brother rose from his chair and walked up to Charles with his hand extended. "I regret if I have done anything to hurt you or Adanna."

Charles wanted to laugh at the half-hearted apology and refusal to own up to his part in the kidnapping, but this was probably all he was going to get. He clasped Emeka's hand. "Thanks, man. I love your sister, and I plan to treat her with nothing but kindness and respect."

Emeka nodded, and took a long sip of his beer. "I should leave now. I hope you will keep me informed of the wedding plans."

He and Adanna stared at each other as she closed the door behind him then burst into laughter.

"I don't think you and Emeka will ever be friends, but at least he won't try to sabotage us anymore."

"We hope. It's amazing how even when you're an adult a parent can lay down the law and make you toe the line. In my family, it's my mother who wields that power. We tend to buck against my father's orders, but none of us questions Mama, because she's always right. And we know she's the only one who can influence Daddy." He moved behind her, kissed her neck, and squeezed his eyes shut against the prospect of going back to his apartment alone. Now that they had been together, he hated sleeping by himself. He loved waking up and finding her warm body next to his. "I've been thinking since Randy showed some interest in Femi, it might be to our benefit to hook them up. Then he could stay here and you and I could spend the night together." They both snickered at the idea.

"Don't go. ChiChi is already asleep."

"Yes, but Femi isn't."

"Do you really think Femi cares if I spend the night?"

"Probably not, but I do, and I don't like the idea of having an audience.

"It's kind of sexy to me," Adanna said

Adanna wasn't giving up. She caressed his arms that were still circling her waist. "We don't have to do anything. I'll wake you up early enough to get to the hospital on time."

He spun her around in his embrace. "There's nothing I want more, but you know if I stay we won't get any sleep.

Tomorrow is another full surgery schedule." Charles lowered his head and nibbled on her bottom lip. "We're going to solve this problem—soon, but you're trying to tempt me is not helping at all." He deepened the kiss until she was leaning against him and his body was the only thing holding her upright. "I need to get going—now." He held her by the shoulders and stood her upright. "Love you."

♥

When he released her, Adanna felt as if she was standing naked in the middle of a snowstorm. She actually shivered and hugged herself in an effort to replace the warmth of his body. Charles was right. They had to solve their problem before one of them did something terribly embarrassing. Her waking hours were constantly disturbed by flashbacks of them making love at the hotel in London. And these visions always seemed to make their appearance at the most inopportune times, like when the doctors were giving patient updates. Not being able to concentrate wasn't just a nuisance. It could be a life or death matter.

By the end of the week her life jumped into fast forward, which left her little time for navel gazing. The adoption agency called to say they were sending someone to do a home visit. Since she worked, it was necessary to schedule a day and time. She chose the upcoming Friday to give her time to alert Femi and to tidy up her own bedroom.

A few days after the adoption agency called, Mrs. Stafford sent her an e-mail full of links and information on setting up the charity. Just reading all of it would take several days. Ever since Charles presented her with the idea, she'd felt as though she'd been shot out of a cannon with no idea where she might land. All of their plans were open-ended. It was still too early for a definite word on the adoption. She was engaged, but they hadn't set a wedding date. They had no clue where they would be living or working. And it irritated her that Charles, the eternal optimist, didn't seem to be bothered by any of it. But she couldn't live not knowing where things stood on the major issues in her life. The only thing she had any control over at the moment was getting the foundation established, so she jumped into the research.

An investigator from the Youth and Social Development department paid her a visit and didn't appear concerned that she shared a flat with Femi. What bothered Adanna were the questions the woman asked about ChiChi's daily care. When she said someone in the village where the hospital was located was caring for the baby during the day, the woman asked for the babysitter's name and address. That's when she noticed Adanna's ring.

"Beautiful ring, Ms. Okoro. Is it an engagement ring?"

"Thank you. Yes, it is," Adanna answered with the sudden awareness of her oversight and the possibility that this might become an issue.

"You didn't think it was important to tell us you were getting married?" the woman asked with a furtive smile.

Adanna exhaled a long breath, then did her best to explain. "We just got engaged over the Christmas holiday. It was somewhat unexpected, but my original intention was to adopt Chichima as a single parent."

"But your fiancé will become the baby's father when you marry. It is vital that we also conduct a thorough background check on him and interview him in person. Is he a local?"

Panic shot through Adanna's body, but she maintained her outer calm. "No, he's not, but he is a volunteer doctor at the hospital where I work. He's American."

"I see." The woman frowned and scribbled in her notebook. "I need to arrange a meeting with him as soon as possible if you don't want our decision to be delayed."

Adanna didn't want the investigator to be suspicious of any hesitation on her part. "Of course." Let me call him now and see if he can talk. He's a surgeon, so he might be in the operating room," she said, intentionally allowing the investigator to hear the pride in her voice.

"Hi, honey. I guess you're not in surgery now."

"No, we just finished one. The next one is in two hours. What's wrong? You sound funny."

"The investigator for ChiChi's adoption request is here. She seems a bit concerned because I didn't mention our engagement on the application."

"Oh, hell," he mumbled. "What does she want?"

"She wants to set up an interview with you before they run a background check."

"No problem. Let me talk to her."

She handed the woman her phone. "He'd like to speak to you."

"Hello. Yes, doctor. I explained to Ms. Okoro that since you two will be marrying in the near future, it's necessary for us to also investigate you." She listened for a moment, her eyes widened, and then she checked her watch. "Yes, I suppose I could be there within thirty minutes. Since I also need to visit Chichima's babysitter, I could do both. Thank you, doctor. I'll see you soon." She handed the phone back to Adanna.

"Charles, is everything straight?"

"You need to come with her and take her to the babysitter. Don't let her go alone, because she doesn't even know this woman is coming."

"Okay. We'll be there soon. Love you too."

Thirty minutes later, Adanna drove up in front of the hospital. Once she introduced Charles and the investigator, she made a fast trip to the babysitter to warn her of the woman's visit then turned around and went back to Lagos.

Charles' surgeries ran late again that night, but he stopped by her flat on his way home and gave her a rundown on how the interview had gone. Before he left, he said, "Don't worry about this, baby. It makes sense that they would want to check me out. Everything's going to go according to plan. Wait and see."

Epilogue

While Adanna carefully dressed ChiChi in the white satin and lace dress, she thought back to five months ago when they were waiting for approval on her adoption. The entire time she'd had the dreaded feeling that something was going to go wrong. Each additional request from the State, and there had been several, had thrown her into a tailspin. They had asked ChiChi's babysitter to make some minor adjustments to her home, which Marc and Gianne happily paid for. Charles had passed their scrutiny with flying colors. Finally the adoption was approved and the final papers had been signed. The matter of the private adoption between the two couples still needed to be worked out, but that would come with time. Adanna had retained a US attorney to help with getting her citizenship papers and initiating the adoption.

After much soul searching, they decided to make Atlanta their home. Charles was vying for a position as a staff surgeon with the Atlanta's children's hospital, because it specialized in juvenile reconstructive plastic surgery.

Today she and Charles had the honor of delivering the ultimate gift to the newlyweds. No longer a baby, ChiChi had started walking and could even string a few words together. She was walking down the aisle between them to meet her new parents at the altar wearing a dress designed to mirror Gianne's gown.

From the beginning, Marc had been dead set against having a Vegas wedding, so he and Gianne chose to have the wedding and reception outside on South Shore Beach at

Lake Tahoe. Marc had asked Charles to serve as the best man, and Gianne had asked her best friend, Stefanie, to be the maid of honor. Vic and Jesse were acting as groomsmen. Adanna and Gianne's cousin, Tanya, had the honor of being bridesmaids. Nick and Greg took care of the usher responsibilities.

The ceremony began with Charles and Adanna bringing ChiChi to the front. They had to take small steps so it would look as though they were pulling her down the aisle that separated two sections of white chairs. It took them a while to reach the podium in front of the clear blue lake, but their leisurely stroll was met by the exclamations of the crowd about how beautiful the little girl was. She smiled at the guests with a smile that was now as close to perfect as Charles' surgical skills allowed.

Adanna had been concentrating so hard on keeping ChiChi from pulling her hand free, she hadn't noticed that Gianne and Marc were both crying until Charles lifted the little girl into his arms and let Adanna kiss her cheek. Before he handed the mini-bride to his brother, the emotion in his eyes spoke clearly. He wanted babies, and she wanted to give them to him. She smiled and held his gaze long enough to let him read her answer.

The minister gave a brief blessing over the three of them then Mrs. Stafford stepped forward and took the baby to sit with her before the ceremony continued. Marc and Gianne pledged their love and commitment to each other then; in true Stafford fashion, the indoor reception lasted until late into the night.

In the morning, the family checked out of the hotel and the caravan to the airport commenced. Charles and Adanna flew into Atlanta so he could meet with his real estate agent to talk about moving back into his apartment. He'd chosen not to renew the current tenant's lease when it had ended in February. All he and Adanna needed to do was repaint and refurnish his former thirtieth-floor home overlooking the city.

She and Charles didn't reveal their plan to Drs. Ijalana and Pategi until the non-profit foundation was approved. On the other side of the globe, Mrs. Stafford threw herself into helping Adanna plan the first fundraiser to introduce the foundation to an organization of Atlanta doctor's wives. She wanted Adanna to start small, and this event would only host fifty women at best.

The best part of all the changes was that she would never have to wait for the man she loved to come back to her.

The End

Credits

[1](http://zahmad.com.ng and http://facebook.com/zahmadcrafts)

An excerpt from

Don't Stop Till You Get Enough

Coming Late 2014

Chapter One

Greg Stafford slammed the door to his upper east side Manhattan apartment, engaged both locks then dropped his head to the door and banged it several times—hoping the pain might snap him out of his nightmare. No such luck. He dragged his body to the sofa, slumped down and tried to concentrate on the tinkling sound of the ceiling-to-floor Asian fountain in the foyer. Even that did nothing to calm him. He'd just spent the past four hours at the local police precinct, waiting for his attorney to get him released. His arrest would surely be headline news. He wasn't a major star, but he had become a fixture on New York television and in the markets where the show was syndicated.

At a complete loss for what to do next, he picked up the remote for the TV and turned the channel to the network to which he'd been contracted for the past five years. Would they report it? Or would they ignore it? That was just wishful thinking. They couldn't ignore breaking news that involved one of their own. Could they?

His co-host, Arianna Wolfe, with whom Greg shared the desk every day, said, "*A member of The Scoop family is off the air tonight, as authorities investigate indecency charges. He will not be at the desk until the investigation is complete. We will bring you up to date when new information becomes available.*"

Thankful that they avoided the details, Greg changed the channel. Sadly, he knew the other stations wouldn't be as kind.

> *"In breaking news, the wife of New York Senator Carl Price was arrested this weekend for having*

engaged in sexual relations in broad daylight in an alley not far from Bloomingdale's. The man has now been identified as Gregory Stafford, the host of the top-rated magazine show, The Scoop. Both were charged with indecent exposure and public lewdness and released on their own recognizance.

We contacted Senator Price's office, but received no response. Stafford has been unavailable for comment. Legal issues aside, these arrests raise questions about the stability of the popular senator's marriage, which has been under scrutiny for some time. Mrs. Price, who is twenty-five years younger than the Senator, has been seen frequently on the New York club circuit alone. Stafford is single and is a well-known regular on the club scene."

The report hadn't ended more than two minutes before his phone started ringing. *His boss.* Then it rang in succession ten more times. He stared at the screen--*his publicist. The station manager. His co-anchor. His father. His mother. Charles. Marc. Vic. Jesse. Nick.* Coming from a big family could be a blessing, but it could also be a major curse. The Scoop was syndicated in most major markets, and inevitably, members of the family watched the show every night. Right now he didn't want to speak to any of them. What could he say to explain the situation he'd put himself in? If he wanted to hang onto to his job though, it was necessary that he respond to his boss and station manager. He pressed his head between his hands as though he could squeeze the condemning voices out, then got up and walked into the kitchen. Vodka. Yes, vodka was appropriate now. Even though he wasn't a big drinker, but he kept a bottle around for when he had guests. The freezer always held a bottle or two of Stoli, his favorite. After he poured enough for three people into a water glass, he swallowed three times and picked up the phone. No, not yet. He had to think for a while before he spoke to anyone.

From puberty on his sexual appetite had been what most

people considered normal. But in the past few years, he'd graduated from a serious relationship, to casual dating, to serial dating, to strictly sexual relationships, to one-night stands, then to online porn when he couldn't find a hook-up. He avoided thinking about the reasons why he'd gotten to this point. Normally he didn't allow his mind to venture into that kind of introspection. His outlook was more on the *don't cry over spilt milk* side. But recently he'd begun to question his escalating sexual appetite, which had begun after his breakup with Addison.

Why couldn't he be more like his brothers? All five of them were committed to just one woman, and they all seemed happy. Not just happy, but satisfied. Marc and Gianne were always thirty seconds from jumping each other, but they were newlyweds. Cydney's perpetual pregnancies proved that doing the wild thing topped her and Jesse's list of favorite pastimes. Vic and Mona had been married for ten years; yet sometimes, the strong sex vibe between them could be sensed by anyone within ten feet. Even his single baby brother, Nick, boasted about his upcoming second anniversary with his girlfriend, Cherilyn.

What was wrong with him? No woman held his interest for more than a weekend or two. Weren't they all raised in the same home with the same lofty moral values? And why hadn't he always been like this? The third oldest of the six, Greg had managed to keep his problem a secret from his family; although when Charles came to New York to stay with him not long ago, he'd taken his brother to a couple of his favorite clubs. When he invited two of the women they'd met back to his apartment for the night, Charles begged off. He didn't come right out and say anything, but his facial expressions, tone of voice, and early departure made it clear that he obviously disagreed with Greg's lifestyle. Hopefully, he hadn't discussed his suppositions with the rest of the family. Not that it mattered now. Everyone would know within a matter of hours.

He gulped down the rest of his drink in an effort to fortify himself before he listened to the voicemail messages. *Might as well go in order.*

"This is Ken. I supposed you've already heard that the Scoop had to put you on administrative leave for the immediate future. You, me and the people from legal sit down and figure out where we go from here. Get back to me as soon as you get this message."

He forwarded to the next message. "Please pick up, Greg," his publicist, Belinda pleaded. You know why I'm calling. I have to speak with you before I can figure out what kind of spin to put on this…*event.* Call me ASAP."

"Greg, it's John Hanke. It's imperative we talk as soon as possible. Your attorney informed us of the situation. Your arrest has brought up some legal concerns, not for the station, but for you personally. I want to discuss them with you immediately. I'll be waiting to hear from you."

"Hi, Greg. It's Arianna. We tried to gloss over the details as best we could. Let me know how you're doing. I'm worried about my co-host. Please call me back."

"This is your father. What the hell is going on up there? Your mother is frantic. She's been crying since we heard the report. Couldn't you at least have warned us? Why did we have to find out from the television? An explanation is in order, son. I expect a call tonight."

The tremor in his mother's voice when he forwarded to her message told him she was still crying. "Sweetheart, I know Daddy called, but I wanted to talk to you myself. Are you all right? I hope your absence from the show isn't permanent. Let me know that okay, please."

He couldn't face his father's reproach. Calling his mother would be less painful.

The calls from his brothers, except for Charles, were of

the WTF variety. Charles merely said, "You're out of control, man. It's time you thought about getting some help. If you want to talk, I'm here."

The cold empty glass in his hand mocked him. Icy and vacant. Like his life at the moment. He didn't understand whether the empathy he felt was for the glass or for himself. Nevertheless, he wandered back into the kitchen and refilled the depleted vessel with chilled liquid. Why couldn't he be filled? What was it that had him feeling so void?

What was I thinking? I knew who she was, but I wanted her so badly that l I didn't care what the repercussions might be if we got caught. Why can't I control myself? He threw the glass across the room, and it shattered on the red wall over the black Chinese symbols for peace.

He had been on his way into the studio and stopped at Barney's to buy a new cologne at the men's fragrance counter when she appeared next to him and inclined her head exposing her long, creamy neck.

"What do you think of this fragrance?"

He leaned closer and inhaled. "Intoxicating."

She studied his eyes for a long moment, then breezed away leaving an enticing trail of expensive fragrance behind. He followed it like a cartoon character drifting on a visible ribbon of scent that wrapped itself around his head. Her gaze locked with his as the elevator door opened and she stepped inside. Greg quickened his steps so he might enter the cab before the doors closed. They rode in silence for one floor.

"I know you," she said, giving him a blatant head-to-toe scan. "You host that TV show…The Story…The Chat…"

"The Scoop," Greg corrected her with a smile. "And you're Mrs. Carl Price."

"Melinda. You are a very good-looking man."

Greg couldn't believe what happened next. She pressed the stop button. The elevator halted its descent, and she took two steps toward him so there wasn't even an inch of daylight between them. When she put her palm against his chest and raised her chin so he felt her breath on his face, he curved his right arm around her back and pulled her body against his. "And you're an extremely beautiful woman."

"Are you on your way to an appointment?" she asked, her lips brushing his.

"I am now." With his free hand, Greg cupped her booty and pressed her hips against him. He backed her against the wall of the elevator and raised her dress up around her hips.

"Not here," she said between raspy breaths and yanked the dress back down. The wife of the state's wildly popular junior senator pushed the button to restart the elevator. "Let's leave." When the door opened on the first floor, she strode out and headed for the main store entrance. Greg followed her like a starving dog panting after a rare steak.

Out in the sunshine on bustling Madison Avenue, she slipped her sunglasses down from the top of her head and picked up her pace until she shifted into a jog. Greg's heart thundered as she turned onto E. 61st Street and glanced over her shoulder to see if he still followed her. The suspense of where she might be going threatened to kill him. She turned the corner again and disappeared into an alley.

When he caught up with her, she had dropped her shopping bags to the ground and was standing with her hands on her hips as though proposing a dare. Unable to slow his pace, he slammed her against the brick wall of the building. The way his head spun from the chase and the headiness of the challenge, he had to press his hands against the wall on either side of her head to get his balance.

"Hurry! We can't stay here long before someone sees us." She wriggled her dress up and stepped her feet apart. "Hurry!"

Greg rubbed his eyes. He needed to start returning these calls. The station manager wouldn't wait; and neither would Belinda. She needed to know how to respond to the media.

That's where he started. John said he wanted them to meet first thing in the morning, so Greg called his publicist and asked her to meet him. He wanted to avoid speaking to his father for as long as humanly possible, so he dialed the house number instead. When his mother answered, he cleared his throat and simply said, "Hey, Mama."

"Is it true, Gregory?" she asked in a tone that sounded like she was heartbroken.

He closed his eyes and dropped his head back so it thumped against the wall. "Yeah."

"I just have one other question." She exhaled a long sigh. "Why?"

The muscles in his throat constricted, and his eyes welled. "I don't know, Mama. I'm—I'm not like my brothers."

"I'm so worried about you, honey. We heard them say on the show tonight that you'll be off camera for the time being."

"It's not a permanent decision. I'll find out tomorrow. Don't worry about me, Mama. I'll be all right."

"I'm not so sure, Gregory. Maybe you should talk to someone about this."

"I will. I promise. Look, I have to go now. Talk to you later." He clicked off the call overwhelmed by the shame that had become his constant companion. Whenever he had a hook-up with someone, afterward there was no elation or even a sense of satisfaction. Just shame and emptiness, and hearing the disappointment in his mother's voice multiplied that shame ten-fold.

Greg didn't even go into his bedroom. Most of the night, he sat up with the television on but not really watching what was on the screen. He'd sunk to his lowest level. Sex in broad daylight with a married woman—a married woman whose husband was famous and adored by his constituency.

Charles was right. He was out of control, and his sexual appetite had escalated to the point where it felt unmanageable. The press had been kind to Melinda Price since her husband's election as senator. The media had downplayed her fondness for the party life in favor of her involvement in many high-profile charitable causes. Greg didn't understand what the pretty thirty-year-old saw in the fifty-five-year-old politician, but to each his own.

He might have slept two hours, before the alarm clock startled him back to consciousness. Following a long, hot shower, he dressed, put on his shades, and one of his favorite duckbill caps. He put the lanyard, which held his studio ID, over his head then took the elevator down to the lobby where Roland, the doorman, hailed him a cab. Greg wondered if Roland knew what had happened to him. If he did, he didn't let on

When the taxi pulled up in front of the towering building that held the studios of most of the network shows, he spotted two men outside the entrance who stood out. One wore a gray vest, khaki pants, sunglasses, and running shoes. The other was dressed in jeans and sneakers, and a white shirt with tails out—nothing out of the ordinary except for the cameras hanging around their necks. Paparazzi for sure. Greg paid the driver, pulled his cap down low on his forehead. It wasn't much of a disguise, but at least he didn't have to look them in the eye.

"Greg!" Khaki Pants yelled. "Can you tell us what's going to happen now that you've been taken off the air?"

"Have you spoken to Mrs. Price since your arrest? Will you two continue to see each other?" the other one hollered as he rushed past them.

Greg bypassed the newspaper box, his normal stop on the way into the revolving doors that opened into an enormous lobby. His automatic instinct was to punch them both, but it was better not to respond than to give them more fuel for the fire. Once he flashed his badge to the security officer at the main desk, he jumped on the first elevator that opened. Two other people followed him in before the doors closed, but he didn't bother to look at either of them. He pushed the button for the twenty-sixth floor and rode up feeling as though he'd swallowed one of the boulders that decorated the fountain outside the iconic building. Hopefully, his attorney and his publicist had already arrived.

Greg mumbled good morning to the few people he passed in the hall on his way to the conference room. The door was open, and the aroma of coffee greeted him as he walked in.

"Morning, Greg," John said, sounding as if it was a struggle to be pleasant.

He removed his sunglasses and hat and nodded to the station manager, Thaddeus Jones, his attorney, and Ken Peterson, his immediate boss. "Morning."

"Fix yourself some coffee," John continued. "We're waiting for someone from Legal and your publicist to get here."

Thankful for the brief reprieve, he went to the table in the front corner of the room and poured two cups, mixed in cream and sugar and covered one with a plastic top. This morning he needed the extra fortification. Before he found a seat at the long table, Belinda entered. After Greg introduced her, she greeted the men, and headed right for the beverage table still carrying her portfolio and purse.

Greg didn't know the last person to enter the room and assumed he must be the legal eagle. John pointed to the coffee and waited until the man seated himself. "We all know why we're here. This situation doesn't only give the Scoop and the network a black eye, but it's also a breach of contract on your part," he said, pinning Greg with a hard stare. Confusion drew Greg's face into a frown, and John went on to explain further. "A morality clause is a standard inclusion in the contracts of all on-air personalities. Unfortunately, almost no one remembers reading that clause before they signed it." He slid the papers in front of Greg, and Thad picked them up before he had a chance to take a look.

"This is pretty cut and dried," Thad said after a few minutes. "To give you the short version, it's a provision in the contract which curtails, restrains, or forbids certain behavior. The clause is used as a means of holding you to a certain behavioral standard so as not to bring disrepute, contempt or scandal to the network and their interests."

"Breaking this clause is grounds for disciplinary action or termination," Ken added.

Always one to think ahead, Thad asked, "Doesn't he have any recourse?"

John squinted. "What kind of recourse, Mr. Jones?"

"What if Mr. Stafford was willing to submit to counseling for a specified period of time?"

"That would play well with the public," Belinda chimed in. "Any kind of rehab does."

"Rehab?

"There's rehab for everything these days—not just the big problems. They have rehab for rudeness, stupidity, racism, homophobia, you name it." A chuckle echoed around the table.

"Would the network be willing to reinstate Mr. Stafford if he completed a mandated course of therapy with a reputable therapist?" Thad asked, directing his question to the station manager who in turn glanced at the corporate legal with raised brows.

"That decision would be up to you, John," the corporate attorney said.

Greg had held his tongue long enough. "I don't get any input in all of this?"

John sent him a snide smirk. "It's your gift for *inputting* that got you into this mess, Greg. I'm afraid your judgment can't be trusted."

Embarrassed, Greg averted his gaze and fiddled with his phone

A tense silence hung over the room while the station manager contemplated his advice. After what seemed like an eternity to Greg, John replied, "Listen, Greg, I haven't been aware of a lapse in judgment on your part since you've been with The Scoop until now. I don't make it a habit of judging another man's personal life. The women you sleep with is your private business, but since this story broke, the rumors about you and women on the staff have become the number one topic of discussion in this building. From what I hear, there are even pools going on now to guess the number of women in the company you've screwed. You need to face the fact that you have a problem." He stopped and pushed his glasses up on his nose. "This mandated therapy has nothing to do with the women you've been involved with on the job. It's the result of your arrest only, but I have to warn you that some of the women on staff are going to talk if TMZ or some other outlet offers them the right price. You'd better be prepared for more fallout. And, he slid a newspaper in Greg's direction. "It looks as if you have another complication."

Greg lifted the paper, which was folded to the headline, *Senator Price makes an official statement.* He quickly read the text of the article, which said that the senator was accusing Greg of pursuing his young wife then passed it to Thad.

"There's nothing he can do to you legally, Greg, but he can make your life miserable. I don't want you to respond to him personally."

"But he's accusing me of being the aggressor in that little escapade, and I wasn't." Greg protested with his balled fists on the tabletop. "She was. The whole thing was her idea."

"Let Belinda create a statement that talks about the station's decision to allow you to return to the air after you finishing counseling."

Thad cleared his throat and offered, "I know of an excellent therapist another one of my clients used. Is that acceptable?"

"I don't see why not," John answered tentatively, then said, "As long as he's certified and reputable."

"It's a woman. If you want to check her out, I can give you the link to her website," Thad offered.

"How does that sit with you, Greg," the station manager asked.

"I'll go along with whatever you decide." What else could he say? If he bucked against the idea, it would appear that he was being difficult and wasn't serious about remaining employed with the network. He had no other choice.

Coming Late 2014

About the Author

Shades of Romance Magazine 2011 Author of the Year, Chicki Brown has published six novels and one novella, all of which have made different Kindle bestseller lists.

A voracious reader since she was a child, Chicki grew up in New Jersey reading everything she could get her hands on. Now she concentrates on romance, women's fiction and suspense.

Mother of two and grandmother of five, Brown was born and raised in New Jersey and now calls suburban Atlanta, Georgia home.

She can be found at any of the following sites:

Blog: http://sisterscribbler.blogspot.com

Twitter: http://twitter.com/@Chicki663

Facebook: http://www.facebook.com/chicki.brown

Google+: https://plus.google.com/+ChickiBrown

Pinterest: http://pinterest.com/chicki663/

Amazon Central Author Page: http://amzn.to/l2kjXQ

Goodreads: http://bit.ly/qcsiMD

75522467R00238

Made in the USA
Columbia, SC
18 September 2019